About the Author

Andy Oppenheimer AIExpE MIABTI is an author and consultant in counterterrorism. An Associate Member of the Institute of Explosives Engineers and a Member of the International Association of Bomb Technicians & Investigators, he has written and lectured worldwide on terrorism, weapons of mass destruction, bombs and explosives since 2001. Long ago in a galaxy far, far away, he worked in futuristic science publishing. He has also been a singer-songwriter of electro-pop music since 1982 and a painter of surrealist pictures since childhood. *Fields of Orion: An Odyssey* is his first science-fiction novel.

FIELDS OF ORION
An Odyssey

FIELDS OF ORION
An Odyssey

ANDY OPPENHEIMER

ISBN (Paperback): 9781686106965

Cover design by Mariel Foulds

Cover images:
©cond1
Pixabay

To my beloved Jane

*"Over the edge of the World comes forth
Great Orion..."*

Henry Wadsworth Longfellow, 1866

Chapter 1

London: 7 July 2005: 8:23

On a warm morning in early July, four men arrived at King's Cross station in central London. With rucksacks loaded on their backs, they embraced, parted, and boarded one of three Underground trains.

8:25

Dan Boland charged down the four flights of stairs of the terraced house he shared with his older partner, Duncan. He strode out of the house and pounded up to Highbury Fields, the park at the top of the street.

Just a little park in north London. But to Dan and thousands of others, Highbury Fields had a magical quality. It provided a refuge from the growing pressures of work; a place for daily exercise and contemplation. The bustle and traffic of the tube station was just audible beyond the quiet rustle of the ring of trees that separate this green haven from the terraces of big Georgian and Victorian houses on its perimeter.

He strode an extra lap round the Fields, the music of David Bowie's haunting album *Low* pounding in his ears. Then amidst the bustle of traffic beyond the trees he looked momentarily upwards. He stopped dead in his tracks.

High above the trees he saw a cascade of shimmering flashes in the sky. No thunderstorm, or solid object hovering as in UFO folklore, but a sea of red, crackling waves - in broad daylight. He was transfixed.

8:50

A gigantic white flash, then darkness. Silence, and then the screams from hell. Within one minute, three bombs exploded on three Underground trains, each trapped in the twilight zone of tunnels between stations. In those blinding, deafening moments, forty-two lives were blown to oblivion. Over six hundred and seventy more lives were shattered, horrendously blighted by injury.

Dan continued his walk, step by step, still looking up at the sky, stopping now and again to watch the deep red glimmering waves high above the trees. Then he pressed on, walking purposefully towards Highbury & Islington station. He saw mayhem and chaos breaking out before him. He pulled off his headphones. People were running out of the station, some silent, others shouting.

"What's going on?" Dan asked a fleeing passenger. "Power surge, mate," was the hurried reply. Dan didn't believe it. Announcements were barely audible above the din. 'The Underground is shutting down. Please leave the station.' As he ran through the escaping crowds, Dan heard his mobile's ring tone. A call from Sky News. After only two years in his new career in counter-terrorism, he was interviewed by the media when something went bang.

"Three bombs have just gone off on the Underground, Dan. There's been mass casualties. Do you know what kind of explosive was used?" shouted the young journalist on the phone above background noise. Dan felt his blood run cold. In the midst of unfolding multiple attacks in the capital he was already being asked that. He moved away from the stream of commuters.

"The most powerful terrorist explosive in small devices was Semtex," he replied, shouting above the din and hoping he wasn't in earshot of the dispersing crowd. "It was the IRA's favourite explosive, but it isn't readily available now." He had to think harder, and fast. "Some are using homemade explosives, made from household items. We won't know yet." He thought, *it's only just happened...*

"Did you hear any of the bombs?" The guys Dan knew in the bomb disposal community said, you don't just hear them, you feel them – booming and cracking through your very soul.

"No. I was on my way out of town."

9:10

Dan sped back home, across Highbury Fields, past the big Tree of Hope. He panted out whatever replies he could muster to the string of media callers. He had to get home and see what had happened – and what could still happen. Already three bombs, all on London Underground trains, mass casualties, and there could be more.

Dan ran up the stairs. He glanced at Duncan clacking away on his computer in the lounge at the top of the house. "There's been three terrorist attacks. On the tube. I'm getting calls." Dan planted himself in front of the TV in the big reception room on the floor below, next to the house phone.

"I know," Duncan said wearily. "It's terrible. And the land line hasn't stopped." Having retired, Duncan was in most mornings. He kept out of Dan's work.

Dan saw the news. A massive attack, the likes of which Britain had never seen, even after thirty years of the IRA campaign. Dozens killed. Dan knew all about the IRA. This year they had finally decommissioned their weapons. This time the perpetrators were violent jihadists: suicide bombers.

The city screamed with the sound of ambulance and police sirens. The hospitals filled with the blood-soaked victims of terrorist carnage. Dan felt a wave of nausea. He realised that had he not run the extra lap round Highbury Fields and stopped to watch the shimmering lights in the sky, he would have been in the Underground network in the midst of one of the explosions.

9:20

A call came in from CBS. "Were any of the bombs radiological or chemical?" Al-Qaeda had been threatening to attack major cities with what later became an almost comical term, WMD: weapons of mass destruction. *Good God, surely not.* Dan had amassed a fair bit of knowledge about CBRN – that unwieldly acronym for chemical, biological, radiological and nuclear weapons.

"The forensic teams will test the sites of the explosions for that."

"The second bomb exploded between King's Cross and Russell Square." Dan had lived in that area for ten years with a feisty New Yorker called Teresa.

"Hang on... Stop!" Dan cried, halting the interviewer's flow. He looked out into the terraced street and saw an image flash before his eyes.

A vision of mass slaughter. A bus exploding, its roof blasted and fragmented into a million pieces, showering the street with lumps of red and black metal, body parts...the pavement stained with blood... then he heard the screams of the wounded...

He gasped down his mobile: "Please call me back later!" He called Teresa. It was her day off work. She picked up.

"Don't go out!" he yelled at her down the phone.

"I'm just on my way out. Seeing the physio."

"Don't go anywhere! Bombs have gone off on the Underground. There will be more... stay in; stay put! Put your telly on."

"OK, yes. OK."

Tavistock Square, central London: 9:47
"A fourth bomb has just exploded. On a bus in Tavistock Square."

The street next to where Teresa lived.

The gut-wrenching scene unfolded before Dan's eyes as the report came through on the TV network he was simultaneously watching and being interviewed by. The top of the bus blown off. The casualties... he heard his own voice on the live TV broadcast analysing it, having already seen the explosion twenty minutes before it had happened...

But not in Tavistock Square. In his own street.

4

Nausea was tempered with the relief of having possibly saved a life, one he greatly cherished. He often wished he hadn't strayed while they had been together.

After an afternoon of media calls he phoned Teresa back. His earlier call had interrupted her as she was about to leave the flat. She would have been in the path of the bus explosion.

"Does this make up for the ten years with me?" Dan asked.

"No," said Teresa.

The glittering red lights over Highbury Fields were forgotten in the ghastly turmoil of 7 July, 2005.

Undisclosed location: 7 July 2005, 11:00

Immediately after the worst terrorist attacks ever launched on British soil, a high-level emergency government crisis meeting was called. Closeted in the corridors of power were the army top brass, high-ranking officials, and the country's leading lights in counter-terrorism, security and intelligence.

Among those stepping out of bulletproof, bombproof cars was a tall, fair-haired, well-built, confident and impressive-looking military figure. He blinked against the sun's rays as he strode, his heart pounding, into the meeting room. Nobody could see beneath his hard exterior the knife-edge tension that coursed through every cell and every sinew of his mighty six-foot-four frame.

His reputation as an oft-decorated bomb disposal technician on several military campaigns had led him from the horrors of the battlefield to high places. He had become a leading light in countering improvised explosive devices – IEDs – and the ways in which those responsible for these blots on humanity are dealt with.

Major Adam Jerome Armstrong answered with machine-gun-fast delivery a barrage of questions and requests for guidance. He rattled through the questions as though on autopilot. The explosives, the terrorists, and –the suicide bombings, which Britain had never suffered before.

What he did not mention at the meeting was the horrific scene that had raged before his eyes on waking that morning. *A flash vision of three explosions on three London tube trains. The aftermath of chaos. The shattered limbs; the blood; the smoke. And then, the screams.*

One hour before they happened.

Undisclosed location: 7 July 2005, 11:45

A tall, stylish, dark-haired woman dressed sharply in a tight-fitting black skirt suit walked out of her house somewhere in the outer limits of London. Her high heels clacked in the driveway as she strode purposefully towards her car, a black 1960s Mercedes. She checked the underside carefully, just as she and her unit and hundreds of others had done while stationed in Northern Ireland. This process used to make her heart flutter. Now she was immune.

Immune to just about everything, as it was soon after that time that the affair with Adam Armstrong had begun. Even today, with the devastating attacks on everyone else's mind, flash memories of that tempestuous liaison flitted in and out of hers. Checking her handbag for her security pass, she took out the photo of him that she had kept – goodness knows why. She glanced down at the standard ID picture of his even, classically handsome features, ruthless confidence shining out of those penetrating blue-grey eyes. She stifled tears, crumpled the photo, tossed it onto the floor and started the car. She would probably recover it later. She couldn't bear to discard it.

And she couldn't discard the memories. The endless, frenetic lovemaking; his boundless energy and strength. Sheena liked her men big, strong, highly trained, hard. Only this one satisfied her limitless appetite. Boy, was he good. Adam epitomised her ideal of high-octane, potent alpha-male perfection. The scene kept returning: riding atop the smooth, muscled body of a Greek god, grasping his golden hair, her long nails digging into his back, biting deep into his broad chest and shoulders… she climaxed not once, but twice, three times, in rapid succession. Their exhaustion was short-lived before they

6

began all over again. She liked being on top. She wanted all of him, to devour him. She adored him.

She wished the memories would go away. Especially the ghastly scene, flashing before her eyes as he swiftly moved on top of her, going in deeper, holding her down, ramming her hard. Mesmerised by the blue-grey eyes gazing down on her as they soared towards the all-devouring zenith, she saw it.

A horrendous vision of warfare. Terrible, blood-soaked, body-torn warfare, soldiers blown apart, the smell of blood, civilians mutilated. Only when she was with him. Only when he was inside her. As she pulled him deeper inside her and screamed and thrashed her way towards her climax.

Worse than the ghastly flashing scenes, she relived the moment daily when she had found him in bed with another woman – from her own unit, damn it. Had she been carrying her firearm she would have shot him dead there and then.

She tried to dismiss the thoughts, blacker each time, as soon as they appeared. She had a job to do. And despite the tragic events of the day, she was about to take up a new post on a highly covert new project. This would enable her to carry out her plan.

Revenge, they say, is a dish best served cold. The heat of passionate love burnt out of her, Sheena was ice-cold. All feelings frozen. But now she was fired up again, as everything Adam touched got fired up, set alight, burning like the sun.

Now she was plunging back into that white-hot heat. But in a way that neither she nor anyone else could have imagined.

Chapter 2

"I wanted to be the guy who everyone looks at and thinks: 'Holy shit, that guy was fucking mental, fearless and, most of all, a leader.'"

Soldier, 26, British Army

Iraq: August 2005

At the baking roadside, looking through his binocular lenses, Adam could see the IED in some detail. Taking them away, he could still see it. And it wasn't the first time. It was the third time in so many high-threat roadside operations. And also… he could see the devices in the dark.

Today, he and his team ventured out into another relentless search for devices. Hidden in houses, by roadsides, in corpses, bins, prams. The constant watch for the presence of the abnormal.

Dozens of bombs and mines had been uncovered and rendered safe by Adam's troop in just one week. The crackle of gunfire was almost eternal, in every setting. Until it all went eerily quiet.

The insurgents had begun setting off IEDs from some distance away, by mobile phone or key-fob. These would send a signal to close the electrical circuit inside the IED, setting it off. The tangle of dirty coloured wires was sometimes visible, and could be disrupted from a relatively safe distance. EOD – explosives ordnance disposal – operators often shot them with a hand-held disruptor, a vital piece of equipment. They combined the strength and stamina of their Army training with technical brilliance and delicacy.

But the devilish thing that lurked metres away from Adam was something else. It was a roadside mortar, triggered by a motion sensor found in alarm systems. This was wired up to a detonator to make it explode when anything disturbed the beam.

And this was no ordinary roadside mortar. This thing, lurking in scrub, was an explosively formed penetrator - which would fire a white-hot kinetic slug at 8,000 metres a second. The thing only metres away from Adam's shaded, glaring eyes could incinerate a tank and everyone in it. The Iraqi insurgents detonated some EFPs by remote signal. But this projectile was on a passive sensor. Deadly ingenuity. The moment Adam stepped across that beam, *boom*. These moments could be his last on Earth.

The adrenaline burst came again and again, flooding his bloodstream. He had to find a way of interfering with the device without setting it off, and while carrying a fifty-kilogram weight. All this time, a crowd wasn't far away. One of them could have his hand on another trigger in case the bomb tech disabled the sensor. He couldn't blow it in place or jolt it. His team waited in the Control Point vehicle, covering him and jamming signals that could trigger the IED. Gunfire crackled.

His face, a perfect amalgam of rugged and 'matinée idol' features, was reddish-brown from the merciless Iraqi sun, which had turned his hair a lighter shade. Sweat ran through his helmet, skirting his blue-grey eyes as they squinted behind his wraparound shades.

Sweat poured; his heart banged; then it happened.

He could *see* the beam of the sensor.

Only for a second, but long enough for him to avoid it and crawl further towards the twin-box device, sweat pouring, breath coming in short gasps. He could make out the charges inside and a small pack with wires leading to a detonator. He wanted to get it back without blowing it up so that it would give a host of forensics clues about its diabolical maker and where the bits and pieces came from.

As he edged closer, he moved, almost an atom's width at a time, the tool for separating the bomb's components and preventing detonation, tensed to apply it in a split second and render the IED useless. He had helped to design this item of kit, dubbed the 'Strong Arm' to play on his name. The lads liked the Strong Arm even though they took the piss out of its name – strong arse, all of that.

Only yesterday, he'd used the Strong Arm erroneously.

Because he had severed the wire with a glance from his eyes.

He didn't know how. It was too incredible, too ridiculous for him to believe, and it didn't always happen.

But this time, on the baking ground somewhere in Iraq, sprawled in front of the tawdry, scruffy little box of lethal tricks that could end his life, it did. He avoided the beam, a beam that he could see; a beam which is not visible to the human eye. He clipped the connector inside the box. Job done.

The elation of success was soon followed by exhaustion. Adam sat on a rock with his team, his outer protective gear discarded, his suntanned body drenched in sweat. He lit a cigarette. Once a few weeks back, his mum had said that smoking was bad for him. After dismantling several IEDs that day, he had said that it was probably OK. He was indestructible.

He looked out over the rocky desert. It was like the surface of another planet.

In an instant, filling the unlimited emptiness, he saw it.

The desert before him turned a deep, boiling red. Mile after mile of vast canyons, mountains, craters. An ancient people – if they were people – walked slowly through ruins on the endless vermilion sands. Lines of warriors marched under a sickly yellow sky filled by a gigantic white sun...

As soon as the vision had appeared, it had gone. Must be the unrelenting heat, the pressure of this job. Later, in the freezing night, the dreams came again.

The nightmares were still there, and they came unannounced. Some came when he was asleep. The ones which came when he was awake were worse.

PTSD – post-traumatic stress disorder – was not yet well known as an affliction suffered by many veterans. And there would be more experiencing it in years to come, along with thousands from past wars. And so young: early thirties and already a veteran of several conflicts. Tough, hard, trained; visible strength, unseen damage.

Nightmares, flashbacks, waking dreams, rapid heart rate: these were just some of the dreaded symptoms. Friends he served with shot, blown apart; villagers massacred.

And that other dream. *Falling, falling... no parachute. Falling thousands and thousands of feet, 200 miles an hour, through clouds of ice, cocooned in flames. Gasping for breath. Falling, the force of gravity tearing him apart, crashing to earth, his strong body blasted into pieces as he slammed into the hard desert ground...*

They were nothing to do with drugs. He never touched drugs; he did the usual round of heavy-duty alcohol intake, end of. His medical record was pristine, physically and mentally.

Neither had he made the extra skills, insights and powers known to a living soul. He never knew when they were about to kick in. Maybe they had always been there, from childhood. And were increasing, by the day.

He wore his military shades not just against the sun's glare but most of the time, as he could see in the dark. Photophobia was a PTSD symptom as well, but he'd been able to see like that for years. Wearing the shades constantly provoked banter in the desert: "Looks like rain, boss" and worse. Some worshipped him; others were not so sure. We just get on with the job. Teamwork makes the dream work. We're all human, after all.

Chapter 3

Liverpool: 1975

Thirty years earlier, Dan was sitting in the lounge in his parents' house in Liverpool, watching a documentary called *Cracked Actor* about David Bowie. He was transfixed. Not just by the enigmatic rock star's music, but also by his fantastic ability to morph and masquerade.

Once he'd left university and the constrictions of family life, Dan descended on the nation's capital and took on the look. As a skinny man with high cheekbones, an expressive mouth, a sharp nose and slightly odd, photophobic eyes that often needed shades, Bowie was an easy fit.

His first Civil Service job in London got him into the lower realms of intelligence work. He was bored rigid. One day he marched into the office with Bowie's slicked-back orange-and-blond hair, eyeliner and theatrical make-up, wearing a sky-blue bum-freezer suit with big multi-pleated trousers. The chit-chat stopped instantly, and instead of cringing with skin-prickling embarrassment, Dan drank in the shocked silence through every pore. He left that job soon after.

Bowie propelled Dan's talent for reinvention: to change from one image and identity to the next, and to mimic and absorb ideas and make them his own. And to accept and enjoy his new-found bisexuality, which had been there since his school days. Back then, you kept this to yourself. He had a string of girlfriends and boyfriends, but not at the same time.

"You're a serial bisexual," said Duncan, when they first met.

"I swing both ways while eating cornflakes."

He liked hard sex with big, masculine, moody men and soft, lingering, tender sex with feminine, feisty women. He fell in love often. Women stole his heart; men, his soul.

London: 1985

He met his first real love, Jane, while DJ-ing in a club. There she was, at the back of the cellar disco, stunning in a pink plastic mini-skirt, with dark curly hair and luscious red lips. She came up to Dan's turntable while he spun a mix of New Wave, Bowie and soul. "Let's go for a drink," she said, pulling him down off the stage. "I love Bowie. But I'm not your *fan*!"

They cut a striking pose as they hit the nightclub scene. As they swaggered down the stairs of Studio 21 in Oxford Street, the basement dancefloor shook to the thumping beat. They moved on to that shoebox of a club, Blitz in Covent Garden, a hangout for the arch-poseurs, the famous and the wannabe famous. It was London's most exciting time in music and fashion since the 1960s. The notion of fifteen minutes of fame ran riot.

They grew apart, and Jane married someone else. Then Dan met Teresa, a Humanities teacher from New York City. She came to his gigs, grew her curly brown hair into a bigger Afro because Dan loved Afros, and in exchange, got him to lose the Bowie make-up.

Her practical influence also got Dan thinking about his future. One night, down the packed Bell pub in King's Cross, as he downed the night's first pint of lukewarm lager, Dan said, "I want something more solid."

"They don't serve food in the Bell." Teresa was always literal.

"I'm talking about something more challenging to do. I want to work in defence."

Teresa had a sister in the US Air Force. "Well, the green flying suit is quite fetching."

"I'm not talking about joining up." A spikey-haired punter pushed past, spilling beer on Dan's sartorial remnant of the Bowie spaceman era. "I mean, *look* at me. I'm a disgrace."

"I am doing," said Teresa.

"I'll have to do a load of research first. And meet some very different people from this lot."

His hair was returned to its natural dark brown, cropped in military style to fit his lean face. He was still bone-thin and dressed in smart Mod vintage suits and shades.

"You won't be able to wear those all day, for a start," said Teresa. "Unless they deploy you in some desert somewhere."

Chapter 4

Thirty years on, the heady days of the eighties were a distant memory. Dan was doing something more solid. He had undergone a transformation of ambitions. He had managed to get into defence. He was now working alongside a military brotherhood, no longer hanging out with night-clubbers. He had made it his business to learn about every kind of explosive device known to man and beast. Who made them, and why, and all the godawful stuff that made up the weapons of war and terrorism.

He couldn't have had a more different background from his new colleagues – mainly Army, first-responder Forces and corporate defence types – if he had tried. He was getting booked to speak in places he'd never been before.

Sometimes a conference coincided with a music gig. Like once in Berlin, where he still had a following. During the day, he lectured on bomb attacks to a military crowd. At night, he weaved his skinny body onto the stage, clad in Bowie's white shirt and dark waistcoat and belted out songs in a smoke-filled cellar in the former Eastern sector. Stepping onto a podium to deliver a talk about IEDs and weapons of mass destruction propelled him to an equal high, but without the mascaraed eyes and clouds of dry ice.

Dan's propensity for change also led him to hanker after men again, this time older, distinguished types. Teresa told him to leave. After a string of one-night stands, he went to live with Duncan in his big terraced house in Highbury. His new work swept him up onto another plane of existence, another life. Duncan hated it.

"It gives you the illusion of power. Like an arms dealer," he said. Dan swigged back a gin and tonic prior to another dinner party. "I am *not* an arms dealer. I'm trying to help save people from weapons – to protect them against terrorism."

"Exactly what I mean. It gives you the illusion of power. Save people, saving the world."

As the intensity of his work grew, Dan took refuge in his walks round Highbury Fields, often late at night, music pounding in his ears. The volume was barely turned up, though, as he could hear a gnat fart in the next county. He revelled in the work he had dedicated himself to. By 2005, he had met and worked alongside dozens of Army veterans.

He laughed off his unconventional past: "He won the Queen's Gallantry Medal, I won the queer's gallivanting medal." Such campy references were as far as he went. Bisexuality was not admitted to; not in these circles.

Not that he wanted to 'come out', another term he disliked. He told friends, "I will not be tagged or labelled in any way, by any tendency, group, origin, or belief." He believed in keeping such things private, while showing off other attributes. His personal life was his own.

And he had a far bigger secret to hide.

Dublin: 2006

On a chilly April morning, Dan took a taxi through streets bustling with people in a modern, prosperous capital of a nation approaching the sixtieth year of its independence. It was also eight years since the Good Friday Agreement, which had ended over thirty years of near-civil war in the North. The incongruity of what he was about to do was almost palpable – to see, handle and photograph one of the biggest arrays of seized terrorist weaponry ever assembled.

He had the highest level of escort. Declan Murray, the former commander of the Irish Army's counter-terror unit, met him. He had arranged with the chief of the Gardaí, the Irish police – to take Dan into the vast Aladdin's cave of death and destruction below their magnificent headquarters in Dublin: a vast arsenal amassed by the most ruthless terrorist group of its time – the Provisional Irish Republican Army, the IRA.

Down several flights of stairs they tramped, down, down, into a warehouse of bombs, explosives, rocket-propelled grenades, mortars, and acres of guns. The IRA's final act of decommissioning had come almost at the same time as the London 7/7 attacks, a year earlier.

Dan took his sunglasses off to gawp at drawers full of detonators and timers, whole rooms full of guns, fully built IEDs, and even a torpedo. All the weapons had been seized before they could inflict death and damage. Like in an old apothecary, jars of explosive samples were lined up on shelves and clearly labelled. Declan and the police chief led Dan over to a display of IEDs that the Provisionals had custom-made. They looked strikingly familiar.

"We seized this lot at Clonaslee – and enough weapons to start a medium-sized war," Declan said in his lilting Cork accent, adding, "I did more than most to put the bloody IRA out of business." He picked up one of the box devices.

"This is the most ingenious. The Semtex went in there." Declan indicated the middle compartment. "They were going to plant thirty of these in London electricity substations." The devices would have been dormant until the detonator, housed in a metal tube, was moved to connect with the explosive charge. The boxes had been mass-produced to precise specifications.

"Had they got all three, the level of chaos would have been almost unimaginable. Just searching for them would have shut down the Underground. These devices were expertly made." For a brief moment, as Dan examined the substation IED, he saw something else. He swayed and turned white, almost dropping the remnant of the IRA's bomb-building prowess.

This time, in front of his eyes, a blinding flash. *An explosion in an Underground station. King's Cross. Top of the escalators. Dozens of passengers blown apart; hundreds more running away.*

Then the scene was gone.

19

Declan said, "You all right there, mate?" He knew about Dan's past. He wondered if Dan was about to faint, now that he saw once again the familiar instruments of IRA death and destruction.

"It's OK," said Dan. "I didn't sleep well."

He had been kept awake the night before by memories of an ill-gotten past – of secrets that lurked in his other world. When he finally slept, an old dream resurfaced. He steps off the plane after a trip to Belfast and goes through Passport Control. Travelling alone, he wears what many IRA men and most of the male population, wore then – a black leather jacket and jeans. His hair is cropped short. He is stopped and taken aside by two burly cops eyeing up selected passengers. He feels the colour drain from his face.

"Where have you been?"

"Belfast." They know that, it's where the plane's just landed from.

"Why?"

"Going to my father's birthplace." They had a file on him that you could see from space.

"Where do you stay in London?" They knew that he lived in the capital.

"Bloomsbury."

"Passport." Dan hands it over, having already had it checked in the arrivals hall. He takes off his shades and looks straight up at the cop. They handcuff him and take him away.

Dan always awoke from this dream – a memory of an actual incident, apart from being arrested at the end – drenched in sweat. That's because in past years Dan wasn't just dallying with men and singing in a band. He also held Irish Republican sympathies. This came from hearing family stories in Liverpool about the Irish Civil War. A genuine love for Ireland – as well as for the country of his birth – turned into a misguided allegiance with radicals. He went to the smoke-filled bars and the meetings, and heard the rebel songs, loaded with nationalist sentimentality. He knew all the words from childhood.

He felt a heated rush of embarrassment at revelling in the sweaty green-and-white fog of Celtic shirts, the baying of the crowd to badly played Irish music ringing in his sensitive ears. He did not support their violence, but he felt an affinity, and was curious. So he ventured down the risky road of a self-appointed infiltrator – and learned every detail of how they made their explosive devices..

On one trip, an old IRA commander met him at Armagh bus station. Shame mixed with naive excitement as he climbed into the man's car. They drove across the border, no longer heavily guarded by troops and barriers, but watched by more cameras than at the Academy Awards. They walked for a while, discussing the Movement, the bombs and the bullets. Looking out over the hilly, emerald-green scenery, Dan said, "My dad used to say that, if you look at Ireland from space, it's all one beautiful island, one geographical entity. If only it were that simple."

His activities were watched and recorded. By 2005 Dan was on the side of the angels. The IRA had decommissioned its weapons, well most of them - and had officially disbanded. He lectured on the IRA's bombing campaign to military and civilian audiences far and wide. In an interview with a military magazine, the editor asked Dan, "How, as a civilian...?"

"A soft civilian," said Dan.

"...did you gain such a vast wealth of knowledge and insight into the Provisional IRA?"

"Long story," said Dan.

On successive trips to Ireland he would approach Passport Control with pounding heart. On these occasions he wasn't stopped. They already knew where he had been.

North London: 2006

Dan moved out of the big terraced house in Highbury. Duncan came back from holiday to find neat piles of removal boxes lining the four flights of stairs.

"I want to go out with women again. We haven't been right for some time. And you've found someone else, anyway," was

Dan's succinct parting shot. "But I hope we can still be friends."

The removal van drove up and around Highbury Fields. Dan looked through shaded, tear-filled eyes at the little park that still held his heart. He knew he would come back – to the Fields at least. As they headed for the south coast, he reflected on two rumbustious decades in the nation's capital.

Then he remembered the strange, shimmering red lights he had seen in the sky over the park on the morning of 7/7. And the night when he had been forced against one of the big trees by a psychotic knifeman threatening to kill him. He had managed to talk the lunatic round by saying that he worked in counter-terrorism. He had peed himself with the knife pointed at his throat. But he still went back to the park for his walk the next day.

And he had seen the lights again, undulating in the north London sky, crimson bands of energy. Must have been the shock of the attack the night before.

Nothing would keep him from Highbury Fields.

Chapter 5

"Superhuman effort isn't worth a damn unless it achieves results."

Ernest Shackleton

Iraq: 2006

Adam Armstrong was brought in to see his commanding officer, a Colonel Richards. He was a big man, only slightly shorter than Adam – just six feet. He motioned to him to sit down.

"I'll get straight to the point. I understand that you have shown some extraordinary RSP skills in theatre."

"What are we talking about?" Adam froze momentarily. There was nothing worse than standing out from the other high-threat operators in anything other than the job at hand. No one was special; you were in it to do your bit until you retired, often cast aside. They say that the Forces fight for Queen and country, but many say, above all, they fight with and for their mates. The best and closest friendships emerged out of Army service. Brotherhood for life: a bond for life.

Somebody in his troop had noticed that Adam had somehow, miraculously, disarmed an IED without the usual kit and render-safe procedures – RSPs. How had they worked it out? They worked as a team, and lived cheek by jowl. Maybe it was more obvious than he had thought.

When Adam's packed audiences heard him describe his missions fighting the terrorists, told at breakneck pace, he never mentioned those extraordinary instances when the tools in his bomb disposal toolbox were supplanted by an unnamed, but not untracked, set of skills. He felt it was something to be ashamed of – something beyond his training and well-honed abilities.

"I'll not piss you about. We're looking to develop those skills. I know it sounds bloody off the wall, but the Americans are already looking into this kind of advancement."

"Are we talking about Supersoldiers?" said Adam. He knew that the Pentagon was hatching some daft Arnie-Schwarzenegger-style project to develop troops with super-strength and telepathy, existing without sleep, even immunity from pain.

"Well, we Brits can't afford their bonkers projects. It's only just a bunch of so-called blue-sky thinking ideas as yet. But we want to get ahead of the game. There's a unit set up to hand-select some talented officers like you and, well, develop and use those skills. Along with some of the new technologies."

Richards went on. "I also understand that you knew at a hundred-metre distance in a row of vehicles in that street which one was carrying the VBIED. We were able to clear the area and blow it."

"Anyone could have done it," said Adam.

Colonel Richards went on. "I doubt it. I know it sounds like fringe nutcase crap, but they're interested in ESP – extrasensory perception."

"I've been in Intelligence," said Adam. He was good at it, very good, but he thrived on action. "Perception is part of the job."

Then the flashback came. Right out the blue, as he was being briefed by his commanding officer. They were out at the crack of dawn. His second ammo tech ventured out to a roadside device. Adam saw into its internal workings, from a distance. He yelled through the comms to his comrade to run – as the device was about to explode – which it did, within seconds. His ATO 2 just got out of harm's way in time. Several civilians didn't. They were blasted to pieces. He couldn't save them all. He wished, above everything, that he could.

Adam didn't flinch during the mind-shattering flashback. His CO, oblivious, went on. "You are a prime candidate, as you seem to have these abilities naturally. I'm surprised they didn't come up in training."

Adam's head cleared and he focused on what Richards was saying. He was proud of his achievements without the ESP or whatever it was. He had worked hard to become a bomb tech, one of the most dangerous and rewarding of Army roles. He had been decorated for showing his abilities and courage. Being singled out for anything weird like this would not sit well. He had won his medals through his own efforts and through teamwork. Like every other British serviceman, he was here to do a job – nothing more, nothing less.

And he had learned to rationalise what he witnessed and experienced. He was highly knowledgeable and calm under pressure. Those were the qualities that drove the EOD operators out into the forbidding climates of Iraq and Afghanistan every day. The more they were exposed to stress and trauma, the more resilience they built up, and the higher their tolerance. Or so it seemed. Amidst the chaos of battle, they were focused on the systematic clearance of lethally cunning explosive devices. Adam plied his trade along with dozens of others who could said to be 'half a stroke off normal.'

"We need everything – every one – we can get. I don't like it, but if it doesn't get results, they'll suspend the experiment."

"Experiment? Sounds like something out of Frankenstein. Or worse," said Adam.

Super-soldiers weren't science fiction. Some projects, funded by the Pentagon, were aiming to create the 'ultimate killing machine': soldiers who were immune to stress, shock, sleeplessness, even guilt. The 'Brain Machine Interface' project was aiming to develop computer chips that could connect directly to the human brain via implants. As well as enabling soldiers to control robotics with thought alone, this was supposed to allow squads to communicate via… telepathy.

Such ideas were not new. Since the élite Spartan force of ancient Greece, military chiefs had long thought of ways to shorten or enhance the demanding training of soldiers and to create a 'warfighter' – the customary US term – sent in to kill and carry out dangerous operations without remorse, regret, fear, and fatigue.

This was the very antithesis of the British Army ethos, despite advancements in military technology. Creating a soldier who was more machine than human was, to Adam and his mates, a form of cheating. They had enough on their plate without this. More funding for vital equipment would hit the spot far better than some half-arsed scheme to create supermen.

"I'm sorry, sir, but this isn't for me."

"It is voluntary, of course."

Voluntary – no such thing in the Army. Adam thought of the ancient joke: I want three volunteers – you, you, and you. He marched out of the office, knowing that this wasn't the end of the matter.

Months later, he was back on his next tour in Iraq, this time in an even more dangerous area of operations in Basra. Adam and other high-threat operators were regular targets of the insurgents, as they had been while patrolling the sniper-ridden streets of Northern Ireland, when he was very young, on his first tour. On this mission, he was even more of a target for the terrorists hiding among crowds, lurking on rooftops and peering through broken windows. Crowds of Iraqis would gather above the streets he trod and drove, looking down on his long walk to remove a bomb threat. Hidden among them were snipers, ready to take his head off or blast his chest apart with a single well-aimed round.

And along with the snipers, there were the scorpions, lurking in bombed-out buildings and under tents, ready to strike. As he slept fitfully, the crackle of gunfire shattering the still air, the snores of his mates almost deafening his hypersensitive ears, the ten-centimetre monstrous yellow thing came at him. Its spiny tail coiled, its sting seared his lower shin.

And again.

He jolted awake and swiped the creature off his leg, smashing it with his hand. There was no way to get antivenom –

no time. He slapped a dirty rag over the sting and held it there, squeezing the punctured skin, gasping for breath. The piercing neurotoxin coursed through his bloodstream. Sweat poured down his tanned face, which was contorted in pain. One sting is agony; the second from this species is lethal.

Minutes later, he rolled over on the rocky ground and fell asleep.

The pain in his leg was forgotten as another bastard day dawned, a day when the bat-shit-crazy insurgency got a whole lot worse. He and his team ventured out on operations under fire from grenades, RPGs, snipers in doorways and on rooftops, the whole fucking lot. In a split-second reaction, Adam blew at least one sniper's head off. It exploded in a cloud of dark red blood and blasted tissue.

As ever, he was high on the danger. He wanted to hunt down every terrorist on the planet.

A sharp pain pierced his right shoulder as a round slashed through it. The pain faded after an instant – the adrenaline kicking in as they came under fire again. Grenades screamed. Two of his men were down. He had to reach them. But the hole in his shoulder was gushing blood; a chunk of his upper arm had been shot off. The bullet had just missed the bone. Another round had lodged in his shoulder. As he lost consciousness, and the paramedic's morphine jab kicked in, a thought streamed into his mind of the mates he had just lost, their blood and remains scattered in the street. And then the images returned: a child's face looking at him from the rubble. No body; just a face.

Then he was falling, falling through the sky, hundreds of miles through clouds, ice, rain and blinding light... crackling flames surrounded him... fighting for air, feeling his diaphragm crushed... dropping at the speed of sound... like a bullet shot from a rifle barrel... no parachute...

Chapter 6

"Danger gleams like sunshine to a brave man's eyes."

Euripides

Iraq: 2006

When he came round in 34 Field Hospital, the bullet had been removed from his strapped-up shoulder. He called his family and girlfriend. *I'm OK; just a flesh wound.*

A mere two days later, when the medic came to change the dressings, it appeared that he was fitter than a butcher's dog. Both wounds were almost fully healed. Although he'd lost a lot of blood, he didn't need a transfusion. Even the flesh that had been shot off his upper arm had begun to regenerate.

"Jesus Christ," was the response, as the bandages came off. "Are you for real? This sort of injury usually takes weeks to heal up, even with our tender loving care."

Another medic saw a makeshift dirty bandage around his lower shin. It had been missed in the melée of the gunshot injuries. "What happened here, mate?"

"Scorpion stings. Night before last operation. Fucking yellow bastard."

The two medics tried not to look fazed. "You said *two* stings. From a yellow jobbie."

Adam muttered something and feigned the need to sleep.

"Better enjoy it while it lasts, mate. We'll be kicking you out tomorrow."

With his hypersensitive ears, he heard the medics mumble a few metres away. "*Leiurus* whatsit. The deathstalker. Bloody hell. First sting hurts like fuck. The second, you're history. No antivenom. But just *look* at him!"

His next thoughts were for the mates he'd lost. As he tried to sleep his head swam with the images of the latest battle he had survived. One comrade had been killed. He hadn't been able to save him. That would take far more getting over, if he ever could.

Adam knew that he was lucky not to have been left limbless or dead in that dusty boiling Iraqi street, as could have happened so many times before. Many were left without limbs and spent years undergoing lengthy treatments and rehab.

He hoped his rapid recovery would not bring him one step closer to being drafted into the nascent Supersoldiers project. He didn't recall having had any serious injuries as a young lad. He seemed to have the ability – he didn't know why or how – to recover from two gunshot wounds and two lethal scorpion stings in short order.

So rapidly and so well that his case notes were transferred up several levels until they reached a small, faceless office on the outer limits of London. Staffed by an agency known only to the core of the intelligence services, this unit had no visible presence – in public or in the wider civil service or anywhere else.

The dark-haired, sharp-suited woman appointed as deputy head of the unit was sitting, legs crossed elegantly, in front of multiple computer screens. She took a paper file from a colleague. All were working at the highest level of secrecy and security. They didn't even know if the names on each other's badges were made up. The legend on hers was simply 'Sheena'.

"Do we have his DNA records?"

"No. He refused to give a sample," was the functionary's reply. "It is voluntary, remember. DNA samples are taken from Forces personnel, if they consent."

A colleague chimed in. "For storage in case we need to identify bodies or body parts after a soldier is killed in action, accident or combat death, where remains are unrecognisable."

"Some object to it. Voluntary samples aren't passed on to the National DNA Database or used to help police with criminal inquiries. But to some, it has those connotations."

"Well, we need one from our star ATO. Arrange it ASAP," Sheena responded curtly. "He's just what we need on this project."

"Has his medical history been checked? At the selection centre, when he first joined up? Anything unusual?" Only the unusual pace, power and frequency of the fantastic sex we had, Sheena thought. And that unusual effect... the scenes... she fought to put that out of her mind.

"He'd have to have a more extensive test, which isn't SOP. Something like a brain scan."

Sheena left the group for another meeting somewhere in the bowels of the gleaming office building. She reflected for a few moments on her earlier years, on her struggle to get past male competition to get to the top, and still falling just short of it. This had spurred her on to even greater efforts with growing ruthlessness and determination.

She had had a string of male lovers, but none had got so near to taking her soul and her heart as the man who was the subject of that meeting. How love and lust so easily become hate, but still love, and still lust, and then more hate... Her heart and her soul may have gone, but her mind, her cold, logical mind, remained intact. Her patience, the long wait to get even, would be tested to the full. And she was prepared to wait, poised to strike.

Adam Armstrong was itching – both literally after his bandages had come off, and figuratively – to get back into action. His shoulder needed minimal physio and he was somewhat annoyed to be called into Colonel Richards' office. He hoped he was being promoted or sent on another vital mission.

"Sit down, Major. I see you have made quite a remarkable recovery."

Not only did he see the big fit man fully recovered, he'd seen the full medical report, which elicited the obvious response, "Fuck. I don't believe this." He had been obliged to send it further up, much further up, following a directive received only months ago from his superiors. He immediately regretted this as soon as he'd done it.

He had heard other sundry accounts of Adam's seemingly prescient and telekinetic abilities in the field, but these were all hearsay. He had to tread carefully. Major Armstrong had already been decorated for actions in the field which were wholly down to his own skill and efforts. He wasn't easily persuaded.

Only occasionally, and at random, had there been an intervening – or internalised – transient extra ability to perform what civilians would call miracles. Dodgy stuff, and not for those whose lives in service, taken as a whole, often teetered between long periods of waiting and sheer hell. And ceaseless banter.

The Supersoldiers project had been put on hold, but its protagonists continued to monitor its most desired recruit. Now, Adam Armstrong was off operations and launched into the outside world of Civvy Street.

Until the big mission, several years down the line, sheer hell could wait.

Chapter 7

"I have seen The great Orion, with his jewelled belt,
That large-limbed warrior of the skies, go down
Into the gloom. Beside him sank a crowd
Of shining ones."

William C. Bryant

Central London: 2018

Twelve years on, Dan was at his umpteenth conference. This time the event, populated by the usual corporate and military delegates, was not overseas, but in a London hotel overlooking the Thames and the London Eye.

The delegates took their seats. He gave his talk just before lunch, on the poisoning of the Russian dissident Alexander Litvinenko with polonium-210 twelve years earlier. It served as a case study along with subsequent examples of Russian poisonings of high-profile individuals. He brought a teapot on the stage and poured out two cups of tea.

"Anyone care to join me for a brew?" he said, deadpan, and handed a cup to a lady on the front row he had chatted up earlier. Women were always in the minority at these events. "One or two sugars, love?" His cheeky northern bluntness overrode political correctness. "One, please." Dan's chosen delegate was a good sport, and he made sure his audience saw him pop something into her cup from a tiny test tube hidden in his jacket pocket.

Then he got serious and reeled off brightly coloured slides packed with facts and figures about radiation, how the victim had suffered, how the agencies had dealt with the incident, and how many people and places in London had been affected not too far from where this meeting was taking place.

The lunch break brought the usual mingling and chit-chat. A delegate gulped down his wine and asked Dan, "I hope you haven't slipped any of that stuff in here, mate. Have you served? Which regiment?"

"Me? Are you kidding? I can manage a sharp crease in the trousers, but that's about it."

"Well, you know your stuff, like you speak from experience," said the delegate, whose name badge indicated that he worked for an equipment company. "I saw you speak a while back on the IRA's bombing campaign."

Dan flushed with pride. He could never quite believe he'd got this far. He was reminded of his past involvement with the Provisional IRA. For many years now he had been on the side of the angels. But nothing could replace actually going out on mission. His role was mainly communicating what his colleagues actually did in the field. And he loved to communicate, to perform – whether singing on stage or talking about bombs and radiation. He revelled in the round of talks and meeting people.

But as he wandered in and out of the chatting groups, he still felt like an intruder. Like a distant, ice-cold comet crashing through the Earth's warming atmosphere, he needed to feed off their warmth. And like a comet, he feared being cast out again into the frozen wastes of space. He was outside the brotherhood. He wanted to win approval and annihilate his past dalliance.

Then out of the huddle, a very tall man of obvious military mien came up to Dan, smiled and introduced himself.

Most people Dan met at conferences were forgettable. But this one was different. Better looking, for a start. Well over six foot, broadly built, dark blond hair, penetrating grey-blue eyes, straight nose, and a perfectly shaped mouth that could bark orders despite a hint of Cupid's-bow delicacy. He flashed a dazzling smile that could stop traffic – and probably stop bombs from going off as well. A rugged, dynamic elegance. They made the usual introductions and exchanged brief pleasantries.

"Great talk," said Adam. "Let me know if you're organising anything. Give me a shout." Flattery aside, the tall Army officer come across with a natural charisma and an easy eloquence. He asked no questions.

He handed Dan a card. Ares Consulting. Ares: the Greek god of war. Well, this man certainly looked like one. Ares: a dangerous force, insatiable in battle, man-slaughtering. Adam turned to move on, clearly restless, and shook Dan's hand.

In a split second, a flash of blinding light bore into Dan's skull. A scene of battle. Bloodied soldiers. Then it was gone.

Dan steadied himself, pocketed the card along with the others, and thought nothing more of it or of its imposing purveyor. That is, until Adam gave his talk in the afternoon. He belted it out in a clipped machine-gun style of delivery that was more a performance than a talk. In these normally dull events, this was rare and in stark contrast to his easy chat earlier. Adam paced up and down the stage.

"The rush you get dealing with a device is fearsome. It's living on the edge of a world…"

A line from a poem flitted into Dan's mind, from a Greek legend. *'Over the edge of the World, comes forth Great Orion…'*

"…where everything is in monochrome. Every device I could neutralise took me one step closer to tracing and bringing down the groups responsible. I wanted to hunt down every terrorist on the planet."

The big screen behind him lit up with slides and breath-taking videos of operations to remove unexploded ordnance, assault entry ops – another area new to Dan – and Special Forces actions. The stuff of heroes, like in the movies – but this guy and the operations he had led were real. Dan was mesmerised. He almost forget to breathe.

"Then, when you reach the IED, you can feel your heart pounding as your eyes take in and follow the tangled wiring of the bomb's circuitry. Then you can cut in to the deadly device and render it safe. Complete success or total failure. "

Dan had seen and heard dozens of accounts by military people but nothing like this. To applause, Armstrong thanked his audience, jumped off the stage and left with his entourage. Dan wondered if this was what Brian Epstein had felt like when he walked into the Cavern club in Liverpool and first saw John Lennon on stage. The raw masculinity, the unbridled energy, the awesome talent, the barely contained violence.

Much later, after the worst day of his life, and of Adam's, he would think back to that day when he had first heard the bomb squad veteran say on that central London stage,

"If you're lucky, you see the signs and know it is time to pull back and step away. But maybe by then it's already too late."

Chapter 8

"Whatever is well said by another, is mine."

Seneca the Younger

Brighton: 2018

Dan walked out of the Art Deco apartment block in Brighton. It was twelve years since he had settled into the spacious ground floor flat. The English Channel was now his front garden. Headphones clamped onto his ears, he breathed in sea air and took his daily walk down to the harbour at Shoreham, past the brightly coloured beach huts that reminded him of liquorice allsorts.

In Brighton, hailed as 'the most liberal city in Britain', life was slower, more laid back, a perfect antidote to the constant travelling. The wind blowing in off the sea cleared his lungs and the sun browned his skin. He had put on weight, mainly from hotel food and seaside fish and chips, going from bone-thin to slim. In his early fifties, he looked and felt ten years younger and was dating women again. One of his dates was Bea, the granddaughter of a Nobel-Prize-winning British scientist. Instead of having a fling, they became close platonic friends.

Dan made supper and brought it into the sun-drenched west-facing lounge decorated with 1930s ocean liner posters, Deco mirrors and towering tropical plants. "It's like The Day of the Triffids in here," said Bea.

"Ah. Invasion of the Bodysnatchers," said Dan. "Don't fall asleep or the pods will steal your mind. They took mine long ago."

"Why don't I help you out with all this work?" Dan was giving talks or instruction somewhere in the world every other week.

"My glamorous assistant!" said Dan, pouring another glass of wine. "You're on." So Bea came to Dan's one day a week as much for cooking and for the gossip that went on in Dan's parallel universe as to do research on areas not deemed sensitive.

Dan's mobile rang with the opening bars of Bowie's 'Heroes'. Bea wished he'd turn it off.

"Do you know Major Adam Armstrong?" said the caller.

Dan's heart leapt. Why, he didn't know.

"He can't make the date and he's recommended you." Dan had seen his email to the organiser, which had made him glow with pride. *"Dan is extremely knowledgeable about IEDs – a fascinating speaker."*

"What are you looking at me like that for?" said Dan, dropping the sickly smile he'd worn throughout the call.

"It isn't the plants that are stealing your mind, darling," said Bea. "What's all that about? You been asked out on a date? You look like the cat that got the cream."

"It's a conference date, standing in for Adam Armstrong. That's like my little band headlining instead of Bowie."

Then he remembered the split-second flash vision of carnage when they first shook hands.

West Country: 2018

The country hotel was a luxurious step above the usual conference venues. Dan weighed up the executive crowd seated in the warm, wood-panelled lounge. Delegates were sitting in armchairs rather than in lecture-room rows or around a boardroom table. He welcomed the chance to address a different audience from the usual hard-bitten military and technical types.

His hypersensitive ears heard someone say, *sotto voce*, "I thought we were getting Major Armstrong today."

"I'm his body double," said Dan with dry northern aplomb, raising a subdued chuckle from the audience, prior to scaring them half to death with bombs and terrorism and the End of the World as We Know It.

Joking done, he could feel Adam's inspirational influence. He sharpened his vocal delivery into a crisp military tone, feeling the spur of his charisma. He felt his heart rate increase as he paced. The phrase 'cultural appropriation' was now in regular usage; Dan was committing something like it, and was as high as a kite.

Then, glancing for a second at the well-tended gardens outside, he stopped. Gasping for a split second, he saw the scene.

The hotel greenery suddenly mutated into boiling, dusty desert. Soldiers firing, bodies exploding in combat, blood gushing, mutilated civilians. Then it was gone.

Brighton: 2018

"How was the country hotel gig?" Bea had got used to Dan's casual use of the term for both work and music events. Dan brewed coffee and brought it through to the big study, which was neatly lined with books, files, certificates and model rockets. They looked through the diary. Dan was to host a series of workshops on IEDs: how they are made, who makes them, and how to stop them. Bea showed him an email from Adam, unbelievably offering himself as a co-instructor.

"Him? My co-instructor? That's like Bowie going on as the support band," said Dan, reversing the earlier music analogy. "Anyway, I've already got someone else. I'll invite Adam as a guest."

London: July 2018

In a July heatwave and fuelled by double espressos, Dan welcomed his old friend and co-instructor to another central London hotel. Rick, an Army intelligence veteran, was built like a brick shithouse and had a voice that could smash a shatterproof window at a hundred paces. They greeted the handful of delegates who trooped in and seated themselves around a boardroom table in yet another faceless conference venue. Dan would rather perform in front of thousands than a dozen any day. In this setting he was under closer scrutiny: he could see the whites of their eyes, and they could see his.

Adam breezed in, flashed his dazzling smile, and briskly shook Dan's hand. Immediately a scene flashed before Dan's eyes.

Again, a limitless desert: soldiers fighting, being blown up, civilians mangled. This time the desert was deep crimson. A huge white sun beat down on them from a golden sky. The hand was released. The mundane setting of the hotel boardroom returned.

Dan hoped that no one had heard him catch his breath as he shook hands with his charismatic guest. He fobbed off the vision – he avoided the word hallucination – and blamed it on an over-active imagination. Then he remembered the undulating bright red lights he'd seen over Highbury Fields on the morning of the 7/7 bombings, and the vision outside Duncan's house of the bus blowing up just before it did, several miles away, in central London. And the battle carnage scene when he was lecturing in lieu of Adam to the industry executives. *Let's crack on. Just forget it.*

Adam sat at the top of the table, nearest to Dan and Rick. He faced Dan's other guest, Dai – another old ex-Forces friend and psychologist who helped veterans with PTSD. Dan felt Adam's presence. Even seated, the big man exuded power; he was a restless tower of energy. Dan snapped into top gear and introduced everyone. "Major Adam Armstrong GC: he's been decorated more than my mum's front room."

The unease he felt after the handshake was replaced by pride at having such an important guest. Dan had no operational experience in those lethal objects that Adam and many others had spent much of their young lives disarming and dismantling, in so many conflict zones at so much personal risk. All while he was swanning around nightclubs.

He ploughed through the programme: the IRA, al-Qaeda, and all points in between. Detonators; explosive charges;

timers; targeting; acquisition; booby traps; firing circuits; trigger mechanisms. Wires snaked their way through an IED, like the double helix spiral of DNA.

Dan noticed the deep frown on the Major's handsome face, as he blinked away the light streaming in through the window. *Never question the look in his eyes*, someone had once said about veterans. He fired questions after each session and Dan managed, breathlessly, to answer them. Then Adam suddenly left, flashing his smile and making his apologies.

"Elvis has left the building," said Dan, relieved at his guest's early exit. Rick went on to talk about intelligence. Two delegates who had arrived together took exception to this.

"What do you mean, the intelligence failed?" one of them barked.

"Well, after some attacks the terrorists were already on the radar." Rick added quickly, "That said, we can't stop everyone given the limited resources we have."

As they bade farewell to the delegates, Dan asked the terrible twins on their way out, "Do you have a card?"

Smirking, one replied, "Sorry, we don't carry cards."

Rick collected up the handouts, which they had left behind. "Are you thinking what I'm thinking?"

"The drinks are on me," said Dan.

"They're from Intelligence," said Dai.

"Yes, but are they extrovert or introvert?" said Dan. "You're the psychologist."

"Well, they certainly aren't what they said they were on the list," said Rick. "Let's go down the pub."

Had they not been mired in the day's class they would have seen Adam being shepherded into a black car with blacked-out windows. Or, later, the terrible twins getting into theirs, and messaging their brief report to Sheena in the Supersoldiers unit.

And immediately after that, a message under tight encryption to the director of another, even more covert programme.

Chapter 9

The day after Dan's workshop Adam emailed, apologising for leaving early and thanking Dan for a 'brilliant job'. There were things Dan had said in the class that even he didn't know. Whether one of the country's leading counter-IED experts was just being flattering or not, Dan felt like he'd just won the Oscar for Best Actor.

And more events came, thick and fast. Not all on Adam's recommendation, but several were, at home and abroad. Adam would come over to chat, rapidly, exchanging information. Dan's heart raced as he felt heat radiating from the man; he could feel his boundless energy. "How's it going mate?" Even casual words transmitted undiluted strength, power, charisma.

Maybe being called 'mate' meant some form of inclusion, and Dan liked it. The Army banter was reserved for others; this would be the nearest Dan got. He knew that the friendship men in service have for one another is one of the greatest loves on earth. They went through hell for each other and could joke about it. Dan had no place anywhere in that brotherhood, even on its outer limits.

Adam fired snappy compliments and insults alike with a heavy sarcasm as though they'd known each other for a long time – an ace charmer. "Don't put yourself down, mate. We need academics like you."

"I'm not an academic," said Dan. "Or a journalist. If I may quote, 'Now I don't know who I am, I've never been happier'."

"Who said that, then?" said Adam, his frown deep, his piercing grey-blue eyes darting around. Probably, Dan thought, in search of higher-powered people to talk to. "Other than you just now." He crammed cake into a mouth that still managed to be finely shaped while he was shoving standard-issue conference food into it.

"Why, David Bowie, of course," said Dan, daring a wind-up. "Didn't they teach you anything at Sandhurst?"

"Do you take your inspiration from anything other than David Bowie?"

Only you, mate.

"I'm going to have to wean you onto Guns N' Roses," said the big man.

"You'll have to shoot me first," said Dan.

Dan was riding high on the acknowledgment from a hero – yes, a hero – that term that army people often avoid but which has few handy substitutes. But the flashes of terrible scenes, when they shook hands? What was all that about? Something he felt – he didn't know what – something was going on in his head, something...

Toronto: August 2018

"You won't be allowed into our talk, mate," grunted the burlier of the two cops Dan had shared a cab with from Toronto airport to the conference hall. 'Mate' again. This time not friendly. These officers from the Met were giving a talk on the investigation into the Litvinenko murder.

"But I was the VIP speaker on Litvinenko, for the US Civil Support Units. And in London." Once again, Dan felt like a frozen civilian comet feeding off the heat of a military sun, then cast out once again.

This didn't wash. "You're not security cleared. Everyone else is." So when the two made their way through the delegate tables onto the podium, one tapped Dan on the shoulder, as though feeling his collar – while the other gave him a highly visible 'out' signal. They reminded him of the two cops who'd questioned him when he landed from Belfast all those years ago. He walked out and was sorely tempted to blow them a kiss.

He wandered down empty corridors and saw that a convention was taking place at the other end of the hotel. Stands displayed all sorts of paraphernalia for what had since the dawn of the Internet become a resurgent breed – UFO enthusiasts. The folks at this particular gathering probably believed that much of science fiction is actually science fact, including the notion that flying saucers and aliens have already landed.

Dan walked up to a stand when a lady behind it called him over in a Home Counties accent. "What are you doing here?" she asked. "Don't you remember me? I was at one of those lectures you organised in London, when you were with that futuristic space magazine. Years ago," she said.

Dan cheered up immediately. It was Allison – lovely Allison Hardy. He remembered the attractive geneticist, who had been bemused by his slicked-back orange-and-blond hair and the baggy suits he sported back then. She had also had red hair, but hers had been long, wild and curly – and still was. She had hardly changed decades on. She still had the same full, shapely figure. She was alluring in a tight, low-cut cream sweater and a long burgundy skirt. Dan was amazed that she recognised him, several incarnations later.

"Of course – Dr Allison Hardy, I presume," said Dan, giving her a formal kiss on each cheek. "I'm at the other conference – the Explosives Engineers of the Canadian Army."

"Wow! How did you get into that? You were the embodiment of that futuristic weird mag you worked for," said Allison. "Oh, and I'm Professor Hardy now."

"I see congratulations are in order. What I'm in now is even weirder. Counter-terrorism. Well, as an independent. I'm not in a government agency. That's why they've just chucked me out. Fancy seeing you here, in a parallel universe."

"Well, it's still flaky, but there's some interesting stuff going on," said Allison. "What you would probably now call pseudo-science in your new military guise," she teased, and Dan made a mental note to thank those cops tomorrow for kicking him out. He was having a lot more fun than them.

"I'm also researching exoplanets – finding planets like ours with intelligent life," she said, as they made their way in the direction of the hotel bar, which was empty in mid-afternoon.

"If they're intelligent, that explains why they haven't come here," said Dan.

"You organised one of those lectures by Arthur C. Clarke all the way from Sri Lanka."

"He did 2001: A Space Odyssey writ large, didn't he? On alien civilisations in antiquity, influencing human development."

"Well, that's all the rage here," said Allison.

"All we got in 2001 was bloody 9/11," said Dan.

Allison sighed in agreement. "But sticking with my main field, I've just given a talk on genetic engineering. And the dangers of creating the superhumans of the future."

"How about a drink? I'm done here until the evening. You'll be a change from the old-hippy brigade."

Drink they did; first gin and tonics at the bar, then a bottle of wine in Allison's room. That was after the first clinch as the elevator doors closed behind them. "I've never had a woman in a lift before," said Dan, pulling her close.

"Or an elevator," she said. "When do you have to get back?"

"I'm giving my talk tomorrow, then I fly home," he said as she put her arms around him. "Nothing else on today."

"Nothing on sounds good to me," said Allison. She began pulling off his shirt as soon as her hotel room door banged shut. He kissed her hard as she pulled him down onto her, into her. He was amazed that an attractive woman not only recognised him from decades ago, but actually found him worth having in one of those glorious afternoon sessions in bed that so many conference attendees are said to indulge in.

He was so amazed that, as he got dressed and made to leave, he did not notice Allison reach for a phone she had concealed behind the desk. Or that she tapped a message that would wing its way across the ether to a scientific colleague in a highly covert, nascent terrorist group in Washington, DC.

Chapter 10

Brighton: August 2018

"How did you get on?" said Bea, tucking into the fish supper Dan had bought in from the seafront chippie. "You said you'd met up with some professor, the red-haired geneticist."

"More than met up with," said Dan drily.

"Ah, so what was all that pious talk about not getting off with anyone at conferences? That it wasn't your style?"

"She wasn't at my conference."

"Not your bloke then," said Bea, grinning and waving a forked chip at Dan while he topped up her wine glass.

"He is *not* my bloke." Dan tried hard to fob her off with a pompous reply. "I like women, for crying out loud. He's just an occasional colleague. *Very* inspiring." He did his mock camp voice. "And anyway, I'm not his type."

"So, what about the lady with the red hair?"

"She's doing genetic engineering, oh, and ancient alien civilisations influencing human development."

"Sounds sexy," said Bea.

"Ah well, then we were otherwise occupied in more worldly pursuits."

"When did you first meet her?"

"She was at a lecture I put on way back for dotty scientists with barmy ideas. Like the paranormal, ESP and UFOs. All the weird stuff we used to do for that American futuristic magazine I worked for."

"Well, not so barmy. I was reading articles about gaps in human intelligence from way back in our evolution, and interfering with DNA in GM experiments. And ESP isn't barmy either."

"Yes, she did the DNA thing. Before she started interfering with mine."

"And as regards ESP, have you looked into those odd experiences you've been having?" said Bea, bringing him down to earth. "The flash scenes, and those strange lights over Highbury Fields?"

"I've been looked at, but I haven't been seen to."

Dan had almost forgotten the lights and the scenes. He was busy, and he thought he was done with all that nonsense as he hadn't seen Adam in weeks.

"Well, not just strange lights. In the night sky, if it's ever clear, you can see the constellation Orion."

"Funny you should say that. I was reading they've found dozens of Earth-like planets there."

"What, on Highbury Fields?"

"In the constellation Orion," said Bea.

"That's what Allison was on about – exoplanets, she called them," said Dan.

"Didn't some nut-job try to knife you up there?"

"What, in the constellation Orion?"

"No, in the throat. Oh, meant to say, some woman rang to invite you to give some talks in Washington. Something to do with an Intelligence meeting."

They polished off their fish and chips.

"US Intelligence? Blimey, that's heavy duty," said Dan. "Back to the capital of the western world again."

"Very high-powered," said Bea. "But I bet you can't get fish and chips like these in Washington."

"Or in the constellation Orion," said Dan.

"Was I recommended?" Dan asked the woman who had called from the agency. He tried not to sound astounded to be called in to talk to assorted US Intelligence people. At least it was weeks away, in early December.

"No, we found you from your work on the IRA." *Yes, and the rest*, thought Dan.

"Any other speakers from the UK?"

"Yes. Do you know Major Adam Armstrong?" the agency lady said breezily.

Dan put down the phone. Bea brought in coffee and saw his face. "What's up with you?"

"He's giving a talk as well," said Dan. "They've put us in the same hotel and on the same flight."

"Who's 'he'? Your bloke? First class, I bet," said Bea.

"He might be. I'll ask to be put in the hold," said Dan.

"And he is *not* my bloke!"

Chapter 11

"No attempt should be made to out-manoeuvre an unidentified aerial phenomenon during interception."

MOD report, Unidentified Aerial Phenomena in the UK Air Defence Region, 2000

Washington, DC: December 2018

On the flight, Dan put on his headphones, listened to the loudest rock music he could find and forced down indifferent plastic food. The requisite gin and tonic and rationed wine failed to settle his nerves. Restless, he walked up and down the aisles amid sleeping passengers under an array of dreary blankets. Adam was splayed out over four seats, so tall that his ruffled fair head protruded into one aisle and his feet dangled off into the other. A sleeping giant.

Dan walked further up the aisle. In the suspended animation of transatlantic flight his thoughts turned to space travel and how little humanity had actually done. *Will we ever be able to travel near the speed of light? And reach the stars... of the constellation Orion?*

Suddenly the plane lurched, shattering his daydream and throwing him off balance. The window shades aligned with Adam's sleeping form snapped open. Out of the aircraft, they appeared. The red, shimmering lights he had seen over Highbury Fields.

Now, over the Atlantic, wave upon wave of deep vermilion, not flashing but glowing. No solid object or UFO. Pulsating bands of energy weaved their way across the path of the aircraft. Like the aurora borealis, but he'd seen that before; they weren't that.

The aircraft dipped, losing altitude. Then dipped again. Dan expected the oxygen masks to leap out of the overhead compartments. No one stirred.

Dan steadied himself. He was transfixed – and afraid. This had never happened on an aircraft. He had first seen the lights on 7/7, on the morning of Britain's worst ever terrorist attack.

And this time, they were 33,000 feet up, en route to Washington, DC.

The announcement came: "Please return to your seats and fasten your seat belts."

Dan staggered back to his seat, gasping for breath in the recycled, cold air. He belted up, feeling trapped, and gazed out of the window at the mesmerising lights. Although it was daytime he completed the famous Bette Davis line, "It's gonna be a bumpy night."

"...We're going through a bit of turbulence." *True British understatement,* thought Dan. This was the worst he'd experienced after dozens of flights.

At least the pilot had seen them. The wavering bands of deep red energy lit up the sky. After seeing them before from so far away, high above the Fields, Dan was now flying through them. The plane lurched from side to side and dipped, rocked and rolled. Dan wished he could have another gin and tonic to calm him down. At one point, it felt as though they had rammed into a wall. Then again, and again.

Dan took his eyes off the sky for a moment to look around. He was amazed to see that most of the passengers were still asleep. Then the fear left him as he thought: *Adam's on this flight. Nothing bad will happen.* He relaxed and let the aircraft lurch and dip as he drank in the beauty of the furious quivering sky.

He thought about the man stretched out over four seats a few rows back, fast asleep. He wondered what the hell was going on in his own head. He was mesmerised by Adam. It was probably just hero worship. But that was still filed under inappropriate.

Adam and his ilk were as straight as it's possible to be in a curved Einsteinian universe. If this was some sort of love, it was the love that dare not even *think* its name. Dan froze at the thought, and was almost physically sick. And not from the undulating force raging in the path of the aircraft.

What if Adam had some sort of special insight, a kind of ESP? Could he sense how much he affected Dan? And others? Dan couldn't be the only one.

The plane began to nosedive.

The lights vanished. The aircraft steadied and resumed its smooth passage.

The hours passed. Dan nodded off for five minutes, then they landed. During the scramble for bags, Adam strode over to Dan's seat, flashed his brilliant smile, and they chatted as usual. The handshake didn't produce any strange scenes this time.

"Did you see those red shimmering lights? What about all that turbulence?" Dan asked, wondering if he'd dreamt the whole thing in the statelessness of flight – the scenes, the lights, all of it. Nobody seemed to turn a hair.

"What turbulence? Nah, caught up on my sleep." Well, Adam was used to flying military helicopters. He pointed at Dan's headphones. "Shimmering lights? You should go easy on the Bowie albums, mate."

He even knows I've been listening to Bowie, Dan thought. *Then again, the Pope is of a Catholic persuasion.*

The two travellers waited in parallel lines at US Immigration, each with British passports and totally different lives, admitted onto American soil for the umpteenth time. Dan wondered how they'd got here in one piece. Adam smoked a cigarette while they waited in the freezing January air for a cab to the hotel. He offered Dan one. "No, ta. I gave it up years ago," Dan said. *Some things are easy to give up.*

Dan took his things up to his room, got changed into a clean shirt and jeans and sat on the hotel bed. This must stop: the lights, the visions, the effect. Adam's effect. Whatever it was and why it happened he had no idea, but he must man up, for heaven's sake.

They met up in the hotel bar, where a Mexican barman concocted big bowl glasses of fizzing green dayglo cocktails that could turn Jekyll into Hyde. The drinks relaxed him and they chatted until Adam's friend, an elegantly dressed blonde, arrived. Dan quoted again from *All About Eve*.

"I guess at this point I'm what the French call *de trop*."

"Not at all: have another drink with us," said the lady friend, and they put Dan at his ease. Maybe she liked Bette Davis's films as well. Fasten your seat belts…

As the drinks flowed the conversation turned to London. Dan said he had last lived with a previous partner in Highbury.

"That's near where I'm from originally," said Adam in his usual rapid, brusque tone. "Do you still see her?"

"Her was a him," said Dan. And with the dayglo drinks talking, he thought – *what the hell. I'm done for; may as well be hung for a sheep as a lamb. Then again, he probably knows anyway. Who cares.* "I've got two she-exes, Jane and Teresa, and a he-ex, Duncan. He said I'm a serial bisexual."

"You swing both ways while eating cornflakes," said Adam, totally unfazed. The couple made to leave. Dan reckoned that Adam had had more women than he'd dismantled IEDs, and that's just on Wednesdays. Adam flashed his smile and barked, "See you down here for breakfast: seven o'clock sharp."

Dan stayed on, chatting to the barman, who brought him a plate of pasta. He ate only half of it. Dan endured another sleepless night, kept awake by the noisy heating system. The next morning, eyes propped open by sheer force of will and slim frame sharp in his dark grey suit, tab-collar shirt and tie, he walked downstairs and into the dining area.

Adam dwarfed the small table among the breakfasting guests. He was clean-shaven and smartly attired in a navy military blazer, light beige slacks and tan brogues, open-neck shirt showing a broad suntanned neck. As he wolfed down an American breakfast piled high enough to see from space, Dan sat down opposite him and asked the waitress to bring what passed for black coffee in America and a slice of toast. Adam's blue-grey eyes glowered at Dan's meagre plateful.

"I'm on a bit of a diet at the moment," said Dan.

"You're always on a diet," said Adam, demolishing a skyscraper of pancakes. *Only when I'm round you, mate. Most days I can eat for England.*

They walked on snow-covered sidewalks to the nondescript office venue. Dan tried not to slip on the ice as he struggled to keep up with the big man striding along at breakneck speed. Nervous, he gabbled on about how he got into Bowie and the London nightclub scene. Once inside the centre he was first on, nerves gone. All was well once he was on stage.

He looked out at the unsmiling corporate and intelligence officials. Then he pitched in with his well-aired account of several decades of terrorist bombings. Fully fired up, he saw from the front row Adam's lightning smile, gone in a second.

And then he saw the scene. Flashing before his eyes in the middle of his presentation – this time a vision not of soldiers' bodies broken, bloodied and blown apart and civilians mangled. This time something very beautiful.

Mile after mile of desert, crimson rocks and canyons under a golden sky, filled with a huge boiling white sun. And there are people – or something like people – in white, from heaven knows when or where. Ahead of them, a giant man strides over the endless sands. Far above his fair head are vast, undulating bands of deep red light, shimmering in the ochre sky.

Chapter 12

"They don't care. The fact that you have fought for your country, done three combat tours, that counts for nothing."

Former Corporal in 33 Engineer Regiment (EOD)

West London: January 2019

Deep in the bowels of an unmarked address in the outer limits of west London a collection of sundry officials gathered in an airless room. Sheena sat at the head of the table, which, like the rest of the fittings, fixtures and walls of the facility-cum-office, was bombproof.

The candidates for the secret Supersoldiers project were being selected. The project was now in full swing after an unsteady start back in 2006. The main focus was on Adam Armstrong, whom they had long tried to tempt onto the programme due to his prescient and apparently supernormal skills.

The exclusive group of experts, civil servants, scientists and intelligence officials had been picked from the highest levels in their fields. Their aim: to explore the incidence of individuals with very high performance abilities and how best to use them in the service of their country. But so far, no other candidate had the extent, number and variety of skills that Adam was reported to have – naturally.

Sheena began the meeting, chipper as ever in a tight-fitting navy suit with her undone jacket revealing ample cleavage, her mass of dark hair piled up, her heavily mascaraed light grey eyes piercing enough to penetrate the bombproof wall. "These skills, or should we say, tendencies, manifest themselves in varying kinds of extrasensory perception and other effects."

"Isn't this stuff logged in the annals of the weirdo paranormal brigade?" An intel colleague in a cheap suit intervened.

"It's not just in battle and EOD situations," was the reply. "And we've had reports of colleagues witnessing it."

"This soldier may be, if I dare say, unique. So far we haven't found any other examples in other walks of life, or in the wider military. Our little group here is focused only on the military."

"Reminds me of a film," said the civil servant from the MoD, who was doodling on his tablet. *"The Midwich Cuckoos."*

"The Midwich what?"

"You know, that old fifties film with those kids from outer space born in a village with white hair."

"A village with white hair?"

"Oh for Christ's sake." Sheena intervened. "And the film was *Village of the Damned.* The nineties remake was terrible, mind."

"Aren't we looking into his genome, if something has intervened in the DNA? Has he given up a DNA sample?"

Sheena shifted in her seat. "We'll get it." *But not* that *way. It has to be with his consent.*

A bioscience rep from Porton Down chimed in. "Well, we are looking into the genetic code of individuals with special skills, but so far there haven't been any DNA oddities."

"We can only look at how we could benefit from these skills. But you can't keep anything secret these days. If this got out... I mean, if it came out that a soldier had these extra abilities from birth..."

"Other countries could be way ahead. The Russians have been cultivating experiments in psychotronic weapons for decades. Back in the 1960s, electromagnetic waves were used to transmit simple sounds into the human brain. In another test, messages were sent in ultrasound frequencies which the human brain perceives, but the subject isn't aware it's happening."

"The Americans are already way ahead in using professional soldiers and spies with these, er, so-called mental and physical abilities. And who knows what the Chinese and the Iranians are up to?"

"That's up to our friends in MI6," said Sheena. "I've done my stint there. One thing I know: our soldier is the prime example of one we are going to need, and very soon."

"How do we know that these powers, if we can call them that, are going to be to our advantage? I mean, are they focused, or random? Couldn't a brain impulse to disarm a bomb... er... couldn't it also set one off? Can we measure it? Is it on some special frequency?"

"And who's to say a terrorist group doesn't have a proponent with these... talents? How many of these people are out there worldwide? Could they set off a bomb with it? Or worse."

"Well, indeed," said Sheena. "And it's an IED. We're all professionals here." She corrected her colleague with an expression she had picked up from Adam.

Yes, the abilities were random. They were unpredictable. And so had been the flash scenes of carnage and mayhem when they made love. She couldn't just put them down to overwork or the heightened excitement of the moment with the most thrilling man she would ever meet. Despite her intensive training, the scenes had been terrifying. But they had never stilled her desire for him. They had made her crave him more.

Her past liaison with Adam must remain a secret. Her other role was an even bigger secret – and an act of supreme treachery. Sheena looked around the table at her colleagues, feeling the thrill of that unfolding life, hidden deep inside her cold, calculating mind.

Somebody asked, "What's his drugs history? Autism? High-functioning Asperger's? Any sort of gene therapy? Did anything show up in training? Surely that would have brought out these qualities."

"No, none of that. Nothing untoward," retorted an Army brigadier who was predictably sceptical about the whole business. He had been the first to see the reports from Colonel Richards about Adam's prowess and his rapid recovery from two gunshot wounds and a double tap of lethal scorpion stings. He didn't believe any of it. Adam was an able officer in his own right. Now these observations had been passed up – hence this meeting.

"According to all available reports, a clean sheet; normal family background," said Sheena.

"Whatever that is," said a psychologist.

"What we know of him, and it's still hearsay, is that he can bloody well stop an IED mechanism with his eyes or something other than the gear they normally have out there. And he can see in the dark and his wounds heal up like a sodding miracle."

"Don't exaggerate. See in the dark my arse. Lots of people can do that. And my mum healed up really well after her hip was done."

"Can he get a copy of his medical record?"

"Yes. They get that when they leave the Services, but this stuff won't be on it."

"If he has a GP, there may be some account of him reporting PTSD or some other problem, or he might have reported it to the medical officer."

"That will still be confidential."

"It isn't here, "said Sheena.

"By the way, do we have a name for this project? If it is a project," asked one of the Intel guys.

"Well, don't laugh," said Sheena, smirking at the title they had dreamed up. "But as we are primarily looking at our bomb disposal star, and want to exploit his, er, gifts, and as it's all in the DNA – once we get it – we are Double Felix."

"Oh, for crying out loud," said the brigadier, and the rest groaned along with him. Felix was the name given to bomb disposal squads – first in the British Army then others around the world. Felix, the cat with nine lives, as bomb techs have, according to legend.

"The double helix, well, that's the structure of DNA." As if they didn't know that.

"Catchy, isn't it?" said the confident Sheena, bored with her colleagues.

"There's something else very serious we need to look at. Let's revisit the PTSD thing. How does this relate to PTSD? Does it have any connection? Has he reported any symptoms?"

Adam had kept his nightmares – and his waking dreams of horrendous war scenes, falling through the air without a parachute, and of crowds of strange people walking on desert sands under a gigantic sun – to himself.

Another military official chimed in. "Soldiers may feel guilt from surviving when their mates got shot and blown up, often right next to them. Or they know they won't find an understanding ear or a practical solution for their suffering. Maybe this officer doesn't want to attract any undue attention."

Sheena knew that Adam would tough it out. Although PTSD was no longer the great unmentionable, if his unusual skills were mistaken for symptoms, his Army career could be over. She said, "Well, he's done that all right."

The psychologist said, "We think there may even be a new, rare, form of PTSD – one that actually advances the shocking memories and visions onto, er, a higher level of perception. Sort of PTESP."

"That's worse than Double fucking Felix," said the brigadier. "I suppose you've never had PTSD or know anyone with it. You want to see how some of our lads are doing themselves in, dozens a year, from PTS fucking D."

He went on.

"There's 350 EOD techs in the British Army. They're some of the most highly trained and decorated soldiers and half of them have PTSD." Thoughtful silence.

"What sort of mission are we thinking of, where we are going to need these, er, special individuals?"

"We need him for a big counter-terrorism operation," Sheena concluded. "We haven't had his consent to be involved on this project. But we will."

What she didn't mention was that Double Felix had been long in the making. Exploiting the special skills of Adam Armstrong and others was just the beginning. Because there was an even more important, far more secret project to look into how all this had come about.

And Adam was its first Subject of Special Interest.

Washington, DC: January 2019

In a booming voice that resounded over the heads of his audience in the packed lecture hall, Dr Carl Murrow concluded the demonstration of his latest invention. The delegates – mainly scientists, technicians and military officials – trooped out, exchanging impressions of his new product. Murrow strode up to one of the delegates who had stayed behind, still tapping vigorously into his tablet.

"Looking good," the delegate said. "How far on are we?" He kept his voice low, even though the hall had been checked for bugs before the meeting.

"Once I'm free of these commercial shackles, it'll be a full-on operation," Murrow replied in his elegant Boston accent. A small, grey-haired man casually but smartly dressed, his lack of stature was compensated by the hard, determined look of an elder statesman. His reputation as a scientist specialising in radiation protection went before him. He ran his own company, which regularly attained Pentagon funding and support for his inventions. Now a multi-millionaire, he had made enough money to fund many of them himself. But his day job was about to take a back seat.

"We're gathering pace," said Murrow. "But it will be a steady process before our plans come to fruition."

"We're in it for the long haul," his colleague said, excitedly.

"Indeed. And it will put everything that's happened to date in the shade," Murrow replied.

Chapter 13

"Everyone thinks of changing the world, but no one thinks of changing himself."

Leo Tolstoy

North London: February 2019
Dan woke up in his study in Jane's Victorian maisonette in Islington. He now had a London base to do business, socialise and fly overseas at short notice. He recalled with joy when, at Christmas over three years ago, Jane had called, saying she had a spare room to rent out. Dan jumped at the chance.

Days later, on 10 January 2016, David Bowie died. As Jane quietly wept among a sea of flowers, candles and mementos given up in tribute to the great rock star at the impromptu memorial set up in Brixton, where he was born, the tattoo on her back of his lightning-flash face was snapped by the press agencies. The photos appeared in every newspaper in every country the next day. This was small comfort to her.

Just days after Bowie died, the spectre of jihadist terrorism returned, when seventeen people were killed in four separate shootings in Paris. The rest of the year was relentlessly tainted by attacks in several countries. It never seemed to end. As for politics, the world metaphorically spun off its axis in 2016: the Brexit vote, the election of Donald Trump as the 'leader of the free world', and the rise of extremism, both right and left. One talk show host said with gallows humour that after Bowie died the world went into meltdown.

The brightly decorated house in the quiet, terraced street lined with may trees was a perfect escape for Dan and an ideal bolthole. As well as a gallery of Bowie photos in the hall, the orange wall in the upstairs lounge sported a six-foot-high Aladdin Sane lightning flash. Dan was back in the capital again sharing a home with the beautiful, bohemian lady who was his first great love and his friend for life.

Jane had to acclimatise to Dan's new work and image, so different from when they first met. She worked in a posh jeweller's shop in Chelsea, selling costume pieces to everyone from Princess Diana to Yoko Ono.

"I told my boss we had a bloke from the SAS round here for dinner last night. He went, 'Fuck-off, Jane darling'!"

"What, not Who Dares Wins?"

They sat at the red formica table in the big kitchen over one of their weekly takeaway suppers washed down with a vat of wine, much of which was drunk by Jane. "And we saw you on the shop's telly the other day on Sky. I said, 'That's my Dan, going on about bombs again'."

"Well, Major Armstrong wasn't available," said Dan.

"Oh, no, not him again. What's with this Adam bloke? Do you fancy him or something?"

"Or something," said Dan. "And don't you start. I get enough of that from Bea."

"Well, we both know you. I've known you since I was seventeen." Jane never tired of saying that, pouring her nth glass of red wine and one for Dan. She had taken her wavy black hair down after her day at work and looked resplendent as ever in a metallic silver pleated dress, diamanté lizard earrings and the bright red lipstick Dan had got her for Christmas.

"No I do *not* fancy him. I've been through all this before. OK, he's very good-looking... he's charismatic. It's different. He's spellbinding. He has a sort of, er, well, an *effect*."

"Oooh, an effect, very groovy. You've been in Brighton too long. What sort of an effect?"

"You wouldn't believe me. It's not what you think."

Jane had swigged enough wine to miss Dan's reply, to his relief. He didn't want to try to explain having visions of strange gory battle and desert scenes when he was in the same room as Adam.

"Anyway, the girls in the shop said, 'Isn't the bloke on the telly talking about bombs your old flame with the bright orange Bowie hair?'"

"Who, Adam? Blimey, Adam Armstrong with bright orange hair, that's a turn-up. Ziggy Sandhurst and the Soldiers from Mars, ha-ha."

Jane ignored him. "Anyway, the girls in the shop couldn't believe I still know you, now you're doing all this terrorism stuff. But here we are, after all this time. We've come a long way, haven't we?"

They never tired of talking about the old days, going down the clubs, the fantastic music, and Dan getting beaten up by skinheads. Anyone who looked like Bowie and had Dan's slim build was fair game.

"If my lot could have seen me back then," said Dan. "Mind you, some of them will have. You can find out most anything about anybody these days, even if you're not in the intelligence service. And that lot will know pretty much everything from my tawdry past – if they can be arsed."

A few weeks later, Dan was getting ready to go on another US trip. He marched into the big orange lounge and sat down with a glass of red wine. An Indian takeaway was ordered. He had to fly off the next day.

He was wearing a navy military-style blazer, beige slacks, a light-blue shirt, tan brogues, and a chunky black watch you could launch a cruise missile off. As usual, he proudly wore his Bomb Technician Association badge in his lapel, the nearest he had got to a regiment. He had put on weight. Against the backdrop of the lightning flash on the far wall, his hair shone in a fetching shade of dark blond.

"What are you looking at me like that for?" he said.

"Oh my God, you're morphing again," said Jane, back from work and curled up with Charlie the dog on the big sofa below a painting of Judy Garland and a poster of Aladdin Sane. She was wearing a red silk kimono with a gold flower pattern; her hair was down and a pair of pointy glitter specs sat atop her head. She was used to Dan's ability to grow a new image like the cracked actor he was.

"Cheers," he said, and bolted down his wine.

"It's sort of Bowie and somebody else. Who is it?" said Jane.

"Somebody else," said Dan.

"Ah, it's your bloke, isn't it?" said Jane, pouring more wine, some of which splashed Charlie, who ignored it. "I see. You don't fancy him – you want to *be* him."

"Well no, it isn't. And I don't. It's a long story. Of course I want to be like him. Who wouldn't?" He couldn't resist a wind-up. "I'd get more birds, for a start."

"Birds?" blurted Jane. "What century are you in?"

"Anyway, all my heroes are blond. My dad, David Bowie, Daniel Craig, Princess Di, Marilyn Monroe..."

"I've served her in the shop."

"Who? Marilyn Monroe?" said Dan.

"Diana," said Jane. "And don't change the subject."

"You just did." Dan struggled on.

"Look, he's an occasional colleague. I haven't seen him in ages. He's an inspiration. Some people just are. And he said I know a lot about IEDs. And he is *not* my bloke!"

Jane ignored this and came over and inspected Dan like he was a specimen in a test tube. "It's also styled different, and it goes with the blue eyes. And you've had your eyebrows done. You're almost unrecognisable."

She stood back, wine glass in hand. "And you've put on a bit of weight."

"I needed to."

She sat down on the sofa again. "Suits you, mind. You look years younger. And more butch."

"Let's not get carried away," said Dan.

"It's still a bit Bowie; you've still got the cheekbones, crossed with the officer types I get in the shop, the Chelsea crowd, pwah pwah."

Then she peered at Dan again. "So, are you morphing again?"

"That's the idea," said Dan. "Now I don't know who I am, I've never been happier."

"Who said that, then?" she said. "Apart from you just now."

Dan pointed to the poster of Aladdin Sane on the wall.

"Oh, right," said Jane, and drained her wine glass.

"I'm off to the States again," said Dan. "See you in a week or so."

"Safe journey," she said. "Oh, and what are IEDs?"

"You don't want to know," said Dan.

Chapter 14

Washington, DC: March 2019

Dan landed at Dulles International Airport and went through the usual rigours of US Immigration, this time on his own: no Adam in the parallel line this time. No strange lights in the sky on the way; no turbulence to speak of.

The dreary officers were as brusque as always. "What is the nature of your visit, sir?"

"Giving a talk at a conference on counter-terrorism." At this, they changed their tune. "Thank you for keeping us safe, sir." Dan felt a warm glow as he stepped onto US soil once more.

He collected a hire car, a neat silver Jaguar XF in the Hertz 'British collection'. He took the tourist scenic route through central Washington. The familiar journey past the White House and the towering Monument and all the classical magnificence of America's capital was so different from the architectural chaos of his beloved London. He drove further out into a far duller area. As he had done before, he tried to settle into his bog-standard hotel.

This time it wasn't just for a conference. He had also come to visit companies making equipment. His first port of call was a physicist who had left Britain for the wealthier climes of US military research and development. He reached the scientist's office at one of the Beltway research institutes early the next morning – after little sleep, but he was used to that. Fuelled by an American breakfast, this time more ample than the one he'd struggled through with Adam two months before, he felt relaxed – but his senses were sharpened.

"Thank you for coming all this way," said Dr Carl Murrow, welcoming Dan into a utilitarian, faceless office. "Delighted to meet you." Dan didn't mention that he had other people to see as well. Better stroke scientists' egos; this lot make the military lads look like blushing violets.

"I take it you're here to chat about my new product. Coffee?" It wouldn't be Dan's usual weapons-grade espresso, but he needed anything with caffeine in it today. Murrow looked more elder statesman than stereotypical boffin. Neat grey hair, lined face, hard thin mouth, ruthless dark eyes, and shorter than Dan. Probably in his seventies. He was dressed in a casual expensive pullover and slacks, probably Brooks Brothers. Dan noted a mixed British and Boston accent, like a male Bette Davis, if such a thing could be imagined. Just a tad camp. Dan recalled that Boston also had a well-connected community of genetics specialists.

Murrow had developed a coverall for first responders at a radiation incident. These were long established, but his promised to be better. He had laid on the desk a sample of the black-strapped, kitted-out garment to show selected visitors. Dan had at long last figured out how to record meetings on his mobile.

"It's got a rad detector and dosimeter combined," Dan observed. "Did you get US government funding for this?" Most of the companies he met benefited from Pentagon funding.

"No. We have self-funded it," said Murrow, eyeing Dan up.

"It looks like an improvement on existing kit. It's much lighter. Does it also detect alpha and beta?" Alpha radiation had been the problem with the substance used to poison Alexander Litvinenko – polonium-210. It gives off a kind of ionising radiation that is hard to detect. It doesn't penetrate the body but if you swallow it or breathe it in, you're done for.

"Yes, it does. Alpha as you know is often overlooked."

"Does it have a brand name?"

"Well, we've called the whole system the Gaia," said Murrow, looking over at Dan's notes. They were in a self-taught shorthand, his own invented hieroglyphic code. He didn't rely solely on mobile recordings.

"Ah, Mother Earth, which – who – will survive whatever we humans chuck at her," said Dan, launching into another pet subject, Greek mythology. "Gaia, goddess of the Earth, who sent a scorpion to sting Orion the hunter to death when he said he would kill all the animals on the planet. She didn't think much to that."

"You've done your Classics," the scientist said. "I've always liked that story."

"Well, I came top in Latin, but the rest is all Greek to me."

Murrow frowned. "Sorry. Joke," said Dan. "But Gaia failed, didn't she? The scorpion didn't kill Orion. He got over that, then got himself shot dead by an arrow fired by his lover Artemis when she found out he'd had a go at another lass."

"Hmm, indeed - the lustful Orion. The great golden celestial warrior; the handsomest of all Earthborn men."

Dan sensed that the scientist was looking at him strangely. He knew that look. He'd been with enough older men in the past to know. This guy was undressing him with his dark eyes. Unflinching, Dan chattered on.

"Yes, Orion. You can see him up on Highbury Fields. The constellation, I mean. Chasing the Pleiades – the Seven Sisters. You can usually only see eight stars, mind."

"Where's Highbury Fields?" asked the scientist, looking irritated but intrigued.

"Oh, just a little park in north London. I walk up there." He smiled as he said under his breath, "Down from Seven Sisters Road, as it happens."

Murrow moved the conversation on, his icy, penetrating dark stare renewed.

"We certainly have made a mess of our planet. And some day, she will hit back. Already is doing."

"Global warming, pollution of the oceans, deforestation, wars, and that's not including nuclear testing," said Dan, breezily.

The technical chat about Murrow's radiation protection outfit seemed to have morphed into politics. Amidst terrorism and everything else the environmental crisis had been side-lined.

"We're overpopulated, that's the main problem," said Murrow.

Dan was making chit-chat not just to be polite but also to keep in with his host, but was, as ever, incurably voluble – if only to countermand his host's unnerving glances.

"Great that a lot of us are living longer, though. Well, at least the old folks are. Don't know about my generation, mind," said Dan. "I don't think my lot will. All the crap in our food, obesity, and we've done ourselves in with drink and chemicals, not all of them legal."

"The old balance has gone. There will be massive movements of people from land turned into desert into northern parts."

"Newcastle," muttered Dan. "They'll cool off a bit up there."

The scientist suddenly asked, "You work with counter-IED and EOD as well, don't you?" Dan had only heard those terms from the military crowd he was honoured to work with. "You must get to meet some interesting army people."

"Yes, and some more interesting than others," said Dan, and immediately regretted saying it.

"I assumed you were a veteran as well, or serving. Very smart. And from the way you talk. Are you?" Murrow looked Dan up and down, his eyes wandering south. Dan kept forgetting his new look; it fit him like a glove, like he'd always had it.

"Thanks for the compliment," he replied with a half-smile.

He turned to leave. Murrow's dark eyes followed him down the corridor. He was relieved to get the hell out. He was blissfully unaware of the old boy repairing to the bathroom next to his office and jerking himself off.

Dan went out into the street and tried to remember where he'd parked the car, blending in with Washingtonians going about their business. This was as different from his last visit to D.C. as a trip to the moon.

Then he saw it.

The device, sitting under trees encircling a little park in north London. A big shiny metal thing, humming, the rays emanating... an explosion ignites the sky and rends the land apart. A mushroom cloud, ghastly, growing, red, black. The silent delay; the rush of a million tons of air; the crashing, bone-shattering boom...

The vision dissolved. Dan went on his way. *Not enough sleep*, he thought. *That's why this happens.* But if this latest scene of horror was because of the effect Adam had on him, how the hell could it leap into his mind from a distance of over three thousand miles?

An hour after Murrow finished indulging himself, he showered, returned to his office and poured himself a large whiskey. He picked up his cellphone and looked at an old text message sent some weeks back by Dr Allison Hardy. He went into another room and dialled her number on a phone that looked like something from a museum.

"Can we recruit him, Carl?"

"Possibly: he could be useful. You'll find out more."

"Well, he's on his way to me now," said Allison, putting fresh coffee beans into a grinder. No bottles of wine from the hotel minibar this time. She knew all about Dan. "He's got a previous record with the most, er, efficient group in history. And he may be amenable."

Murrow said, "Keep it to business, Allison. You need to have him clear of mind, if not of body." At that thought, he started to get hard again.

His contact signed off with, "We'll get him."

Chapter 15

Dan had indeed booked a return match with the vivacious professor. After his encounter with the radiation specialist and apparent part-time ecowarrior Dr Murrow, Dan was more than relieved to visit Allison. This time, unlike the previous time in Toronto, it was purely for business – although he would have welcomed pleasure as well.

He walked up four flights of stairs to the spacious open-plan apartment, thinking that the equivalent home in his own capital would cost a cool two million. As a Brit working in the US for half of the year Allison had done well, as did many scientists from the UK.

She welcomed him in with a peck on the cheek. She was as alluring as ever, in a clingy sweater and a long floaty skirt, her curly mass of long red hair surrounding her heart-shaped face. It was difficult to forget what had happened between them.

"You look gorgeous as ever," said Dan in a sharp, clipped tone.

"Thanks," she said. "You're not so bad yourself. Like the new look."

"Well, all my heroes are fair-haired. My dad, David Bowie, Daniel Craig, Adam—" He stopped dead.

"Well, you've also gone a bit military." She smiled as she brought in coffee, her skirt swishing deliciously around her long legs. "Even the voice. it suits you. Like you've always been. You've got a real talent for change," she said.

"That's what got me into Bowie. I'm just a cracked actor. More a tendency than a talent," said Dan with a grin. "I've put weight on as well. Hope you still fancy me."

"We'll see," she said.

Dan sat facing the picture window, which overlooked green, gently rolling Cleveland Park. It was automatic since his Belfast days not to sit with his back to the door or a window. Allison sat opposite.

"And, speaking of change," Dan said, seeing that Allison wasn't up for another afternoon romp. It would have been a nice diversion, but this wasn't the time. He launched into the reason for his visit. "Genetic manipulation. Specifically, for modern warfare and possibly terrorism. How far are we on towards this, or is it still science fiction?"

"Human enhancement? No longer science fiction. It's possible, and it's going on."

She went on to explain. "As early as 2001, the Pentagon planned to do experiments to maximise soldier performance. Back then, the breeding of genetically modified troops was predicted within a generation."

"And go on, tell me – we can do it now," said Dan.

"Well, yes. They're aiming to get round our genetic limitations. Like, say, adding cat DNA to human eye cells for soldiers to see better in the dark."

"Blimey, that'll probably make the soldiers climb into boxes as well," said Dan, who adored cats. "Extra cover." Just at that moment, a big fluffy ginger cat sloped in and jumped onto Dan's lap.

"Gosh, she really likes you." Allison smiled. "She hisses at everyone else who comes in."

"I love cats. She's beautiful. And she's got lovely red hair like you," said Dan, gently stroking the huge cat, which purred loudly. "You can jump up on my lap as well if you like."

Allison gave him a glance that signalled 'steady on' and reverted to Terminator scenarios. She looked at her watch, which after an hour of discussing genetically enhanced humans was not unexpected. But she seemed uneasy. The cat mewed happily and gazed up at Dan with her huge elliptical eyes.

Allison suddenly said, "I just try to do the good stuff. You know, to benefit mankind. The technology is here, and it's up to the people in authority how it's used."

"Like nuclear weapons, you mean," said Dan. "What could possibly go wrong?"

"Well, you're the expert on the dark side... you know, humanity's ignorance, malice, hunger for power, terrorism, and addiction to killing."

"Yes, but mainly on the M.O., er, modes of attack. I leave the ideology stuff to the academics," said Dan. "And I leave the dark side to the goths."

"I thought you were an academic."

"Don't you start," said Dan. "I've had all of that from Adam. No, I'm not."

"Who's Adam?" The cat jumped down.

Dan wished he didn't have such a loose tongue. Being from the north and half Irish probably didn't help. But it sometimes helped to make light of a sticky subject.

"Oh, he's just an Army bloke I sort of know in the field," said Dan. "And I do mean, in the field – a war hero, bomb squads, all of that."

He didn't add, *a man you would lay down your life for. The most charismatic man I've ever met. A powerful, beautiful, dangerous man. When I shake his hand or see him I get weird visions of desert warfare and Christ knows what else.*

"I meet great guys like him all the time, to do with all that stuff that goes bang. That's when I'm not being an academic."

Something told Dan she knew who he was talking about.

"He's quite a star. And, speaking of stars, what about those planets of yours? Have we been invaded by aliens, or is it just Brighton on bank holidays?"

"It's exoplanets, and the search for extraterrestrial intelligence – you know, SETI. The great Dr Carl Sagan started it. You met him – do you remember? Back in the day when we first met."

"Yes. He was great. I'm in another world now."

"But we don't need aliens to teach us how to kill." Allison poured more coffee. Dan needed it. "Ordinary humans are capable enough of mass murder and executing the means of our own destruction."

"You as well? I've just had a basinful of eco-doom and the End of the World As We Know It from that Murrow bloke," said Dan. "He can stare through a nuclear bunker as well."

"Probably fancies you," Allison said, smiling. "He likes military types, but not too rough. You're just his type."

"Well, he isn't mine," said Dan. "You are, though. And I can do rough with the best of 'em." He added, with a grin, "Not with you, though."

Allison ignored him, so he thought it best to recap the End of the World As We Know It.

"Mind you, it won't be war and terrorism, but a natural pandemic or environmental disasters that'll do for us. We're certainly having enough of those, what with global warming kicking in."

"But not all of us," said Allison. "Some of us will survive it, a mass-casualty event or war or natural catastrophe. And the Earth will survive it all, even with the punishment we're dishing out at her."

"Ah, that Gaia thing," said Dan. "That's what Murrow called his new invention. Gaia; Mother Earth. The Earth goddess who sent a scorpion to kill Orion, the mighty hunter."

"Eh? Didn't know you'd done the Classics."

"Well, I may be a northern savage but I went to a posh school. I love all those Greek gods, goddesses and heroes. And stargazing. You can see the constellation Orion up on Highbury Fields. In eternal flight, chasing the Seven Sisters across the sky. Only in winter, mind. Even with all our pollution. "

"Highbury Fields? Where's that?"

"Oh, just a little park in north London." He returned to the Earth goddess. "Well, the Gaia thing, as you say, is probably right."

"The Earth will survive and we'll probably go the way of the dinosaurs."

"Some already have; my music fans. They're still stuck in the early eighties. Most of them are goths now."

"We've got to do something about it," said Allison.

"What, my music fans? I think I'd rather deal with the terrorists." Dan shrugged.

"Mind you, our intelligence services manage to catch most of them, although they can't stop everything." He remembered the two guys at his workshop on IEDs who didn't carry cards and didn't take kindly to criticism of 'their' intelligence efforts.

"I mean, we have to help Gaia," said Allison.

As Dan made to leave, Allison turned to kiss him goodbye. He couldn't stop himself, and put his arms round her waist, pulling her close, tenderly caressing her hair, kissing her long and deep. She could feel his arousal and gently pushed him away.

"Not today, love," she said. "I've got a lecture to write. When do you fly back?"

"The day after tomorrow," he said. "Terrible film, that, speaking of global warming."

"Come for dinner. Tomorrow evening," she said, and kissed him again, tender, tantalising.

On the ride back to his hotel he longed for the next day, when he would be in her arms again. Meanwhile, as he tried to stem his desire for her, he reflected on the array of nasties which they had talked about. He thought about supersoldiers, and realised that he had forgotten to ask Allison about mind experiments and ESP. *Tomorrow, I'll ask her tomorrow. Before holding her again.*

A local music station on his car radio played assorted country and western. He switched to another station and put his foot on the gas. A rock band was belting it out.

"Oh no, it's bloody Guns N' Roses..." Dan remembered Adam's recommendation for his listening pleasure as an alternative to David Bowie. He rammed his shiny silver car into the back of a truck.

"Oh shit."

Once he had left, Allison picked up the phone and called Murrow.

"I think he might play."

After concluding the brief call, she sent a message on a separate secure cellphone, the one she had used in the hotel after the carnal afternoon in Canada with Dan, to an MI5 unit somewhere in London.

It read: "He may be our man. I don't know if we can get him to play, though."

The text reply read: "Thanks Allie. We'll see about that. Cheers, C."

Chapter 16

"Once superhumans appear, there will be significant political problems with unimproved humans, who won't be able to compete."

Dr Stephen Hawking

Ministry of Defence, Central London: April 2019

Adam walked into the office and sat down. He was energised after his morning run round Highbury Fields and a high-octane night of sex with his slim, lithe girlfriend, Anthea. She waved him off to yet another tiresome meeting about the most hare-brained idea he had come across in twenty years of military service. He waited restlessly. He felt he was only passing time before he went out on a worthwhile mission again.

But this wasn't it; he was being pressganged into this project, something nobody had ever done to him before. He poured a black coffee from the machine and fidgeted, wanting to go outside for another cigarette. He ran a large hand through his fair hair and tried to concentrate on the report on his laptop. He reflected on the thousand and one times he had felt the adrenaline rush. Not just from EOD but from the stand-up fight, firing your weapon, coming under fire... He tried to focus on what lay ahead.

As he waited, behind a glass screen a specially selected board of military officials talked through that hare-brained project they were about to try to persuade Adam to join.

"Supersoldiers: the official Pentagon project intended to revolutionise warfare."

"We haven't been involved so far. Way off beam for us and way too expensive."

"It kicked off in 2009, after the troop surge. The Pentagon's defence agency experimented on pigs in Afghanistan, to see if they could stem blood loss."

"We brought it up with him back in 2006, after his second tour. No joy. We've focused on the technologies in the meantime, with no recruits as yet."

The officials rattled through it in turn. Technologies to maximise physiological performances. The breeding of genetically modified troops within a generation. Enhanced overall fitness without noticeable augmentation. Increased tolerance to environmental extremes. Increased endurance. Nanoparticles in an integrated-powered exoskeleton to repair physical damage.

This was the stuff of video games and Marvel comic superheroes, not the reality of Army service. Several of the officials knew this. Some were reluctant to press ahead; others embraced the futuristic project. Seemingly mocking their efforts, someone had inserted a slide on the screen of a seven-foot-tall genetically engineered cartoon figure, power-armoured, wielding a full-auto armour-piercing explosive-round pistol, and with a fist to kill a tank.

"Reminds me of the Bionic Man. We have the technology; we can rebuild him."

"It's more *The Matrix* and *The Terminator*. But gene therapy and smartphones were futuristic not so long ago."

Enhanced senses. The ability to transmit thoughts through electronically-aided telepathy. Seeing in the infrared; night vision without special goggles.

Adam already had all of these. And they knew he had.

"Whatever, our chap won't want to do this. It goes against Forces culture, at least in the British Army. He'll be asking questions. Like, how do we integrate both enhanced and unenhanced soldiers into the same unit?"

"He's already enhanced," said a uniformed woman seated closest to the screen, which flashed up a service picture of

Adam in fatigues alongside his unit details: rank, regiment, number, awards.

The chairman cleared his throat. "It's also about consent. Our command structures mean a soldier can't say no."

"Our lad can. He already has."

"I wouldn't say no to him," the uniformed woman persisted, gazing at the screen and wondering when their Boy Wonder was going to make an appearance.

They ignored her. "We must avoid precedent. Servicemen were fed LSD without their consent in mind-control experiments."

"When was that? Sounds like the late sixties hippy era, Vietnam and all that."

"No, before then: in the 1950s, and without their knowledge. Some received compensation. They were fed drugs to reduce the need for sleep."

"Do we know if he has PTSD?"

"He hasn't reported it. He's a force of nature. Unstoppable."

"Even if he hasn't got PTSD, he'll want to know how he and his mates will cope with this, er, extra situation after they retire and in between missions."

"Enhanced soldiers would be put into riskier situations when their normal counterparts are not. The 'enhanced' troops will become an elite force. It'll be the SAS on steroids, for crying out loud."

"Yes. Isn't it marvellous!"

"They can still be bombed from the air, mind, and there's snipers and IEDs."

"Every officer knows that cohesion is the bedrock of fighting units. Everything is about the team. If any of the team has unusual skills or resilience…"

Adam had tried hard to keep his 'hidden' skills just that. But they were no longer hidden; they'd been noted, which was why he found himself here. He felt a residual stab in his lower shin, a reminder of the dual sting by the deathstalker scorpion.

Until now, he hadn't known if and when the shots apparently emanating from his eyes would render an IED safe. He didn't know if his visions and premonitions were from PTSD. Until now, they had all been random. But on that last mission, the impulses had been focused. They came on demand. He waited impatiently.

Suddenly he was back, back, back in a scene he had relived many times. This was a flashback, horrendous. The convoy coming out of Basra runs over an IED. He sees one of his best mates killed, blown apart, the explosion. He can smell the blood, the stench on the desert wind. He sees the medical guys pushing fluids into burnt and haemorrhaging flesh, plugging holes, pushing organs back into broken bodies. He'd saved one of his mates before when he saw an IED by the roadside... but not this one. Years on, the flashbacks were still there.

Then it stopped. He took a deep breath, stood up straight and poured another coffee. He didn't want to be the mad guy in the troop and now, the mad veteran; you didn't do weakness, not in the Forces. Just when he thought the nightmares and flashbacks were diminishing, they returned. Nobody really understood other than your mates. Going back on mission helped to an extent. On the outside, all the booze and the banter with colleagues were just as before.

The banter, others outside the brotherhood would never understand. It was all about the action and the teamwork, and bringing out the best in his lads, and treating them to a cook-out in the desert in the rare moments when the crackle of gunfire and explosions abated.

For years he had tried not to think about why and how the fuck he had got this other, this special, stupid fucking thing.

Then it had come. On that last tour, walking out into the Iraqi desert after dealing with a daisy-chain deployment of IEDs. The black clouds of explosions littered the scorched skyline.

He is falling, falling, falling. Out of the sky, falling, at 200 miles an hour. Through ice and fire. He fights for breath. No parachute...

The force of the signal knocked him to the ground.

He blacked out. For several moments, as the signal blasted his eardrums and split open his very soul. He opened his eyes, gasping for breath. Had he hit an IED? No. His limbs were still there.

It had come. The message. Why he had the skills.
And how and where he would have to use them.

He was chilled to the bone while the sun beat down on him. He devoured the air, doubled up on the rocky ground. He felt the desert earth beneath him shudder. He thought his head was exploding. Not like him; it took the intensity of battle to get near that. It wasn't PTSD. Not this time. He didn't believe it. But he had to believe it.

After long centuries, the signals had arrived.
And he wished, he really wished, they hadn't.

The ground below him shook. He felt it sucking him in like quicksand. He staggered to his feet, the sun searing his eyes. Fighting the monstrous pull of the Earth, he ran for cover.

Chapter 17

Undisclosed location, USA: April 2019

In a shabby, functional room of 1990s vintage on an American university campus, a small group gathered for a meeting. The group comprised academics and others, mainly from the sciences and engineering, but not exclusively. Only a water jug and tumblers were on the formica table for refreshment; there was no coffee or food, and certainly no alcohol. Although the group was a mixture of ages, and equally split between male and female, they were all white.

The chair, a middle-aged man, began to speak. He wore casual clothes and had no distinguishing features – not even a central-casting prof's tweed jacket with leather-patched elbows. He made the briefest of welcome pleasantries. The men and women present were all equally unremarkable in appearance. You would pass them without a second glance in the street, in an airport or on CCTV. But their expressions today were intense.

Dr Carl Murrow sat to the right of the chair. The room had been swept for bugs by a hired hand with security expertise. But he did not discover the listening device secreted on the person of Dr Allison Hardy, who was sitting near the back.

Allison saw the meeting was private. They had booked the room for an evening in the middle of the semester. There were few people left in the building - just the caretaker, the occasional security man and some desultory students hanging out in the coffee bar at the other end of the corridor. Holding a meeting like this during a vacation period would have looked odd.

Up to now the group had had no official name, only random numbers which changed every week. It had a substantial number of followers in America and Britain who could set up encrypted communications, so members could maintain transnational contact. But online comms were generally discouraged. Written or face-to-face communication was encouraged to avoid interception.

The only way they recognised each other as a group, if a group they were, was by certain modes of expression – not unlike jihadists using a cookbook recipe code for bombing plans. Their plans had been long in the making.

These were no kindly Sir David Attenboroughs warning the world about climate change. These were a new breed of scientist fanatics, although they wouldn't want to be called that.

The group was disciplined – as far as sundry scientists could be – and most members were in top jobs. Like the IRA and al-Qaeda, they were fighting a long war, although they didn't think of themselves as warriors. Arguably far worse, they thought of themselves as saviours – but with no established religion.

"I think we're all here," said the chair. "Welcome to Adrestia."

"What's Adrestia?" asked a physicist from MIT. "I didn't do Classics. I'm a scientist."

Typical, Allison thought. *He's a scientist, so he didn't do Classics.* C.P. Snow's *Two Cultures* – science versus art; two different worlds. Yet many great scientists were polymaths of cultural stature. Even old Murrow knew his Classics as well as his physics. He called his product Gaia – Mother Earth. And as well as rattling on about weapons, Dan knew about Gaia and Orion. When he managed to keep his hands off her.

Murrow intervened. "Adrestia accompanied her father Ares, God of War, into battle. She is the goddess of revolt, revenge and retribution." Ares. Allison recalled Adam's business card when he came into the London office. He ran something called Ares Consulting. *He's as near to a god of war as it gets.*

"This name must not be used online or in any communications that might be intercepted. We are now well on with our plans. At this crucial point, we must make sure you are all on board. You have huge responsibilities, and in the coming months, everything will be coming to fruition and we must not risk any weak links. We are growing support in science and, er, adjunct communities."

"Going global," said a blonde woman who could have been anything from a cop to a teacher.

The chair went on. "Our world is being destroyed. And in cleansing our precious Earth, albeit at great cost, we are launching a broadside that we hope and trust will shake up all those who are polluting it. We will send a message that will make 9/11, Chernobyl and the 1918 flu pandemic look like a pinprick. If anyone has any doubts, they must declare them."

Nobody responded, other than the fervent nodding of heads.

Murrow took his cue from the chair. Allison recalled the dark, penetrating eyes, the neat grey hair and bristling grey eyebrows, the hard sneer of the thin mouth. The scientist could turn on the charm, but mostly he was terrifying.

"For too long we have blundered along with mere protest and stood back while peace-loving researchers pushed out scientific reports on global warming. We watched ineffectual protests by eco-hippies and well-meaning environmentalists."

"Like Deep Green Resistance," said a delegate with too many pens in his top pocket. "And something called Extinction Rebellion in the UK, stopping the traffic on London's bridges."

"Yes, those idiots, bunch of anarchists. They just see world capitalism as the enemy, not their stupid selves using up the world's resources. Or the hordes of incomers overwhelming our societies. We are taking this way beyond that. Our greedy consumer culture and inability to control our populations have exhausted our natural resources, wrecked our climate, and left a trash heap on the planet. We are diluting our excellence with mediocrity and idiocracy.

"And worse, mass immigration and overpopulation is tainting our beautiful planet with hordes of, well, the wrong kind of people. By that, we mean the imminent mass movement of whole populations northwards from Africa and the Middle East once climate change really hits, way beyond the wars of today. The Syria business has already haemorrhaged swarms of refugees to Europe. But the mass move north will make that pale into insignificance. America is not immune, with our own Hispanic invasion. We will end up losing our identity and being swamped, and our precious resources will be decimated.

"There are too many people in the world, and all the problems and industrial effluvia come from populations which are increasing exponentially. Now we can cure the old and the ill, there are even more, on top of those in the Third World," he used that archaic term, "who can't stop breeding.

"So now is the time to redress the balance – for Gaia. It's not enough to persuade people to recycle their goddamn bottles and paper. And we are not, like the eco-hippies, warring against the techno-industrial system. We are not technophobes; we embrace technology and science. We will use science for our ends.

"And we're not standing by for the next world war, flood or pandemic. Gaia will survive all of that, but we must make sure we do, along with the planet, before it's too late. We're taking control."

"Who have we got?" asked a senior woman at the end of the row. "Who will actually be making that possible, or, er, carrying out our message?"

"We have people in place in the military and other institutions."

"What about people in the security services?" the woman in the white blouse piped up. Allison froze as she went on. "Could they infiltrate us?"

"We have to tread carefully," answered the chair. "The downfall of many a plan has been informants and untrustworthy so-called supporters." Allison felt his eyes bore through her as she listened, unflinching.

"The intelligence services know how to infiltrate most organisations. Especially in the UK. We've got members with insider knowledge on how they are monitoring us."

Then, as abruptly as they had begun, the delegates left. Everything Allison feared was coming to fruition.

She made sure she was well away from the university before she sent her encrypted report to the MI5 unit.

Chapter 18

"Be secret and exult, because of all things known that is most difficult."

William Butler Yeats

London: June 2019

Dan stood in Jane's kitchen, waiting for the espresso machine to churn out his third coffee of the morning. He had a feeling that something unexpected was coming. Maybe thinking about it would make it less unexpected. But that attempt was in vain, because it still came out of the blue.

His mobile phone rang, jolting him out of his reverie. The call was from a woman in an office Dan had never heard of, but he had a good idea what it was. He still couldn't believe it, and the colour drained from his face.

"We're sending a car for you now," said the woman's bland voice, calling from a withheld number.

"What... er... what should I bring?"

"Just yourself. And your knowledge and aptitudes. We'll be there within the hour."

Knowledge and aptitudes? You must be joking, thought Dan. He knew straight away that this wasn't going to be like doing an interview at Sky, even those tricky breaking news ones straight after an attack. The adrenaline normally carried him through those without a hitch. This was different. The call ended briskly, and Dan realised that they already knew his address.

He grabbed his keys and watched a silver Ford Mondeo crawl to a halt outside the terraced house. He'd expected a black car with blacked-out windows, probably from watching too many spy films. He wondered if he'd ever see this street again, and the bustle of Islington, and the serenity of Highbury Fields.

Then, nerves gone, he felt a twinge of excitement as he was driven through congested streets to somewhere in central London. The driver didn't speak to him, which was a relief. He tried not to think about where he was going. Passing time, he flipped through a talk he'd printed out in a vain hope to impress his interrogators with his knowledge of IEDs. As for aptitudes, what was all that about?

When he got to the nondescript building, he underestimated how wound up he'd been during the journey. He knew he would never remember how he got there. With a nod, the driver pointed towards the entrance where Dan would be met. It was like any ordinary London office, with a revolving door, large swathes of glass, and a neat reception area staffed by a bored receptionist and security guards.

Bypassing the normal security procedures, he was escorted down several flights of stairs by two unassuming women, one wearing a strong perfume which permeated the stale air. *Armani,* he thought; his favourite scent. They ushered him into a room.

"Reminds me of a film," he said. They ignored him.

A group of people was seated at one end of a long boardroom table. Their mutterings subsided as he was motioned to sit down. He wondered if they were all going to read from a script. *I hate these boardroom gigs,* he thought. He much preferred working a large room to a small group.

Especially when it was MI5.

Among them, seated right opposite him, was Dr Allison Hardy.

"You?" he said. "Blimey, have you found... intelligence on other planets?" Dan glanced around to see what reactions he'd got with his lame attempt at a pun. Silence.

"Sorry – joke. I assume that isn't why you've brought me here.""No. A bit closer to home than that," said the red-haired prof, suppressing a grin as she looked straight at Dan. She looked gorgeous – and distracting, even in this tense setting.

"Will I need to ring my solicitor?" said Dan. He couldn't have, anyway, as they had taken his mobile phone from him. The man who had shown him in smiled for a split second and said, "No, you don't. We have some business we rather think you'll enjoy."

That's all right for you to say, mate. He had met intelligence officers in his current roles and MI6 staff in his first job. But these had brought him in, and it was far scarier. They must know about his past. At least the coffee tasted good. They must know he liked a double espresso. And everything else.

"I suppose there's only one way to say this," said the stocky woman at the head of the table. "We've called you in to help us. There's a very serious threat to our nation. We're looking at a form of terrorism that you may know something about, Dan."

She spoke in a lilting Newcastle accent. Dan loved Geordies; you don't mess with them. She had short, dark auburn hair cut in a fringe to soften a square, resolute face and wore a white blouse done up to the neck and a loose scarf. She looked over fifty, a senior operative with years of experience, and Dan guessed, mostly with the police. The others were bright young things, part of the new intake. As their boss flashed the occasional tight-lipped smile, Dan felt she suppressed a natural warmth in favour of her job. The only evidence of her name was on a small card placed in front of her, first name only: Carolyn.

"Me?" said Dan. "I mean, *look* at me."

"We are, pet," Carolyn said. "You look all right to us." Dan had forgotten that his appearance had morphed into something like a veteran military officer, albeit a lean one.

"I'm not exactly undercover material. I'm just a bit too visible." Dan had never thought of himself as well known, but a Google search brought up dozens of pages. Much of it was information about his old foibles as a musician as well as articles and interviews. Two identities already – and counting.

"And, as I've been told more than once, I'm totally inappropriate."

"You know your stuff," said Meena, an attractive woman of Indian origin seated on the other side of Allison. Mid-thirties, Dan thought. *Beautiful, elegant and classy. The ladies here sure are good looking. Especially Allison.* He had to suppress any physical manifestation of his desire for her. He tried to focus, which in his ludicrous situation wasn't easy.

He said, "Don't you know all about this new threat with, er, all your methods?"

Meena ignored him. "You know how to analyse a load of complex information. And you know more than some of our lot about IEDs." That's what Adam had said after that workshop in London. Dan had thought he was just being flattering.

"Well, most of that knowledge is as an upstart civilian. I don't know much about cyber-attacks. I can just about turn my mobile on." Dan wondered if he would get his back. He shuddered for a moment at what they were finding on it.

"As for terrorism, I know much more about the IRA than other groups. They're more or less gone now, except for their bastard offshoot progeny. But I got into all their methods and how they carried out their bombing attacks."

"We know," said someone at the end of the table. Dan reckoned they used his file as a door-stop.

"And what's all that stuff about attributes?" asked Dan, recalling what the woman had said during the call.

"You appear to have a higher level of intuition. Possibly, to see rapidly in the midst of a crisis how a situation will develop. That's of great value to our Service," said Carolyn.

"How do you work that out?" Dan blurted out. *They must know about that vision of the exploding bus on 7/7.* Was he under surveillance to the degree that they saw inside his mind?

"Let's just say, we've heard high praise of your work. You come highly recommended."

"Who by?" said Dan, holding his breath, thinking, *no, no, not him… it can't be… not this time…*

"Do you know a Major Adam Armstrong?"

Chapter 19

"Motivation is the art of getting people to do what you want them to do because they want to do it."

Dwight D. Eisenhower

Dan burst out laughing. Not a good move, but he couldn't help it. A long, throaty, manic laugh. His interviewers either glared or suppressed a snigger. This time Adam wasn't putting him forward to give some conference talk. This was heavy stuff.

He stopped abruptly. He knew that Adam had been, or maybe still was, involved in Intelligence as well as his EOD missions. Maybe he was serving with, or had been contacted by, this unit.

Did he know that Dan had foreseen the bus bomb exploding in July 2005? And that he had weird visions of battle scenes? Dan shuddered. They must know. They seemed to know everything else. So he decided not to pursue it or he might get put away. But why him? Surely there were much more able operatives they could use? Did Adam want to get Dan killed? He wasn't *that* annoying, surely?

"How do you know Major Armstrong?" Carolyn repeated. Dan thought, *surely you lot must know already.*

"I met him at a conference." Dan wanted to keep this brief and neutral. He hoped they weren't monitoring his heart and eye blink rate, which they probably were. "He used to put me up for talks at events." He put the print-out of his last talk on the table. Nobody looked at it.

"Well, he spoke highly of you. But he said you needed some discipline and purpose and that you wanted to do something more substantial to really stop the bad guys," said Carolyn.

"And I bet he said I should stop listening to David Bowie and get into Guns N' Roses," said Dan.

Then he remembered the chat with Adam in Washington. Dan had thought, but not said, those very words: "I want to do something more substantial to really stop the bad guys." If Adam could read his thoughts word for word... Christ, how had he got into all of this! So that's what they meant about 'a higher level of intuition' – that's why Adam had recommended him. But why did he see those scenes?

The military man motivated him beyond measure. Dan far preferred that this was for talks and media interviews, not this – a role he wouldn't have chosen in a thousand years.

"Which bad guys are you talking about?" asked Dan. "If not the jihadis, or the IRA offshoots making a comeback."

A bearded chap, who looked like a cop and who had been weighing Dan up, responded. "The jihadists keep us all very busy 24/7. And as if we didn't have enough problems with that lot, this is what we've got you in for. We've got wind of an amorphous group. They're based in universities and a host of other institutions we believe they're in the process of infiltrating – Army, police, civil service, companies. We think they are planning some kind of mass disruption, an eco-attack."

"An eco-attack?" said Dan. So at least he wouldn't be sent to fight jihadist maniacs with beards, just another bunch of maniacs with beards. "Does that mean they use biodegradable bomb components?" He was met with another stony glare.

"This is serious. We are getting intel that this crew really means business."

"Well, we've got the Green Party in Brighton," said Dan. "Can't I just join that?"

"We are not talking about the sodding Green Party!" barked Carolyn. "Do you have to make a joke about everything?"

"Well, not quite everything," said Dan. "I draw the line at Liverpool getting relegated."

"There's nothing new about eco-terrorists," said Allison, suppressing a smile. He kept wondering about her. Did she have sex with him back in Canada as part of her appraisal of him? They'd had a good time, and they really clicked together. So beautiful – that mass of curly red hair; that lovely face, the shape of a heart. She aroused him so much that he averted his eyes as she went on.

"They've been around for years. The Earth Liberation Front was classified as a domestic terror organization in the nineties. There's shedloads of eco stuff all over the internet. But so far it's been mainly protest groups. Some have done civil disobedience. Like Extinction Rebellion's giddy games in London this year, blocking the roads and sending drones up to disrupt Heathrow. The animal rights groups were so far the most violent. And we're all so busy with the real threats, the jihadists and the Russians, that it hasn't been top priority."

Each operative round the table took it in turns.

"We'd like to think they're just a bunch of cranks. Most people think of eco-warriors as peaceniks, left-wing hippy weirdos. These we think we've got a handle on are anything but. They have an apocalyptic philosophy, but they're not religious nut-jobs, nor do they have a recognisable cult leader."

"They don't stand on street corners handing out leaflets. They don't sound off on the internet, although we've picked up some presence online. On stuff like GM research."

"They are arguably even more dangerous, or potentially dangerous. We're afraid they've infiltrated companies as well."

"And what's more, they're white supremacist Fascists. Sounds like they will be into eugenics as well. You know – gene manipulation, creating supermen. Er, superpeople."

"Some of them, as far as we know, are involved in genetic engineering projects," said Allison. "That's what I've gleaned, and for some time. So we're looking at that."

"That's what I talked to you about, isn't it?" Dan stopped himself, but too late.

"We know," said the unit head.

"But what have I got to offer in all of this?" asked Dan. "You seem to know a lot already."

"You did a bit of intelligence in your first job in London." A 'bit of intelligence' sounded like being a 'little bit pregnant'.

"Yes, and I was lousy at it and they kicked me out of that section," said Dan. "When I went into the office one day with bright orange hair."

A man seated next to Allison was so fat that Dan could hear him breathing and thought he was going to explode. He panted, "Yes, you're good at reinvention. And imitation."

"But I can't be a spy. I've got a mouth like the Mersey Tunnel."

"We know," said three of them at once. A ripple of laughter reduced the tension.

"Don't come the false modesty with us," said Carolyn. "You're better than you think at keeping your background quiet in professional circles. You like intrigue, you've been around, you like a bit of adventure, and you're good on detail. Not everyone has all of that." A lone wolf trying to find his pack. They'd recruited that type before.

"And speaking of getting around, there's the little matter of me being bisexual. Isn't that a problem?"

"We've moved on a bit since the days of the Cambridge spies," said Carolyn, although Dan sensed her male colleague at the end of the table did not share her liberal attitude.

"They were MI6," said Dan.

"We also know you visited a Dr Carl Murrow a while ago, who we have strong reason to believe is high up in this group. You went to talk to him about an invention of his, to do with protection against radioactivity. You've already made contact, and you would be a likely recruit for them."

"How did you know all that?" gasped Dan, then, in Allison's direction, "Oh, I get it, you must have been monitoring me. I thought there was something not quite right about him – all that political Gaia stuff."

Carolyn said, "There is potential here for bioterrorism, this genetically manipulated diseases business, or a dirty bomb."

"Radiological dispersal device," said Dan, but stopped short of adding the phrase he'd picked up from Adam: "We're all professionals here." Nobody took any notice.

Meena pitched in. "Everything we thought al-Qaeda was going to do, but this lot may have enough tech abilities to pull at least one of those off. We're most concerned they could get hold of nuclear. They may have access to American facilities, and ours. Or a state programme of WMD."

"That's the hardest to do," said Dan. "I think they would go for something easier which doesn't involve intercepting a military shipment. Or stealing from a high-security facility. Like most terrorists: even with brains the size of planets, they will probably go for the path of least resistance."

"Unless it's going to be cyber," said the bearded chap.

"A cyber-attack on a nuclear power facility is very possible. The Russians could do it."

"The bloody Russians can do anything," said Dan. "Pity they don't find a cure for cancer while they're at it."

"This new group isn't anti-nuclear, so probably not that. If they were to launch a violent attack, like a bombing, they would need to bring in expertise and obtain illegal materials."

"That's where you come in," said Carolyn. "You know your weapons of mass destruction. They could use experts like you, and from other terror organisations."

"Won't I be in danger? Won't they cotton on about me?" said Dan, desperately trying to fight his way out of this. "As you say, I've met this Murrow guy. He'd suss me out. He's sinister all right." Dan remembered the stares.

"Aye, he took quite a shine to you, didn't he, pet?" said Carolyn, unable to restrain a smile.

"But surely you can find out about them without the likes of me? And what about my usual work?" Dan was freelance, unlike many other experts.

"We'll make sure you are remunerated," said the large chap, who looked like he would rather be down the pub. "And yes, we can monitor them; we are doing – with our American colleagues. But there's nothing like HUMINT."

"Human intelligence," said Dan. "But what if I'm not human?"

"Or intelligent," muttered the fat bloke.

Then he got serious, at last. "What if I refuse?" Dan dared to say. He knew he was onto a loser there. "And how will I get through the vetting? You know I've got a bit of a dodgy past."

"If you refuse, we can make your, er, dodgy past public," said the fat bloke. "Especially all that business with the IRA."

"I see. That's me bang to rights then, so to speak."

"Look, Dan, you've done a lot to absolve yourself," said Meena. "And we've already vetted you. We also know you acted with considerable bravery under an extreme threat."

"Bravery? What did I do? Watch a Liverpool away game in the middle of the home crowd?"

Meena ignored him again. "You were challenged by a knife-wielding criminal whom you managed to disarm."

"Oh, that nut-job up on Highbury Fields. I didn't do much."

"Well, nothing violent. But you persuaded him, while he had a knife at your throat, to desist."

"I told him I was in the SAS. He believed it. I've been to confession over that one." Then it dawned on him. "How did you know about all that?"

No response. Dan shuffled in his seat.

"Oh, and by the way, I'm terrified of spiders."

"We're not deploying you in the bloody desert," said Carolyn. "Not this time."

Then Dan thought: *if Adam said I wanted to do something more substantial to really stop the bad guys, then that's exactly what I should do. Boy, can that guy motivate.*

"Well, I'll do my best. And at least I haven't got a criminal record. Except Adele's first album," said Dan, brightening up.

"And we have it on good authority that you want to serve your country."

"Well now, you should have said," said Dan, rapping on the table. "Marvellous. Can I start on Monday?"

"You start tomorrow."

Chapter 20

"Espionage offers each spy an opportunity to go crazy in a way he finds irresistible."

Kurt Vonnegut

Undisclosed location: September 2019

Well, not quite tomorrow – at least not 'out in the field'. Carolyn was in charge of his recruitment. She told him he wouldn't be needed in the role for long. That was a relief. But she also said he needed intensive training, which wasn't. He was basically untrainable.

But somehow, he got through several weeks of rigorous instruction before being sent out on assignment. He was slim and fit for his age, and drew on hidden resources. One day he rocked up in a navy T-shirt, tactical cargo pants and desert boots. For once the military shades went with the gear.

"I think you're overdoin' the image a bit, pet," said Carolyn, trying not to laugh.

"I need these shades; it isn't just a pose!" said Dan.

"It isn't sunny today."

"What would you know about the sun? You're from Newcastle. Last time it was seen up there a record number of UFO sightings were reported."

Carolyn sighed, eyeing him up. "You're looking fit, I'll grant you that."

"I'm just a lean mean fighting machine," said Dan, frowning and deadpan.

"In your dreams, bonny lad."

"Well, I've dragged myself off to your excellent gym as well. It's got to be a matter of life and death for me to do that," said Dan. He'd made a valiant attempt to build up his scrawny frame to something more substantial. The insuperably boring tasks of treadmills and lifting weights were made bearable with headphones on, blasting Bowie into his mousy-coloured head. And he was doing it for his country. Him, of all people.

He was even taught to fire a weapon, something he'd always wanted to do. Even with his ambidextrous clumsiness he was, surprisingly, more successful than he'd ever dreamed. That is, apart from the first session. "Take your bloody shades off!" Carolyn yelled, watching his instructor dive to avoid his erratic firing. "Good job they're dummy rounds."

He was well organised despite his various eccentricities, which, in any case, were sometimes put on for effect and to make life more colourful. While he had never served, he had a military mind as far as a civilian could have one. He got things done on time, and had an eye for detail without getting bogged down in it. And he had some special sort of intuition, albeit random, which was what the MI5 unit was tapping into.

"I think you're ready," said Carolyn when he was brought in for a final briefing. He was always taken down to some basement room, and he reflected on past times when the only basements he descended to were nightclubs in London, Berlin and New York. He'd come on since then.

His regular work was put on hold. They had prepared a suitable reason for him to give. Bea took on some of his work and looked in on the flat occasionally. He gave her a farewell call. "Don't forget to feed the Triffids, or they'll swallow up the world. Brighton and Hove, at least."

"Look after yourself," said Bea. "No more Mr Nice Guy."

"Let's not get carried away," he said.

Central London: November 2019

He made a double-strength coffee in the espresso machine in Jane's big kitchen and brought it down to the study. Everything was exactly the same as it had been when that first call had come in from the MI5 unit months ago, but he was now transformed. His hair was short and sharp and he had bought new suits to fit his broader frame.

He packed up the laptop he had been given and sat at the white desk. A giant poster of the Saturn V rocket taking off and a black frieze of troops and helicopters were emblazoned on the white walls. The bookshelf housed work files, military memoirs, and a copy of *Pocket Bowie Wisdom*. He would miss all of this, and Jane – and everyone else.

While he waited to be taken to Heathrow airport he savoured the mundane for a few minutes, something he found himself doing as he got older. Charlie the dog was curled up on the bed and they both stared out of the big sash windows onto the tree-lined street.

"You could probably do this job better than me, Charlie," he said, stroking the little poodle cross's curly fur. Highbury Fields was just up the road. He had been back earlier that morning, pounding laps along the path of hallowed trees. Nothing kept him away from his beloved Fields. He was relieved to see that there were no more strange red lights in the sky.

He got more excited with each day's training. But now that the time to go on mission was upon him, hard reality was kicking in. He felt the huge burden of secrecy, of having to act out a role which he hadn't chosen. He enjoyed being a cracked actor, but he wanted to choose the roles.

He didn't dwell for too long on how much danger he'd be in. And what he would do after… after what? Stopping an attack? Who really were these people he had been sent to infiltrate? And what if they came for him… after? Or before? And could he keep a secret? What would he tell, or more precisely, not tell, his friends? The 5 unit had worked out a cover story which Dan would have to keep to. He was the most unlikely agent that had ever been.

Dan got in the car. He kept wondering about Allison. She knew that he had visited Carl Murrow before he had visited her in D.C. Was she secretly working on the side of the eco-terrorists? Who was she loyal to? He really wanted to see her again after all of this, to hold and kiss her.

He knew that even if he were to serve his country, this was his final chance. His new bosses must have known that Adam's compliments would motivate him. Or maybe they'd made that up just to recruit him – because they knew about the effect the war hero had on him.

But now he was self-motivated, and ready for anything. Even spiders. Just not the big ones.

Undisclosed location: November 2019
Sheena convened a meeting for her unit after sending a brief, encrypted message to her main contact in Adrestia. She had been in regular touch with the domineering Dr Murrow for some weeks now. She was used to patriarchal bastards like him. But she had well and truly nailed her colours to his movement's mast.

She curtly welcomed the small group into the dimly lit, spacious basement office. Whatever light there was emanated from Adam Armstrong's entire DNA genome sequence, enlarged and backlit on a huge wall screen. He had finally consented to giving a sample, albeit reluctantly. This had been put through the most extensive analysis available.

Next to charts of helix spirals and endless humdrum lines, bars, coloured blocks and letters which elicited the very essence of Adam's being, both now and centuries past – a standard service photo half-smiled across the room. Infuriatingly normal, ruggedly and elegantly handsome, a very British face frowned with ruthless determination as if to say, *don't waste my fucking time here. I need to crack on.*

The specially selected experts and officials drafted into the UK's version of the Supersoldiers project were held to an even higher level of secrecy than their usual security clearances. This had taken weeks.

The members of the group who understood DNA and genetics looked up at the wall screen, and breathed out audibly.

"Shit," said one.
And the predictable, "Oh my God" from another.
And another: "What the fuck…?"

"…Eight?"

Chapter 21

"If somewhere else in the universe, life is also coded in DNA, it's not going to be exactly like what we have here on Earth."
Steven Benner, US Foundation for Applied Molecular Evolution

The group gaped at the screens. Stunned silence was punctuated by whistling *phew* sounds, and occasional mutterings not intended for others to hear.

"This is more than just a genome variant," said one of the genetics experts.

"We'll need some extra letters for a start," said one of the scientists, as though he had run out of his hand at Scrabble, struggling to make light of what he saw.

"We're looking at *eight base pairs* here. This is unbelievable. Probably never been seen before."

The usual double helix – the big DNA spiral ladder – filled the screen. The familiar coil had been recast in an attempt to portray Adam's profile.

Eight, not the established four, coloured protein molecules danced together in a multi-armed, tangled helix like the coloured wires in an IED. They'd double-checked and triple-checked everything. But there it was. The presence of the abnormal.

A government scientist broke the silence. "Could this be a mutation that we're only just seeing now?"

No response. Everybody just kept staring at the screen. He added, "Well, I'm just trying to stay calm and, well – scientific."

Another scientist came to his support, equally struggling for words. "Our human DNA is just a programme consisting of a code for our species. We're looking at a totally different genetic code here."

"They've just created a helix with eight bases, but it's synthetic. Called the Hachimoji DNA, put together in an American lab. Not in a human being."

"Oh, yes, I read up on that. The eight-base DNA has a much greater capacity to store information, and—"

"It also meets the Schrödinger requirements."

"What, like the cat? Is he dead and alive at the same time?"

"The eight building blocks can support molecular evolution. Vastly enhanced ability for information storage and transmission, and physical resilience. The possibilities are endless."

"But eight-base DNA can't possibly exist outside the lab anywhere on Earth."

"Well, this guy does."

They were desperately trying to explain in scientific terms what they were seeing. Someone tapped the screen and a full-length blown-up photo of the British Army officer, his classically handsome face almost mocking, stood alongside a genome chart that beggared belief.

Some of the delegation sat down, although they really needed a lie down. They stared at their folders, then up at the chart. Sheena was the least shocked: nothing surprised her. Especially if it was about Adam Armstrong.

"He must be some sort of genetics experiment. Some secret project. Christ knows what the military are up to."

"We *are* the military."

"Could he have had extra genes introduced, by some form of therapy or a virus?" asked the government geneticist. "Or artificial transfer of genes in an experiment? Or from way back?"

"Reminds me of a film."

"A film? Ah, yes, *Gattaca*."

"They were already genetically manipulated before birth in that film, to create perfection – an élite."

The biotech company scientist pitched in. "Simply speaking, artificial genes can be introduced by direct injection of DNA via a virus. But that's for gene therapy, for specific diseases."

"Usually, chromosomal anomalies signal genetically inherited disease."

"We're not looking at predictive genetic disease here. He's clear of all that. A perfect medical specimen, but as you specialists can see here, er, different."

"You bet: this genome looks like an explosion in a ladder factory."

"There must be others who have it. He can't be unique. He must have forebears, ancestors with it."

The gene man launched on his pet topic. "Most of the mutations in a million DNA samples arose in the last two hundred generations. Almost three-quarters of all genetic variation arose in just the last five thousand years. Much of human intelligence is an accident."

"Much of *our* intelligence is a sodding accident," said somebody, *sotto voce*.

"That's unfair. Our security services do their best."

"We would have to find out if this is being duplicated, elsewhere in the world by other institutes and defence research."

"We are doing," said Sheena. She did not add that another, even more covert, unit, above Top Secret, had been set up to do the very same. And that she had a starring role in it.

"What about the lab which analysed this? Are they security cleared?" asked the biotech man. "If this gets leaked..."

"We've taken care of that," said Sheena.

"Why did you decide to look at his DNA? By rights it's only taken from servicemen so that they can be identified if killed in action. It won't explain much. Could someone have contaminated his sample?"

"They wouldn't dare," said Sheena.

"Hasn't he been reported as displaying, er, special characteristics in the field?"

"What characteristics?" an Army official barked.

"We've got reports on his ability to disarm an IED – only occasionally, mind – with some sort of psychokinetic energy on a specific electromagnetic frequency." Several groaned. Sheena did not mention his ability to transmit – if it was transmitting – rapid 'scenes' to someone else.

"As well as that, he's shown a rapid ability to recover from injuries."

"Good grief. Am I hallucinating, or is this real life!" blurted an Army brigadier, who had been in the earlier Double Felix meeting and hated the entire business.

"Well, he's been decorated many times. Iraq, Northern Ireland. Everything fits the normal profile of a thoroughly effective officer – quite normal, but exceptional in terms of his service. Exemplary record. Especially in EOD," said Sheena, still unable to blot out the memories of him.

"Has he agreed at least to be in the Double Felix project? Does he know we know?"

"Know about what? His special qualities? Well, yes, probably."

"If he can bloody well read your mind he will," said the Army man. "I mean, does he know about this result?"

"That's under review," said Sheena. *God help us if he does.* "We need him for an impending vital task in counter-terrorism."

"Indeed. I advise we leave well alone and let this man get on with his job and make sure he's fit. We also need him in Iraq, and soon." Full-length pictures of Adam in fatigues flashed up on the screen.

"He's fit all right," said a lady at the back who had been staring at the screen throughout the session, more at the man's stature than his molecular depiction. "Genetic mutant or not, I wouldn't kick him out of bed."

Sheena sighed. She'd heard it all before.

"If I may continue," she said, glaring at the woman. "The Double Felix project has been set up to engineer an individual through various interventions. Like the Pentagon's Supersoldiers."

"But hasn't he already been, er, engineered?"

"Well, he *looks* normal enough," said a military psychologist.

"I think I've seen him on the telly," said a lachrymose scientist from a biotech firm.

"What about his mental state?"

"I think we ruled out PTSD. He hasn't reported it. But a lot of veterans don't report it. Anyway, the extra skills would be separate. He probably had them before going into service."

"There's no proof of that. We don't know. We'd have to ask him."

"Best of luck with that," said Sheena.

"What is his family background?"

"Very normal, solid, some veterans, and anyway, we're not doing DNA ancestry, are we? Or are we?"

"That's been out a while – commercial kits for people to find out where their forebears originate, anywhere from Tottenham to Timbuktu. They were imprecise a few years ago. Now they're much more accurate."

"We would need to know if the parents carry this profile. If they don't, it must have happened after he was born, through external interference. God knows how. Maybe from a comet. They carry viruses which can interfere with human DNA."

"Or it could have reappeared after centuries, or been re-activated by something."

"Re-activated? Centuries? Who on Earth had eight-base DNA centuries ago?"

"Where *was* he born?" asked the military psychologist.

"Somewhere in north London," said Sheena. "Highbury, I think. One of those trendy places."

"God, how mundane," said a burly man, a government scientist who looked nonplussed throughout the whole session.

"What if he's among the first of the next, advanced stage of human evolution?" asked a young, very keen-looking geneticist.

"Not if he's from Highbury," said the biotech man.

"...the first of an upgraded species. Or..."

"Blimey, Kate, that's a bit far out," said the government scientist, who thought he was being very hip saying 'far out'.

Seated near the back, Allison Hardy flinched. She had been co-opted onto this project once Armstrong's genome had been analysed. As well as being an experienced MI5 operative, she continued her work as a high-achieving, respected geneticist. She had seen Adam several times in meetings in the office. An impressive man indeed.

The geneticist continued. "We need to think for a moment that... what was once science fiction could now be possible."

Allison's throat constricted with suppressed shock. She looked at the man on the screen and meant to say nothing. But she could hardly contain herself. Chilled to the bone, she almost choked as she blurted out,

"We may be the first to be seeing something like this. He may be the first..."

Then she pulled herself up short, avoiding the most outrageous theory of all. For now, Allison would keep that to herself. How, she did not know.

"This is getting farcical," said the brigadier. "We had better proceed with his participation in the so-called Double Felix effort and make use of him, if he'll consent. But I'm not keen, and I've had enough of this."

"As I hardly need to remind you," said Sheena, seeing a natural end to proceedings. "You are all at the highest level of secrecy on this."

"Much like everything else," someone said.

She waited until the meeting members had left, and pulling down the blinds in her office, called a number on a secure line.

"Have you confirmed it?" Murrow asked her.

"Yes."

"Evidence?"

"It's in the DNA," said Sheena.

"Right. You know what to do."

Chapter 22

"Being natural is simply a pose, and the most irritating pose I know."

Oscar Wilde

Washington, DC: November 2019

Dan arrived in DC. Again, there had been no shimmering lights, no turbulence on the flight over. He got through Immigration with additional papers explaining why he carried special kit. The rest of the techie stuff and service weapon he needed – a new, compact model of the Glock 19 – he was to collect next day from a rigmarole of keys and safety deposit boxes. This may be gun-toting America, but not for a British visitor of any stripe.

He felt upbeat about his new role. His first main task was to make contact with the dreaded Dr Murrow and sound him out. Was there anything going on while he was visiting? Just casual-like. His aim: to get invited to one of their closed meetings and get signed up. He wished he was back in the Angel with Jane, or in Brighton with Bea. But he wanted so much more. This was a real mission – to actually prevent a bomb attack, or worse.

Dan arrived at an ivy-covered, detached – well, they all were over here – house on the outskirts of Washington. He enjoyed his umpteenth cab ride across the US capital; his handlers had made sure he had enough cash dollars. Carolyn drew the line at him hiring cars after he smashed up the last one.

Last time in the Washington suburbs, he had been in Allison Hardy's apartment to chat about genetic manipulation and exoplanets. Then, a glorious evening of long, languid lovemaking. He wished he could see her again.

Meeting the radiation scientist back then had been chilling. This time, Carl Murrow was not surprised to hear from Dan. He had already been tipped off about his arrival by Allison. Dan remembered his lascivious stares. Dan was here for the biggest challenge of his life. And now he was trained up for it.

The spacious, traditionally furnished wood-panelled lounge was adorned with giant plants twice the size of Dan's in his seaside flat. Classic decoration – pictures of family, award ceremonies, and landscape scenes – gave off a mundane, innocuous sense of pleasantness that belied the real reason for the gathering. Around fifteen guests quietly took coffee or water – no alcohol, as was customary in the States – and sat down at two large mahogany dining tables.

All the attendees were unremarkable in manner and appearance; all were white. These days at any scientific gathering you would expect many more south and east Asian, black and Middle Eastern faces. Somebody welcomed him without introducing themselves. Nobody said their name, and there was no preliminary chit-chat. It felt like a cult meeting. Dan feigned interest.

The illustrious Dr Murrow did not officiate. Dan wondered if he had freed himself up to observe the attendees, as he was seated near the back – and to observe Dan and any other newcomers in particular. Dan felt his eyes boring into his back. There must be a leader, a director, somewhere. Dan tried to act naturally. They had trained him to conceal his real thoughts and take whatever acting talents he had to a new limit.

He avoided taking notes at first, until he saw a few others scribbling. Nobody used a laptop, although some used a tablet. They were probably not writing to the cloud, or anything that could be intercepted. A nondescript middle-aged man was talking about overpopulation.

"...the fittest will survive. The original out-of-Africa human bottleneck created a period in which natural selection diminished. Then the global population boom, curing of disease, extended life expectancy and mass immigration. This has only just begun. It's already gone too far. Now that our precious, polluted world is on the brink of self-destruction we have to free it from the burden of human beings, and we all know which type of human beings we mean."

What the hell am I getting into here? Dan's hackles rose, but he had to conceal his anger. This smacked of the Holocaust and all the other racial massacres scarring human history. African and Asian peoples had far less impact per capita on the world's resources. Eco-warriors were left-wing, surely – not far-right.

This bunch went totally against the grain of most scientific communities or eco-campaigners. Not only was the Right usually anti-science and not very eco, but the scientific establishment had little or no tolerance for racism. Many scientists past and present were Jews. It had been truly international for decades. These people were about to prove his intuition about terrorists: to prepare for the odd, the unprecedented.

"We are running our own genetics experiments, and as well as these, we know there are already some extra-special people in the world – other than us, that is." This was their attempt at humour, for heaven's sake.

"These special people have extraordinary skills such as ESP, the ability to transmit their thoughts, and self-healing. The reason why is to be confirmed very soon, in a way you would never imagine. They are supermen, and superwomen."

Dan felt a sudden wave of nausea. *Special people... transmit their thoughts... in a way you would never imagine...* He thought of the flash scenes and Adam. But self-healing? What was all that about?

The attendees all looked and sounded frighteningly normal, rational. This was no science fiction or UFO convention, but Dan wished it was. He tried not to look around at the gathering too much. He didn't want to look like he was an observer.

This network went by the term 'research group'. Beyond this leafy mansion in the heart of the 'free world' there was no indication that they intended violence. No one would imagine such an unholy alliance, such a corrupt fusion of what was supposed to bring good to humanity, not to destroy any part of it. But these were odd times, and bizarre alliances and ghastly chimeras were appearing everywhere.

Dan's skin crawled as he listened to the speaker. He felt his cheeks and face prickle with disgust.

"We want to foster and recruit these special people. If they aren't willing, if they're on the side of the authorities, we have to make sure they don't stop us achieving our aims."

"And, ladies and gentlemen, the main purpose of our gathering today: to update you on how far we've got with our main, imminent, project."

Carl Murrow looked over at Dan occasionally, but saw only nodding approval. As a master of masquerade, Dan could act out his new allegiance. They were planning something big in a major city. And of any group, they could launch a CBRN attack.

This had been the great fear since 9/11, and he was in the thick of it. He heard with concealed horror the heavily coded language about shaking the world up, and waking up those in power as to the state of that world. It came back to him: *the grey, gleaming metal thing he saw after he left Murrow's office... an explosion ignited the sky...*

The meeting over, Murrow sidled up to Dan, sitting too close and making his flesh creep. *What does he see in me? Ah, it must be the look and the re-fashioned body shape.* Dan was wearing a sharp dark-grey suit, his new fair hair cropped short. Murrow probably saw him as a delicious fusion of military discipline and loose cannon. He was just what the group, and Murrow on a more salacious level, was after. And maybe he knew that Dan was bi. Dan hoped he hadn't made that obvious – although it might prove useful.

"You're looking smart as ever," said the scientist, eyeing him up. "Well, what do you think? Would you like to be involved?" He lowered his voice, and Dan almost expected him to put a hand on his thigh.

"You bet," said Dan. "I've been out in the wilderness for too long. I've never been accepted into the club" – referring to the Army people he loved working with. For an instant he thought of Adam. He could almost feel his insides tearing at the thought of betraying him. He hoped, almost prayed, that they wouldn't want to know more about him. And that no one here could read minds.

"Good man. You need a purpose, a mission." *Not you as well*. Then Murrow did it, that thing Dan had been dreading. He put his hand on his thigh and squeezed it.

"I could tell when we met, that you'd see where we want to go," the scientist said, slowly moving his hand further north. Dan knew not to flinch.

"We will need you here again next week, but it will be a closed meeting. And I'd like to see more of you."

I bet you would.

Chapter 23

Washington, DC: November 2019

Dan was taken back to his hotel on the other side of town by another silent driver. He wondered if he was FBI or with one of their intel agencies. He went up to his room and sat at the small desk at the window, overlooking an ordinary street of office blocks and eateries. He quietly moved the desk away from the window, checking carefully that no one was observing from the buildings opposite or the street.

He removed the first of the tiny listening devices. He had dreaded Murrow touching him anywhere other than the thigh and finding it. He'd have to put it somewhere else next time, especially if the scientist was going to, er, see more of him.

After a lot of swearing, he managed to connect the bug to his government-issue laptop after logging on via a secure site. Using facial recognition to sign in, he smiled as he thought how this may not have always worked for David Bowie.

Over an encrypted connection, he sent over what he had just witnessed. He felt no excitement, just relief. Now trained in counter-surveillance, he had checked his room for bugs, which needed special equipment as they would be minuscule. He checked everything again and again. There would be more meetings in colleges and remote offices in assorted locations across the US. He filed off encrypted intel after each one. He avoided bugging the rooms, as they were always checked.

Rendezvous of another order took place at Murrow's second home – a plush apartment in another suburb ten miles away from the home he shared with his wife. Dan was driven on the long, slow journey through the familiar Washington cityscape, Murrow's free hand occasionally straying.

As he was shepherded into the scientist's refuge, Dan noted with some relief a fully stocked bar at the end of a living room big enough to stage a game of five-a-side football. A floor-to-ceiling window shone bright light onto solid expensive furniture and traditional paintings. Dan took off his shades and steadied his nerves by looking at the pictures. One in particular caught his eye.

"That's a famous work by Poussin, isn't it?" said Dan as Murrow prepared drinks. "Blind Orion, Chasing the Sunrise."

Murrow drawled in his Bette Davis Boston accent, "Yes. That's not all he was chasing. Orion was blinded by the king of Chios after he made sexual advances to his daughter."

"Aye, he was a bit of a lad. Then his sight was restored by the sun god Helios," said Dan, playing for time as he gazed, transfixed, at Poussin's depiction of the semi-naked, muscled giant Orion striding through gloriously painted countryside. Tiny Cedalion stood atop his broad shoulders, steering the big man's sightless eyes towards the dawn light, pointing to the sky. *Standing on the shoulders of giants...*

"I've seen the original, in the Metropolitan Museum of Art in New York. And the constellation up on Highbury Fields, as I think I said before. The brightest stars in the sky."

Dan refrained from adding that Poussin was the favourite artist of the infamous Cambridge spy Sir Anthony Blunt, purveyor of the Queen's pictures. Poussin had given the towering Orion the face of a very handsome modern man. Dan noted an uncanny resemblance to Adam. But the painting was nearly four hundred years old.

"You're quite a cultured guy." Murrow motioned Dan to sit next to him on a wide brown leather sofa. "A Classics scholar, stargazer and art historian. And weapons expert. No end to your talents." Dan knew where this was going. And to put the tin lid on it, in sloped – of all things – a big white fluffy Persian cat. Dan burst out laughing.

"What's amusing you, young man?" said Murrow, handing him his drink. "This is America, and it's the early evening cocktail hour." Dan took it. *Please don't let it be a vodka martini...*

"Reminds me of a film," said Dan drily. "Maybe she's been expecting me." The cat nuzzled Dan's legs and mewed as he sat on the sofa and stroked its thick fur. It gazed up at him with huge blue elliptical eyes and purred as loudly as a train.

"Well, she's a he, and he sure likes you," said Murrow, ignoring Dan's allusion to Bond villains and white cats. He sat next to Dan and began kissing and pawing him.

"And so do I. I think we're going to get on very well."

It wasn't long before the old guy's seduction routine kicked in and its inevitable culmination. At least the cocktails were good. Dan had been ordered by his new boss to limit himself to just one, to keep his head clear. So he had three.

Dan had known long before his MI5 crash training course the power of the spy who could offer sex. He knew not to cringe while Murrow went through the routine of slowly unbuttoning his shirt, grabbing his nipples, then groping breathlessly inside his trousers and going down on him. Dan's bisexuality meant he'd seen and done it all before, and with older, high-status men. As the cracked actor, he could feign ecstasy. The old guy wasn't bad looking. Alcohol and a luxurious setting helped.

The kissing was the worst, but mercifully brief. Dan's superior strength and dedication to his mission kept him in control. Like many men who exert power over others by day, Murrow liked to be dominated and treated roughly by night, often by a man in uniform and out of it. If he tried anything that Dan didn't want, all it took was a sharp command or the pressure of Dan's polished shoe. The scientist always obeyed. He got off on Dan's image, and Dan got his momentary kicks from knowing he could break the old creep's neck with one rapid snap. He was tempted to do it several times.

Focusing on his assignment, he used the tedious liaisons to gradually extract information from Murrow. Not just from talk. When the old guy was in the shower, away or asleep, he would don gloves, take photos and rifle through books, drawers and desks which, to Dan's amazement, yielded a treasure trove of information that the group kept off the world wide web. But nothing about planning an act of terrorism. Even Murrow's laptop files, which Dan hacked, were heavily encrypted.

Dan had to make sure that he wasn't being watched or filmed while he took these risks. A tiny hidden sensor allowed him to trace the presence of bugs, cameras and mobiles in any of the rooms he found himself in. It also detected guns and other weapons – and a miniature detector spotted traces of chemical or biological poisons and aerosols. Equipment he had written about and lectured on, he was now using – for the Service. These were things he had never done before, but had now been trained to do.

He even checked Murrow's white cat, which kept following him around. He gently examined its collar and stroked its voluminous fur while it snuggled up to him and mewed and purred with delight.

Murrow also liked to show his new recruit off at academic functions and fundraising dinners as his new 'executive'. Dan now had to maintain a double cover story, hence two layers of subterfuge. As a master of masquerade and fused identities, he revelled in these multiple roles.

But he had to keep alert, his super-keen ears tuned to the info and gossip as he mingled with the Washington luminaries. From prancing about on stage years ago in a faux-Bowie white shirt and waistcoat, he graced a totally different arena, equally sleek in faux-Bond black-tie, tuxedo and hidden mike.

"You look dazzling, young man," said Murrow as they quaffed champagne with the great and the good. He noted Dan's pretend look of effete boredom. "I take it this music isn't to your raucous tastes." Decorous background music was played exquisitely by a hired chamber combo of good-looking women whose plunging necklines and easy conversation provided Dan with a welcome distraction from his spying duties – and from Murrow's attentions.

"Bach suits me," said Dan. "I love his mathematical precision. I may be a northern savage, but I went to a posh school."

"Cultured as well as savage," said Murrow, sliding a hand over Dan's back. "That suits me. And I see you've quite an eye for the ladies."

"I did say I was versatile." Dan sniggered, returning a smile from an elaborately adorned official's wife who eyed him up as she sashayed past.

In turn, Murrow assumed his new associate was malleable enough to be manipulated. Although twenty years the scientist's junior, Dan was no 'young man', and the older man's flattery meant he had to be aware of being fed misinformation. And it wasn't long before he knew what he had been selected to do – apart from support Murrow's cause and provide sex.

Dan endured several weeks of feigning compliance, both with the group's aims and with Murrow's sexual needs. One afternoon, after a mercifully quick session on the leather sofa, he was back in his hotel room. Before he got set to transmit more encrypted intelligence back to base, he lay back on the bed. Despite being sucked to oblivion by the cock-hungry scientist, he wanted Allison. At one of the receptions in town he espied her at the other end of the ornate room. He burned with desire for her but knew he had to avoid any contact, even communication via hidden mikes, in case they were intercepted.

He wished she was lying next to him, her long legs wrapped around him. He wanted more than anything to hold her again. And he worried about her. Like him, she was undercover and in danger. He fell asleep, then was woken moments later by the customary slamming of doors along the corridor. He turned on the TV to see what passed for news. A call came from Carolyn on a secure line in her office. She was fuming at her sizeable phone console.

"Where the bloody hell are you now?"

"Back in Washington," said Dan. "DC."

"I didn't think you meant Washington County Durham, man. You're all over the place like a chimp's tea."

"I have to go where the action is," said Dan, unable to resist a wind-up. He was relieved they weren't on a video link.

"Who's that in the background?"

"I'm basking by the pool with a vodka martini in one hand and a blonde in the other. There's a cool band playing... No, I made that up. I'm watching the news on the telly in my luxury penthouse suite."

"Listen, you Scouse layabout, I need more reports from you after those meetings and functions he takes you to," she barked. "And cut down on the cocktails!" She slammed the phone down and poured herself a glass of Scotch from the bottle she kept locked in her office drawer.

Dan got off the bed, turned off the TV and opened the safe where he kept his laptop, checking after turning it on for any form of interference. As ordered, he rapidly filed off his latest report. His thoughts turned to the power of scientists. Some inventors were already billionaires, and ran their own research and space projects after the big state-funded programmes declined. It only took a few rich benefactors to get up to some very serious mischief.

This Adrestia bunch was no lone-wolf-in-a-lab operation. Their tentacles were spreading. Most of the scientists, engineers and functionaries wouldn't get involved with terrorism itself. If they were going to blow people and places up, and more besides, they got others to do their dirty work.

And soon Dan was to become one of them.

Chapter 24

"Tomorrow belongs to those who can see it coming."

David Bowie

Outer London: May 2020

The secure MI5 facility monitoring unfolding terrorist activity in Britain was hopping. Staff numbers had swelled to interpret the mass of information feeding in from the police and other agencies. The normally hushed tone rose to an occasional shout against the hum and buzz of the workstations. Operatives broke off from staring at multiple screens to rush around intermittently.

Vague intelligence on something brewing had been coming in for weeks. An attack looked probable, but no one knew when, or where it would be. So the threat level remained Severe – likely – but not yet Critical – imminent.

Their hands were already more than full. They had pre-empted dozens of attacks – over forty in 2019 alone. The latest atrocity, in April, was wrought by three jihadis who went on a shooting spree in the Westfield centre in Stratford, east London, claiming twenty lives. A gang of neo-Nazis shot five worshippers dead in a mosque in Leicester. In February, a chemical device was dropped from a drone over a stadium in Dortmund, Germany, killing over twenty.

In Iraq, a new incarnation of ISIS was on the rise. Donald Trump was heading towards a second term. Putin – still in power – gobbled up more of eastern Ukraine with no opposition. Cyber onslaughts from the Russians and North Koreans were putting the internet itself under threat. A snap referendum on a united Ireland just missed a majority vote, propelling more violence from the dissident Republican groups.

Dan went back and forth to hurried rendezvous in dreary locations. He was dispatched back to England to await further instructions from his Adrestia masters. He slept most of the flight home to recharge his batteries for the next crucial mission. Sleeping came easier these days.

Carolyn awaited his arrival in an unmarked car. He sat next to her in the back. She saw he had grown into his role.

"Lookin' sharp as ever, bonny lad. Make sure you don't cut yerself." But she also saw behind the façade of confidence and the smart suit that he was more keyed up than usual.

They were driven into London and descended to yet another basement: no windows; soundproof; guarded. They had only a short time before Dan's Adrestia minders, two thugs in predictable black hoodies, would meet him somewhere seedy and take him to another remote, dreary location.

What he had to tell Carolyn was top secret: the ultimate task that Adrestia had lined him up to do. That MI5 had lined him up to do. Once Dan's work was done and an attack was imminent, they had to know when, how, where.

"Right," she said, taking a deep breath and trying to look unfazed.

"So, am I to do it?" Dan could hardly believe what he was telling her.

"And I fear I may soon be outed." He knew he was totally expendable by both sides. He had to be ready – for anything.

"Something that's never been deployed before," said Carolyn. "Do you know where?"

"I assume London."

"Bloody hell. Pinpointing where will be like trying to find a—"

"—subatomic particle in a football field." Dan finished the sentence for her. "I don't know who is telling what to do. They only have one-use mobiles and everything is encrypted. Maybe they're using ESP, for heaven's sake. I can't nail any of them for planning terrorism."

Carolyn looked exhausted. "Right. You know what to do, don't you, pet." She handed him his latest firearm, a sub-compact Glock 26.

"Nice and neat," said Dan.

"You bloody watch yourself, sunshine. You're not supposed to have this. But we're up against it. And I want a daily sitrep from you – and your exact location at all times."

"Why aye, man," said Dan, in a passable Geordie accent.

"Oh, shut up and get out of my sight," said Carolyn.

He called Jane. "The Westfield attack was awful. I'm so sorry I couldn't call you. You know why," he said. "But then again, you don't know why. Just as well."

She said, "Is it ever going to stop? And are you in danger?"

"No and no," said Dan.

"I'll take that as a no and a yes," said Jane. "Stay safe, darling."

From his past he had attained the ability to fulfil Adrestia's deadly plan. Now he had the training to put paid to it. And he was ready to risk his life to do just that.

Chapter 25

Dan sat in yet another basement. He guessed he was somewhere in southern England. He had no idea exactly where, as he had been brought hooded in the back of a van. If that had happened just a year ago, he would have crapped himself. Not now: he was getting hardened to his role. He wore an old pair of combat trousers, a black roll-neck sweater that had seen better days, and a pair of battered trainers – all disposable apparel.

He now sat in a scruffy room with a table laid not with dinner cutlery but with bomb-making equipment. In mundane contrast, a coffee maker sat on a kitchen surface. He recalled that the IRA had used coffee grinders as well as cement mixers to mill the ammonium nitrate fertiliser for their huge vehicle-borne devices. Next to a microwave the sink was piled up with unwashed pots. *Why don't bomb-makers ever wash up?* He hadn't lost his knack for finding irrelevant light relief.

Apart from the usual components he recognised, he also clocked the main bomb-maker seated at the table. He was Provisional IRA and he'd done time, then released under the terms of the Good Friday Agreement. Now he was back in business.

Why the hell had the Provos bought into the hare-brained schemes of the eco-terrorists? The IRA and its bastard offspring, the dissident groups, were gangster outfits with distinct nationalist aims. They had helped other terrorist groups, but not this sort. Dan assumed it was for the money, to keep the 'armed struggle' going.

Three devices in varying stages of completion were laid out on the workshop table that filled most of the room. Along with the usual array of wires, batteries, timing and power units, switches and duct tape, Dan noticed that the pen-shaped detonators were a reliable commercial type, not homemade ones. The main charges took up most of the adjoining room: a piled heap of at least a hundred wrapped blocks of PETN – pentaerythritol tetranitrate – and a batch of TNT. Both top-of-the-range explosives.

They must have their contacts jumping through hoops to acquire this lot. The real McCoy. This big batch was a newer, heat-stable version of PETN – as easy to handle and store as the IRA's favourite explosive, Semtex. The scruffy, ageing man facing Dan was experienced in fashioning most types of explosives into all manner of IEDs – from small devices left in shop doorways to the big vehicle-borne monsters.

Dan had devoted himself to stopping bombs, not making the bloody things, although he knew how to. He kept thinking of how many people had died or been left limbless dealing with these very devices. The thing Dan was now tasked with producing was far worse – years after renouncing his past.

He felt a short, cool rush of panic.

What if Murrow or someone else in this group found out what he was about to do? If he failed, he wouldn't be saving lives – he would be aiding and abetting the possible deaths of thousands. Then he became calm. He must succeed. If only he could save lives...

One, or maybe more, of these 'ordinary' bombs that a convicted terrorist was building in this squalid room in a broken-down lock-up was the come-on. The second – the big one – sat outside in the makeshift lab in an adjoining room. This was the gross, grey gleaming thing Dan had seen in that flash moment as he left Dr Carl Murrow's office some years ago. The thing Dan was going to build.

And it was no ordinary bomb.

"Put your gloves on. And this," said Dan to the veteran IRA bomb-maker, who glowered back. If he was meant to be advising on the construction of a weapon of mass destruction, at least Dan would make sure they followed procedure. He handed over the garment that Carl Murrow had invented for protection against radiation. This version was the full cover. He heard a beep.

"And turn your mobile off, for crying out loud." Dan was not certain if the bombs could be triggered by mobile signal. So far, only timing and power units were visible, but he couldn't be sure they would use mobiles.

"Come on. You know the rules. I've seen the original list in the old training camp in County Donegal. Gloves, eye protection, no mobiles, burn all your clothes, leave no trace."

"We didn't have mobiles back then," said Patrick, as he plied his black art on the bits and pieces on the table.

"Just testing," said Dan, coldly. "We fucking well have them now." *Blimey, you can't get the staff these days.*

"For a British fella, you know a heck of a lot about us," said Patrick. His wizened, pointy face frowned intensely over his fiddly, devilish task. "How do I know you're not British Army? Or Intelligence?" he growled. "You got a military way wit' ya. Reminds me of someone."

"Who's that, then?"

Patrick peered up at Dan. "Ach, you've a wee look of some Brit Army bastard I've seen on the telly. Major somethin'."

"Oh, him," said Dan, suppressing a smile. "Well, apart from me being nearly a foot shorter and almost a foot narrower, and he's much better looking, we're completely alike." He wondered if the IRA man's eyesight was too poor to make the coffee, let alone a roomful of IEDs. It could make Dan's later job a lot easier.

"You're going to need far more protection against the dish I'm cooking up out there." Dan thumbed back at the monstrous object in the lock-up, waiting to be connected up.

135

"We never touched that stuff. But then, you'd be the expert on what makes you glow in the dark," said Patrick, soldering a wire. The whole place smelt of burning and something else, although the PETN explosive was odourless. It was probably the washing-up.

There the old bomb-maker was right. PIRA did not touch CBRN, for many reasons. But this group was aiming for just that. Dan hoped with all his heart that he could get back to his handlers the details of the device that he was helping to craft, if he lived that long. He just didn't know where it was going to be deployed.

His orders had not come from Murrow, as this would have put the scientist directly in the frame for planning an act of terrorism. Instead, the communication came from an unidentifiable source, on paper – not from any mobile or via the internet – which he had to collect from a dead drop in a grimy part of the American capital. His miniaturised DNA test kit failed to yield any human trace off the note.

At least there were no more visions. Dan had felt in control, exerting a modicum of power. The Adrestia mastermind's domineering manner had melted as he slaked his lust on Dan's newly honed frame. But Dan had to be extra careful now. He was in the most danger of his entire life.

He began his work on the cumbersome chimera of explosives and radioactivity sitting in the lock-up. He hoped that the garb the sinister scientist had invented – the Gaia – would protect him. If he were contaminated by radiation after unshielding the material, his days were numbered. He wouldn't be allowed contact with anyone. He would spend his last days in agony in a hospital bed like the poor man he had lectured on so many times, Alexander Litvinenko.

And how the hell had they got the rad part here? He wasn't privy to that information, and assumed they must have criminal gang connections, possibly in Eastern Europe or the FSU, where smuggling of nuclear materials was rife, and insider help. It seemed very odd that an environmentalist group wanted to pollute his beloved capital city with radiation. That was assuming it was going to be London. But, scientists or not, they were fanatics with a toxic ideology.

What would Declan Murray, the Irish Army chief, make of it all? The IEDs being crafted by Patrick were almost copies of the one that Dan had been given to examine in the IRA inventory below An Garda Síochána HQ in Dublin. Most of the IEDs in this ramshackle room were too small for a vehicle-borne attack. But they could be used, like the Dublin inventory bombs, to knock out London's substations.

Not for a moment had he thought he would ever be in a situation like this. But his military friends and colleagues had risked their lives many times and saved many lives. It was his turn now.

An hour after Dan had completed the first phase of his deadly handiwork, two black-clad, masked and gloved operatives entered the ramshackle lean-to where the device sat, waiting. They went through to the room of IEDs, checking each one.

But, squeamish about radiation, they omitted to check Dan's partially constructed device.

Chapter 26

"She turns about in the same spot and watches for Orion."

Homer, The Odyssey

Undisclosed location: July 2020

Adam stood at one end of the room, which resembled a converted gym. His muscular form was attired in a blue T-shirt, combat pants and desert boots. Despite the size of this mundane testing ground, he appeared to dwarf his surroundings.

Connected to his blond head and broad, frowning brow was an array of wires and electrodes. His blue-grey eyes were narrowed, determined as ever. He was not wearing his customary military-issue shades and the bright, clinical white light that bathed him and the room was intense. He wore no protective clothing or gloves, nor did he carry bomb disposal tools. He might as well be naked.

At the other end of the room sat an average-sized training IED. Not quite a Hollywood bomb with red digital clock read-out and toy 'dynamite' sticks, but a realistic tangle of brightly coloured wires, chunks of simulant explosive charge and detonator, the requisite switches and an ancient Nokia mobile phone taped to it. Beginner's stuff.

With a group of carefully chosen and high-security-cleared experts and military medics on the upper gallery, Sheena observed her former lover through a glass screen. Double Felix had finally got Adam Armstrong on board. Not to turn him into the supersoldier he almost already was, but to explore and expand his special skills, which were being put to the test here in this converted gym.

She gazed down at Adam, his tall body and broad fair head encased in wiring, his brain waves about to be monitored, scanned, and measured. A momentary rush of lust and longing indicated that she was not over him. Nor had she got over the bitterness of how it had ended. She had found him with someone else, the bastard; someone in her own unit. Then he had finished with her, just like that. Binned her off, as it used to be called in student days.

She still ached with desire for him despite everything. Riding that big, powerful thrusting frame, devouring the Cupid's bow mouth. Being flung to the ground by him, pinned down, almost crushed by the huge, smooth body, pushing him back up as she was strong as iron… looking into those searing, hard eyes as she pulled her golden giant deep, deep inside her…

Those eyes… and then the flash scene… soldiers bloodied, screaming, torn apart…

Adam took a deep breath and reflected for a few moments on the utter ridiculousness of his situation. Unlike his temporary overseer, he hadn't expended as much as a nanosecond on the dalliance he had indulged with her some years back. He merely noticed her up there, watching him. *She's done well for herself. So let's give her a show, fucking man-eating bitch.*

Her colleagues stared down as voyeurs at the performing-seal test they were putting him through. He felt like some experimental animal in a lab, a specimen being observed by a bunch of flabby officials and wanker boffins who had never seen a moment of service in the field.

He cursed his extra skills. But now he knew why he channelled the energy impulses, why he had extrasensory perception, and why his wounds healed up many times quicker than those inflicted on other soldiers.

It had taken days to absorb the unbelievable shock of that terrible knowledge.

If this were his origin and his destiny, so be it.

So long as they didn't probe further. He had reluctantly given up a DNA sample. It was only a matter of time before they knew.

Sheena already did.

He stepped up to the line. He would channel this humiliating experiment into his eternal desire to serve his country. If it had to be through his unusual skills, so be it. The energy impulses were the least controllable of these qualities. They didn't quite come out of the blue as before, but they weren't guaranteed to happen.

This Double Felix crap broke all the rules, the culture, the brotherhood. It was all about teamwork. He wanted to be the soldier he had dreamed of being from childhood – through his own efforts. He hoped above all that his close mates, his muccas, would not find out about it. But somebody must have said something, or he wouldn't be here. Those incidents in service in Iraq had somehow been logged. But no jibes about Uri Geller. Not even out of earshot. They didn't dare.

"Device will be activated in five," called out one of the nerds from behind the glass, his voice resounding through a PA system. Nothing they witnessed and recorded today would be committed to any system that could be hacked, only noted in writing and on secure computers with no cloud access. Could his telekinetic ability be measured? The team monitoring the equipment connected to their first supersoldier was attempting to do just that.

He looked at the simulated device fifty metres away, propped on top of an exercise bike. The light was blinding. He screwed up his eyes. Suddenly the yellow wire connected to the commercial detonator was snapped apart. The device was disarmed.

Applause and cheers resonated from behind the screens above.

"Let's try another sequence," called out the same voice said through the PA. Once more with feeling...

Another device was placed, to be set off by a mobile phone hidden out of his line of sight. His task was to stop the signal, and not with jamming equipment – just himself.

They were waiting for him to perform the impossible – to block the signal. Adam still assumed that this ludicrous task would be way beyond even his extraordinary abilities. But it wasn't. An invisible impulse, travelling at the speed of light, shot from his eyes. No mock detonation flashed up on the receiving mobile on the device: the signal had been blocked.

Adam fell forward, almost dismantling some of the wires on his head, wanting to clip every one. Again, the moronic applause: it had worked, fuck it. His head was splitting fit to burst.

Then he was falling again. Falling, falling through icy clouds, encased in flames, at 24,000 miles an hour... ... the burn of friction... the murderous gravity... gasping for air... his head bursting, his eyes bleeding... no parachute...

He straightened up. He knew that this was no premonition or waking dream.

This was a flashback.

Gazing down at him, Sheena said quietly to nobody in particular, "Isn't he magnificent."

And looking at the reading on the laptop in front of her, and with her advanced knowledge of electronics and frequencies, she knew exactly what to do next.

The team had omitted to test him with an IED on a timer.

Chapter 27

"This work… in eight-base DNA… expands our understanding of the types of molecules that might store information in extraterrestrial life on alien worlds."

Steven Benner, US Foundation for Applied Molecular Evolution

Outer London: July 2020

Adam's former commanding officer was shown into the brightly lit office, which one of the members of the Double Felix unit occupied in their day job. Sheena and two colleagues sat at a table. The imposing Colonel Richards sat opposite them.

They were meeting at the request of the project head, her colleague to her right. A young Cambridge graduate, he was among the academic mafia who still rose up in the intelligence and security field. She did all the hard work; he got the credit. He had a beard, which still hadn't gone out of fashion. Sheena hated beards. His first name was Glynn.

Colonel Richards gulped down a substandard coffee and came straight to the point. He had been handed the expanding – and redacted – file on Adam Armstrong. He did not for one moment like what he saw. They wanted some more background to that file, and who better than his CO to provide it? But they would be wrong.

"I hope you know what you're doing here," said Richards, "playing at modifying a veteran officer into some bloody freak performing act. And I hope you realise that Major Armstrong also has some PTSD." Again, 'some PTSD' sounded like 'a little bit pregnant'. Adam hadn't reported PTSD officially, but maybe it showed to his CO and colleagues. They had enough experience of it.

"Have you any idea what that means? You've probably no notion of it."

You bloody civilians, he meant. "So go easy, if that's at all possible, if only to make the best use of him. He's also sustained injuries in the field. I want him back in service – preferably in one piece – when these tests are concluded."

"Of course," said Glynn. "We need to marshal anything against the current threat."

"You've got the whole RLC to choose from." The Royal Logistic Corps' 11 EOD Regiment: highly regarded as the world's premier bomb disposal squads.

"Veteran officers of his calibre, if you'll pardon the pun, are rare, and Major Armstrong hasn't showed any adverse symptoms since we ran our last tests."

"Adverse symptoms! You've no idea, with respect," said Richards. "And he's not as rare as you think. He'd be the first to tell you that. It's a job."

Sheena thought, *so he's got a sudden fit of modesty. That's new.* She wondered if there were more like him. One ex-lover with magical bomb-disposal powers was quite enough to cope with. But maybe they were like London buses; you wait half an hour then three come along at once.

The colonel's booming voice pierced her reverie. "Our specialist units have not only the right skills, they go through umpteen tests. And they also get trained up on the equipment to get them through most operations. We don't put a bomb tech in harm's way unless they're in a very poorly equipped arena. Don't do what a robot can. And Armstrong has trained up squads as well. I don't want this interfering with that vital work."

And he went on. "Then there's something else. He was a target for the insurgents in Iraq, but before that, for the Provisional IRA in Northern Ireland, actually during operations. Their bastard offspring are making another comeback since the border got hardened, and are back up to what they enjoy best – settling old scores."

Colonel Richards didn't fail to notice something didn't quite tally in the expression, or lack of it, of the tall, shapely woman with the piled-up hair. "He's tough enough to deal with it," she said.

She should have showed a modicum of concern at this point, albeit merely professionally for the sake of the mission. Especially if terrorists had targeted a high-threat EOD operator – and were still targeting him. Maybe her Double Felix unit already knew this.

But Richards felt that something in the woman's cold mien, her off-hand attitude, wasn't right.

Central London: October 2020

Adam breezed into the MI5 office. The unit knew nothing of his extra skills. The more people who knew, the more likely that he – and the Double Felix project – would be compromised. The intel people were more concerned with the information coming in, of variable quality, about an impending attack.

Adam assumed that the meeting would be a whole lot more normal than the ludicrous circus that had watched him perform his party tricks a few weeks ago. That session had left him restless and irritable, with an intermittent splitting headache.

Carolyn bustled into the office, wearing a sloppy green jumper over her stocky shape and carrying a bunch of files. She looked worn out and harassed. Always down-to-earth, she wasn't spellbound by Adam and didn't stand on ceremony.

"We've got your bloke in there. Dan Boland."

"Good," said Adam in his brisk tone. "And he is *not* my bloke."

"Well, you recommended him. And he's feeding back info about the devices we expect will be emplaced any week now."

"Do him good," snapped Adam. "Keep him focused, doing something useful."

"Yes, we're pulling him out soon." And almost in passing, "Oh and he's building the main one. But we're still trying to find out where it will be deployed."

"The main one?" Adam looked straight over Carolyn and her colleagues and groaned. "Are you serious? Not CBRN; not him! Please don't tell me… he's not making a CBRN device!"

"Aye," said Carolyn, her dark eyes returning his icy glare.

"I only recommended him as a civilian consultant who knows his stuff...and only suggested he…"

"…should stop listening to David Bowie and get into Guns N' Roses," Carolyn mumbled, restraining a smile.

The colleague sat to her left said, "And as far as we know from his latest intel it's going to be some sort of dirty bomb. He's been tasked with sabotaging it."

"Radiological dispersal device," Adam sighed, with the slightly bored look he had when he wasn't out in action. He wished he were back in theatre doing something normal, like dismantling fields of IEDs. "We're all professionals here."

He added, "And if he's meant to fuck up that RDD, if that's what he's been tasked with, he's going to be a target - probably for life. I know what that's like."

"We know, pet," said Carolyn. Adam screwed his eyes up against the bright overhead lighting. He wondered which was worse, Dan quoting Bowie lyrics all the time or Carolyn calling him pet.

He snapped, in his clipped voice, "But I'm highly trained for all that. He's anything but."

"Aye, we know," she said. "But we've trained him, remember. He's toughened up. You wouldn't recognise him."

"I think I would," said Adam.

"Anyway, he'll be all right. He'll do the job. And *you* recommended him."

MI5 may not have known about Adam's special qualities, but Adrestia's directors certainly did – from one of their most loyal agents based in London. They were gathered in the basement of a Beltway office block where one of the group's scientists worked in his day job.

"He is a remarkable case, according to our contact. Pity he's on the other side."

"Yes, terrible waste. He would have been perfect for our purposes."

"Well, whatever team he's leading will be instrumental in stopping us," said the man sitting next to Dr Carl Murrow.

"And his special skills we've been told about by our source will be harnessed to stop what we are about to accomplish. She has attempted to disable them."

"We have a unit out in the field to take care of him. Just two: they've been paid off."

"Only two? What can they do against a highly trained Special Forces guy with special skills? You'll need two dozen."

"They'll do it. They're professionals. If they fail, there are more. And we have to keep the cells compact. The bigger they are, the more prone they are to infiltration."

"We also have good reason to believe we've been penetrated by at least one informant: our prime bomb expert. He's a British intelligence operative."

"He will also need to be taken care of, once his work for us is done."

Chapter 28

"Keep your eyes on the stars, and your feet on the ground."
Theodore Roosevelt

Southern England: October 2020

Dan sat for long hours in the cold, dirty lock-up. He was clothed in full NBC protective gear while he plied his dreaded, deadly art.

The final part of the deadly chimera he was fabricating had been delivered. Security guards at a local hospital had disabled the physical perimeter and cyber systems under cover of darkness. Having been paid off by an insider working for the group, they had moved the therapy machine out of a door secured only by a swipe card. The machine was not secured to the floor. It was loaded onto a truck near a loading dock.

Several detectors used to X-ray goods for explosives, each with a radioactive source, were also scattered around the lock-up. *Must have nicked them from an airport insider.* He'd lectured about it; now he was the one doing it.

He had to extract the radioactive cesium-137 ceramic pellets and other isotopes from the various stolen pieces of equipment. Either he would grind them up into a powder or just fit the detonators and the other components to each device to blow them up with enough explosive to breach the shielding – and disperse the deadly particles.

Dan didn't want to go out with a bang now, not with the appalling shame he would bring. So he must do what had become his duty at all costs, and he must survive – at least this time. He had to keep his nerve. There were no flash scenes. It was as though they'd never happened.

He trundled back into the room which the press would call a 'bomb factory'. He wondered why the place hadn't been raided, but he couldn't ID his location. And he was unaware if there were other Adrestia bomb-makers duplicating this operation.

He surveyed the table laid with IEDs, the wires and taped-up charges and other lethal innards in an array of varying shapes like some bizarre exhibition in the Tate Gallery. Each bomb's tightly knit components were bound together in a muddle to avoid a clear path for any of the bits to be disrupted.

These were the 'ordinary' IEDs fashioned by Patrick to divert the responder services and cause injury, death and mayhem, with the first attack requiring cordons, evacuation from nearby premises and stations, and the diversion of traffic. And the taking of many lives. Or knock out London's electrical supply – or both. Dan would not be able to interfere with these; only one or two would be used, and he daren't try to guess which ones as they were checked by hired hands each night.

Dan's RDD would be set to go off next, amidst all that initial chaos. He knew what would happen. Dozens could die from radiation, as well as those killed by the explosion. All the areas affected by the fallout would have to be decontaminated or sealed off until the radioactivity had decayed away. The time taken for the material that sat only inches away from Dan, cesium-137, was thirty-seven years.

Whole districts would be evacuated. Many people could lose their homes, workplaces and whole streets. All affected would have to be identified, decontaminated and tested for radiation. Probably for life.

The weather on the day was important. If the day was hot and still, the particles would drop onto surfaces in concentrated, lethal clumps. They were approaching winter, and Dan wondered if they had planned it for summer but couldn't get the materials in by then. But winters were already becoming delayed. Electric storms in November were the norm, and after they abated, the air was still. Ideal for concentrated radioactive fallout.

Dan looked at his device. The responders were really up against it if the bombs - and especially his bomb - were on timers. He was to substitute at least one of the timers and detonators with very convincing mock items he had been supplied with. Keeping these concealed had been an almighty task. His RDD wouldn't function – as long as the terrorists didn't do a preliminary test.

Then his heart rate leapt. He saw something else, taking up all the rest of the space at the end of the lock-up. A mortar, like the ones he had seen in the IRA inventory. This one looked top of the range.

An EFP: an explosively formed penetrator. A cylinder like a chopped-up missile with a curved copper disc fitted on the end. The Iraqi insurgents, with help from Iran, had taken them to the nth degree. The mortar was designed to shoot out its deadly white-hot slug of explosive when anything disturbed the sensor, destroying everything in its path. *How the hell did they get hold of this? Did Paddy fabricate it? And how am I going to mess this mother up?*

He bent over the empty mortar tube, the NBC suit crinkling around him, sweat pouring, gloves clammy. Dan peered at the sensor component. He thought of bomb techs wearing their heavy, cumbersome suits. He wished he was in a spacesuit instead, stepping out onto the surface of another planet…

Then he staggered, almost falling over onto the shabby instruments of death. Of all places, here in this bomb factory, his mind and eyes were pierced once again.

The desert. In Iraq, baking under a blazing sun. A tall soldier crawls on the rocky ground to a point near the roadside. He edges closer, gasping for air, and stops for a second. A beam shoots out from a hidden device. The soldier sees the beam. Just for a microsecond.

The soldier works his way around the device, avoiding the beam, and clips the connector inside the box...

The soldier is Adam.

The scene dissolved. Dan was still standing up. He swayed, gasping, almost choking inside the suit. He looked down and saw that his hands were gripping the small unconnected box in the mortar that held the sensor. He had no idea how he'd got to it. He looked down at the ingenious component in his clammy gloved hands. He set to work.

After Paddy was escorted off the grimy premises Dan's protective suit was removed and he was similarly whisked away in the back of a van, hooded and handcuffed once again – although he couldn't have seen where he was being taken. He breathed evenly, to stop his heart pounding. Would they slot him now his work for them was done?

The van arrived at a safe house in the middle of nowhere. He was dragged out and frogmarched into a ramshackle building, the handcuffs and hood removed, and ordered to stay there until further instructions. He had little choice, as he was locked in. He checked himself for tracking devices. Then he began to search for ways of escape.

But first, he had to find something to eat; he was starving. The days of swanning about in a tuxedo at grand receptions with Murrow were a distant memory. He went into a grubby kitchen to make a strong black coffee and found some stale bread and mouldy cheese in a cupboard. This looked more likely to kill him than the radioactive pellets.

As he sat down at a ramshackle table, an ordinary-looking young man in jeans and a black hoodie arrived. Dan drew his firearm. He had managed to secrete it from the Adrestia goons who, unbelievably, failed to search him again. The operative jumped back, looked aghast at Dan and said, "I'm from C. The name's Mark." Hands aloft, he waved his ID. "I've come to extract you to safety. Interim address."

Dan handed him his false ID. Mark checked his weapon. "The latest compact Glock, eh? You must be some asset."

Just as Dan thought one operative to collect him wasn't going to be enough, his sharp ears heard footsteps at the end of the scrub path. Within a second, he dived under the table.

"Get down!" he yelled as the door crashed open. Two men in black balaclavas burst in. Dan fired several rounds into two sets of invading black-trousered legs, shattering ankles and shins. Mark fired a single shot from where he hid behind the door, catching one of the Adrestia goons in the shoulder.

Dan rolled out from beneath the table, finished the first attacker off with a double tap to the head – and applied the same to the other hitman as he writhed on the ground, his legs shattered, screaming for mercy. There was blood and spattered brains everywhere and the smell of cordite.

"Fucking hell," said Mark, looking aghast at Dan. "We'd better get the hell out of here."

"Can I finish my mouldy cheese sandwich?" said Dan.

Chapter 29

"Throw two planets into space, and they will fall one on the other."

Jules Verne

Central London: October 2020
Allison Hardy gazed with sleepless eyes over the patchwork of southern England as her flight descended into Gatwick airport. She was exhausted.

She landed and caught a train to the small town in East Sussex where she lived. She was longing to see her two sons, aged five and twelve, who were looked after mostly by their father. The marriage had failed because she was hardly ever at home, the penalty paid by so many women who were devoted to their careers if they wanted children as well. And Allison had more than one career that took her away. Every time she got to see them, she wondered if it would be her last.

Countering her relief to be home at last was a feeling of profound depression. She longed to go back in a time machine to a time before Adrestia. She'd had many a job in intelligence, but this one put the tin lid on it.

The group's eco-fascism made her more angry than she could ever have imagined undercover work would make her. Especially as these were scientists – the same supposedly noble profession as hers.

And on top of all that, they had kicked off another obsession. The Adrestia élitists wanted to aim for some pristine new existence for future, white – whatever that was – generations. So some had infiltrated astrophysics projects searching for Earth-like worlds. The idea was to migrate to some la-la land before Earth – Gaia – became uninhabitable. In the lead-up to climatic Armageddon, they would first purge its marauding dark masses.

As a researcher into exoplanets, she was an ideal plant in the group. Her undercover role had led her down this path once again – and to studying Adrestia's intended destination: a distant world in a constellation familiar to stargazers the world over.

At the same time, she had been seconded onto the Double Felix project, where she had begun to uncover the truth behind Adam Armstrong's reported extra skills, ESP, and powers of recovery.

That in turn had led her to be seconded onto an Alice in Wonderland project run by her own side. Her high-level clearance was renewed, and now that her work in Adrestia was done, she was fully involved in that project. Many of her old scientific colleagues would have been excited at being a vital part of it. She was terrified.

She made the ultimate decision – what to do with the most sensitive, world-changing information any human being could ever find. After hugging her kids goodbye, she left her East Sussex home and checked into a faceless central London hotel under a false name. She went up to her nondescript room and called the number of a journalist working for a reputable science publication.

They arranged to meet the next night. She smiled as she thought momentarily about Dan, still working undercover. So shocking was the new information she was privy to that even he wouldn't make light of it. He was fun in bed and out of it, but if he got out alive it would be a miracle.

Allison knew that there would be terrible consequences for her actions. This was above Top Secret, but she couldn't keep it to herself any longer. She'd had enough. She checked her room for bugs. Then she called the journalist, a young woman. Together with a male colleague, the journalist came up to Allison's room to hear the most fantastic story anybody – in their or any other profession – had ever heard.

Southern England: October 2020

Dan grabbed the car keys off Mark and they jumped into his new colleague's car. Mark was too shaken up to drive after Dan's summary dispatch of the invading hitmen. But their rapid departure from the safe house hadn't gone unnoticed. Another Adrestia enforcer unit was after them.

Dan jammed his foot down on the accelerator. The vehicle in hot pursuit of them was left behind momentarily, then gave full chase.

"Fucking hell! C was right," yelled Mark in the back seat, clinging on for dear life.

"Stay down!" snapped Dan. The tranquil Sussex countryside whizzed by. "Who's C?" They were touching 100 mph. "Isn't he head of MI6?"

"Carolyn, yer daft twat," Mark yelled, putting his hands over his head. "She said you were a fucking awful driver and *not* to let you drive! Under any… cir-cum-stances! And that you were a mad bastard—"

"She's bang on there, mate." Dan snarled back. "Fasten your seat belt. It's gonna be a bumpy—"

"At this rate you'll get done for speeding," Mark stuttered helplessly as they screeched round a narrow bend.

"Hope they don't take my wasting of them two back there into consideration," said Dan. The vehicle behind was rapidly catching up.

An hour later Dan was hooded. This time, not in the back of a van – but in a disused barn. His hands were tied with thick wire behind the back of a broken chair. His shoulders felt like they were being yanked from their sockets. But they didn't hurt as much as his battered, bleeding face and splitting head.

His MI5 companion was similarly restrained at the other end of the ramshackle shed. They'd put up a fight after the pursuing car overtook them, and lost.

"Take it off." A voice resounded from somewhere. A familiar voice with a low, drawling Bostonian accent. A voice Dan wouldn't forget in a hurry. The disembodied voice of Dr Carl Murrow. One of the masked goons ripped off Dan's hood.

"Reminds me of a film," croaked Dan through swollen, bruised lips. The goon punched him in the solar plexus and growled in an Eastern European accent, "Shut the fuck up."

Through a heavily blackened eye he saw that the scientist was Skyping from the luxury apartment where he'd conducted his trysts with Dan. Murrow must have discovered the bugs he'd planted in the room and on his laptop. And everything else.

"Missing me already?" gasped Dan at the screen, breathless from the beating.

Murrow nodded, but not in agreement. It was an order to the hired thug to whack him across the head again. Dan yelled.

"You can cooperate, young man, or suffer the ultimate indignity," said Murrow. "Which I promise will be long-drawn-out and painful. It's your choice." He sighed and said very calmly,

"What have you done to my bomb."

"*Your* bomb?" Dan gasped, fighting for air, his head, face, shoulders and guts bursting with pain. "You mean *my* bomb."

Another nod. The second thug's gloved hand lashed his face with a cosh, further lacerating his mouth. Dan fought to stay conscious. He remembered being beaten up two decades ago by skinheads. That was nothing; he wasn't tied to a chair then. Somewhere in his splitting head he recalled how to resist interrogation. Not just from his MI5 training, but from years before that – during his dalliance with the IRA... Play for time. Resist.

He began to sing, very loudly and very badly. 'Starman': the ultimate singalong Bowie hit. *If I'm going to go out now, I'll be raising the rafters.* The scientist on the laptop screen winced and nodded again to Dan's captor – pointing to the area of Dan's body he had enjoyed not so long ago.

"Do it."

Dan stopped singing and fought the urge to throw up. The thug parted his legs. *So this is it. Torture and death by castration. The dirty old bastard.* He hissed, "I suppose you'll enjoy this more than yer man here. I don't think I'm his type."

Then, as his torturer turned to retrieve a hunting knife from the table, Dan saw a blur of white fur suddenly leap onto Murrow's lap. The Persian cat mewed back at Dan, then launched its big fluffy body at its master's head, screeching, biting and clawing. Murrow's pierced eyelid and lacerated cheeks and head gushed blood. His efforts to bat the cat away failed. It clung on, goring his face. He screamed.

With the last ounce of strength left in him, Dan lunged with his left foot and tripped up his captor, who fell headlong into the table, smashing his head. The other thug, who was holding a gun to Mark's head, turned to fire on Dan. Mark kicked out at his captor's feet, similarly up-ending him. Dan ducked as rounds whizzed past his ear. He smashed the chair to pieces against the wall and stamped his boot on the fallen knifeman's hand, crushing his fingers, relishing his scream – and kicked him in the head. The knife skimmed across the floor.

Dan then wrenched his hands free of the wire ties and grabbed the semi-automatic dropped by Mark's captor – and in an instant fired rounds into the heads of both prone thugs. Then he untied Mark, who was shaking uncontrollably. The screams via the laptop had stopped, the connection to Murrow cut. Blood, brains and sundry tissue stained the floor and walls.

"You saved my fucking life. Again," said his companion.

"Let's not get carried away," said Dan, wiping blood off his face. "It was really Blo-job's cat."

Mark passed out.

A day later, Dan was lodged in a faceless B&B somewhere in Holloway, north London. Carolyn called him on the secure line.

She was furious. "You've just knocked off four blokes inside of 24 hours! We had to extract you both by heli."

"That was great," said Dan. "Better than that spin I once took in the Grand Canyon."

"I've no time to mop up after all your misadventures, my lad. Your body count is getting beyond a joke!"

"It was them or me," said Dan. "And Mark."

"Aye, I'll give you that. That poor sod's going to be in counselling for a bit."

"They forgot to tie our feet to the chair. Big mistake – huge. And that Murrow bastard was going to, you know, stop anybody else enjoying my charms."

"Oh, get over yerself, man." Carolyn grunted and fidgeted with papers on her desk. "I don't know what he saw in you."

"Well, he made the ultimate cute pussycat video," said Dan. "Can't wait to watch it on YouTube."

The facial wounds and battering Dan sustained during his internment by Murrow's thugs healed up within two days, leaving him with a slight headache. Against orders, he went out the next morning for the first walk he'd had in weeks. Dreary old Holloway: it was great to be back, once again breathing in the pollution from the traffic. It was vastly preferable to inhaling his own sweat encased in the NBC suit. And to enjoy something resembling normal life just for one day after his brushes with death at the hands of Adrestia's thugs.

He had been allowed to collect some things from Jane's and was wearing his standard navy blazer, beige slacks and shades, his dirty-blond hair neatly cut after weeks undercover. After being decontaminated following his sojourn in the lock-up he thought he would never need to shower again. He put on his headphones. The unit had given him back his mobile, which had been wiped except for music and a few innocuous apps. He would catch the news later. He knew it would be only a matter of days before he was brought in again and the news would be part of him – and he, part of it.

So he missed the early morning headline: a respected British geneticist, Professor Allison Hardy, had been found dead in a hotel room in central London.

He made his way up to Highbury Fields. Somehow, he was still being drawn there. After the mayhem of his recent life as an agent he had almost forgotten the lights in the sky above the little park. Then he remembered what had happened on that heart-stopping flight to Washington, DC. The blazing red waves of pulsating energy pounding the aircraft. He glanced upwards...

So he didn't see the black car accelerating towards him as he walked across busy Holloway Road just down from the Fields as the light turned red. The car rammed hard into him, sending him flying through the air and into the path of an oncoming bus.

Chapter 30

The bus braked suddenly, just inches away from Dan's prone body. This threw the passengers standing at the front onto the floor as per Newton's First Law of Inertia, mobiles flying, buggy-bound babies crying. Pedestrians, long used to seeing moped thugs and terrorists in vehicles mowing people down, gave the collision a momentary glance. Just another road traffic accident in another London street – and at least this time the car did not mount the pavement. It screeched away and was gone.

One man rushed into the road, managing to stop the lines of traffic, horns honking. He bent over Dan, who was spread-eagled in the middle of Holloway Road. Vehicles were in gridlock at Highbury Corner, now stripped of its century-old roundabout.

"You OK, mate?" he said. Dan tried to roll away, if only to avoid being run over, and yelled. Good sign: he was conscious. The man rapidly dragged him onto the pavement. His hip joint and broken ribs down his right side screamed in pain where the car had rammed into him. After interminable moments he heard the squeal of an ambulance siren.

They raced to nearby Whittington Hospital. The paramedics worked efficiently on him. He became alert; he felt a line go into his arm for the pain, and for fluids, and an oxygen mask was clamped on his face. He was told to keep still, *we'll be there in a minute mate*. At least he wasn't chucking up blood, which would mean that a broken rib had pierced a lung.

Dan thought, *Murrow's gang again*. The car driver had seen him crossing and revved up at speed rather than slowing down to let him cross the road.

"Thanks, mate," mumbled Dan to the man, who had jumped into the ambulance to go with him to the hospital. "You were quick."

"I'm a security guard in the shop opposite," the man replied in a Glaswegian accent. Dan instantly felt safe. "I saw the whole thing. I've called the cops."

"I think it was deliberate," Dan said, pulling off the mask. It hurt like hell to speak.

"Looks like it, pal. I'm ex-Army, by the way. You in service? Have I seen you somewhere?"

Dan was groaning quietly. "Blimey, not you as well. Thanks mate." Starting to laugh, he cried out with the pain.

A day later, his broken arm strapped, Dan was propped up in bed – amazingly, in his own room - at the Whittington. His ribs hurt most. Several were broken or cracked, but not strapped – or you end up with pneumonia or worse. But it was nothing compared to the beating he'd received in the disused barn. He was on drip-fed painkillers, which made him high.

Jane came in to visit him after his handler cleared it. She sat down on the other side of the bed, wearing her big red faux-fur coat. She reached over to give him a brisk kiss and said straight out, "I said you were in danger!" *If she ever finds out I've just shot four blokes dead...*

A young police officer who looked like he'd just left school was sitting at the end of the room near the door. The doctor, whose accent and name badge – Dr Abboud – suggested he was from an Arab country, gave Dan a cheery diagnosis.

"This is amazing, Mr Boland. In fact, *you* are amazing," said the doctor. "We saw on the first X-ray when you were admitted, and doing a lot of shouting, that you had a cracked pelvis. But this latest X-ray shows that the fracture has shrunk! The car went straight into you there." The doctor raised his hand to demonstrate the impact of the car. "You're lucky to be alive."

"Somebody up there... likes me." Dan was high enough on the painkillers to ignore the pain in his ribs and spout a favourite Bowie song, but without the fabulous saxophone backing. And without the imminent threat of castration and death.

164

"You must be getting better," said Jane. "Just not the vocals."

"Well, that security guard stopped the traffic and got me to hospital, or I wouldn't be here."

Dr Abboud went on breezily. "Those ribs will hurt for a bit. But the arm is healing up great. So we're kicking you out tomorrow. We'll book you in to see the physio."

"Hope she's nice," said Dan. "Or he."

"Should be four weeks on, but at this rate it'll be under a week."

The young constable gazed bemused at Dan and said, "Sir, this is a serious RTA in terms of it being a hit and run. My colleagues will update you." And in came two far more seasoned officers. They reminded Dan of the Special Branch cops who had questioned him after he had stepped off the plane from Belfast all those years ago. One of them muttered to Jane and the doctor that they had to see Dan in private. He stank of cigarettes.

"I'll get us some coffee," said Jane. "You can still drink coffee, can't you?"

"Make it a triple espresso," said Dan.

"Flat white for us, love," said the bigger cop, whose enlarged middle reminded Dan that, while he had put on weight, he was still slim.

"Is that your ex?" said the leaner cop, who looked keen as mustard. "She's very nice."

"Yes, isn't she," said Dan, wincing as he pushed himself up in bed. "She's one of my exes. And you're not her type." He didn't add, *and you're not mine either*.

"I'm DCI Collins, and this is DI Thornbery. We know who collided with you. The driver and passenger were from Northern Ireland. They're wanted north and south – and here. We've arrested them and handed them over to Counter-Terrorism."

"What, not Adrestia? Oh, it must be Paddy's old pals," said Dan, rambling on. "The artists previously known as the

Provisional IRA. Patrick and the group I'm working undercover in must have got the hump because I tampered with his device."

"What's all that about, mate?" asked the big cop, the DCI. "What device? Who's Patrick? And what group? Who's Adrestia when she's all at home?"

Dan sighed, realising he should have kept his mouth shut. He handed the policeman his government-issue mobile phone.

"You'd better get in touch on that number," said Dan. "They'll fill you in on what I've been up to. Well, some of it."

DCI Collins looked at the phone and glared at Dan. Jane handed out the coffees while the DCI called the number. She went out into the waiting area to take a call on her phone.

"Oh, and I told him he should get his eyes seen to," said Dan, high as a kite.

"Told who, sir? The driver of the car?" said the big cop, wondering when he was next due to go on leave.

"Nah, Paddy the bomb-maker. He said I looked like a military bloke he'd seen on the telly. I told him he should've gone to—"

"Did he mean a Major Adam Armstrong, sir?" said the other, leaner, cop, peering at Dan as though he would also benefit from a trip to an optical retail outlet.

"Yes, him," said Dan.

The big cop took a deep breath and said, "Well, that's the man the driver said he'd been instructed to target. Settling an old score. He's spilled the beans. That he was told to top a well-known Army bloke with fair hair wearing a navy blazer and beige slacks.

"His target was Major Armstrong."

Jane had walked back into the crowded private room and spat out her coffee all over the lean cop who fancied her.

"Oh well, apart from me being about eight stones lighter and nearly a foot shorter, and him better looking and he's got medals from the Queen, we're exactly the same," said Dan, trying to mime Adam's height and broad frame with his good arm.

"You'd get into less trouble if you went back to looking like David Bowie," said Jane.

Then he asked the detectives, "And just one more thing, Inspector, as they say. Why did these IRA hitmen come all the way up to Highbury Fields to run Adam, er, Major Armstrong over, for crying out loud? I'm the one who goes up there, not him."

"Well, sir, they say they received intelligence that Major Armstrong goes on an early morning run round those Fields. He's been a target of theirs for years."

"Well, I've never seen him up there, and I lived down the road from those Fields for ten years." Dan was really high now. "Mind you, I've seen some strange red lights in the sky up there."

"Strange lights? Highbury Fields? When was that, sir?" The lean cop was enjoying this, having wiped Jane's coffee off his face. At least it wasn't as boring as the usual run-of-the-mill day on duty in north London: the stabbings, moped muggings, burglaries and car thefts.

"The morning of the London bombings on 7/7, all those years ago," said Dan, suddenly feeling queasy. "I saw red shimmering lights over Highbury Fields. And a few times since."

"Just watch out, mate. You need to get back to your, er, bosses and stay out of trouble. They're picking you up in a day or so, I'm told."

Nobody had told Dan about Allison.

Chapter 31

Dan's recovery was so rapid that he was discharged after two days in hospital and taken to Jane's in Islington. Dr Abboud told him he could go out after a night's rest. Carolyn told him he couldn't.

The painkillers kicked in and he awoke from a dreamless sleep. Showering and dressing was a performance in itself, but with a hot breakfast down him – his first in weeks –and smartly dressed in a suit again, he felt refreshed. He was determined to complete what he had failed to do the day he was sent several feet into the air by that car: to run – or, at least walk – round his beloved Highbury Fields.

His ribs hurt more than the fractured arm and pelvis, now almost healed, but he could walk. *Nothing will stop me coming here,* he thought. *If it's my last breath, it will be here. Don't ask me why. It's just a little park in north London.*

Carolyn had called him again, this time about Allison's murder. He sobbed quietly for some minutes. Poor lady. He'd really, really liked her. Well, more than liked. He had fallen in love with her, and had wanted to ask her out properly when all this was over. The media were saying it was the Russians, but Dan was sceptical.

He had escaped death several times – but Allison was gone. He feared her life had been lost in vain and that his attempts at sabotage had failed. Where the hell were the devices going to be planted? And the big one? He didn't know. Murrow wasn't playing. Despite being able to get the old bastard worked up, Dan wasn't able to extract this final, vital piece of intel from him. He had tried to identify which vehicle was going to carry his bomb and plant a tracking device under it. But – he sniggered grimly – like Carolyn, Murrow's men never allowed him near any operational vehicles.

His encounters with Adrestia's hired hitmen showed they had a reach to gangsters from Eastern Europe and the kind of criminals that still crawled through the sewers of terrorist shit in Northern Ireland. Like Patrick the bomber, the ones who had run him down were old Provisional IRA, aiming to settle an old score. Adam was their target and, like Dan, he was also a prime target for Adrestia, who had probably killed Allison. Their luck could be rapidly running out.

He looked out at the familiar terraced street and longed to be back among bustling Londoners and traffic. He left the house before Jane got back from work. He smelt still, polluted air – precious little rain in weeks.

Jane arrived home and saw a note on the kitchen table. She took Charlie out for his evening walk and called Dan on his other phone.

"I'm out for a walk as well," said Dan.

Jane tried to put her foot down. "You should also be put on a lead, never mind the dog! You shouldn't be out, you idiot. They told you to stay in. Watch the telly, for fuck's sake! Listen to some music, put on a box set, have a glass of wine. You're in danger!"

"I'm bored!" protested Dan.

"What do you mean, *bored*? You've just been run over! You've got broken ribs. Somebody tried to kill you."

"I know. It's all right. I'm… armed."

"You're working for some secret service somewhere doing Christ knows what." Then it dawned on her. "What do you mean, armed? Who do you think you are, James Bond?"

"Only on Wednesdays," said Dan.

"I'm being serious. And it's Thursday today."

"Look, I'm trained in self-defence now. I want to be up on the Fields, just for a bit." He did not say they were bringing him back in tomorrow and that any day now all hell was about to be let loose. And he was drawn to the Fields and he didn't know why.

As he approached the central avenue of trees that cut through the park, his service mobile rang. It wasn't Carolyn this time. It was a younger woman, speaking coldly.

"Dan, you must go back and stay in. You know what they tried to do to you."

"That was meant for Adam," said Dan. "And what about poor Allison? She worked for you and got herself killed."

"That's why you need to stay out of harm's way until we come for you tomorrow. We can't follow you everywhere."

"I've got my service weapon," said Dan.

"Yes, and we'd rather you didn't have to use it."

Christ, I already have. Several times.

Adam knew that something was wrong. The blinding flash of pain kept returning. The same lightning bolt of agony that had seared through his head the very moment he had disarmed the last device from a distance during those fucking stupid Double Felix tests in the disused gym. With what looked, to the onlookers, like his eyes.

The goons behind the screens on the gallery above had made him perform the act of seemingly miraculous EOD another four times, even on an IED set behind a car door and another in a car boot. This usually needed either a controlled explosion or a high-power disruptor, brought up to the vehicle on a robot – to fire a lightning jet through the innards of the bomb, rendering it useless. Adam did it without the kit.

But now, something had been done to interfere with his ability to transmit that 'signal'. Something. Or maybe he'd overstretched himself, now that he knew where the impulses were from and why he had them. That moment as he walked back to base in the Iraqi desert. When he was flung to the ground. The searing vision, the terrible, unbelievable message.

His ultimate mission wasn't here in London. But it wouldn't take place until after the big threat to the capital had passed.

Thank goodness his girlfriend understood. Many past ones hadn't. Anthea was nothing like Sheena or the others who wanted to possess him, to devour him. She took it all in her stride.

He had one last day with her before he got called up for the impending counter-terror operation. They sat down to a gargantuan breakfast in his spacious, ultra-modern steel-and-glass penthouse apartment.

He was quiet, moody, distracted, his screwed-up eyes staring out of the picture window into some undefined distance beyond the city streets.

"Are you all right, darling?" Anthea said, her arms around his broad neck, nuzzling his golden hair.

"I've got a headache," he said, rubbing his eyes.

"That's what I'm supposed to say." She kissed him hard. She never wanted to stop kissing him. She was afraid, so afraid she would lose him. "No girl in their right mind would say that after a night with you."

She didn't mention what had happened two nights before. When he had suddenly woken in the early hours, sitting bolt upright, a deep, terrifying yell rising from his throat. The nightmares and flashbacks of military combat had returned. Soldiers' bodies torn, severed, civilians mutilated, blood-spattered walls, deafening gunfire.

And that other flashback. *Again, falling. Falling through the clouds, fighting to breathe... encased in flame... his lungs bursting, as he plummeted down at 200 miles an hour. Falling, falling; no parachute...* Then he screamed.

She had held onto him for some minutes as he panted, gasping for air. Then, realising he was safe, he had turned to hold her, almost crushing her. She had heard him breathing steadily and deeply, the glorious sound of male arousal. Their lovemaking, long and tender, calmed him. At the first light of dawn they fell asleep, his muscled arms wrapped around her.

He knew he was once again a target. The Adrestia directors would prefer to have both him and Dan out of the way before their plans were executed. They weren't going to make the same mistake twice. But Adam was used to it: Northern Ireland, Iraq, he'd always been a target for the bombers and the snipers.

The word from Carolyn at their next meeting was that Dan's attempts to tamper with the radiological device had probably been discovered and overridden. He'd been run down crossing Holloway Road by some IRA scrotes who'd thought it was Adam, for fuck's sake. Adam avoided that bloody awful road anyway.

And there was worse. Their operative Allison Hardy had been found dead in London. It was not known whether she had killed herself, or if she was murdered, and if so, who by. They suspected that Adrestia had rumbled both her and Dan. The official word for now was that it was the Russians.

Then Carolyn said, almost in passing, "Oh, and by the way Dan Boland recovered very rapidly from his injuries."

"What do you mean, very rapidly?"

"He had a broken arm, what looked on X-ray like a fractured pelvis which seemed to have healed up within the day, and broken ribs – and he walked out of hospital after two days."

Adam flinched at this. But he knew why. He left the office and tried to put these thoughts aside. Before the balloon went up he headed off for a last evening run with Anthea around the little park beyond Highbury Corner.

Dan savoured his last evening walk before being brought back to base. He pounded the other side of the Fields from where, unknown to him, Adam and his girlfriend were approaching, running like Olympic athletes. Dan wore no headphones – must keep his acute hearing clear for situational awareness. He should have always followed that rule, but he was as addicted to music as he was to Highbury Fields.

For the first few minutes the sky was clear. Dan stopped to look up at the stars, up there in the southwestern sky, over Highbury tube station beyond the trees. He could just make out the eight brightest stars in Orion. He thought about Allison and her search for planets like ours. *Poor Allison. She's up there among the stars now.* His eyes filled with tears.

Then he saw them again. Glowing above the trees, the red, undulating waves of light, moving, glittering. Like sizzling, frenetic flames, as though the whole sky was on fire. They reminded Dan of the fields of Orion – the vast magnetic clouds in the heart of the constellation's beautiful Nebula. Then the bands of energy crackling above him fractured. The stars of Orion faded behind the gathering storm.

Dan walked on, trying to ignore his twinging ribs. The sky rumbled with approaching thunder. It was November, but climate change meant winter storms. When they came, they were sudden. Lightning began to streak through the clouds over the little park.

Dan saw the two thugs in dark hoodies and balaclavas come at him. One wielded a knife, the other a handgun – that in a rapid glance Dan saw was military issue, the real deal. Highbury Fields – his playground, now his graveyard…

Dan dodged the knife in a micro-instant. A fork of lightning blasted through the sky next to the ring of trees, striking his stabbing assailant. The thug screamed. His knife dropped to the floor. His head and shoulders were partially carbonised.

The other thug was thrown by the bolt and his weapon went off, shooting him in the thigh. Dan drew his firearm and shot him through the kneecap, spattering fragments of blood and bone all over him and his fallen accomplice. The sky exploded with a searing thunderclap. So nobody heard his screams or Dan finish him off with a single tap to the head.

Then sped down the road he used to live on and banged and rang on Duncan's front door. "Let me in! It's Dan!"

Several agonising moments later, Duncan opened the door.

"The bastard with the knife just took a lightning strike… I just shot the other one…" *The fifth.* Dan fell over the black-and-white cat in the hallway. Duncan helped Dan up as he vomited onto the tiled hall floor and all over Duncan's feet.

"This is why I couldn't cope with your work," said Duncan.

Chapter 32

"Three stars mark Orion's head, which is imbedded in high heaven with his countenance remote."

Manilius, 1st Century BC

North London: November 2020

Just minutes before, Adam and Anthea had turned away from the Fields, their late-evening run completed. They stopped metres away from the beautiful Georgian terraced street near the tube station to begin kissing hard, pulling off clothes, grasping and grappling each other. He pinned her down, entering her against the Tree of Hope. She pulled him in deeper, her legs wrapped around his big, thrusting frame. The thunder cracked overhead; she cried out in the ecstasy of climax.

They started laughing at that old 'Did the earth move for you, darling?' joke. As they kissed, happily and tenderly, Adam heard a shout on the other side of the Fields. Even on his last night of freedom there had to be some commotion somewhere.

Then he saw the forked lightning strike the ground a hundred times brighter than Dan had seen it. It hurt his eyes for an instant. Despite his night vision he didn't see two hooded yobs fall to the floor, one of them with his head blackened – and their intended target fleeing.

But he did hear the three gunshots in rapid succession, despite the deafening thunderclap. For once, he did not intervene. His next mission loomed close and the second, the really big one, soon after. There was so much street crime these days. His attention was on his lady. Some poor devil had taken the bullet.

Later, at yet another emergency meeting at MI5, Carolyn told him that the 'poor devil' had been one of Dan's assailants, whom Dan had shot dead. She was more dishevelled than usual, her scarf tied whichever way around her stolid neck.

"*Shot dead* one of his assailants? Dan Boland? Are you serious?"

"Well, as I keep sayin' – you recommended him, pet."

Adam was restless and dying for a cigarette. "Where the hell did he shoot him?"

"In the kneecap. Then in the head."

"I meant *where*?"

"Oh. Up on Highbury Fields."

"Oh, not *there* again." Adam remembered the three shots that had rung out while he was enjoying some al fresco high-energy intimacy with Anthea. And the blinding fork of lightning that had seared the far end of the Fields.

"So that's what I heard last night. When I was, er, with my…"

"Spare me the details." Carolyn glared at him. "Your star recruit's chequered love-life is quite enough to get me head around without yours an' all." She leaned back and frowned unflinchingly at the restless, handsome officer sitting opposite.

"Oh, and there's more."

"How many more, for Christ's sake?"

"Two Adrestia goons who ambushed him and the operative we sent into the safe house to extract him. He shot the hitmen's legs to bits, then doled out a double tap apiece."

"Who does he think he is, James Bond?"

"Aye. And there were two more who chased him and Mark after they escaped in the car. Dan fought back and finished them both off with one of their own semi-automatics after they started torturing him in some isolated farmhouse."

"I've heard it all now. The whole world's gone mad!"

"Well, that's as may be. We trained him. Well, tried to."

"Easier to train a fucking cat," mumbled Adam.

"You're still a target," she snapped. "And not just of the New IRA – or the bloody old one."

"They'll need more than a short-sighted IRA car driver to get me."

Carolyn sighed, wishing she was back in the good old days chasing Russian poisoning gangs across London. "I'm talking about the Adrestia mob." She added, "Oh, and it *was* easier to train a cat, but he's done OK. And we're bringing him in tomorrow."

Dan put his bloodstained trousers and other items into a London Borough of Islington recycling bag. This time the police could be involved and at some point he would have to hand over everything for forensics. He showered and put on a suit left behind for overnight stays. He had never been so glad to knock back the large gin and tonic Duncan handed him. How his life had changed since he last sat in Duncan's elegantly furnished lounge, adorned with Afghan rugs and surreal pictures Dan had painted of the cat.

The meal was taken in an uncomfortable silence, broken by thunderclaps and the scream of an ambulance and a police car rushing by to shovel up what remained of his assailants. There was none of the usual chatter about holidays, dinners and Duncan's social life.

"If the police come, just give them this number," said Dan, handing Duncan a card. He was careful to keep his service weapon out of Duncan's sight, but his dishevelled jacket worn the night before had revealed it.

"I take it you've been issued with that," said Duncan, tapping Dan's sore ribs. As a former civil servant with friends who had served in Intelligence, he was unfazed.

"It gives me an illusion of power," said Dan. "Remember, you said that a while back. And without it, I wouldn't be here."

"Well, the sooner you're out of here, the better." And Duncan added, quietly, "I don't want to know what you're involved in, but I hope you'll be looked after."

"Thanks," said Dan. "I owe you one."

Dan called his handler.

"Someone from the unit will pick you up in the morning," said Carolyn wearily. She was too exasperated to ask if he was still all in one piece. "Report to me for a proper bollockin' then. Meanwhile, I'll get onto the local police." She wished she was in her first job, scraping drunks off the pavements in Newcastle city centre of a Saturday night.

Duncan put Dan up in the spare room. The thunderstorm and his multiple encounters with Adrestia's hitmen prevented any attempt at sleep. In the hours before dawn, sporadic unconsciousness was permeated with bad dreams. He struggled out of bed and looked out over the terraced houses at the night sky, intermittently pierced by fork lightning.

He staggered back to bed and dreamed he saw Adam shot down in the street, a fountain of blood gushing from his chest. Looking down at his agony-contorted face he saw his eyes staring back, unblinking… then saw it was himself. He woke up with what always feels like a bloodcurdling scream but which was probably just a gasp for air, struggling back into the real world.

The black-and-white cat came in and jumped up onto the bed, gazing at him with her huge eyes and snuggling up to be stroked. He had never been so glad to hold on to the little purring animal, his favourite during all the years with Duncan. *A cat saved my life. I love them – and for some reason they seem to like me.* Then at last he fell into a dreamless sleep.

He was taken into protective custody in the morning. A nondescript man and woman sat on either side of him in the unmarked police car, saying nothing to him or to each other, throughout the journey.

He looked back at the house, remembering when he had left with all his belongings to move to the flat on the south coast so many years ago. The bad dream about Adam – if it was a dream – was still fresh and ghastly in his spent mind, his stabbing ribs a stinging reminder of the car ramming into him. This was offset by a twinge of pride in having dispatched his assailants.

He was brought into a different basement office from the glass-fronted one where he had first been recruited. This faceless premises had blacked-out windows and more armed guards than the other locations. He tried not to limp down the iron spiral stairs, which reminded him of the helix of DNA.

He was given a strong black coffee. Carolyn and two other operatives he hadn't seen before sat at the table – a big bald guy called Colin and a young, attractive black lady with Afro hair whose nameplate declared that she was called Jill.

This time there was no cursory welcome or preliminary chat. Carolyn bolted down her coffee. She looked exhausted; her short dark auburn hair was dishevelled. Her dark eyes glared at Dan and her mouth was set in a furious line.

"We told you not to go out!" she said, banging the desk, the Geordie accent not so lilting this time. "You're bloody lucky to be alive."

"That's what the doctor in the Whittington said."

"You won't be so lucky next time."

"The IRA used to say that. We only have to be lucky once."

"We can't follow you everywhere," said Jill. *I bet you did back then*, thought Dan as an unwelcome memory of his dalliance with Irish republicanism loomed in his head.

"Anyway, never mind that. We need to talk to you about Dr Allison Hardy," said Carolyn.

"Yes. I was very upset to hear about what happened."

"That's as may be." Carolyn and her colleagues looked straight across the table at Dan.

"But you are the only one working with the group who knew she was one of our agents."

Chapter 33

"The universe is a pretty big place. If it's just us, seems like an awful waste of space."

Dr Carl Sagan

Outer London: November 2020

Sheena got into her black vintage Mercedes outside her home in northwest London. She made sure to check the car's undercarriage for bulges and affixed devices. Now that the dissident Republican and other threats were back in full flow, it was once again an essential habit.

Ever fastidious, she checked her make-up and piled-up hair in the car mirror. She espied the crumpled photo of Adam and picked it up. She glowered at the elegantly rugged face, the half-smile mocking her. She still couldn't bring herself to throw it away. With stabs of residual desire for him coursing through her, she shoved it into the glove compartment and banged it shut.

She drove to a disused warehouse on the outskirts of west London somewhere near RAF Northolt. It had once stored tons of goods for one of the numerous stores which went bust years ago. It had a vast underground area.

An emergency meeting of the highly covert unit had been called. Not so much a unit – more a full-scale programme whose findings would be sealed Above Top Secret in perpetuity.

It had a much larger counterpart in the US, which they collaborated with, but the British version had grown. A few foreign scientists had been cleared, but none from Russia. As with everything else, the Russians had their own version of the project. The spate of poisonings and other forms of extreme

181

antisocial behaviour meant that they were excluded from these programmes. A separate division had been set up to prevent them hacking into it.

Sheena got processed in. It took twenty minutes before her fingerprints, DNA and biometrics were checked at three entry points and scanners. People moved purposefully among rows of workstations and dedicated impenetrable servers in the huge operations hall; it was like NASA Mission Control. A massive bank of screens covered an entire wall, where a familiar star system sat above a conglomeration of graphs, charts, photographs and videos.

It had taken the first signals over nineteen years to get here. Now things were moving fast. The James Webb Space Telescope had begun feeding in a multitude of images. One showed, in extraordinary detail, an exoplanet superimposed onto a blurry point in the constellation just below three brilliant stars set in a distinctive diagonal line. Lines of code littered one side of the screen.

An astronomical map of the solar system's asteroid belt stood alongside a map of the Middle East. A photo of the desert in northwest Iraq looked like the red surface of Mars.

And next to all of that the vast screen boasted a floor-to-ceiling 3D poster, and the eight-based DNA genomic sequence, of Major Adam Jerome Armstrong.

Sheena walked through the vast ops room, casting no more than a quick glance at the display dominated by the cinema-sized picture of her former lover. She joined several scientists and intel officials in jeans and sweaters, uniformed military, and the odd nondescript suit seated around a table at the side of the main hall.

"How many more do we have for sure, as well as our bomb squad veteran? And from where?" Sheena asked.

"There's only one more that we know of so far, in Iraq. He's an Iraqi Army officer, and with EOD skills. In service from the

182

insurgency through to ISIS and their offshoots still operating. Amazing he's still alive."

"Well, these subjects can survive almost anything. They'll both be invaluable, or should I say irreplaceable, for the big operation coming up."

"What's the Iraqi's DNA like?"

"Similar to your guy down there," said a US Army official, thumbing back at the giant screen. "It's possible they were in combat against each other during the insurgency. Then allied in the fight against ISIS and in the multi-agency demining efforts."

He meant the efforts to clear the thousands of IEDs that the worst terrorist group in recent times had laid in cities and certain areas of Iraq. "I'm assuming they may have come across each other, especially if they now know that they have this special connection, so to speak."

"Before we get to that we've got a big counter-terror operation in train," said Sheena. "Our Action Man down there is going to be an essential, er, component. It's an interruption, but, let's say, a dry run for his special skills." The very skills she believed she had disabled from behind the screen up on that gallery as she watched him shoot forward impulses at IEDs on a frequency that was previously unknown.

"Indeed, and we hope that this doesn't compromise our main operation. This isn't far off, judging by the signs we've been getting from below the desert out there. And from up there in the asteroid belt where the signals are emanating from." A government scientist in jeans and a sweater pointed down and up to produce something resembling dramatic effect. He went on.

"And among that barrage of signals, those multiple lines of code." He pointed to the wall-high picture of Adam.

"And what about these sightings in the sky? Mainly over north London, but also in the Middle East, mainly Iraq – despite everything else going on there. We don't want anything to draw public attention to what we're doing here."

"The red lights? Still, dare I say it, a mystery. Not UFOs."

"They're called unidentified aerial phenomena now. It's some sort of energy force, like an EMP."

"Electromagnetic pulse? Christ! They're massive plasma surges from the sun. Or nuclear weapons. Have there been power outages in the areas they've been seen?"

"Intermittent. Also sighted by pilots."

"Regardless, we won't be able to keep the underground phenomenon hidden. Geologists and seismologists the world over are tracking it."

"Good God, that whole area and some of the cities are still chock full of IEDs left behind by ISIS! As well as below-ground mines."

"And that's after successive missions to de-mine the area. Armstrong's teams have already shifted shitloads of IEDs and he's trained up some of the squads."

"Sounds like quite a guy," said an American scientist.

"He's that all right." Sheena sighed, glancing at his picture composed entirely of deciphered code. *And you don't know the half.*

"Well, we'll need more than those two, good as they are. But they will be the only ones, unless we find more subjects to disarm it."

A military official sounded exasperated. "Signals from out there, signs below here – this is more than the UN or even a world government will be able to cope with. How are we going to deal with all of this? And what about the bloody Russians? And the oil?"

"The PM and the US President are regularly briefed."

"God help us," said a military psychologist. As well as the teams of astrophysicists and other scientists and droves of electronics and other technical people, Dai was one of the psychologists on hand to deal with the effects of the programme's discoveries. Not just the effects on the teams working in the converted building, but the eventual mass psychological trauma if the truth came out. He specialised in trauma counselling and other psychological effects of warfare.

He had also briefly met the 'subject', as the programme called them, under examination. At Dan's IED workshop two years ago Dai remembered the impressive Army officer showed signs of something exceptional, as well as being wound up like a spring and emanating pure, unadulterated charisma. He had also seen Dan suddenly wince for a moment as he shook hands with the big man before the workshop began, and put it down to the latter's superior strength.

He had assumed that this programme, with its space connotations, would recruit Dan as well. Instead, MI5 had got to Dan first, and Dai had no idea where his old friend was. He missed the long chats over his home-cooked curries and field walks outside Woking where the Martians landed in *The War of the Worlds*.

"How far have you got with his Supersoldier progress?" asked a military chief Sheena didn't recognise.

Sheena launched in. "Major Armstrong demonstrated all the skills in the RSP tests we ran. He really is exceptional. His medical records show rapid healing from bullet wounds. He also recovered within minutes from a double sting from a lethal scorpion. A deathstalker. Without antivenom."

"What?" barked one of the medics. "Where the hell did he get stung by a deathstalker scorpion?"

"In Iraq."

"No, I mean *where*?

"Oh, on the lower shin."

Welcoming a diversion onto a pet subject for light relief, an astrophysicist in the group pointed to the Orion constellation, its eight brightest stars lighting up the huge wall.

"Well, that's apt. According to Greek myth: Orion, the giant hunter, born with superhuman qualities. Stung in the ankle by a scorpion."

Her colleague joined in, gazing dreamily at Adam's giant form gracing the screen alongside the glittering stars.

"…And placed in the sky forever. The handsomest man ever born. The celestial warrior, fleeing from Scorpio, the constellation next door. But not at the same time."

"If we can get back to the medical specifics," snapped Sheena, her ice-grey laser glare boring through them. "I've no time for myths, Greek or otherwise. Or horoscopes." She suppressed a smile as she imagined her golden giant fleeing her own scorpion.

She ploughed on.

"He refused a full brain scan, and we don't know how far or exactly when the ESP works. We measured his brain waves during the tests. We couldn't detect anything untoward."

"Reports indicate that he has premonitions, as well as the telekinetic abilities. With his DNA result, we have as much as we need to know with regard to this operation." She waved a red-talon-tipped hand at the brain-packed hall.

"I don't know how long we can keep this from going public."

"What – the signals, the underground phenomenon, or our Army officer?"

"All three," said a NASA astrophysicist, and, looking over at the decoded photo of Adam, "I think I've seen him on TV."

"Look, he's a decorated British Army veteran with complete loyalty. His reputation goes before him," said Sheena abruptly as the memory of that horrendous battle scene as they reached the zenith of their rampant lovemaking intruded on her thoughts.

Dai chimed in. "He'll be in a state of transition. He may have blanked it out at first, if only as a coping mechanism while caught up in theatre operations. We don't know how he's coped with the extra skills along with the ESP. But now the entire process may be taking its toll. So I hope you aren't expecting too much in this forthcoming operation in London or wherever it is."

"And if he will be fit for the big one," said the military chief, like a football coach.

"He's fit all right," chirped the young scientist who had led the distraction into Greek myth and hadn't stopped staring at Adam's wall-high depiction. Sheena shot her an acidic glance.

Dai went on.

"If he's suffering from PTSD as well, he's also keeping that dark. If he knows what the skills are all about, and why he has them, he could be traumatised. Without exaggeration, he's carrying the biggest secret known to mankind. He could be in denial in order to maintain the resilience expected in his profession. And to prevent anyone finding out. This is a perfect storm in terms of his mental health."

"We haven't time for him to go into counselling," snapped Sheena.

Dai rebounded on her. "Do you know what PTSD does to these veterans? Most of them never get any help, let alone counselling. And now he's got this other shit happening!"

"He won't need it," said Sheena. "He's the toughest there is."

"Does he know this programme exists?" asked Dai.

Sheena didn't reply. *No, but he knows I do.*

"And the underground thing?"

"We've a way to go yet. Our teams are fully occupied with interpreting the signals coming in from out there right now."

"How long have we got?"

"Two months, top."

Sheena was relieved to leave. Her killer red heels clacked down the dingy corridor and through the checkpoints. As she waited to collect her coat, she glanced briefly at her tablet notes jotted under the heading 'Orion'. She deleted that word before closing the app.

There were bound to be people connected to the programme, albeit loosely, who would find out its true mission. One already had: a young, vibrant geneticist who was in at least one of the Supersoldier sessions. Better known as a researcher in the now well-established science of genetic manipulation, she had written and lectured on the search for intelligent life on exoplanets.

This had brought her into the highly covert programme gathering pace in the disused warehouse outside London. And there, she was privy to what it was all about: the discovery of signals emanating from an Earth-like planet located in the constellation Orion.

She had discovered what was sending them, and to whom, and why.

And in the course of this research, she had also uncovered the astonishing and history-making reason for the extraordinary skills of Adam Armstrong.

Her name was Professor Allison Hardy. And now she was dead.

Chapter 34

Central London: November 2020

The MI5 unit was accusing Dan of getting turned by the Adrestia group and giving them information about Allison being an undercover agent.

"Me, going over to those eco-fascists? I loved Allison!" There – he'd said it. And he meant it. He lowered his voice. "Well, I really liked her. I wouldn't do a thing to harm her."

No response.

"You made no attempt to sabotage the RDD. You've been undercover with Adrestia for a long time. They turned you."

"I told you only last week that Paddy the bomb-maker probably found my fake components on the IED I connected up to the radioactive materials. He probably replaced the components with real ones. They must have found out I'd sabotaged them. So then they tried to do me up on the Fields," said Dan.

And, as though in passing, "Oh, and at the safe house and then at that other place as well. They were about to slot me and Mark. I wasted the lot of 'em."

Carolyn sighed and looked down the table. "Slot... Wasted the lot of... Bloody hell, what is he like!"

"You've also got form with the Provisional IRA," said Colin. This was like police interrogation, only worse as Dan didn't have access to a solicitor. "Your loyalty isn't guaranteed."

"Well, you recruited me. You vetted me. It was your idea. I didn't turn up off the street trying to join MI bloody Five," said Dan. "I'm an independent consultant. Well, was. I know I was an idiot back then. I've redressed the balance in that regard. I'm devoted to my country, to the mission. And it was the bastard IRA who ran me over!"

"Those IRA idiots were trying to run someone else over, not you," said Colin. "Settling an old score."

"Yes, and that 'someone else' recommended me to you! And anyway, what about those other scrotes that came for me up on Highbury Fields?"

"Those scrotes, as you call them, are dead. We've had to hold off the police. You're lucky you're not in jail."

"One of them shot his bloody self. I just finished the job."

Dan was empowered by his recent dances with death. He was hardened now, no longer the reluctant lightweight they'd dragged in off the street. He sat back, pleased with his defence and his efforts against his assorted assailants.

"And I had some help from Mother Nature. I bet the media have a field day. 'Forked Lightning saves MI5 Agent from Terrorist Gang.'"

"Come on, Dan, never mind the lightning. You used your firearm."

"Yes. Thanks for the training. Nice weapon, that."

"Oh my days," said Carolyn, turning to her colleagues, exasperated. "Who does he think he is, bloody James Bond?"

"Only on Wednesdays," said Dan.

"It's Friday today, sunshine."

"Well, I've got one big thing in common with Daniel Craig."

Colin snarled back. "And what would that be mate? Other than your first name."

"He's a Liverpool supporter."

"You also can't keep it in your pants," said Carolyn.

"Excuse me?" said Dan, turning cold. Surely she wasn't referring to his glorious time in Allison's arms.

"Your, shall we say, liaisons with Carl Murrow."

"Of course, you'd have had a front row seat. I was wearing a bug the whole time. In a safe place. Although with my acute hearing I needn't have bothered."

"How do we know you haven't given a bunch of secrets away there, when he was, you know...?"

190

"That's *how* I got such a lot of information out of him," protested Dan. "And that's not all I got out of him. I'll send you the dry-cleaning bill."

Carolyn banged her fist on the table. "Too much information!"

"Well, I got you plenty. And about a bunch of other infiltrators, in all sorts of institutions. When I was swanning around in my tux among the great and the good. You've had a few cheap thrills while I lay back thinking of England. That's when I wasn't acting on my sealed orders from the Kremlin."

"Well, we know you're versatile." Colin sneered.

"I had to go along with having sex with a man high up in the group. It was bad enough making him a potential weapon of mass destruction. I didn't expect him to *fancy* me, for crying out loud! And the bastard tried to get me killed!"

"Well, sorry, Dan, but we can't think of anyone else who could have tipped Adrestia off about Allison being our operative," said Jill.

Dan loved ladies with Afros. Like Teresa in his past life. His thoughts wandered for a moment back to that terrible morning in July 2005 when he had called Teresa moments before the bus bomb exploded, having seen it blow up twenty minutes before…

And suddenly, it was there. The flash scene. Dan gasped.

A truck explodes. People are screaming, running in all directions. Fire, everywhere, fire. A black mushroom cloud soars above London. Shots are fired in a street. Adam in his bomb suit is down, blood spreading in a pool over his chest…

Dan let out a cry as the pain seared through his heart like a bullet. He clutched at his chest, gasped and caught his breath, and the scene vaporised. A few nights before, it was a nightmare. Today, a vision of hell.

"Are you all right?" asked Jill.

Dan's head jolted forward as he breathed out and looked up at his interrogators, wild-eyed. "I think I know where the RDD is going to be," he said.

Carolyn stepped in, sounding gentler, and put a hand on his arm. "How do you know? What's going on, Dan? What happened to you just now, love? Where's the radiological device?"

"I think it's north London. And I think Major Armstrong may be in danger," he said, his voice cracking, his hands shaking. He had no idea what Adam's role was in the forthcoming counter-terror operation or about his extra abilities. Against all his better instincts, and knowing that Adam could look after himself, a tear rolled down his face.

They looked at him, trying not to appear shocked, while he told them about the scenes. The one on 7/7, and the ones he had seen when he was with Adam or when he shook his hand.

"We know you have some sort of special intuition. One of the main reasons why we got you in," said Jill. And she added gravely, "But this is something else."

You bet it is, thought Dan. He stopped short of telling his handlers, now his accusers, about the other scenes that had flashed before his eyes, both in the presence of Adam and on his own – of a strange people wandering about in a strange red desert under a vast white sun – nor of the red lights over Highbury Fields.

"I mean, I don't understand why." He looked up in desperation. "I know it's crazy, but I'm just an ordinary guy trying to do my best and I am loyal and I don't know when or why I get them."

"Have you had any psychiatric treatment you haven't told us about? Or hypnotherapy? Or drugs?" said Carolyn. "And you're *not* an ordinary guy."

"Well, thanks." Dan recovered his composure. "I did speed and coke back in the nightclub days – nothing since. I've been on something for years to help me sleep. I'm hyperactive.

Insomnia since childhood. I can hear a gnat farting in the next county. But then you know all that."

"Yes. We have your medical records. We know you've got very acute hearing – off the scale. And you can't sit still, and we were told you had a degree of advanced intuition. But you didn't mention any strange visions to us then."

"I was hoping they'd go," said Dan. "I don't want to be put away, for goodness sake. I don't know when they're going to come. Here's the last place I expected to have one."

"So where's the dirty bomb, then?" asked Colin.

"Radiological dispersal device," said Dan in a crisp tone, sharpening up. "We're all professionals here."

"Fucking hell, he even talks like him." Colin snorted.

"I just said. Somewhere in north London," said Dan.

"What? That's where you were attacked."

"That was on Highbury Fields. It could be anywhere in north London. It's a big place. I just saw—"

"Isn't Highbury Fields near where you used to live?"

"Yes, and these days I stay just a mile from there, at the Angel... oh Christ, please, not the Angel!" He thought of Jane and wiped sweat off his forehead despite the cold.

"Did you pick up something from Adrestia that indicated that the RDD would be in north London?"

"No. I've just seen it now," Dan said desperately.

"Probably Arsenal stadium," said Colin. "It's the most high-profile sporting venue in north London. No offence if you're a Spurs fan."

"I said I'm Liverpool, mate," said Dan. "And don't assume it'll be there, as that ground has a lot of security and barriers and the like. Terrorists don't always go for the obvious target. Unless they're planning to drop something out of a drone onto the crowd. But the RDD's too heavy for that."

He went on. "But don't have a go at me about poor Allison, or why I can't tell you exactly where the blasted RDD is. You put me in there. I've defended myself and my colleague against repeated enemy action to take us out. You know I get these sorts of premonitions. I'm working to stop the bad guys. Don't blame me if I'm wrong. I'm not Mystic bloody Meg."

"We're going to keep you here for a while," said Carolyn. "Out of harm's way." *And to see what else I can cough up out of my befuddled brain. Then get me charged with Allison's murder.*

"What about the first device?" asked Jill.

"You don't ask for much, do you? I've no idea. There was a table loaded with IEDs. There's going to be a come-on attack, or simultaneous. You know that's a standard M.O. I couldn't manage the other IEDs, but I put a duff timer and other fake components into the RDD, which will be in a truck or a big van."

Then he said, "But if the terrorists have already spotted what I've done to that RDD, they could override the timers and put in a suicide bomber like the jihadists. Or transmit a radio signal. "

Caught up with his latest gut-wrenching premonition, Dan had forgotten about the mortar in the lock-up.

Washington, DC: November 2020
Dr Carl Murrow looked out from his apartment over the affluent suburb of Washington, D.C. where he lived with his wife, Mary. She was laying the dining room table and fidgeting nervously with the cutlery. She handed her husband, whom she had begun to doubt in most ways, an early evening cocktail. In a split second she imagined, to her horror, stabbing him through the heart with one of the steak knives.

"How's the face now?" she asked, trying to sound as though she cared. Murrow's left eyelid had been ripped to shreds by the cat, his eyeball torn. It was covered by a bandage and a medical eyepatch. The heavily lacerated left side of his face and neck was also patched up.

Mary had picked up the white Persian after the attack, having burst into the room where Murrow was barking orders via his laptop to his hitmen. But only after the cat had done its work on its master's face. It was now safely lodged at her sister's. She had regretted leaving her beloved cat with him so often, but relished its revenge.

"How far on are you towards the forthcoming event?" she asked, sounding very tired, and sitting down with her drink on the sofa opposite him. She drank too much, especially lately.

"How far on are *we*, Mary," he said, swallowing painkillers with his drink. "I hope you're not having last-minute doubts or qualms. Everything is in place."

"What about that woman, the geneticist? Who got killed in London? You're getting to be like a bunch of cheap gangsters."

"We didn't do that," said Murrow, which was true. But what he said next wasn't. "It's not our style." He sat back, wincing from the pain in his gored eye.

"She found out something that is of huge value to us, which is going to shake up the world even more than our little operation – far more. Somebody else did her in just as we had got to her little secret – or should I say big secret. Probably her own side."

"But you found out that she was also working for British Intelligence," his wife said. "I would have thought that was a big enough secret. Enough for you to have her killed. She would have fed back a wealth of information to them."

"None of the nuts and bolts. That was that other infiltrator, Boland," said Murrow. He didn't mention the ham-fisted attempts to bump Dan off on Highbury Fields, and before, at the safe house and the disused barn – or their secret sex sessions. The thrill of yielding to those strong, elegant hands that could break his neck in a split second, hands that could make bombs... and that had shot five of his operatives dead.

"He tried to sabotage the main part of our effort. And he's got away, back to that wretched organisation he serves. I'm only worried that there may be other informants and saboteurs. So we haven't much time." He omitted to tell his long-suffering wife that another hit squad paid by Adrestia to finish off Adam Armstrong was still at large.

"What happens afterwards? After you and your friends have rendered much of London a radioactive desert?"

"You'll have to do your shopping in New York," said Murrow. He treated his wife like a doormat. He was an old-school chauvinist in both sexual and racial terms. Murrow preferred men, and had married Mary for the usual reasons – for show and respectability. He and his colleagues loved technology but did not espouse progressive values. The Trump era had made it a whole lot worse.

"Don't exaggerate, Mary. And that's only going to be the warm-up act. So you'd better get used to the idea."

"This isn't the way I saw the movement in the beginning," Mary said. "We were supposed to be saving the planet, not polluting it even more. And we weren't supposed to kill people!"

"You have to look at the bigger picture," said her husband. He was even more terrifying with one exposed dark eye glowering at her. "There's far more out there than our little planet."

Mary poured another drink, aware that another lecture was coming on.

"We can now, at long last, see that the Earth is no longer the only planet with life. We're living on borrowed time on this one."

"Well, it will be, if your plans" – he glared at her as she stuttered – "our plans go ahead. What are you all going to do, foul this world up even worse than the people we're trying to shock have already done? Find another one? For God's sake, other planets indeed! I'll attend to the dinner."

She stomped out of the room with her third drink. Murrow looked through the sheaf of papers on the far desk and unlocked the drawer. He took out the above Top Secret report written by Professor Allison Hardy about the programme known only to itself as:

Orion.

Chapter 35

"…Artemis, her bow, with points drawn back,
A golden hue on her white rounded breast
Reflecting, while the arrow's ample barb
Gleams o'er her hand, and at Orion's heart is aim'd."

Richard Henry Horne

Central London: November 2020

Adam knew that the extraordinary abilities he had displayed in zapping IEDs, very much against his will, had gone. At least for now. It had happened on the day of the Double Felix tests. When he had felt like a performing circus before a baying crowd. Something, someone, had jammed the frequency he used to knock out the IEDs. And he had a good idea who.

Maybe it was for the best. In the imminent counter-terror operation, any extra skills he displayed would publicly expose him. 'Army hero pierces bombs with his eyes', and so on *ad nauseam*. He'd be the laughing stock of the Forces, already replete with a level of banter not equalled in civilian jobs. He had a reputation to live up to.

He wondered if their using him was a total mistake. There were other EOD operators and team leaders on hand who were still serving, with the right experience. Using a veteran with anything other than the usual abilities and kit could hamper the operation rather than enhance it.

If his extra skills were exposed, the next gargantuan task in the Iraqi desert would be put in great jeopardy. The enormity of that task he tried not to dwell on, nor his bizarre, incredible situation. *Just get on with the job.*

He was driven away in a blacked-out car to another high-level meeting. His thoughts turned to the death of the MI5 operative, Professor Allison Hardy. She had found out something and died for it. Not just the information she had gleaned from her undercover work inside the Adrestia group, but something far bigger than that.

And Adam knew what that far bigger something was. She had been about to spill the beans. It was a race against time before it all came out.

Only a few streets away from where Adam's car was easing its way through the central London traffic, Colonel Richards was in a special meeting at MI5. There were few preliminaries.

"This Supersoldiers business," he began, "is one thing: you may know I'm not in favour, especially as one of my veteran officers has been drafted in. But I'm even more concerned about something much more immediate, from a conversation I had a few weeks ago with a manager of that unit."

And he explained, with as much tact as he could muster – his misgivings about one of the project managers. He had enough experience of men, and more recently women, under his command and of equal rank – to know when something was amiss.

His suspicions about the aloof deputy chief of the Double Felix effort were duly noted, but Richards doubted whether any action would be taken against her, and wondered if he was too late.

Carolyn and her colleagues were also under pressure to solve Allison's murder while the official Met Police investigation was ongoing. Her killing had come just as the terror threat was getting closer by the day.

She now knew more about the Double Felix project after hearing Colonel Richards' misgivings about its deputy director. She had come across the woman named Sheena at HQ once or twice, but avoided her – why, she wasn't certain. Too alpha-female for her; strident, domineering.

But Carolyn knew nothing about the Orion Programme. Neither did she know about Allison's report on that programme and its most closely guarded secret.

Or that Allison's report had been hacked by an Adrestia operative, and was now sitting in the mahogany desk drawer of one of its main directors, Dr Carl Murrow. And that its soft-copy version was lodged somewhere in central London. And that Allison had met two apparent journalists in her London hotel the night she died.

"They're blaming the Russians," said Jill. They were in their umpteenth meeting that day. "It has to be Adrestia, though. They must have found out she was undercover working for us."

"We must keep everything about that under wraps. Let them think it's the Russians for a bit," said Carolyn. She was still shocked by the loss of her colleague, and only her anger kept her from crying.

"The obvious, superficial signs are that it's them. The news and Twitter are in overdrive, as usual."

"Well, it'll seem obvious that it's GRU. Allison was injected with a rare poison, according to the toxicology report. Not a rare nerve agent or a radioisotope this time, but still a classic Russian method."

"The Russians have plenty of form: Salisbury in 2018 and Litvinenko back in 2006, and several others. But this time we've no CCTV of the perpetrators or of hotel intruders, staff behaving oddly, or of any visitors." The journalists Allison had arranged to meet were nowhere to be found.

"Whoever they were, they were real professionals."

Chapter 36

In the western outer limits of London, not far from RAF Northolt, Patricia and Wendy drank their fifth cup of tea of the day in their 1930s semi, which, unknown to them was only a few miles away from the most covert and closely guarded operation ever set up in British military, security and intelligence history.

"I wonder what Dan has been up to lately. We haven't heard from him in ages," said Wendy. The retired couple knew Dan through Duncan. He enjoyed going to their garden parties, gourmet outings, and a night on the tables in the big casino in Leicester Square. They all had an unlimited appetite for London.

"He said he had to go on some operation and couldn't talk about it. Sounded very hush-hush."

"Dan isn't usually secretive. He's got a mouth like the Mersey Tunnel," said Patricia. "He said so, so it must be true."

"Well, things have got pretty hairy lately. There's another load of terrorism going on," said Wendy. "I hope he's all right. He's not even on Facebook or whatever that other new thing's called these days."

"And there was that woman who was found dead in a hotel, a scientist or something," said Patricia, pouring them both another cup of tea, the ladies' equivalent of Dan's espresso addiction. "Didn't Dan know her?"

Wendy missed nothing. "Yes, more than know her," she said. "He had a fling with her, from all told."

"Blimey, another one," said Patricia. "Who does he think he is, James Bond?"

"Only on Wednesdays," said Wendy.

"It's Monday today."

"Oh, and did I tell you there was something very weird the other night, you know, when we had that electrical storm? I was driving back past that old warehouse. There was something in the sky."

"Probably a plane taking off from Heathrow," said Patricia, forever the practical one. "You should keep your eyes on the road."

"You couldn't miss them, those red lights. Not just the lightning, and it wasn't a plane… something glowing up there. I wanted to tell Dan about it. He used to do all that weird space stuff years ago. He said he once saw something strange in the sky over Highbury Fields."

"Hang on," said Patricia. The TV was on, and breaking news on Sky showed a north London street with 'terror alert' emblazoned in larger-than-usual letters on the tickertape.

Central London: December 2020

Carolyn walked into the secure intelligence operations hub buried deep below a nondescript street somewhere in London. It was sheer mayhem with people running around. Her normally calm, impassive colleagues were at breaking point. The level was set at Critical: imminent attack expected. And Allison's death was still unsolved.

Then there was Adam's place in the Supersoldiers project. Like Adam's old CO, Carolyn had a low opinion of such efforts. But his expressed misgivings added another layer of concern. According to the colonel, one of the project operators was not quite the ticket. Just a hunch, but the intelligence services could not ignore hunches, especially from the likes of Richards, and were bound to act on them. With all their technology, IT and training, sometimes intuition was the last resort. Or even the first.

And she had to give more than a passing thought to what Dan had said about the celebrated bomb-squad veteran being in

202

danger. There was no hope if guys like him were. Armstrong was a prime target for more than one group.

And Dan was high on Adrestia's hit list. They had to keep him under wraps and out of harm's way. Especially as that oddball recruit she had been running for some time had just shot five men and admitted to experiencing premonitions about impending attacks.

Now he'd admitted to having hallucinations of battle scenes when he was with one specific person – Adam Armstrong. Why the blazes had Adam recommended such an unconventional chap? He wasn't ex-Army, so she and her trainers had toughened him up. He insisted he was loyal. But those visions… *Maybe Adam knows that Dan has some sort of extrasensory skill. But how could he know?*

Dan was brought into the nerve centre. The unit working under Carolyn thought he might be of some use, albeit limited, with the intel coming in. Amidst all the internet, dark web and surveillance-based chatter, they were told to listen to anything he came up with.

Jill took him into a bare steel-and-glass room bathed in bright overhead light. He put his shades back on. "Take them off, Dan."

Dan squinted as he took them off. "Reminds me of a film."

Jill ignored him. "An attack is imminent. We need to keep you on hand. Help yourself to coffee." She turned to Dan's temporary minder, a heavily-built, dreary-looking chap who looked like another ex-cop.

"Make sure our master spy stays in here. Don't leave him on his own. Go with him to the gents, and report PDQ if he sees something." Dan calmly poured a double helping of coffee from a machine in the corner of the room and put it on the table.

"If he *sees* something?"

"He has extrasensory perception. I've got to go."

The minder looked nonplussed at Dan, who drew an imaginary revolver and growled in a mock Sean Connery voice,

"The name'sh Meg. Mysh-tic Meg."

For the third time in a week, a top-level government crisis meeting was called. Along with the usual collection of top-ranking politicians and officials, Adam Armstrong was, as before, a prime contributor. Also present were Carolyn. This was a big step-up for her – being summoned to this high-level gathering – as she had the most critical information to hand in a rapidly unfolding situation. Also flown in that morning was Dan's old colleague from the Irish Army bomb squads, Declan Murray. He knew more than most about IRA bomb-making and state-of-the-art IEDs.

"We've put in extra armed units at prime locations. RLC units have been on alert all this past week."

"They had hundreds of callouts last year."

"And a specialist unit and equipment on standby to deal with CBRN, with all the bells and whistles, as we have intel it's radiological."

Adam, as a time-served veteran still in action, was set to lead one of several EOD teams.

"Suspected location?"

"A network of streets in north London."

"North London? A network? How do we know it's going to be there? It's a big place."

"Possibly in or near Highbury."

"Christ, we'll have to cordon off half the city," said the Met Police chief.

"We have intel from one of our informants. The group is highly secretive, but we managed to infiltrate them."

Adam said, "Don't go too much on that. Informants aren't always reliable. Who are we talking about? Oh – don't tell me…"

"Your bloke, Dan Boland."

Then Adam remembered why he had recommended him.

And why Dan had said Highbury.

"Oh, him. I'm afraid the intel is reliable," he snapped, his blue-grey eyes penetrating whichever hapless official sat opposite him. "And he is *not* my—"

"The fella I showed round the IRA weapons inventory in Dublin years ago?" said Declan.

"That's the one."

"Jesus, Mary and Joseph! How did he get the information?"

"We put him in undercover with Adrestia. He thinks it's Highbury. Or near there." Carolyn did not say how. "We put in other undercover agents," said Carolyn, wishing she hadn't.

"Ah, yes. Didn't one of them get herself killed? In a London hotel?"

"Yes, which is why we know this is imminent. They know they've been penetrated and that a lot of intel has been fed back to us. They've been planning this for months."

"Anything on the M.O.? Is it actually going to be a dirty bomb?"

"Radiological dispersal device," snapped Adam. "We're all professionals—"

Carolyn interrupted him. "Yes, and Boland has also built it."

"Mother o' God!" said Declan. "Whose idea was that?"

Adam said nothing.

Carolyn rattled off the reply. "And he was meant to ensure it wouldn't detonate. But he's saying they've rumbled him. So it will probably be viable." Declan looked round the table, wondering if they had all lost their minds.

"Anything on the firing mechanism? Where did they get the rad source from?"

"It's on timers, but it could be anything now. The IRA input – one of their veteran bomb-makers – means they will most likely work. But if they've found Boland's attempts to replace them, they could use something else."

"We've had reports of the disappearance of some discarded hospital equipment containing a radiological source. Hospital in Essex. It's weeks since it was removed. And handheld airport scanners, all with a radioactive source. We're dealing with a well-connected bunch here."

From Dan's intel they knew it would be a vehicle-borne threat. It was going to be a monumental task finding and interdicting a lorry or van out of the thousands moving on British roads at any one time. PETN high explosive was hard enough to spot at the best of times.

"What do you know about the likely suspects? This Adrestia bunch of eco-maniacs?" asked somebody from the government.

"They're comprised of a network of scientists, highly covert, very wealthy. Not much on the web. They've cultivated and paid insiders and infiltrators in major organisations. Not just universities, big science corporates and government labs, but also the military, and possibly the police. All clean, so a devil to ID and track them."

"Strewth, as if we haven't got enough shit with the jihadist nutters," said the Met Police chief. "That lot you're on about are still called eco-warriors. Nobody's got round to calling them terrorists yet. We've had a bellyful of protests and idiots blocking bridges. Then there was that drone dropped on Heathrow."

"But bombings? That's not very eco-friendly. Isn't a radiological attack going to cause pollution, not stop it?"

"According to our sources, they want to shake up the powers that be and the public at large who have been ignoring global warming and all the usual. But they've got a whole bunch of much more alarming agendas."

"Like what? There's more?"

"They're white supremacists – at least the directors, as they call themselves, are. They blame everything on overpopulation, particularly by what they call the wrong sort of people."

"They've also got a loony-tune branch claiming to be in touch with some planet with intelligent life on it, for heaven's sake!"

No one saw Adam wince. Then he rapped out, "I'd like to kill every terrorist on *this* planet."

Carolyn felt her blood run cold and met his grey-blue laser glare. *God help them. This Armstrong guy is terrifying.*

Adam strode out of the meeting ahead of the others. He had to prepare his team – and himself. The piercing headaches and residual stabs from the scorpion stings were easing, but had not left him.

But the telekinesis was a curse. But without it how would he meet the ultimate challenge of his eventual mission in Iraq? How much did the intelligence agencies know? And did they know why it had to be him?

Nobody must know. At any cost.

He may not turn out to be a Double Felix – a supersoldier – on the day. For now, he was Felix. The name for bomb disposal technicians around the world. It started out as 'Phoenix', after the 11 EOD Regiment's radio call signal. They lost two operators in a morning and the squadron metaphorically rose from the ashes to conquer terrorism. 'Phoenix' was misheard as 'Felix': equally appropriate; a cat with nine lives.

Adam had risen like the phoenix and, like Felix, was on his ninth life. Just him and his team. No weird extra skills. Not this time.

Words from a talk he had given years ago returned. *If you're lucky, you see the signs and decide it's time to pull back and step away... but maybe by then it's already too late.*

And this time, more than ever before, he feared that it was.

Chapter 37

At the height of the morning rush hour on the Tuesday before Christmas 2020, a middle-aged white man wearing a suit and a plain dark overcoat walked into King's Cross station, central London. He joined the throng of Underground passengers and rail travellers rushing in all directions in diagonal lines, criss-crossing each other with their bags and trolleys and purposes. Some dragged reluctant children as they hustled their way through: just another day. Like thousands of others, the man carried a rucksack. He walked down the escalator into the main Underground.

Just another morning in one of the capital's busiest stations; thousands on their way to work, others to do Christmas shopping. All living their lives, with momentary worries about the tasks ahead or getting to work on time. Those who hated mornings moved as though on autopilot. Only the multiple CCTV cameras saw the nondescript man put down his rucksack at the foot of the escalators, walk back up and out of the station and merge into the traffic and crowds of Euston Road.

At precisely 8 a.m., the short-delay timer ran down on the box device inside the man's rucksack. It triggered in a nanosecond the detonation of 25 kilograms of PETN high explosive, nails, screws and broken glass. An all-engulfing white flash and an earth-shattering boom ripped through the Underground station at 4,000 metres per second.

In that second, one hundred lives were blown to oblivion. A further 300 were injured, some irreparably. Bodies, limbs and brains were shattered in a devil's instant. An ocean of lifeblood spattered. Strewn bags; obliterated lives. Seconds of deathly silence followed the blast. Then the screams, the screams that pierced the fog of terrorist war.

Then the screams of sirens, the screech of ambulances, fire engines, police cars, the media descending. People filming on mobiles, pictures flashed across the world, some too horrendous to show. Each separate, special life now logged as a group of victims in the hundreds of ghastly terrorist tolls of mass murder. A collection of shattered remains that had been lives. Limbs parted from people. Eardrums shattered. Guts and spleens ripped out. Eyes, faces and bodies torn and punctured by shrapnel. A billion shreds, shards and splinters of metal, piercing flesh at the speed of light. Parts of bodies merged with others. Masonry falling; limbs crushed. Bodies flung and shattered against fog-enshrouded walls and pillars.

First responders dashed in, wading through the smoke and the fires, fighting to save lives. Tourniquets, belts, scarves – anything to stem the bloodshed. The injured helping the injured. Forever, the screams and the sirens.

Dan was allowed into the ops room. The wall of screens showed the breaking news bulletins and live scenes of the response. CCTV images; moving grainy pictures of those minutes of hell on earth. The final minutes for over one hundred people. The worst single terrorist bombing in Britain, ever. The ambulances, the sirens, people running out of the station. No suspects; no claim of responsibility. London 7/7 repeated; all praying that there weren't more, as there were then…

Hundreds of converging commuters and pedestrians were evacuated, traffic stopped and diverted. Mobile phones rang eerily, some of them among the carnage. Dan heard nagging tones ringing around the ops room where he sat, helplessly watching the aftermath of the carnage unfold. *This is all my fault… I couldn't spoil the first IED… I saw this all those years ago in the IRA bunker in Dublin. That bastard vision. King's Cross, a bomb…*

Dan's guts lurched. He turned to his minder. "Give me my mobile! I must warn someone I know in the area." He called Teresa, history repeating itself. There was no such premonition this time. He just knew that she, like thousands of others, was in danger.

Teresa picked up and answered in her usual practical tone. "I'm OK. I've seen it on the news. I was just about to go out."

"Thank goodness you're all right. Stay there. There's going to be more. For fuck's sake, don't go to Highbury! Don't go anywhere!" Dan shouted above the din gathering volume in the ops room.

"Why would I go there? That's your patch," she said. "I hope you're safe. Haven't heard from you in ages. It's OK, I don't want to know."

"I'm OK. Long story. Which I can't tell."

"Thank God for that," said Teresa. "You said you wanted to do something more solid. All those years ago. Be careful for what you wish for."

Dan knew that the RDD was next. He snapped, "Keep your windows closed. Don't turn on your aircon."

"Aircon? It's December."

Then he remembered that Jane would be on her way to work. She never had her mobile turned on. He had to warn her to keep away from the area before the cellphone system went down. All he could do was send her a text, his fingers shaking, praying she'd hear the beep.

This, the 'come-on' attack, had come before any agency could find and stop it. The intel people and the counter-terrorism police knew that there would be at least one more. And if it went off, it was going to be far, far, worse.

North London: 21 December 2020, 16:00

Everyone in the ops room was shouting. People were cleared from the environs of the station. Cordons were erected, with traffic chaos and streets blocked off. Hospitals filled with the wounded: the capital was stretched to the limit. Cabinet meetings, crisis meetings – but this time Adam wasn't there. He was at the forefront of the response to what was coming next. Wherever it was. The world's TV networks and social media belted out the breaking news. The commentary followed the usual pattern.

"What do we know so far? What caused the chaos and mass slaughter of over one hundred people in a prime railway and Underground station?"

A police chief replied on camera. "A standard terrorist device. Intended to divert responders and resources."

"So there's going to be another bombing?"

"The Army bomb disposal team are searching for more devices in and around the station."

"What if it's somewhere else?"

In the depths of the ops room, the focus was on finding the radiological device. Was it in a car, van, truck, trailer or some other vehicle? And was it in north London? How could they go on such erratic, unreliable intel? They had other, more tried and tested, methods.

Then the monitoring stations fed back information on a recently rented vehicle that fitted several sightings during the long hours that had preceded the Kings Cross bombing.

Heading towards north London off the North Circular, a large white van ventured down the A10 to Seven Sisters Road. With a typical builders' firm logo on the side, it was like thousands of others on the roads.

It was already dark: the shortest day of the year. In other parts of the vast capital not directly affected by the morning's atrocity, last-minute Christmas shopping and parties went on, the streets and houses lit up with last year's decorations. As well as the myriad technologies and cyber systems the combined security agencies were using, Dan was expected to provide them with some miraculous premonition.

They didn't come to order. But if only... if only he could get the next one right.

Chapter 38

"Be strong, saith my heart; I am a soldier; I have seen worse sights than this."

Homer, The Odyssey

North London: 21 December 2020, 16:30
The white Transit van made its way south from Seven Sisters Road onto Holloway Road. It parked outside Seven Sisters tube station. The driver got out and within seconds armed police descended, pulling him and his passenger to the ground and cuffing them at gunpoint. There was no resistance from the men as they were bundled into a police van. A cordon was set up. At least they weren't suicide bombers.

Responder vehicles crammed the roads and police moved the thronging pedestrians. Thousands had already been diverted following the attack at King's Cross. Every available police officer and first responder was brought in. Shouts for more cordons and the screech of sirens added to the din of people hurrying from the scene. Helicopters and drones whirred above.

Seven Sisters tube station was evacuated. People streamed out onto the streets in the middle of the evening rush hour. Because of the fear generated by the morning attack, some panicked and stampeded out of the narrow exit.

On the TV, breaking news bulletins told people in north London to stay in and close all windows. Social media shrieked with questions and rumours. Close all windows? What did they mean by that? Experts were wheeled on, frenetically questioned about what was going on. This time Dan was not on camera. He was at the heart of counter-terror operations, facing a wall of screens, watching the dreadful events unfold – and felt helpless.

North London: 21 December 2020, 18.00

The bomb disposal unit moved rapidly inside the cordon on Seven Sisters Road, at a distance from the suspect white van. Combined teams and the specialist CBRN unit in response vehicles were stationed at the incident control point. They wore medium-weight NBC gear to protect them from whatever was brought out of the vehicle.

Whatever that thing was, they got ready to assess it from a distance, at the incident control point. The command vehicle was loaded with equipment: bomb disposal robots, their X-ray cameras and sensors set to feed back within minutes what menace lurked inside the vehicle. Two ammunition technicians in bomb suits, their heads encased in helmets with built-in respirators, operated the robots. Everything was pressed into service to keep the ATO away from the threat. Along with an Army infantry escort, Royal Signals soldiers jammed signals that could set off the bomb.

Adam directed the EOD operation from the command vehicle, coordinating with the fire and police responder commanders. He had the authority to act on whatever the robot found. And he was just the man to direct it. This was what he lived for: stopping the terrorists, leading his team. Every nerve, every sinew, every brain cell at the highest level of tension while staying calm. *Now a real soldier again, as before – not some twat supersoldier.* Making rapid judgements to save lives, including the lives of his team. A bad day at the office meant death: instant success or total failure.

Not enough that the van could contain bulk high-explosive. This normal-looking vehicle could also be carrying the means to blast radiation across London. And with so little time. In the glare of temporary arc lights they worked against the clock. The intel indicated that there was a timer, or multiple timers. And that attempts by the undercover agent to stop these working had failed.

They also had to deal with possible booby-trap devices, under the vehicle, or in the doors, or around it. The bomb techs couldn't blow the device in place, as this would release the crap inside. Ambulances stood by, with paramedics equipped to decontaminate responders and civilians.

The Army and the police and the fire service had drilled for such a nightmare. Now it was actually happening, in a crowded, relatively obscure street in north London – after the worst-ever attack only hours earlier, amidst chaos. Darkness was punctured by the arc lights. Adam could see without them, and blinked away their stabbing beams.

From the control point, he tried to see into the vehicle with his extrasensory abilities, as he had done in Iraq. But nothing happened. It was going to be the robot's job this time. And his training and skills long hewn in the field: nothing more, nothing less.

Minutes ticked by. Then he saw the images fed back from the robot. They showed the van was loaded with boxes and bulging black bin liners, the type the IRA used to fill up with ammonium nitrate. No wires, switches, signal receivers, timers, batteries or other IED paraphernalia was visible. Nothing was giving off a radioactive signature. The boxes were loaded with grains of simulant explosive, and the bags were filled with sawdust.

The white van was a dummy. A decoy sent to divert the responder services, already stretched to the limits after the morning's atrocity.

Adam jumped out of the command vehicle. "That useless bastard Dan! This isn't the RDD!" Then he yelled,

"Where the fuck is it?"

North London: 21 December 2020, 18:00
All eyes were on the screens. The heavy-duty radiation-detecting robot trundled its way towards the white van, lit up by the arc lights. Seven Sisters Road had been cleared. The eerie silence in a normally vibrant London area added to the tension.

215

For several aching minutes the teams waited to see the pictures of the van's innards. Then the X-rays loomed up on the centre screen: result negative, no explosives, no radiation. The white van was a dud.

Dan's temporary minder said, glaring down at him as though he was something the cat threw up, "That white van was crap. You said north London."

"Shit. I should have known they'd do that. Probably Paddy's fucking idea. The IRA used to deploy hoax vehicles."

"So is there an RDD? Are they just pissing us about? Are *you* pissing us about? There could be more IEDs all over London about to go off. We've already lost over a hundred people!" Several operatives crowded around Dan.

"There has to be an RDD. I made the blasted thing!" Dan protested. "I saw it taken away, but I didn't see where. I was hooded!"

The roomful of intelligence and counter-terror operatives saw the tall officer in charge of the operation remove his bomb suit helmet, revealing a flash of dishevelled fair hair. Under the glare of an arc light he made to climb back into the response vehicle. The veteran bomb tech commander's unshaded eyes pierced the screen with a furious glare aimed straight at Dan.

Everyone in the ops room heard Adam shout,

"Where the fuck is it?"

Then, in a searing flash, Dan saw it.

Chapter 39

"Courage is fear holding on a minute longer."

Gen. George S. Patton

North London: 21 December, 2020, 18:05

It was more searing than anything Dan had ever seen before. He let out a deep, terrifying cry.

The scene blasted through his head. A vision of hell.

A black vehicle, glowing. Adam's big form in his bomb suit. A metal object metres away. A massive explosion... a mushroom cloud rising over the London skyline. Hundreds fleeing, burned, bleeding, screaming. Shots fired in the street. Adam's suit spattered with blood, his broad chest bleeding out...

The scene vaporised. Dan looked up at his minder's colleagues grouped around him. Someone had grabbed his arms, to stop him reaching for a firearm. Others thought he was having a fit. Amidst the noise of the ops room, a momentary quiet descended. A few heads turned at the sound of his chilling, low-pitched scream before the buzz of frantic activity resumed.

"Dan, what have you just seen?"

Gasping for air, Dan cried out, "The RDD... it's in a black vehicle! It's a big Transit, like an Iveco. Black, black! Not a white van!"

"Do you know where it is?" somebody barked.

"In a street at the back of Highbury station!" Dan gasped, looked up helplessly, breathless, trying to stay conscious. "I know you won't believe this. Ask Carolyn!"

"Not north London again! Is this the actual vehicle?"

"Yes. It's been parked there all last night!"

Somebody thrust a tablet in front of him showing a Google map. He pointed to the street.

"They must have brought it down earlier. It's got over five hundred pounds of PETN in it. And something else, something radioactive. The white van must've been a decoy to distract."

"Something radioactive? What's that, for heaven's sake?"

"I don't know!"

"But you made the damn thing!"

"Not this! No, not this. I can't see what it is. But it's radioact—"

"Why did you cry out?"

"Adam, Major Armstrong, he's in danger." They let go of his arms as he looked at them, wild-eyed. The visions made him feel faint yet super-alert all at once. Carolyn had come down and stood next to the workstation facing him. They had called her out of the central command room above. Dan realised he had passed out briefly.

Carolyn recalled Dan's last hallucinatory episode where he had claimed to see a vehicle and Armstrong being shot. And that Armstrong at the last crisis meeting had said, very suddenly, that Dan's intel about Highbury was "reliable".

She glared at Dan, her short auburn hair dishevelled, her square face resolute. Drowning out the din and breaking every intel rule in the book, she yelled,

"All units to Highbury & Islington station! Close the station! Evacuate the area!"

Police helicopters rumbled above as the evacuation of Highbury station and the streets below proceeded apace. Cars, buses and people streamed as far down as the Angel. Crowds moved like pulsating blood along the north-south artery Holloway Road, spilling over into Highbury Fields. Never before had such a displacement of pedestrians, residents and businesses been executed since World War II, and in such a short time.

So nobody other than the heli pilots flying over Highbury Fields saw the undulating beams of vermilion light spread-eagled across the skies. They were flying through a force that tossed them about like toy planes in the crosswind.

"What the fuck is this? Over!" radioed a pilot to his colleague as his heli was buffeted by the deep red forces being hurled against it.

"We've got to get through it. Please don't tell me they've launched a fucking EMP!"

"That would be invisible. Out." EMP: electromagnetic pulse. Massive bursts of plasma vomited out from the sun, and from nuclear explosions – putting the lights and comms out across a continent. Also a viable weapon. The lights of London below stayed on.

The helicopters ploughed through the pulverising waves, which crackled and flickered like flames in a giant fireplace. The crashing thumps of turbulence almost brought one heli down. Then the aerial display vanished as rapidly as it had appeared.

In the black of night, the black Transit van, which could hold twenty cubic metres of explosive death, was parked in an unassuming street. The team still didn't know exactly what it held. The Emirates Stadium northwest of the Fields was a mere two hundred metres away. People crowding around the football ground were moved on, as this was a prime target. Even if the vehicle were parked streets away, if it exploded, radioactive particles would descend on the stadium and anyone in it.

The scheduled home match had been cancelled due to the earlier attack. Sporadic fights and stampedes broke out. The air was pierced by the sound of ambulance and police sirens. The new road system at the other side of the tube station was in gridlock. The police tried to keep the media away, but the turmoil did not prevent a torrent of mostly meaningless images belching out from smartphones onto social media.

Adam heard the radio command tell him to redeploy to Highbury and set up the ICP at the back of the station. This did not go down well. Going on a hunch transmitted by that bloody joker, Dan Boland, after his first effort turned out to be a dud. This was against all the rules: you go on real intel. Adam's entire training and experience treated it as laughable.

But Dan's intel *was* reliable. Near Highbury Fields – of course. He knew why, and he couldn't tell anyone how or why. He just had to act on it. *We're not playing this one by the book; not this time.*

He barked orders over the radio network. The street was cordoned off. He and his team – joined by police, CBRN and Army support – were left alone to save hundreds, possibly thousands more lives. And to stop north London becoming a radioactive no-go area. The robots were prepared, one in reserve if the first one stalled or failed. They hardly ever did.

This was what he had been trained for, this is what he would give his life for. Hyper-alert, the next tumultuous mission was absent from his conscious mind.

Above the incident control point just ahead, police snipers armed to the teeth were at the ready atop buildings. Through a barrage of helicopters and activity on the ground, they watched for enemy drones and outlying threats.

They were armed with brand new state-of-the-art automatic weapons that could blast anti-personnel rounds through a metre-thick wall.

Chapter 40

"Remember to look up at the stars and not down at your feet."
Dr Stephen Hawking

North London: 21 December 2020, 20:00

After the false alarm of the infamous white van, the multi-tasked specialist responder teams arrived at the back of Highbury tube station. They leapt into gear. The tension they had endured an hour earlier on Seven Sisters Road had never left them. Adam led again. He didn't have to, but insisted in no uncertain terms. When Adam insisted, you shut the fuck up. Not a normal procedure, but nothing about the times was normal.

Each highly trained operator was at the heart of the worst day of terrorism in London for fifteen years. And for the first time, they had to stop a vehicle-borne IED with a suspected radioactive component from blowing up in a poorly lit street in the black of night.

The white-van occupants had not yielded any further information. These hoaxers didn't know what the other operatives were up to: Adrestia operatives worked on a need-to-know basis.

The nondescript black vehicle parked in a quiet street at the back of the station could be set to blow up at any time. Or the driver could be hiding, waiting for the teams before detonating it and himself as they approached. Or it could be detonated by signal. They had hardly any time to ascertain what lay inside its black heart.

Adam watched from the control vehicle several hundred metres away. His energy was boundless; he was wound up like a spring and his headache had dissipated. The EOD robot was sent on its way, duplicating the previous action on Seven Sisters Road. Readings at the control point indicated radiation.

So this was the RDD.

"What the hell's in there?"

"It's not cesium. That's gamma. It's an alpha emitter…"

"Alpha? At this range? Plutonium… shit! It can't be!"

The area had been cleared of civilians – just. No one in the immediate vicinity could send a signal to the van. Internal comms were on a dedicated network. The robot had to picture everything and the team had to act fast on that picture.

Except the road the black van was parked in was dented with potholes. The robot stalled and tipped over.

"Shit! Deploy UGV 2!"

The second robot trundled on its way. A minute later, it came to a grinding halt. This happened in the rugged terrain of Afghanistan, not on an urban street. But the second machine had not fallen into a pothole. It and its scanning systems had just stopped.

As did the hearts of everyone. Distant sirens were hardly heard. Every atom of Adam's being was straining to blot out distractions, memories of lost comrades, flashbacks, signals…

Attempts to restart the second robot failed. Adam took charge, stepping out of the command vehicle to re-set it. Failing that, he'd go up to the vehicle himself. Each step took him closer to the black harbinger of hideous mass destruction. This went against all the ammo tech's rules: you don't go in guns blazing; you stick to the SOP. But this was different. Adam was different.

He marched ahead, his tall frame encased in eighty pounds of black and green Kevlar and ballistic plates. Inside the helmet, he breathed processed air through the mask that protected him from chemicals and radiation. Even the new lighter gear was too enclosed. In the stifling heat of Iraq and Afghanistan they rarely wore it. Too many sharpshooters lay in wait and they had to move rapidly into cover. But this wasn't Iraq; it was north London – in December.

Suddenly he felt the flames surrounding his face. Choking, gasping, encased in the helmet. Falling... falling... through fire and ice...

In a split-second decision, Adam took off his helmet. It contained his voice command system, but restricted his special vision. If he couldn't right the robot and get it to work and if everything failed, he was still mincemeat.

"What the fuck is he doing?" muttered one of the EOD operators in the command vehicle. With his extraordinary hearing, Adam could hear the vocal transmission from the ICP vehicle.

He yelled back, "Shut the fuck up, mate. I'm a bit busy."

"How the fuck did he just hear me?"

Adam's heart was pounding fit to burst. Maybe, just maybe, his eyes could still do the telekinetic work of a directed energy weapon. In the black of that December night, he could still see everything. He began the long walk towards the vehicle containing the bomb.

It was the longest walk he had ever made.

North London: 21 December 2020, 20:20

When the second robot came to a halt, an eerie quiet descended on the ops room. Operators gaped at screens showing the unfolding action, on a knife-edge, as though in a movie or a video game. But this was real. Too real even for the seasoned Gold and Silver commanders and the teams of highly trained police, counter-terror and intelligence experts watching the incident commander and his teams in a race against time.

Dan was placed in front of the main monitoring screen, where everyone saw Adam take his helmet off. Dan's sharp ears heard one of the team mutter from the ICP, "What the fuck is he doing?"

People seated around Dan emitted similar mumbled and shouted expletives. Dan felt sick. He watched Adam, lit by the arc lights, his blond head bare and oddly vulnerable, walking into possible oblivion. At least the rooftop snipers overlooking the scene would protect him.

Seated some distance above in the control room and pretending to care, Sheena saw her prime target take the long walk. She saw him remove his main piece of protection and communication. Her job, the ultimate treachery, was going to be easy. She had no regrets, only the unwanted pangs of physical desire. She wanted to fuck him there and then. In more ways than one.

And in the frenzy of the day, the two Adrestia assassins tasked with doing him in were still at large.

The camera closed in on Adam. The entire control room could see him in the piercing lights. They wanted to stop the frame and replay it. But they couldn't. As though time stood still, but it hadn't. Time was speeding on. Time was the biggest enemy. There were timers inside. Even the non-religious were praying. There's no such thing as an atheist on a sinking ship.

Dan watched Adam move forward towards the van. He was carrying an SAS assault rifle. Not usual for a bomb tech responding to an incident, but this incident was anything but usual. And even with armed support, Adam was still a soldier trained to kill.

But his head was unprotected. He may as well have removed his space helmet on another planet.

Suddenly, Dan's phone pinged. Of all things, an app – one that MI5 hadn't deleted – of a night sky map. Distracted, he saw the eight most brilliant stars of the constellation light up the little screen.

Then he saw a flash of blinding light. He leapt to his feet, pointed up, and from the depths of his soul screamed out one word:

"Orion!"

At the same time, in one, almost invisible rapid movement, Adam looked up at the rooftops. A police sniper on a roof to his left held up a mobile phone. Adam went down on one knee and fired, shattering the cop's hand and the mobile held in it – at the very instant the sniper was about to transmit a signal to the bomb in the van.

Just one second later, a second police sniper on the roof opposite fired twenty machine-gun rounds into Adam's chest. Blood exploded from his upper body.

As he fell – his face twisted in agony, blood spurting from his mouth – Adam returned fire on his assailant on the roof, blasting him apart.

He is falling, falling... falling through the sky: no parachute... his body blasted into a million pieces as he crashes down onto the rocky ground of Earth.

Chapter 41

"Show me a hero and I will write you a tragedy."

F. Scott Fitzgerald

North London: 21 December 2020, 20:25

The control room fell silent.

Spellbound, everyone watched the teams on the scene leap into action. Paramedics ran out of a stand-by ambulance and worked on Adam's shattered body, his bomb suit a spreading sea of red.

"Pressure applied. Must stop the bleeding. Must get oxygen into him..."

The rounds had penetrated the ballistic plates of his suit. His head streamed with blood from a round that had sliced the side of his head.

An air ambulance landed, its rotor blades deafening. He was rapidly stretchered in. Sirens screamed below while the paramedics on board battled to save his life. The heli soared into the sky as wave upon wave of pulsating crimson energy tossed it around above the streets of north London.

Suddenly, the screens in the ops room went blank.

Nobody saw the tall, elegant woman with piled-up dark hair half-smile at the events unfolding on the screen and turn to leave. Sheena's work was almost done.

And nobody heard Dan let out a muffled cry as the pain seared through his chest. It was drowned out by the shouts as Adam Armstrong shot the mobile phone out of the first police sniper's hand. Shouts turned to cries of despair as everyone saw him mown down in a cascade of bullets.

Dan thought his heart would burst. That vision, that bastard vision, had come true. He hadn't been able to do anything to stop it and he couldn't do anything now. Jill saw his distress. She sat next to him. He looked up at her, tears streaming down his face, and she put a comforting arm around him. That made him worse.

"I'm so sorry!"

"What for? Don't you know what you just did?"

"I bloody let him down. I let everyone down!" said Dan.

"We saw you. Something you called out to the screen. Then Major Armstrong spotted the cop on the roof with the mobile and shot him."

Dan looked up at her, totally bewildered.

"That mobile was going to set off the bomb. You transmitted something to him, didn't you? A signal!"

Transmitted? A signal? That's what Adam does to me – not the other way round. Anyway he knows his job. He's trained to the nth degree; he took the initiative.

"Must be something I said," Dan said, rubbing his eyes. Jill laughed out of kindness. Dan had only a vague memory of the flash that had seared his mind as he looked down aimlessly at the sky map on his phone.

Everyone else rushed around, ignoring them. Then he sharpened up.

"What's happening now?" The room was in turmoil. It wasn't over. There could be more devices. The cameras at the incident scene came back on. The screens leapt back to life. They saw the black van being towed away along with whatever they'd found inside. The RLC squad had rendered it safe and hauled it by remote control into a huge black containment vessel.

What was in the device? Was Dan right?

Was Adam still alive?

Sirens screeched constantly. Areas of north London and beyond, and the Underground system, were still in chaos. The breaking news headlines on several networks shouted a breathless commentary and ran endless footage of the scene.

Dan suddenly thought about Jane. *Is she safe?* Then his mobile rang.

"It's Jane! I'm safe," she said. "I'm at home."

"At last. Thank God you're OK," said Dan.

"King's Cross, the bomb, it's terrible! What the hell's going on? What's all that noise?"

"I can't say," said Dan.

"Are you all right?" said Jane. "You sound awful. You're not hurt, are you?

"No, but Adam is," said Dan, unable to hide the quaver in his voice. "Worse."

"Oh. I've just put the news on." The footage, played again and again, of the incident commander gunned down in a north London street.

"Oh no… poor Adam. Dan, I'm so sorry."

Dan struggled not to cry. Not here; not now.

Royal London Hospital, Whitechapel: 21 December 2020, 21:08

He was brought in at top speed. Paramedics ran with his stretcher down the corridor into the Trauma Unit. The Royal London was the nearest hospital with experience of gunshot wounds. It played a major role in treating the wounded from both World Wars.

He was taken into the secure medical unit which had been set up immediately after the shooting.

Still conscious, Adam felt the bits of his bomb suit being cut away. His body bombarded by a barrage of tubes, hands, hypodermics, oxygen mask clamped, blood, so much blood…

He was falling, falling… no parachute… no air…

"We're losing him!"

Chapter 42

Behind locked doors, questions outnumbered answers.

"Why the hell weren't those cops fully vetted?" barked Carolyn. She was facing a roomful of high-ranking security officials, ministers, police chiefs and assorted commanders seated around the table. "They are there to protect the EOD operators, for Christ's sake! Those two were terrorist plants."

"That's your job. You should have found that out." Carolyn wished the Director-General of MI5 was here instead of her.

"The first cop, who tried to initiate the device with a mobile, immobilised the second robot."

"How do we know that?"

"He's talking. He's in bad shape; the IC shot his hand clean off. But he's been questioned after surgery. He's coming clean about who recruited him and how he infiltrated one of the Met's armed police squads."

"How did these two infiltrators get assigned to exactly the right location in a specific operation on a specific day?"

"Turns out the two snipers were ringers in police uniforms. We're getting the gen on a highly placed mole in our service. She installed an infiltrator into the Force. The ringer snipers were deployed ostensibly from a counter-terror unit in support of today's operations. Highly paid. The speed of events would have helped them."

"I know you can't get the recruits these days, but this is outrageous!"

"We're now getting a shedload of intel about this group, Adrestia."

"How come we didn't know more about this bunch of loony tunes before?"

"It's since several arrests after the King's Cross bomb this morning. This has added to the background traffic we've had over the past months. They haven't claimed responsibility – yet. They're a well-educated, highly skilled bunch. Scientists, mainly."

"Jesus Christ! Not jihadists?"

"Is that why they chose the winter solstice? All that Mayan rubbish, the twenty-first of December, the end of the world?"

"No. I said they're scientists. Not jihadists, and not old hippy eco-activists either. December the twenty-first is a coincidence, we think. Anyway, the end of the world was supposed to be in 2012."

"Why hasn't there been more information about this apocalyptic group? If it is a group. How much have Five and you other lot gathered on them?"

'You other lot' meant MI6, often regarded as the more glamorous of the UK's intelligence agencies.

"They set up mainly in the US and UK in the past ten years. A highly covert network of scientists and other high-status professionals. Infiltrated the military, and as we've just seen, the Met."

"They're eco-fascists. Want to cleanse this polluted, warmed-up world of its overpopulation – mainly brown and black people – wake us all up, all that apocalyptic crap. Put experts in charge. More on them later. Arrests are imminent. Also on the other side of the pond, a high-level director of the group. Our American colleagues missed them as well. Too many of 'em in high places."

"Why didn't we – or should I say you – catch these people before this blasted carnage today?"

"There were so many unknowns. We didn't want to blow our informants' cover. The intel just got more horrendous. We've got more now on Adrestia's supply chain. Much of it only today. It's pretty extensive – transnational."

The Met chief got everyone back onto the day's first appalling event. "We got enough CCTV footage of the King's

Cross bomber to track him. Ordinary-looking white bloke in a suit, overcoat, like a million others. Rucksack abandoned. It contained the IED. Top-grade explosives. He's being arrested as we speak, somewhere on the Kent coast."

The security minister grunted at Carolyn. "Why didn't you detain the bomb-maker of that IED? As your man had been working with him, building the RDD!"

"He wasn't able to communicate with us while he was building the RDD. Once we brought him back in, he had no idea where they'd taken the bomb-maker."

Carolyn went on. "And it gets worse. Both those cops on the roof were paid by Adrestia to kill our incident commander. Both were paid assassins as well as being tasked with detonating the vehicle device. One was shot dead by Armstrong; the other is talking."

Some restrained gasps were exhaled. This was an insider job on steroids – something they all dreaded.

Carolyn asked, "What do we know about the device in the van? Our screens went blank."

An uncharacteristic hush fell over the room of top-ranking officials.

The Army chief had waited impatiently while they agonised over the sniper cops. At least it gave him time to think about what he was going to tell them.

"If it had gone off, it would have been goodnight Vienna, London and…"

Vocal backing came from three scientists rushed in from the Atomic Weapons Establishment at Aldermaston. One of them breathlessly added,

"The RLC and CBRN units found the mobile receiver on the IED, which was not of any type we've seen. It was set up to receive an unknown frequency."

"And it had commercial detonating cord connected to six hundred pounds of PETN high explosive—"

The Army chief pitched in with clipped, impassive tones. "The charges were connected to a new radioisotope. Fissionable. Weapons-grade."

"A radioisotope? Weapons-grade?"
"Yes."

"A nuclear device?"
"I'm afraid so."

Groans and muted cries. Even this hard-bitten, high-powered company gathered around the table in the bomb-proof bunker stopped their own flow, as though in a freeze frame.
"Nuclear?"
"Uranium? *Plutonium?*"
"Neither."
"Not uranium or plutonium? What the hell was it?"
"Curium-247. Very small critical mass needed."

Exhalations were audible. "Go on, what's that again?"
"The amount needed for a chain reaction to occur."
"We're talking mushroom clouds here, then!"
"A mushroom cloud can be caused by any big bomb, like the IRA in Manchester. But those weren't nuclear. So, yes."
"Good grief! How the hell—? This is just what we feared from al-Qaeda! For years!"
"Surrounded by det cord connected in a hexagonal configuration to the nuclear charge, the sphere, in the centre."
"Bloody hell. Implosion. Like the Nagasaki bomb?"
"Enough to flatten London. North London, at least. Like a small exploding sun."

"Your informant built a nuclear bomb?"
"No, he did the other one," said Carolyn, on the edge of total exhaustion. "A dirty bomb." *So Murrow deceived Dan in the end*, she thought.

"Dan thought he was building their ultimate weapon, the RDD. We had no intel on this curium jobbie. Our man never got near it."

The security minister asked, "I thought you could only get fissile material from natural uranium?"

"So far they are the only fissile materials used in nukes. This material, curium-247, is very expensive to make. But this group has plenty of funds and shedloads of expertise."

The famous Periodic Table of Elements came up on the screen, with the actinides at the bottom. One of the Aldermaston scientists took over.

"It could therefore be used in a portable nuclear weapon."

"A suitcase nuke! Didn't some of them go missing after the Soviet Union broke up?"

"Yes. And we've seen them in the movies. But this is a new device. They were showing how inventive they are."

His colleague chipped in. "To make weapons-grade uranium or plutonium takes acres of heavy plant. That's why there's only nine countries with nuclear weapons. No terrorists could ever manage it."

"So how on earth—?"

"This thing was custom-made, a highly professional job. We've never seen anything like it outside of a nuclear weapons lab. They set up their own cyclotron. A fissionable material. Alpha emitter. The most radioactive element that can be isolated. It'll take weeks to do the forensics at AWE, with max protection."

"What's its half-life, dare I ask?"

One of the scientists took a deep breath and replied.

"Er... 15.6 million years."

Silence.

"What about biological? If they're scientists, that would be a piece of piss for them to make. Much easier than nuclear. Some genetically engineered epidemic. Kitchen lab stuff. They could do the works. Reduce the world's population without a shot being fired."

"Hang on, we've got enough on our hands with nuclear Armageddon here!"

"How the devil did they make this new stuff? This isotope?"

"We're getting intel that this group set up their own lab in some remote part of Utah."

"All of Utah is remote. And the FBI and security agencies didn't spot it? How did they get it into the UK?"

"Bought off, probably. We're talking about a powerful group here. These aren't radicalised religious losers. They're top drawer."

"I keep saying – it's a rare isotope. First tests by the EOD team couldn't match it on their nuclear ID scanners."

"And it was a bastard to spot, as it emits mainly alpha radiation. This was the reading that came out of the van."

"The Yanks have their Nuclear Emergency Search Teams. We were about to call them in. Our CBRN EOD guys got it out in one piece, them and London too."

"How much was in the device?"

"Three kilos. It only takes as little as two kilos of plutonium, and it's the same with this new one. A 15-kiloton job. Like Hiroshima." More gasps. Despite their lofty positions, the inhabitants of the room in the deepest bunker below Greater London were beginning to feel that this was above all their pay grades.

"This must *not* get out! Christ, and we thought we had problems with Litvinenko. A speck of polonium in a teapot – and we still had to decontaminate over a dozen buildings and close up the rest. That's why we had to decontaminate the squads out of public view."

The Army chief said calmly, "The Highbury bomb was primed to go off on multiple timers; several were as failsafe back-up. By the grace of God they all malfunctioned. We don't know why yet. The driver still has to be found and interrogated to find out if he actually did set the timers – and when."

"Well, something stopped them. When we interdicted the van, they had been set at the same time, er, last week."

Shocked glances were exchanged. "What? Why didn't the nuclear device go off then? When the bloody thing was en route?"

"No idea. We got lucky like never before."

"The high-explosive was stable. And the detonators were also set up to be triggered by a signal from a transmitter."

"That's where matey on the roof came in, as back-up with the mobile."

"Classic jihadist trigger method. But for a nuclear device? I can't believe I'm hearing this."

The Security Services chief took over.

"Failing the running down of a timer, the signal from a transmitting device, in this case a mobile phone, would be enough to set it off. The receiver was linked to switches and det cord and commercial detonators. The high explosive was PETN. That alone, even without the isotope, would have blown up most of the street."

"Surely a bunch of mad scientists couldn't make a thing like that and get it into the heart of London!"

"So far, this group has chosen clean skins. Not like the jihadists, who have all sorts of losers and miscreants with petty criminal records, drugs, etcetera. These guys are clean. We can't get a name from the cop, as they only got need-to-know info before this op."

"The fucking Russians again! They must be in this group. They're in everything else," said the police chief.

The Government Minister for Security answered quietly. "Criminal traffickers in Russia, FSU and the Balkans have been smuggling radioactive materials for years. Adrestia haven't any Russian members, though – unless they've been infiltrated or used gang connections. They made this in the US."

"And are we sure they haven't cyber-attacked a nuclear plant as well? Sellafield?" Everyone was thinking of everything at once.

"Maximum alert there and at all other nuclear plants. Nothing so far, according to GCHQ. This group is very pro-nuclear power, as it doesn't emit CO_2. If that's any comfort," said the security services chief.

"Very pro-nuclear power indeed! Like blowing us all to kingdom come with a nuclear bomb!"

The questions continued to cascade.

"Why Highbury? Why wasn't the nuclear jobbie driven to a more high-profile location?"

"Arsenal stadium, that's high-profile…"

"The cop who's talking says the driver had some sort of fit as he approached north London, panicked, parked the vehicle, and buggered off. Some weird stuff about seeing flashes in the sky over Highbury."

"On drugs, probably."

"Lights over Highbury… Haven't there been a lot of electrical storms in London lately? Was it lightning? Some bloke got killed by lightning up on those Fields."

"No. No storms. You saw – it was dry, still weather."

"Hang on, we got radio calls from the police helicopter pilots. Two of them sighted some sort of red light wave phenomenon. Extreme turbulence. Including the heli ambulance taking Armstrong to hospital. They were lucky not to get knocked out of the sky. Everyone on the ground was otherwise occupied."

"There's been reports about those lights. The usual internet crap about UFOs and, more credibly, pilots reporting them causing massive turbulence. Intermittent power outages. Nothing proven. Not our department."

"Whatever. We got lucky this time."

"The driver probably didn't know what he was transporting. The nuclear device in the van was disguised in an ordinary shipment crate. The explosives and dets were added at a location in Britain, then taken by road into London."

"But he still panicked and left the van before he got to the intended target in the City?"

"Yes. Because, as the sniper cop has said, he had some sort of funny turn near Highbury."

"And he didn't set the timers?"

"I've already said – the timers were disabled when we found the device. They were set at a week earlier, for heaven's sake. It's bizarre. We've got to find that driver – to ascertain when and where he first set them. If he set them."

"This must *not* get out. None of it. Except that it was a vehicle bomb – high explosives."

"It's all going to come out in the media. Twitter is already in meltdown."

"So where's this other so-called dirty bomb? On some sort of mortar? Is that still in London, waiting to blow? How the hell did that get in?"

"Lax hospital security. Hospital security staff bought off, and infiltrators. Inside job. Same with the airport scanners. Shielding meant it wasn't spotted. The mortar was assembled here."

"After that false alarm at Seven Sisters, straight after King's Cross – where the hell is this vehicle bomb? Why was your agent allowed to build it?"

"We had him in undercover, to build it, then to render it useless. He has form as an analyst with bomb-making skills."

"You just said he couldn't make a nuclear bomb."

"This other one isn't a nuclear bomb. It's a radiological dispersal device," said Carolyn, looking to the AWE contingent for confirmation, and mumbling, "We're all professionals…"

Another security official chipped in after taking a call. He called out, hardly taking a breath, "We just got intel on that dirty cesium device. Several arrests. It's just been interdicted. It was in a white truck. Here." A map of London. A white haulage truck parked near Old Street, en route to the Bank of England. A photo of the dirty bomb fitted on the mortar.

More gasps, then restrained cries.

"That would have rendered the financial district a radioactive no-go area for—"

The Army chief put up a slide of a rocket-shaped weapon. "This was no ordinary mortar. It was an EFP."

"This is getting farcical. What the fuck's an EFP?"

"An explosively formed penetrator, or projectile. A sophisticated type of mortar. The Iraqi insurgents used them against our lads and the US troops. Roadside nightmare. A white-hot slug in front of a shaped charge. Triggered to fire by a signal or if you disturb a built-in sensor."

"Classy," said a government official.

"It was set to be fired through the vehicle's undercarriage. It would have gone down into the water supply. With the cesium radioisotope built into the warhead. And possibly into the Underground tunnel system."

Before the exclamations started again, he added,

"But it wasn't viable when it was found. The warhead and the timer had fake components."

"And the sensor in the EFP has been disabled. There was also a tracking device inserted. Superb job."

"Why, ya bugger, man!" Carolyn cried out, banging her fist on the table.

"Pardon?"

"Old Geordie expression. Take no notice. So our lad did it!" said Carolyn. "The only good news of the day. After all this, he managed to sabotage the cesium device!" *And he almost lost his life twice after he'd done it and shot five blokes into the bargain.*

"And speaking of your *lad*, what's this about him sending the incident commander, Major Armstrong, some sort of signal that directed him to spot the cops on the roof? That's a bit off the wall, isn't it?"

"We're looking into that. So far as we saw, Armstrong used his own initiative under extreme pressure."

"What do you mean, *own* initiative? He's trained to do that, with years of EOD and Special Forces experience! What else would he use, for crying out loud?"

Carolyn wished she hadn't said that. "Yes. Of course. But he's also been seen to show, er, extraordinarily prescient skills in EOD missions. In one incident he dismantled one of those EFP things after he was said to have, er, visualised the beam emitting from the sensor."

"Visualise the beam? From a sensor? Are you talking about disabling an EFP?"

"That's what the report from his CO said."

"I can't believe I'm hearing this. Seeing sensor beams indeed! They're invisible to the human eye!"

A military official, who had been taking all of this in, said in a low chilling voice,

"What the devil are you saying? What don't we know?"

"Major Armstrong is in Double Felix. Our version of Supersoldiers." Carolyn sighed, exhausted, wondering if her nearest and dearest were safe. And what had actually happened to Adam? There was no news. She'd been cooped up in the ops room for the past 48 hours, and it wasn't over.

"Oh, that thing," said a security chief. "Well, he was that all right."

"But isn't this weapon also what your undercover agent managed to disarm? The PIR sensor on the mortar, set to trigger the cesium device?"

Carolyn cringed in the silence. They'd trained Dan. He knew his bombs. Adam had seen a PIR beam. *But Dan? Had he also been able to? On the mortar sensor? How?*

The security minister said, "Well, Armstrong interdicted the most dangerous device ever planted in our country – in any country – outside wartime, with extreme courage…"

"…he saved London from a massive explosion, and whole areas becoming a radioactive desert. And beyond."

"And another thing. How the hell did Major Armstrong manage to even see the triggerman up there? And the other

241

police sniper he shot down off the roof as he was being shot to bits himself?"

Carolyn knew she had to answer as best as she could in front of the combined military, security and intelligence might of the nation all looking at her at once.

"Major Armstrong has shown that he has extraordinary night vision."

"Well, he wasn't wearing night vision goggles. And he took off his helmet, for fuck's sake," the police counter-terror chief grunted.

"You say some signal came in, but Armstrong had no comms to receive it. As far as I'm concerned, it's amazing he didn't get his head shot off."

"Why didn't his armed support see those guys up there and take them out? It's not up to the bomb tech chief. They're not usually armed. Or are they?"

"Ammo techs are still soldiers first and can shoot to kill. This was a dynamic operation, the first of its kind, and against all the odds. With only minimal cordon support, we had to get there in double-quick time."

"And he isn't just a bomb tech, he's a crack shot."

"Was a crack shot, more like," somebody said quietly.

The security minister said, "He'll get the highest posthumous honour there is."

Royal London Hospital: 22 December 2020, 00:30
"The head wound is superficial. It's clipped the temple. It's bleeding into his eyes."

"There's some sort of permanent lens here. We've got to remove it."

A medic pulled open his eyelid and shone a pen torch directly into Adam's right eye. He let out a cry of pain.

Another began to remove the grey-blue lens.

Adam screamed, blood pouring from his mouth. "No! No! Not my eyes! Shit! *Not my eyes!*"

The last thing he saw was the blinding torchlight and the medics bearing down on his blood-soaked body.

Chapter 43

Dan was left with a minder in a waiting area several metres away from one of many meeting rooms, in what seemed to him like a underground steel bunker. That's because it was an underground steel bunker.

His mobile was taken away again, to search for what he had appeared to 'transmit' to Adam Armstrong from the ops room. He sat on a plastic chair – no possessions, no news, nothing to drink, nothing to take his mind off this terrible day. Not that he wanted to take his mind off it. It wasn't over.

After constant, frenetic meetings, if anyone remembered, somebody from the unit was to be freed up to take him to a safe address and bring him in the next day for further questioning. Did he have any friends nearby, not in central London? There, the threat level was still the highest – Critical – as more attacks were expected and the Underground was still mainly down; he couldn't get back to the Angel.

He suggested his friends Patricia and Wendy in Ruislip in the outer reaches of west London. It was three o'clock in the morning – too late to disturb them. So someone led him into what looked like a nuclear shelter with bunk beds and very basic fittings.

He lay awake for an hour, the day's horrors churning over in his mind. The bomb attack; Adam shot down; his nightmare had become reality. Sometime after dawn he was woken up during another bad dream. He emerged from the hushed corridors of the bunker into the open air of west London, leaving the great and the good and the operator teams to work through the crisis.

Jill came to process him out. She handed him back his mobile and said they would bring him in the next day after some R&R.

"We'll need to discuss the job you did as well. With the vehicle we pre-empted carrying the cesium device."

"Job I did?" asked Dan. "What do you mean? Did I manage to stop it? And what was in the black van?"

"We'll catch up with you tomorrow," Jill said, but managed a smile. Maybe there was some good news in an ocean of bad. She looked like she hadn't slept for a week. "I've briefed your friends in Ruislip Manor without giving away any details about your role," she said.

"How come you're letting me go? Out of this complex? I could do a runner."

"You wouldn't dare."

"So do you trust me now?"

"We trust you, Dan. And you need a bit of R&R. You're on the brink of collapse. And this is just the beginning."

"But aren't I still a target?" asked Dan. "I don't want to endanger my friends."

"Looks like you can look after yourself," said Jill. "And them."

"Thanks for the compliment," said Dan.

"You're welcome. But – no more shoot-outs please."

"In Ruislip? Are you kidding?"

Dan was given a cover story. He was used to carrying them around, acting out his role. To his amazement, Jill also briefed him for media interviews. He was to go on Sky and BBC lunchtime news tomorrow. For a blind instant of gallows humour he thought, *because Adam Armstrong isn't available*, and wished he hadn't.

"What's happened to Adam?"

Jill looked back at him with big sad brown eyes. Dan thought, *I'd like to ask her out when all this is over.* "I'm afraid I can't tell you, Dan."

"Has he died?" Dan said, trying not to show any emotion as Jill ushering him briskly out of the facility and into the car. He knew he couldn't ask any more.

Maybe they didn't want to tell him. They needed him to have hope – so he'd continue to be of some use. Morale, all of that. They would keep it out of the news, at least for now. If Adam had died, he'd fall apart.

It was nearly Christmas. It takes a lot to distract Britain from the interminably tacky winter festival which starts earlier every year. In the dying weeks of 2020, a primarily atheistic group of sci-terrorists had almost managed it. But not quite – despite their wholesale murder and maiming of hundreds of people only a day ago.

Dan looked out from a blacked-out car window at the bustling streets of outer London. Despite all the carnage and its aftermath, things were beginning to get back to normal. London was like Gaia. Whatever you threw at her, she would survive: the greatest city on Earth.

The driver, silent throughout the short journey, walked him up to the stained-glass front door. Dan wore a tracking device so that he could be found PDQ. He hoped that no remaining terrorist hitman could hack it. Patricia and Wendy welcomed him in and the driver left. Dan tried to put up a front. It was going to be like this for the rest of his life.

He knew his friends wouldn't ask him what he'd been up to. *Oh, nothing much. I've been working undercover for MI5 for several years, infiltrated a terrorist group, built them a dirty bomb, tried to sabotage it. They tried to kill me twice and so did the New IRA. I shot dead two masked hitmen who ambushed us in the safe house and another two in a disused barn. Oh, and another one up on Highbury Fields. The usual.*

"We've got the news on," said Patricia. "And I'll get the kettle on." They each gave him a hug.

"Gosh, you've gone all muscly. Love the suit."

Dan had made an effort to smarten himself up after long hours in the ops centre.

"You look very tired. We'll have some lunch soon."

Dan sat down heavily on the cream sofa, relieved to be in a warm lounge with friends in a west London suburb.

"We know you can't talk about it," said Wendy.

"That'll be a first," said Patricia.

The TV was on, yielding a stream of reports. The media was in meltdown, even more than usual.

"I have to be on Sky News later," said Dan. "About the attacks."

"The morning one, we were here, thank God. How terrible. We were worried about you."

"I was away from it. Jane, Teresa, Duncan, they're all fine. They weren't anywhere near, thank goodness."

Patricia gave him a cup of sweet black coffee. Their black-and-white cat ran in, mewing loudly, and jumped onto his lap. She purred loudly while he stroked her.

"Just look at that cat," said Wendy. "She was unwell today, then you walk in and she's bright as a button now. You really have a way with cats."

With Murrow's white Persian in mind, Dan mumbled, "And you don't know the half."

The news began.

"Only twenty-four hours ago, after over one hundred were killed and over three hundred were injured, a second, even deadlier, car-bomb attack was stopped late last night in the heart of north London. Nobody has seen an act of bravery like it."

The newscaster and various reporters breathlessly described a redacted version of the operation and shoot-out behind Highbury station. Split screens showed reporters with the usual plethora of experts, police officers and politicians at Westminster and at Highbury station.

Dan still didn't know exactly what they'd found in the black van. He knew that the report wouldn't mention anything nuclear or radiological, keeping it to 'five hundred pounds of high explosive'. No way the authorities would release anything else.

Repeat footage showed the black van being towed away, then the white vehicle in the City. The one Dan had successfully rendered useless, but he didn't know that for sure. Then, again and again, the footage of Adam being shot, falling to earth as his weapon discharged well-aimed rounds into what looked like the night sky.

"The officer who stopped the car bomb exploding at the back of Highbury station, the incident commander, Major Adam Armstrong, is now fighting for his life in a secure intensive care unit in a London hospital. He is not expected to survive his injuries."

Dan held onto the little cat. He had begun to shake. He gasped. "Nine lives... please, please..."

"This unbelievably brave Army veteran saved London from another devastating attack by shooting the mobile phone held in the hand of a rooftop police sniper – which was about to trigger the bomb in the vehicle. The police officer was uncovered as a terrorist infiltrator working for an as-yet-unnamed group of terrorists based in the UK and the US...."

"...shot down in a north London street immediately as he was able, unbelievably, to shoot another police infiltrator on a rooftop who opened fire on him..."

An MOD spokesman: "He is to receive the highest military award for valour."

Dan began to cry. At last: great racking, heaving sobs, his throat constricting as though he would choke on his grief. It was as much a release as anything else after months of a strange and dangerous life. Wendy motioned to Patricia to get some brandy. His friends put their arms around him.

"Don't upset yourself, Dan. Your bloke *has* got nine lives."

Patricia gave Dan his brandy and he drank it down in one go. He sharpened up. "Please God. And he is *not* my bloke!" This made them laugh, as he always loved to do.

More breaking news interrupted them.

"We're getting reports from the FBI that a leading figure in the suspected terrorist group behind the attacks in London has been arrested in Washington DC. What do we know about this arrest?"

The US correspondent, with the usual background of the Capitol building, said,

"A Dr Carl Murrow, an eminent scientist in the field of radiation protection, who worked for the Pentagon's top research agency…"

Dan punched the air. "Yes!" The cat jumped down, her comforting role done.

"It emerges he was shot in the kneecaps by his wife, who then handed him over to the FBI."

CNN footage showed the American scientist being carried off on a stretcher amidst a thronging cabal of reporters. Half of his face was bandaged.

"Kneecaps? Blimey, good on her!" said Dan. The last time he saw Murrow was on a laptop screen, ordering his goons to castrate and kill him before being attacked by his big white cat.

"He is now believed to be the mastermind behind a number of plots and attacks, including the recent outrages in London."

"What is this group? What are their aims, their ideology?"

"They are very secretive. It's emerging that they are eco-extremists with apocalyptic aims, and have a far reach into academic and scientific communities here and in Great Britain. They are also believed to have planted infiltrators into police forces and intelligence agencies…"

Intelligence agencies? Dan hoped to goodness they wouldn't call Allison an infiltrator. She'd been put in undercover to spy on Adrestia, like Dan. She was firmly loyal to MI5 and to her country. He still didn't know who had killed her.

"Do you know that chap, Dan?" asked Wendy, seeing how much he'd cheered up.

"I can't say," said Dan, smiling. "If I tell you…"

"Go on, you'll have to kill us," said Patricia, smiling as she poured him another coffee.

"But it's good news."

"You knew that scientist, Allison, as well, didn't you, the lady who got killed?" said Patricia. "Awful business."

"Yes. I did," said Dan, his smile fading, realising how much he'd loved her. "I did."

"You don't half get around," said Wendy. "And here you are, back in boring old Ruislip."

"I could do with a bit of boring," said Dan. "At least some of the time."

It wasn't to be.

Royal London Hospital: 23 December 2020, noon

Adam was taken back into the operating theatre for a third time in the 24 hours since the attack. They hooked him up to heart and lung bypass machines while an army of surgeons and assistants fought to stem the blood loss.

They worked through the night to remove over a dozen rounds that had penetrated one lung. His soft tissue had collapsed inwards, his ribs and tendons were shattered. Over twenty rounds had been fired into him. They say that one round can kill where twenty don't.

"The blood transfusions haven't taken!"

"How much blood has he lost?"

"Too much."

"He's flatlining… again…"

Chapter 44

Central London: 23 December 2020, noon

Dan sat in the waiting area of the Sky News Millbank studio just up from the Thames and the London Eye. He was about to give the official story – not the real one – of what had happened in that north London street, in his first media interview since he had begun his new, crazy life as an undercover agent.

After a proper night's sleep, mercifully free of dreams, he had enjoyed breakfast with his friends, just like old times. He found a suit, shirt and tie in the spare-room wardrobe, kept in reserve for overnight stays. He looked and felt sharper than he had in months.

He didn't feel nervous; he'd been through too much for that. He was at home in front of a camera, but it felt strange after months undercover. In the most painful of ironies, his last interview had been to stand in for Adam, so long ago.

The interview was delayed. Dan poured himself another coffee out of the machine and watched the breaking news zoom onto the TV screen in the reception area.

"The arrest of the American scientist, Dr Carl Murrow, implicated in the devastating attacks in London, came after his wife saw the attacks in London on the US TV networks. Mrs Murrow waited for her husband to return home last night. She shot him through the kneecap to immobilise him…"

"Pity she didn't shoot him somewhere else," mumbled Dan. "Wish I'd done it myself." Maybe she'd also caught him *in flagrante delicto* with another guy. *Hope the cat's all right.*

A counter-terrorism expert, one Dan had met before, came to a stark conclusion.

"If she'd made that call just a few days earlier, this group's plan to attack London may have emerged in time for the British security services to pre-empt the first bomb atrocity at King's Cross station, where a hundred and five people were killed."

The journalist added, "Her decision was finally prompted by the news reports – having already felt deep doubts about her husband's role in the Adrestia eco-extremist group."

Dan fidgeted. Everyone, everything, was still on a knife edge. His mind went back to Allison. Who killed her? There was still no confirmation of cause of death. Initial reports suggested suicide, pending toxicology reports.

Carolyn had blamed him for betraying Allison to Adrestia. It sounded like the Russians had done it, but why would they kill her? As far as he knew she hadn't been a double agent for the GRU. But he didn't know anything anymore.

Another newsflash shrieked onto the screen.

"A high-ranking official on a high-tech military project being conducted here in the UK has just been arrested in London in connection with the recent death of the geneticist Dr Allison Hardy in a hotel in St James' a few weeks ago. She has been named as Captain Sheena Maxwell.

"Our sources are saying she stands accused of colluding in her murder."

Who the hell is Sheena Maxwell? If Allison had been killed by someone high up in the military, this had enormous repercussions. Was this treacherous, elegant-looking lady also behind the attempts to bump him off? He would probably never know.

Then he heard the rest of the report and his blood ran cold.

"She is said to have been deputy head of a project of soldier enhancement – called Supersoldiers in the USA, and codenamed 'Double Felix' here. She was involved in directing our version, set up by the Ministry of Defence.

"They are conducting experiments on serving British Army soldiers and also some veterans, to enable them to withstand the challenges of modern warfare. The aim is to give soldiers extraordinary skills to use in battle, such as extrasensory perception, resistance to pain, reduced need for sleep and rapid recovery from injury. Even inserting cat DNA into the eyes for soldiers to see in the dark. All futuristic a few years ago; now technological reality."

Extrasensory perception? Good grief, was that why he'd seen all those weird battle and desert scenes? Was it some sort of government experiment that Adam was part of? *Could explain it. But it's not like him. He wouldn't go in for such crap.* Then Dan thought, *he must have PTSD, and he's been transmitting horrific visions of warfare to me telepathically. But why me? And how?*

Dan tried to relax while the Sky make-up lady applied powder to his face. He normally enjoyed a chat before going on air to talk about death and destruction.

"Are you here to talk about the bombing, Dan? We haven't seen you in the studio for a while."

"Yes. This is the worst I've ever had to talk about."

"Love the fair hair," she said, trying to lighten the grim topic.

"All my heroes are blond," said Dan. "David Bowie, Daniel Craig, Adam Arm—"

"It was terrible what happened to him wasn't it? What a brave man. Did you know him?"

Past tense.

He went back to the waiting area. He had no idea why the van driver had panicked and left the vehicle in Highbury, instead of driving it into central London. Or what, precisely, was inside it. Jill had only hinted that he'd 'done his job' with the cesium device.

He had been given notes to read, which he had to keep to. Especially the stuff about Adam's response. He shuddered at what his family must be going through. As only an occasional colleague, he knew nothing about his family.

The authorities were keeping quiet about him. They'd done this before. *Some big shot dies and the news isn't put out for days. Even these days. Don't give me that no-news-is-good-news crap.*

Just please tell me.

No… please don't.

Royal London Hospital: 23 December 2020, noon

"He's in VF. Again!"

"Charging to… clear…"

The pumping chambers of Adam's heart quivered uselessly while the crash team worked desperately on him.

"Wait! You can't shock him! The plate… it's embedded over his heart!"

"No output!"

"We're losing him!"

"We can't call it! Try again! Try anything!"

Central London: 23 December 2020, 12:10

At last, Dan was brought in to the studio and miked up. He squinted in the bright lights. As usual, he watched the tail end of the news before the top-of-the-hour headlines. And as usual, the link in his earpiece was deafening. "Can you hear me, Dan? And the broadcast?"

"Loud and clear, mate," said Dan. "Turn it down a bit."

"We're just getting reports of a massive earthquake in the vast desert area in western Iraq. Registered early this morning at eight on the Richter Scale… deep tremors beneath the desert about a hundred miles from the capital, Baghdad. No casualties reported so far. We will bring you updates on this when we get them."

The news reverted to London, terrorism and abandoned vehicles. Then, for the first time in days, something on a less serious note.

"An unusually high number of sightings have been reported of strange waves of light filling the skies over several parts of the Middle East, in particular Iraq."

Dan mumbled, waiting to go live, "Iraq, eh. Suppose it makes a change from Highbury Fields."

"And people have reported similar effects above north London in the days leading up to the terrorist attacks. The unidentified aerial phenomena were also sighted by police helicopter pilots as they flew over Highbury."

The newscaster began his questions.

"We have counter-terrorism and explosives expert Dan Boland in the studio. Thanks for coming in, Dan. Sorry for the delay; we've had a lot of breaking news. What do we know about the bomb in the black van? The one that was stopped? Are there any more?"

"The explosive threat inside the van parked at the back of Highbury station contained over five hundred pounds of high explosive. It wasn't a homemade type; it was PETN, a commercial, reliable explosive. We do not have intelligence on any further devices."

Then the news anchor dropped the bombshell right into Dan's lap.

"What do you think of the rumours circulating on social media, and on the US news networks that it was some type of nuclear device?"

Jesus Christ. Dan took a deep breath. They hadn't briefed him on that. *It can't be.* The thing he'd worked on and tried to sabotage, that was just a dirty bomb, not a nuclear one. *How the hell—?* He skirted around it.

"There's bound to be chatter on social media about any such incident," he said in a clipped voice. "Like on just about everything these days. London's worst ever terrorist bombing

255

had just occurred in the morning, and speculation, as ever, would be rife. It was not a nuclear or a radiological device, what people call a dirty bomb."

"What's the difference?" Dan then gave an idiot's definition of a true fission weapon as per Hiroshima versus an IED connected up to radiological material.

"Do you know how the device was going to be set off?"

Dan breathed out. *Phew, this is the easy bit.*

"There were timers on the device. Similar to the IRA's big truck bombs in the City of London back in the nineties. But this device had a fail-safe mechanism installed: a receiver for mobile-phone initiation."

"So didn't the timers work?"

"No. We're not sure why. That's under investigation."

"Couldn't the driver just set it off as a suicide bomber? Didn't he exit the vehicle before he got to his target? We got reports he saw a UAP over Highbury and panicked, so he got out, leaving the vehicle."

"UAP? Oh, the lights over Highbury Fields... the investigation will no doubt find out more."

"There have been several arrests, including the police sniper who was wounded by the bomb disposal chief. Wasn't that police sniper about to trigger the device?"

"Yes, and the incident commander shot the mobile out of his hand. And his hand with it." It gave Dan great satisfaction to say this.

"We heard that some kind of signal was sent to the incident commander, Major Armstrong, although he had removed his helmet and therefore the means to receive it. Do you know where the signal came from?"

Dan felt sick. He took a breath to answer in the negative.

Then it happened. Again. Here, of all places, during a live broadcast being seen by millions. The scene. The vision.

A vast red desert: mountains, craters, canyons. The night sky. A gigantic star high above. Millions of stars. What looked like people, if they were people, wandering over the endless fractured landscape. And ahead of them, a giant commander. Adam. His eyes shed tears of blood.

The scene vanished like it had never existed.

"I'm sorry, can you repeat the question?" he asked, his voice cracking.

"A signal appeared to come over to the incident commander, Major Armstrong, but he had no communications system to receive it. So do you know where it came from?"

They weren't supposed to ask this. Dan assumed that his 'signal' – the bone-shaking yell of 'Orion!' he had shouted at the screen in the ops room – was being kept under wraps. And he didn't believe he'd done it, anyway. Or that Adam had heard it.

Dan's clipped reply came out at breakneck speed. "He saw the snipers on the roof. He's a highly trained EOD – explosives ordnance disposal – veteran, but a soldier and a skilled marksman first and foremost, and he shot them both. A tremendous act of heroism. The first sniper was about to trigger the detonation of the bomb in the vehicle. The second shot him, and he fired back, killing the b—"

"Did you know Major Armstrong?"

Past tense.

Dan squinted hard under the lights. He blinked through tears as he stared into the camera.

"Yes."

Dan got into the car sent to take him back to Jane's at the Angel. Carolyn had consented to him staying at his London home for some more R&R before they brought him back in.

"Can you stop here, please," said Dan. They could track him wherever he was, but the driver had been told to mind him if he had to stop off anywhere. They approached the crammed streets of north London. Residents and business owners were returning to their homes and premises now that the cordon had been lifted. It was that bit more chaotic than usual.

The driver stopped near the little green haven which Dan had walked around so many times. He got out of the car onto the elegant terraced street – only two days ago in turmoil as its occupants were evacuated – and walked over to Highbury Fields.

He looked back past the Tree of Hope to the bustle around the tube station. Only a few days before, the streets nearby had witnessed the biggest counter-terror operation in London's history. Where an army commander stopped a vehicle-borne bomb going off…

Which could have been nuclear.

Where he, and apparently others now, had seen weird lights in the sky. Where the driver had abandoned his death-laden vehicle when he had seen those lights.

Dan gazed out over the Fields, where he had almost been killed by hired thugs, both recently and in the past. And where he used to go out at night and gaze up at the stars. Just a little park in north London.

He looked up. In daytime he had no idea where the familiar constellation was. And he prayed to whatever it was, some invisible force – no such thing as an atheist on a sinking ship – *please, please… nine lives… please…*

His phone went beep. A text. From Adam's mobile number.

"Thanks, mate. ORION."

Chapter 45

North London: 23 December 2020, 13:00

Dan dropped his mobile, picked it up, looked at it again and threw it skywards. He sank to his knees, looked up and yelled,

"Thank you ... thank you!"

The driver, mildly amused, watched him from a few yards away while he smoked a cigarette. A lone jogger passed by along the central avenue of trees. "Good news?"

"Yes! I think so. I don't know! I don't know anything anymore!"

The jogger smiled and continued her run. "Ah well, happy Christmas."

"And you, love!"

Then he checked his phone again and his stomach lurched. Maybe the text hadn't been sent just now. Maybe it had been delayed; maybe it had been sent days earlier.

Maybe Adam had already gone.

Royal London Hospital: 23 December 2020, 13:00

Two surgeons from the team of specialists assigned to Adam discussed his condition in low tones outside his private room. It had been set up as a separate ICU, guarded by a coterie of armed police and army protection units. Nurses and bodyguards were on shifts 24/7 by his bedside.

He lay, a shattered body swathed in dressings, on life support amidst a tangle of tubes and drips. A dressing covered the side of his head. The cloying heat and quiet of the room was punctuated only by the bleeping of the vital signs monitors.

"The skin has grown over a piece of the ballistic plate, right over his heart. We tried to remove it. What the hell have we got here?"

"The plate lodged in his chest. Tissue has grown around it. It's like an exoskeletal graft. And five bullets we couldn't remove. Those things implode on impact and destroy human tissue. One has fragmented in the chest cavity. No sign of infection. Yet."

"He's arrested several times. He's back in a coma."

"It may be just a matter of time."

"We've done all we can."

A staff member approached them and handed over a file. The first surgeon scanned it, his eyes dancing over the chart. He took a deep breath and handed it to his colleague.

"His DNA profile." He braced himself for the inevitable reaction.

"What the fuck is this?"

"And, more urgent, how can we go on treating him?"

"We can't have him moved."

"What do we tell his family? We can't put them off any longer. He may have to be switched off."

"Do we have any medical history on them? The same?"

"Not yet. We've tested several. We had to get blood from at least two, living locally."

"It also says here in his army medical records that he's on some sort of soldier enhancement project. Top secret. Some army officials are coming in later."

"God, that's all we need. I've heard about that crap to genetically engineer the troops. Make them invincible. Well, it may explain a lot. He's lost more blood than we've ever seen. And we treat gunshot and multiple knife wounds every day here. That amount of blood loss would normally be fatal."

"And we've lost him twice on the table, but—"

"He's started to make his own blood."

"It may also explain those eyes."

"No wonder he could see those cops on the roof in the middle of the night."

"One of those loony Pentagon efforts. Have his eyes been genetically manipulated? It's possible now. They must have overdone it."

"No. Those eyes are natural."

"We had to remove the lenses covering them. Very convincing. The army doctors will have missed them."

"Maybe they're for zooming in on distant objects? They can make those for soldiers now."

"No. It's what's underneath the lenses."

North London: 23 December 2020, 13:30

Dan arrived at Jane's. Islington was bustling again: it was wonderful to see London getting back on its feet, with so much horror so recently and so close by. Jane was at work. He made coffee and a sandwich and sat down in the big lounge adorned with posters of David Bowie.

"It's all your fault mate," he said, laughing bitterly. "Since you passed on, the whole world has gone to hell in a handbasket."

He turned on the big TV. More on the arrest of Sheena Maxwell, and the earthquake in Iraq. The strange lights in the sky had been relegated – too much breaking news for all that nonsense. And still more analysis of the London attacks.

He played back his own interview to see where the gap was when he'd seen the desert vision again. Nothing untoward: just a slight pause before the interviewer repeated his question.

He muted the sound and, plucking up something like courage, called the hospital. It had now been revealed that Adam was in the Whitechapel but he guessed he would be under protection and in a private ICU. He wasn't supposed to call them, but fuck that.

"Are you a member of the family?"

"No," said Dan, his heart pounding. "Nor a friend of the family. I'm only an occasional colleague. But… I've just received a text message from him, and I wondered if…"

"Just hold on, please. What's your name?" Dan told her.

He waited. *It's nearly Christmas; they'll be full-on busy. And still caring for the wounded from King's Cross.* Every hospital was full to bursting.

Someone else came on the line, their tone grave.

"Mr Boland, did you just tell my colleague that you received a text message from Major Armstrong?"

"Yes. An hour ago. I don't know if it was delayed or actually sent in real time. How is he? Can you tell me anything?"

"Mr Boland, he could not have sent you any message. He hasn't access to a mobile phone, neither could he possibly use one."

"But he's alive?"

"I'm afraid we can't say any more." There was a pause, as though the person on the other end of the line was conferring with someone. "But I've just been told that you need to come in. How soon can you get to the hospital?"

Dan called Carolyn. "You weren't supposed to call the hospital," she said. "One word from us and you do as you like."

"I got this text from him! Out of the blue an hour or so ago. But they say he couldn't have sent it, as he's—"

"OK, but where were you, for heaven's sake? The driver was told to take you straight back from the studios to your friend's at the Angel."

"I stopped off at Highbury Fields—"

"Oh no, not there again. Will you ever learn?"

"But it's special. He's special!" Dan blurted out, immediately wishing he hadn't said that. *What the hell? It's all gone totally bat-shit crazy now.*

"And nobody's said if he's dead or alive!"

Schrödinger's cat. Dead and alive at the same time. The bomb squads, Felix, nine lives...

When Carolyn didn't reply, he said desperately, "They want me to come in. The hospital. Why me? I'm not family."

"I'll come for you," his handler said. "We need to talk."

Royal London Hospital: 23 December 2020, 14:00

They arrived at the hospital. Dan had expected Adam to be taken to a military base, but his condition was too critical. This hospital did wonders for gunshot and knife wounds. But, along with the terrorist bombing, looking after a high-profile patient with multiple gunshot wounds who was also a terrorist target was pushing them to the limit.

Carolyn and Dan were met by two doctors and a military official. They walked down an endless corridor lined at intervals with assorted armed police officers and soldiers.

They were ushered into an anteroom.

"I have to leave you now, Dan," said Carolyn. "I'll be just out here. Please do as these people say. It's really important." Inside the anteroom, several staff were wearing blue lightweight hazmat coveralls. They busied themselves with an array of kit.

"Please put this on, sir," said a nurse, masked up. "I'll help you on with the suit."

"He hasn't got Ebola as well, has he?" said Dan. They ignored him. "Sorry, I gave up a failed career in comedy to go into counter-terrorism."

They togged him up, including gloves and hazmat bootees. Except his face, which seemed odd. The main area of protection from infection is normally the nose and mouth, for both patient and visitor.

"We need a DNA sample from you, sir," another staff member said. *That's if he is a staff member.* He briskly opened a small case and brought out a DNA probe.

"What if I refuse?" Dan said, then knew it was hopeless. He wondered why MI5 hadn't done a genome profile when they drafted him in. *It takes mere minutes to process the entire sequence these days.*

"Oh, all right. I always wanted to know if my great-grandad was Russian." He opened his mouth and a hazmat-suited nurse extracted a tiny fragment of his very essence.

"You don't know where that's been."

A hazmat-suited operative, who Dan reckoned was not a hospital staff member, said, "We also need to wire you up."

"Why? Am I recording what we say?" said Dan, desperately trying to understand. "I could film anything on my mobile."

"Please just do as instructed, sir. Your overseers will explain in good time." Dan felt tiny invisible wires and a camera even smaller than the ones he'd been trained to use being applied inside the hazmat covering. Someone else applied two small electrodes to the palm of his right hand, under the hazmat glove, and connected them to the tiny camera. A further eight electrodes were applied to his head, just under the hazmat hood, and connected in turn to the hand electrodes. They were too small to be seen.

He had spent months covertly bugging and recording the enemy. Now he was about to covertly film and record his friend.

"But – how is Major Armstrong? You lot asked me in. Is he recovering?"

"He came round half an hour ago. He keeps slipping in and out of a coma. Come with me, sir. He is critically ill. There isn't much time."

Chapter 46

"Next I discerned huge Orion…
He grasped in his hands a mace of bronze, never to be broken."

Homer, The Odyssey

Royal London Hospital: 23 December 2020, 15:00

Dan strode out into the corridor, flanked by armed police, a nurse and an unidentified NBC-suited operative. As he took the longest walk of his life, his heart pounded and his stomach lurched. He was led into the private room. His escorts returned to the anteroom, where a one-way observation screen had been set up. Another armed police officer stood at the door. A nurse sat close to Adam's bedside.

Even though he had known what to expect, Dan gasped as he saw the big man lying in an ICU bed. His chest and one side of his head was swathed in dressings. All manner of fluids were infused through a panoply of tubes connected to the high-tech paraphernalia enabling him to cling to life. Dan thought about the injured from the King's Cross bomb and about all those who had died in service or were still languishing, parts missing, in hospital beds.

At least he was off life support, an oxygen mask clamped over his face. The monitors bleeped away at his bedside in a barrage of electronic percussion. The TV at the end of his bed was on, showing repeat footage of his heroic action in that north London street. The sound was barely audible.

The handsome face had a ghastly pallor. He was wearing his wraparound military shades, even here. The room was admittedly very bright.

Dan couldn't tell if he was conscious. He must not show emotion. Not here. Adam looked as if, as they said, there wasn't much time.

"Hello, mate," Dan said quietly. He walked over to the bed. His blue hazmat suit crackled as he sat down on a plastic chair.

No response.

Please wake up.

Right, Dan thought. *I'll be really annoying. That'll work.*

"I've never seen you in bed before. It's my lucky day."

A long pause. The big man turned his head very slowly. *Poorly as he is,* Dan thought, *he's still as strong as iron and he's going to thump me.*

"Did I say something controversial?"

Adam blinked at him through the shades, slowly pulled down the oxygen mask and grunted, "Oh, it's you." His words came in shallow, crackling breaths. The usual crisp, sharp military tones were dulled and slurred by pain and painkillers. "You did well, mate."

"Me? What did I do?"

Adam struggled to speak. "The... EFP. Explosively formed... penetrator."

Just go on being annoying. Anything to keep him awake.

"I love it when you talk dirty. The EFP?"

"You got the sensor."

Dan took a deep breath. In the lock-up, standing over the mortar. The flash vision when he was suddenly able to *see* the sensor beam...

"The sensor..." Dan stuttered. "In the mortar... to fire off the dirty bomb?"

"Radiological dispersal... device," Adam slurred back.

And together, they said, "We're all professionals here."

"Don't make me laugh, you bastard. It fucking hurts."

"I'm not surprised. You got shot to bits and saved London from being blown up. Well, north London, at least."

"More than that," said Adam, proudly. "But we didn't get that first one. The IED. Worse than 7/7."

"I know."

It suddenly dawned on him. "More than that?" Dan, said, trying not to shake. Even as Adam had been shot down, he had known what was inside that black van.

"That device in the black van. Something… nuclear?"
No response. But Dan knew.

He hasn't just saved London. He's saved the whole fucking world.

The faces watching on the anteroom screen registered shock. "Nuclear. Oh shit."

"I suppose they asked you to come."
"I rang the hospital after you sent that text. They asked me to come in. They said you were in a coma."
"I was. That fucking racket keeps waking me up."
"That fucking racket is keeping you alive, mate."
"And your interview on Sky woke me up again."
"Any good? Not in your class, I'm sure," said Dan.
"Don't do yourself down."
"You said that once before."
There wasn't much time. Dan breezed on. "You sent me that text. Up on Highbury Fields. It said 'Thanks, mate'. For what?"
Adam's voice trailed off and slurred. His breathing was terrible.
"I don't remember sending you a text. Those goons on the roof. I saw them…"
"And you signed off the text with 'Orion'. What's all that about?"
"You called that out. I heard you."
"You *heard* me? I was miles away in the ops room! I didn't have a comms system. Neither did you! You took your helmet off. And what happened to the timers? I didn't replace them, as they didn't let me anywhere near the black van jobbie."
No response.

The nurse motioned at Dan to take it easy. The heart monitor beeped erratically, and stopped. Dan's stomach lurched. He had no idea how many times Adam had gone into cardiac arrest.

267

The nurse stood up, at the ready. Then it became rhythmic again. He couldn't resist going on.

"Also, how did you see those blokes up there in the dark? You didn't have night vision goggles on."

And then it happened. Adam took off his shades and looked straight at Dan.

Dan saw them. Perfect, beautiful, dark, oval.

The eyes of a cat.

Dan stood up, gaped, gasped, and fell back down onto the plastic chair, almost knocking it over.

"Is this a wind-up? What have you put those in for?"

Then he yelled,

"Where the hell are you from?"

"North London," Adam said, flashing a grimace of a smile through his pain. Still a brilliant smile. "I told you."

"Bit further north than that, mate!"

Adam closed his eyes.

Dan desperately tried not to faint.

Everything suddenly went very still. The heart monitor began screaming. *No, it can't be! No, this isn't happening…* Dan jumped away from the bed as the nurse yelled, "He's arrested again! *Crash team!*"

Several hospital staff rushed in and worked on him. Dan saw that they didn't shock him with a defibrillator. What seemed like a lifetime but was mere seconds later, the bleeps began again, in rhythm.

"He's back."

The nurse glared up at Dan, whose face had gone as white as the bedsheet.

"You must go very soon," she said, totally ignoring Adam's eyes, as though they were quite normal. *God bless the NHS.* "You're tiring him."

"Tiring him? Him? Nobody could tire *him*," sputtered Dan.

The nurse took his arm and moved him closer to the door. "He is hovering between life and death, sir."

Schrödinger's cat: dead and alive at the same time.

Adam opened his elliptical eyes. Dan gasped again. *Never question the look in a veteran's eyes.* The nurse brought him a glass of water. Then she left and was replaced by another.

"Are you part of some secret military programme? And am I?" He pointed to Adam's eyes. "Is this a genetics experiment gone wrong?"

No reply.

Dan couldn't take his eyes off... his eyes... strangely, so very strangely, beautiful. Even in the strong, handsome face: such a normal British Army officer's face. *Am I having one of those dreams? No. This is for real.*

"Is that why I've been seeing all those strange desert and war scenes, those visions? Were you sort of transmitting them?"

A long pause.

"You were receptive."

"No need to get personal," said Dan in a mock camp voice. "And what about Orion? Is that a code word? Or a code name for some sort of secret project? Of course, you can't tell me that. It's secret, like everything else."

"I'm on that Supersoldiers project," said Adam. "It's called... Double Felix." At this point, they both grunted a laugh.

"Double Felix? Well, that fits right in, I suppose. I've written about that project. Inserting cat DNA into soldiers' eyes. So that's it. Mind you, even with those eyes you're still much better looking than Arnie Schwarzenegger."

"No need to get personal," said Adam. "And don't you dare get me started on David bloody Bowie or I'll fucking kill you. Even in this state."

Dan folded his arms. "Well, you're trained to kill in a hundred ways. Can I choose which one?"

"I hear they trained you up a bit as well, mate. Shooting those bastards. Good work."

A compliment. For something Adam had done umpteen times – fire on the enemy. *He's just saved London... by firing on the enemy.* Dan had done it five times – to save himself.

In the next room the officials heard and saw the unfolding, unbelievable scene through Dan's hidden recording apparatus. One said to Carolyn, "Where did you dig that civilian joker up from?"

"Dan Boland? Yes, he is a bit of a card. But he's doing a good job."

"Do they know each other? Why has he been called in? He's not family."

"A number of years back, from the conference circuit. He's not fellow Army, but Dan is here because he's one of the very few people we've recruited who would understand all of this."

At the words 'all of this', Carolyn motioned towards the bomb tech veteran with extraordinary powers, impossible eyes and eight-base DNA, now critically wounded, talking. *At last, he's talking. And we're listening.*

"Dan has also displayed a similar additional skill, this premonition business, and he's recovered from injuries in double-quick time."

"What injuries?" said the doctor, staring at Carolyn, unblinking. "Double-quick time? Like, how long?"

Carolyn stuttered, realising the import of what she was saying, her voice cracking. "An attempt to kill him failed – he was run over. Shattered ribs and a cracked pelvis healed within hours."

A medic came in with Dan's DNA sample result and handed it to Carolyn. She looked inside the file and sat down very slowly.

She breathed out audibly and handed it to the military official.

Chapter 47

"A dream you dream alone is only a dream. A dream you dream together is reality."

John Lennon

The TV was distracting. "Do you want this on?" said Dan.

Adam nodded, slowly putting his shades back on, to Dan's relief. "I wanna hear what we did there. And what the fuck's going on."

"I was going to ask how you could hear it with the sound off, as I can... hear the telly with the sound turned... down." He didn't add, *and I have to wear shades much of the time.*

There was more news on the arrest of Sheena Maxwell.

Adam barked, "I had her. A while back." *Good grief,* thought Dan. *And you've had a shedload more. Then again, you had us all.*

"I had Allison as well," said Dan, trying to sound macho, then immediately relented, looking down at the scrubbed floor. "She was lovely. I really miss her."

"I don't miss that Sheena bitch," growled Adam. "Fucking man-eater. Betrayed her country."

"She's not another one is she? Or are you the only one?"

"Only *what*?" Adam snarled. Dan felt his scorching glare through the shades. He remembered how frightening he could be. With or without cat's eyes. "Go on, say it."

Dan took a deep breath, closed his eyes, stood up, moved nearer the door, ducked theatrically, screwed up his face, said his prayers... and said the 'A' word.

"Alien!"

He actually said it, that ridiculous word. To a decorated British Army veteran who looked like he was dying. Who had just saved London from nuclear catastrophe.

"No, she fucking isn't! And I'm not either. I'm from—"

"North London, yeah, you said."

Then Dan belted out the question he'd wanted to ask from the very start.

"Is this why it all goes back to Highbury Fields? Those lights in the sky. And on that flight we were on, to the States… What the hell are they? Are they a sign?"

"They'll tell you, mate. All of it. All in good time," said Adam, his speech fading, his breath coming in short gasps. "It's just energy. Wish I had some."

"Are you kidding? They could run the National Grid off you."

Dan desperately went on, seeing that his nonsense chatter was keeping the man he loved in a way he didn't understand from falling back into a sleep he may never wake from.

"I'm told you go for runs on Highbury Fields. I lived near there for ten years and walk up there every day. I never once saw you."

"Aren't I the lucky one."

Dan gabbled on.

"Well, it would have been like matter meeting antimatter."

"What the fuck are you on about now?"

"If matter ever meets antimatter, the entire known universe will be destroyed in a massive explosion. So, good job we didn't."

Outside in the anteroom, there were muffled mutterings. With all their experience, they were totally fazed by what they were hearing. In his critically ill state, amidst the daft banter, Armstrong was still not admitting to it.

The medics had called in whoever could fill them in as they were desperately fighting to save him. The unthinkable possibility that they may lose their most valuable 'subject' had got fed through to the Orion Programme. Its Enforcer Section operatives monitored instances of subjects under their scrutiny being 'outed'. And they dealt with leaks in no uncertain terms. No one was allowed into Adam's private ICU room without prior authorisation. They were body-searched, prodded, tested and kitted out in an NBC suit.

He had to recover, to go on the ultimate mission. Misgivings had been expressed about his deployment to the counter-terror operation in London, but Sheena had pushed that through – with his demise in mind.

He had her; she had him. Then, in the end, she was had.

The Orion enforcer despatched to the hospital held the fake identity of an official attached to the Double Felix project.

The hospital's ICU director got stuck in. "What the hell is going on here? Why haven't we been informed about this officer? What do we tell his family? They're already devastated."

Carolyn tried to calm things down. "He's on a project of soldier enhancement. Codenamed Double Felix. Their delegate has arrived, and there's a military rep as well."

"Double Felix? Felix the cat? Well, that sounds about right," the chief medic responded. "And on top of that he's made four pints of blood in two days. He's got five bullets lodged in his lung. And a bloody great chunk of his bomb suit's ballistic plate growing over his heart, with no infection – yet. That means we can't shock him when he goes into VF, which he's done several times."

The other surgeon barked, "And what about his eyes, for crying out loud?"

The Orion enforcer replied, "The eyes are a genetics experiment, sir. To make soldiers see in the dark."

"Well, you fucked up big time there."

Carolyn pitched in breathlessly. "And Major Armstrong's amazing powers of recovery, which we hope to God he will repeat here, were reported by his CO some time ago. From his service in Iraq. And his ability to sever IED mechanisms, his extraordinary night vision and hearing. And the ESP." After blurting all that out, she tried to normalise things. "And his exemplary military record."

"But nobody told us about his... let's say, his origins!" said the medic. "Have you seen his DNA profile? Is some lab technician taking the piss?"

The Orion rep had no time to respond before Carolyn replied. "We had everything on a need-to-know basis, sir. We couldn't risk anything like this getting out. Not just the Double Felix project he's involved in."

"You're telling me," the ICU director said. "But how do you think you can keep this dark? This is a high-profile officer."

The Orion man said, "Everything you've found out about Major Armstrong must stay inside these walls."

Carolyn was tired of it all. She turned to the medics. "Let's stop fannyin' about, gentlemen. If this gets out, talk about going viral – we'll have a soddin' pandemic. And not just the UFO brigade banging on about, well, you know..."

"What?" snapped the ICU director.

Carolyn took a deep breath and said the 'A' word.

"Aliens."

"The military official bellowed,

"We do *not* have aliens in the British Army!"

Carolyn said, "Looks like you do now, pet."

Dan felt the wires inside his hazmat coverall. The hidden listening gear was a betrayal of the man who may soon be laying down his life for his country. After saving it. A man he would give up his own life for.

Now he feared for Adam's safety, big and brave as he was. That was if he recovered. *They'll give him another fucking medal and lock him away in a secure unit like this one, but miles away. They'll prod, poke, interrogate and analyse him like a high-performing exotic lab rat.*

Or if not that, what will they get him to do if he gets over this?

The news on the TV turned to the earthquake in Iraq.

"That's what they'll get me to do if I get over this," said Adam, managing to point at the TV.

Dan blurted out, "I never said anything. I just thought that, just now!"

"That's where I have to be," said Adam, his voice slurred. "Iraq. You think the London attacks were bad. This, out there, is going to be... the end. I have to be there..." He was fading again. "In the desert..."

The nurse motioned for Dan to leave.

Oh God, not Iraq again. The end? What does he mean?

Fuck those bastards waiting in that room, thought Dan, and he moved forward so that Adam could see the wires and the mike. Adam looked straight at him.

The unspoken reply came sharply, like a bullet to the head.

"I can see them, mate. I can see invisible wires, with these eyes. I've severed tripwires and put IEDs out at a hundred metres with these stupid fucking eyes."

Dan took it in. He took a deep breath and said quietly, "You did send me that text, didn't you? You were out cold, but you still transmitted it."

"I need some kip, mate. Another time." Adam slowly reached up a big hand, punctured with drips, for a farewell handshake. One last time... even weak from injury, Adam almost crushed the electrodes hidden in Dan's hazmat glove.

Then came the scene, once again, but this time so vast, so bright, so terrible.

The desert; a huge red desert. Mountains, canyons, under a golden sky filled by a gigantic white sun. People, or something like people, running and screaming... fire, explosions... mutilated soldiers, hundreds of soldiers... so much blood...

Adam marches forward, a golden giant. He bends to pick up the shattered body of a fellow soldier. He looks up at the vast blinding sun. Tears of blood stream from his dark elliptical eyes. His mouth opens to yell a deafening scream...

The hand was released in a split second. Dan saw the nurse move over to the bed, holding a hypodermic. *Something is wrong; he has everything coming in through the drips. She looks wrong.*

The thought shot through him from Adam's eyes. *She's another plant.*

Dan rounded the hospital bed. He launched himself at the nurse, knocking the needle out of her hand. She shrieked as Dan twisted her arm behind her back and yelled, "Need some help in here!"

Two armed cops stationed in the corridor rushed in and, with the armed guard, relieved Dan of Adam's would-be assassin. So much for vetting hospital staff.

"Fucking hell, that was a close one," Dan said, straightening up. "That bastard group gets in everywhere. I've never done that manoeuvre before. Not out of bed, anyway."

Adam was breathing in short gasps. He looked over at Dan. "Thanks, mate."

"You said that once before."

Two more nurses came in and put Adam's oxygen mask back on, checking all the tubes and drips. They glared at Dan. "You must go now, sir."

"Don't get run over by the IRA again," said Adam, his voice fading.

"That was meant to be for you," said Dan, his voice cracking as his throat constricted as it does when you're desperately trying not to cry.

"Fuck off out of here," said Adam.

The heart monitor resumed its continuous scream.

Dan walked out of the room. He did not look back. The scream of the heart monitor penetrated his skull. He would never see Adam again. Or anybody or anything ever again. He'd saved his life. For just a few more minutes.

Suddenly he doubled over, gasping for air. He staggered forward. This time there was no desert, no mutilated soldiers, no gigantic sun, no giant commander striding ahead.

This time Adam is falling, falling through the sky. He has no parachute. Falling, hurtling to Earth. Adam is screaming; blood pours from his nose, mouth and eyes. His lungs are bursting. Hurtling down, down...

The polished floor came up and met Dan's outstretched arms. The vision was gone. He opened his eyes. Everything was black. He couldn't see.

He cried out in terror. An armed cop picked him up roughly while his colleague pointed a gun at his head. He stood up straight and his sight returned, like someone switching the light back on. He glared at them and the guards stood down. He breathed in deeply and walked back into the anteroom crammed with waiting medics and officials.

They began removing his outer hazmat gear. He was shaking. He looked over at Carolyn for help, his eyes wild. "I had to show him the hidden gear. I had to!"

They took off his right glove and removed the electrodes and the ones affixed to his head under the hazmat hood. Somehow, the electrodes inside the glove had remained intact despite his hands breaking the fall. They removed the miniaturised mike and wires that had recorded the scene when they shook hands for the last time. The terrible desert scene, the exploding sun, Adam's elliptical eyes bleeding tears, somewhere... and the agonising moment captured of him falling, falling through space as Dan crashed to the floor.

He rambled on. "I couldn't betray him! Do you understand that? He could see the camera anyway, with those eyes!"

Carolyn took his arm as the operatives put his protective suit into a forensic bag. "You need to prepare yourself, Dan."

"What, that he's... some sort of military genetics experiment?" The colour drained from his face, his voice breaking as he struggled not to break down. "That he's going to die? I can see that. I heard the heart machine go off again. I felt it, just now, out there. He's gone!" He looked around desperately. "I saw him falling... then I couldn't see!"

277

"He's gone blind."

The room was silent. Nobody looked Dan in the face.

"When they removed his lenses... the light they shone in..."

Dan gasped and staggered into a seat. He looked around helplessly. Carolyn tried to comfort him with her softest lilting voice. She put a hand on his arm.

"He was bleeding into his eyes, love. From the bullet wound to his head. They had to take them out. it was the light..."

"So that's why he was only hearing me! And the TV..."

Dan stood up and screamed at them:

"What the hell have you done to him?"

A doctor intervened, trying to sound gentle. "We were trying to save his life, sir."

Dan's head spun. He sat down again. Thoughts poured through his head: irrelevant, deranged. *Orion was blinded in the myth. And the final visions... they have them on film...*

Carolyn nodded to the operatives as they secreted away the evidence from Dan into a heavily protected case.

"It'll be all right, love. He'll be all right. He always recovers, remember."

Orion's sight was restored... by the rays of the sun.

Then he was shot dead by Artemis's arrow.

Dan stood up, relieved of the apparatus of personal treachery. In a clipped, calm voice, he asked, "Oh, and where's my DNA result? I'm entitled to see it, aren't I?"

Carolyn took the file off the table and handed it to him, just long enough for him to read on the front cover next to his name, MI5 ID number and passport photograph:

'RESULT WITHHELD FROM SUBJECT.
ABOVE TOP SECRET. ORION PROGRAMME ITEM 8809.'

"You must go with them now."

Chapter 48

"It is possible that the future of human civilization depends on the receipt of interstellar messages."

Dr Carl Sagan

Undisclosed location: Christmas Eve, 2020

All the teams working on the Orion Programme moved into top gear. Mission Control in the underground HQ of the most secret government project in history hummed with heightened activity. It was Christmas Eve, but nobody here had holidays, turkey and presents on their mind this year. The earthquake in Iraq and the latest welter of signals were uppermost. The giant screens showed a vast stretch of the western Iraqi desert interspersed with videos of seismic upheaval.

The signals from the asteroid belt were intensifying. Each transmission increased its data load, requiring more experts in linguistics and encryption to be security-cleared to interpret them. The transmissions took just under an hour to arrive, but they were coming in rapid succession.

The project managers now knew for sure what lay beneath that desert, why it was there and what it meant for our world.

And what a very special individual on our small planet, fighting for his life, had to do.

Colonel Richards was processed into the labyrinthine complex. He grunted his displeasure at more screening. What he was about to hear would turn his momentary carping into stunned horror, even for a seasoned soldier.

The director of the Orion Programme took him into one of many side rooms from which they could look down into the Mission Control area. The floor-to-ceiling screen displayed a moving collage of the Iraqi desert. A sky map of the Orion constellation formed the backdrop, its millions of stars punctuated by the eight brightest in the December sky. A wall-high photo of Adam Armstrong in fatigues glowered over his observers – formed entirely of composite lines of code, like something produced by an old dot-matrix printer.

Another photo depicted an Iraqi Army officer. Next to this was one of a menacing-looking bearded man wearing dark clothing with a shemagh covering his lower face.

And among all this played a soundless, grainy video of a vast red desert under a yellow sky populated by a gigantic, exploding white sun. A stream of people, or what looked like people, ran over the endless sands, some open-mouthed, screaming in terror. In the forefront was a shaky image of Colonel Richards' supersoldier marching forward. He bent, picked up a blood-soaked comrade, and cried out. Bloodstained tears poured from his dark oval eyes.

"What the devil is going on here!" Richards barked. "Are you starring him in the next Hollywood blockbuster? That wouldn't surprise me in the least."

"No, that would be Pinewood, sir," muttered the intelligence rep drily, who had also been called in as back-up.

The director said, "I have some urgent news for you, Colonel, which I'm afraid *is* going to shock and surprise you, so you need to be sitting down."

Colonel Richards' rugged face darkened as he crashed into his seat. "Nothing shocks me. I've been on ten campaigns. I want to know if he's dead or alive. He's like Schrödinger's bloody cat. And if that Odeon advert down there is anything to go by, in more ways than one!"

"Well, sir, they're still fighting to save him. They lost him for several minutes on the operating table. He's been in cardiac arrest and a coma several times since."

"Good God!"

"Even lost his sight for a while. At least that's now restored. What a fighter."

"He's that all right," said the Colonel. "Got the VC as well now. Pray God it isn't posthumous. Tremendous operation." The project director and intelligence official had been cleared to a high enough level to hear what Richards said next.

"I hope you realise that my officer stopped an improvised nuclear device from destroying London, on his own initiative – and may pay the ultimate price. Proud of him. The whole country is."

"That is so. Now if you would kindly bear with me, sir, what I'm about to tell you is not going to be easy."

The director of the Western world's most secret project began to explain the background to Adam's unusual qualities that Richards had reported to his superiors some time ago. His ability to sever IED wires and mechanisms from a distance, to bat off lethal scorpion stings as if they were fleabites, and all the rest of it.

He added that he had regenerated four pints of blood within two days. A section of his bomb suit's ballistic plate had settled in to cover his heart, like part of an exoskeleton. His heart had restarted without defibrillation. His sight had returned after he had been blinded. And his eyes...

And then he told the colonel why.

"After over twenty years in service, I've never heard such unmitigated, unadulterated crap!"

"I'm afraid it is the result of the highest level and depth of investigation by our programme teams here, sir. Along with the MOD. After he was hospitalised following the attacks in north London, we were able to further our observations on this very special officer.

"He was our first subject, and it is now confirmed."

Colonel Richards gave a deep sigh. He wished he was doing something normal, like fighting a war.

"And there was me thinking I was only coming in for a chat about him being on that blasted Supersoldiers project, Double Felix. Felix the cat. Huh, appropriate code name, at least."

Then he barked, "Have you and your crowd of geeks down there got genetic proof?"

"Yes, sir." The director proffered a redacted version of his star Major's genomic profile.

Richards glowered at it. "You chaps have been waiting for this for ages, haven't you?" he said. "What about his family, for heaven's sake?"

"We've acquired testimonies from family members, and witnesses and colleagues like your good self, about the special skills and qualities of some of these individuals. They are usually very high-achieving, in professions involving high risk. Like EOD. We're still investigating this subject, sir."

"Subject my arse!" shouted the colonel. "This man has won the VC, the highest military award!"

The director went on, wondering if he would get out of the meeting in one piece.

"Yes, sir. Indeed. But I also have to inform you that Major Armstrong is under even more special attention and investigation than the other subjects."

"He *would* be."

Then the director told him why.

On the screen, the colonel could see fragments of the final agonising vision that Dan had recorded of Adam falling through the sky with no parachute, his face inside his helmet twisted in agony and terror, fighting for the very breath of life.

The director sat back, quietly, waiting for the thunderclap.

"*Fucking hell!* Are you sure?"

"Yes, I'm afraid so, sir."

The colonel was reduced to staring at the display of a perfectly normal, strapping Army man, with his ruthless, mocking half-smile, the blue-grey eyes frowning against the desert sun, ready for action.

"I once told him he'd come a long way," Richards said.

Then he said in an uncharacteristically gentle tone, "What now? What's his future?"

"He has to be out there very soon." The director waved a cursory hand towards the images of the Iraqi desert below.

"What? Oh, Iraq again," said the colonel, gazing, bewildered, at the assorted scientists, technicians, and encryption teams beavering away at their workstations. "He's been managing clearance of hundreds of IEDs left by ISIS and Co. Then we had the loony eco-mob's attacks in London. I assumed that he wouldn't pull through after that. And if he does, he won't be fit for further service."

"He must be, Colonel. It's absolutely imperative that he is. The mission he's being assigned is even more dangerous and has far greater implications. Not just for Iraq, but for the entire region."

He avoided saying, *for the whole world*. And that stopping nuclear bombs in London didn't compare.

The intelligence man interjected. "And I'm afraid it's something far worse than ISIS, although it is connected."

"Worse than Daesh? ISIS have regenerated; isn't that bad enough? They've already killed and enslaved thousands. It took seventy-nine countries to beat those bastards. What in the blazes are we talking about? Not Adrestia, surely? I thought we'd caught the big shots in that loony science cult."

And the director told him. What lay below the Iraqi desert. "And Major Armstrong is the main, er, emissary who can lead the teams to deal with it."

Seeing that the colonel had calmed down – as much from sheer shock as anything else – the project director pressed on.

"There's another subject we've identified. An Iraqi Army officer. He graduated from the insurgency that Armstrong was pitched against on his previous deployments, and will now be instrumental in this imminent mission."

"Now this is getting farcical," said the colonel. "You'll be telling me next that there's one of these subjects, as you call them, in fucking ISIS... no, Jesus Christ, please don't tell me – that chap down there in the shemagh..."

"Yes, I'm afraid so, sir. The subjects are not all good guys. Also, as well as ISIS, the Adrestia group are not down and out. They infiltrated at least one astrophysics project before we commandeered those sundry efforts. Which is why Major Armstrong will be indispensable in this desert operation. Due to his special place in..."

Richards' brief period of calm came to an end. The implications of what he had been told were sinking in.

"Are some of these, er, entities the bad guys, then? How do you know you're not getting just one side of the story? Are they just one group or are there others with ill intent? And in contact with their ISIS chap down there? Good grief, maybe all of ISIS are from—"

"These individuals are very rare."

"It only takes one. A few mad scientists just tried to incinerate our capital city."

"Indeed. Not all the subjects we have uncovered have our best interests at heart. But if it's any comfort, what we have received and decoded so far is basically an admission of us being left with a devastating legacy. And one that only their – our – 'good guys' can eliminate."

And as if it couldn't get any worse, he added, "But we don't know what sort of contact has been made with that ISIS commander."

Richards glowered and sat bolt upright.

"Before you told me all this appalling claptrap, I came in to talk to you about the arrest of one of your team directors – the now infamous Captain Sheena Maxwell."

The intel rep took over from the harassed Orion Programme director.

"Yes, for her part in the killing of Dr Allison Hardy. I understand Ms Maxwell is being held at an undisclosed detention centre. And that you reported your suspicions about her."

Richards was relieved to be talking about something much more earthbound, as bad as it was.

"I relayed my doubts about that operative some weeks ago. I was concerned about her attitude. Something didn't seem right."

"We understand she's been working on the side of Adrestia. She arranged the emplacement of the infiltrator cops on the roof in the north London operation."

"Good God! Where our man down there got shot to pieces."

"Yes, sir – massive infiltration."

"Like some female Bond villain. Happy to see London reduced to radioactive rubble. She isn't another one, is she?"

The director jumped in. "Another what, sir? No. So far as we know, she isn't an Orion."

"A what? Is that what you're calling these… individuals?"

"Yes, sir, the subjects. Orions. But this is all Above Top Secret."

"Now he tells me," said Richards.

The intel guy said, "She's been carrying through your Double Felix project as well."

"It's not my Double flaming Felix project," Colonel Richards replied. "I was never in favour of all that superman shit."

"Dr Hardy was also involved in our programme."

Richards thought he'd heard it all. "So may I assume our Ms Maxwell has also compromised this comedy clown circus you're running here?"

"No, Colonel. You can be assured of that."

Undisclosed location: Christmas Eve, 2020
Sheena sat in the interrogation room and robotically answered the steady stream of questions from the two security officials tasked with her case. Her long dark hair fell untidily over her shoulders and her clothes were bedraggled after a night in a high-security prison cell. Her elegant mien was shattered.

She admitted to enabling the emplacement of police infiltrators and to betraying a security service operative to a terrorist group which had attempted to blow London up with a weapon of mass destruction, following their murder of over a hundred people in a bomb attack on the Underground. After being rumbled by the colonel, she had decided to confess, arrogantly hoping that she would get a shorter sentence.

Sheena had almost facilitated the destruction of London. But she also confessed to something she hadn't done. Sheena hadn't killed Allison, or had her killed. The scientist had, in fact, been dispatched by handpicked Orion enforcers – because she was about to reveal the Orion Programme to the media. Anything related to the programme must be protected at all costs. Its teams had made the biggest discovery in world history. Everything had to be done to keep the Orion operation covert – until the ultimate mission was concluded. Sheena had taken the rap for the murder of an MI5 operative and, hence, had got the programme's enforcers off the hook.

Allison's sudden death invited endless speculation. It was initially reported as suicide, like Dr David Kelly back in 2003. Then there was talk of a cover-up. Then it was the Russians, then a Brit conspiracy to make it look like a Russian hit. Toxicology reports confirmed that a rare, rapid-acting poison had killed her, administered by injection after she drank a spiked drink. The Russians theory was dropped, as she'd had no connection with Russia. Whoever Allison had met, she'd known them well enough to have a drink with them. Her training would have precluded her taking drinks with strangers.

But the Orion enforcers were just colleagues, working alongside the scientists.

There were bound to be leaks, so the Orion Programme set up its own enforcer unit, seconded from hand-picked, highly trained military operatives. There was too much at stake to risk anything getting out, especially in an era when what you had for breakfast went round the world within seconds. The longer the loony output on websites about UFOs and the like stayed in the realms of unreality, the better.

Now it was real. And Allison was about to release it. Whatever got out of the Orion Programme, the enforcer unit was tasked with silencing it – both the leak and its perpetrator.

But it was only a matter of time before the truth got out.

"Can you absolutely confirm what you have just told us, Sheena?"

Sheena turned her ice-grey eyes on her interrogators. Exhausted, she croaked out,

"Yes."

"Are you prepared to sign an affidavit to confirm your testimony?"

There was a long pause as the dishevelled woman, on the brink of derangement, took a deep breath and yelled back at them,

"*Yes*, for fuck's sake!"

They pushed a document in front of her. The file cover was emblazoned Orion Programme: Above Top Secret. She looked up at them, then down at the file. Someone opened it and gave her a pen. She saw the standard Army ID photo of his face frowning ruthlessly up at her from the page.

She scrawled her signature at the foot of the text on the paper. The ultimate betrayal of the man she desired above all others.

"Thank you, Captain Maxwell."

She swept the document off the table onto the floor and shouted,

"Now fucking well leave me alone!"

When they left her alone in her cell, it came again. The repeated, bizarre scene of battle and shattered soldiers' bodies as she pulled Adam further into her. Explosions, ripped limbs, blackened sands... Looking into those terrifying eyes while they sprawled, pulling off clothes, writhing in union on the floor of her apartment, his big, unusually smooth body pinning her down...

She dropped the crumpled photograph from her clenched fist. Sobbing uncontrollably, she let out a piercing, strangulated cry, which nobody heard.

"Adam!"

Chapter 49

"Two possibilities exist. Either we are alone in the Universe or we are not. Both are equally terrifying."

Arthur C. Clarke

Undisclosed location: 3 January 2021
A group of around thirty hand-picked intelligence, government and security officials settled into their seats in a heavily guarded lecture hall in the headquarters of the Orion Programme. Like the project building, the hall was protected by bombproof walls. The entire room had been repeatedly swept for surveillance devices. The Christmas period had come and gone, but there had been little to celebrate. Nobody had the faintest idea what they were about to be told. Mobiles, tablets and any means of recording had been removed.

Standing on the podium with a sheaf of papers in her hand and a laptop on the lectern before her, Carolyn began. Her lilting Geordie accent was gentle on the ear, almost serving to soften what she was about to say.

She had long dreaded this moment. Her sudden promotion and transfer to the nation's most secret programme did little to lessen that dread.

"Good evening, everyone. What I am about to tell you we trust will not be heard, read or communicated beyond this facility." She held the papers high above her head for dramatic effect.

The screen behind her displayed a sky map of the constellation Orion and a backdrop of the Iraqi desert.

"I am going to read to you the report that my colleague, the late Professor Allison Hardy, was about to leak to the world's media before she was killed by the group we sent her to work undercover in: the eco-terrorist organisation known as Adrestia. Before we begin, a minute's silence, please, in Allison's memory. She died for her country."

These are the last moments of silence I will ever enjoy.

"This report is a verified account of the Orion Programme, its origin and mission. This information is Above Top Secret, as you all know. It is going to shock you all in varying degrees. You have been specially selected to hear it under the strictest secrecy rules.

"We don't know Allison's motive in wanting to release this. It was purloined by one of Adrestia's leading lights, Carl Murrow, now about to stand trial in the United States for plotting and instigating acts of terrorism. After his wife handed him over to the FBI, she mailed it to us.

"We have not been able to find digital versions of this, so we converted and encrypted it. It may be out there in some other format."

She trotted out Dan doing Bette Davis in a final moment of levity. "So, fasten your seatbelts – it's gonna be a bumpy night."

She took a deep breath and tried to stop her hands from shaking.

"To whoever reads this, I am prepared to testify that everything in this report has been researched, verified and comes to you from the highest level.

"The Orion Programme.

"Around 2012, a large-scale secret project was set up, called the Orion Programme. This followed the interception of decipherable signals by several astrophysicist teams. The signals were investigated exhaustively. We conclusively proved that they emanated from an Earth-like planet situated, in sky map terms, in the constellation Orion.

"The earlier programme, called SETI, was headed up by the renowned astrophysicist Dr Carl Sagan. This was closed down in 1993, then replaced by Project Phoenix, which concluded without success in 2004. Others continued as the public face of the search for extraterrestrial intelligence. Orion is the real deal, however, and is as top secret as it gets – and, arguably, the biggest intelligence-gathering operation in history.

"The project consists mainly of UK, US and European scientists, and security and intelligence people vetted to the highest level. The Russians and Chinese have their own versions. It is not to be confused with the ongoing NASA Orion Spacecraft project."

"I was co-opted onto the Orion Programme as a geneticist and researcher into possible life on exoplanets and contact with them.

"There have been many exoplanets discovered in the Orion constellation. Many are situated in the turbulent magnetic clouds in the Orion Nebula – the fields of Orion."

The screen filled with the constellation in the night sky. The hallmark eight stars were joined up in an imaginary framework of a mythological figure depicted as a modern, clean-shaven warrior. Many more stars and a lonely planet lit up his gigantic form. His muscle-bound right arm wielded his unbreakable club aloft; his left arm thrust his shield forward. Three bright stars glittered on his belt. The vast Nebula lurked in plain sight on the scabbard of his sword.

A NASA photograph appeared on the screen. Streams of undulating magnetic waves stretched over hundreds of light-years in the Nebula. The beautiful fields of Orion.

"The Transmissions.

"We began receiving and interpreting signals from a planet in this constellation in 2012. It was given the astral catalogue name of HD8889 b, or 'Planet Orion'. The transmissions from this planet comprised far more than the usual bumps and

crackles received to date. They came at regular intervals like a heartbeat. Not unlike pulsars, which also emitted regular signals – discovered by Dr Jocelyn Bell in the 1960s.

"But these signals were not from pulsars, or regular FRBs - fast radio bursts. In the UK, we deciphered the barrage of signals and our encryption, AI and linguistic teams translated them into English. Details about the frequencies and electromagnetic spectrum are in Appendix A.

"Planet HD8889 b circles a newly found star, designated HD8889. It appears in the Great Nebula in Orion's sword, but is much nearer to our solar system than the stars in that nebula. The planet circles the star in a 316-day year orbit, a relatively 'close' 19 light-years away. So it took 19 years for the first signals to arrive, having been transmitted from this planet in 1993."

A star glittered brightly behind her from the cross-guard of Orion's sword. An impossibly distant sun in the midst of gargantuan, super-hot stars. A gigantic white mass of disintegrating hydrogen in a vast ochre ionising sky, incinerating and irradiating a dying desert world.

To stem the mutterings and snarls from her audience – some of them offensive with regard to Allison Hardy's sanity – Carolyn cried out,

"This is just the start, so grip onto something firm.

"The senders of the signals from Planet HD8889 b are humanoid. That is, human-like in almost all respects, but not human."

The crowd exhaled gasps, grunts, jeers and wows in equal measure. Carolyn paused and gulped from a glass of water, wishing it was a large neat whisky.

"Please. If I may continue." She went on.

"Astrophysics teams began receiving more signals later in 2012 – like a beacon – much closer to home: from an odd-shaped object in the asteroid belt in our solar system. We

identified this structure as an activated signalling point, which we call 'Asteroid Station'. The signals from this object take only one hour to get here.

"Every effort was made to close down all information about this discovery after it was commandeered by the Orion Programme.

"Our teams of encryption and radio frequency specialists deciphered the signals being transmitted from Asteroid Station. The language was in the form of a type of computer code. The translated transmissions are in a series marked OR8000."

Carolyn had seen the tower-block of print-outs that comprised the appendices to Allison's report. But she hadn't read them all. Nor had she previously read all of the report she was delivering today.

"Our translation of the signals indicates that they come from a highly advanced civilisation. They tell us of its former existence and of its past visitations to Earth, its technology and – its descendants. The planet's atmosphere is like ours, so they breathe in oxygen like we do and the gravity is almost the same as on Earth. But the planet is brighter and hotter than ours. They had oceans of water. Much of it has been turned to desert."

Carolyn shushed the expletives flying at her from her high-level audience as she continued to read out the most sensational report in history. Her hand shook as she clicked slide after slide that formed its backdrop.

"They also set up the signalling station in the asteroid belt to be timed to send out more regular transmissions once our world was deemed to be on the brink of a specific catastrophe."

Silence.

"The signals from Asteroid Station were configured to be received by our teams – 'for your eyes only', so to speak – so other projects may have missed them. They have given us a vast new trove of data after long months of work.

"The Landings.

"Our translation of the signals reveal that the first landings by inhabitants of Planet Orion were made on Earth around the eighth century BC. There have been several more since. The vast distance meant the interstellar journeys were spent in cryogenic suspension."

"I hope they brought sandwiches," said a wag near the front. Carolyn ignored him.

"UFO mythologists and writers have long lavished attention on this possibility, on the idea of ancient alien landings – and on first contact with another world. We had the 1950s flying saucer mania, Ancient Astronaut Theory, Erich von Däniken's best-sellers in the 1970s loaded with biblical analogies, numerous films, and endless ravings on the internet. Even some professors have lectured on the notion of alien-human hybrids.

"The stuff of decades of UFO folklore has now actually happened. From the transmissions, the earliest landing site was the area we now know as the western desert of Iraq. Originally Mesopotamia – the site of the earliest Neolithic human settlements and the world's first agriculture. The constellations and astronomy have great significance in medieval Islamic culture. Orion has figured in several ancient mythologies. Some peoples even believed humans originated from Orion.

"As far as we know, the senders of this vast amount of data once became an integral part of ancient Middle Eastern and Greek civilisations. Their proximity to an expanding star – there are many in this constellation – meant that their days were numbered thousands of years ago. They spread out to other worlds and set up interim stations like the one in the asteroid belt."

The exploding sun. Carolyn had viewed the last, short piece of footage from Dan's hidden camera.

"Why weren't any of these incursions logged? Where's the evidence?" A heavily-built official shouted as he rose to his feet. "This is loony-tunes territory."

Carolyn looked helplessly at the script inherited from her murdered colleague.

"There's a shedload of it, sir. In the Appendices." She struggled to say, "And much of it is still under investigation. I know none of this is in our comfort zone. So do please bear with me.

"From the history lesson decoded from the Orion signals, the first settlers on Earth were warlike, and brought weaponry skills to the Middle Eastern region. However, we have learned that more recent visitations have occurred, as recently as..."

The mutterings in the auditorium stopped.

"...the nineteenth century."

Then the shouting began. "Where, for fuck's sake?"

"Southern England," replied Carolyn.

Chapter 50

"Somewhere, something incredible is waiting to be known."

Dr Carl Sagan

She drank more water. Derisory questions and expletives were hurled at the podium.

"I assure you, everyone, this is for real. If I may continue. We've a long way to go. Questions at the end, please.

"The visitors from Planet Orion hunted us down millennia ago. Then, in our time, we searched and we found them. We can now put paid to the Fermi Paradox: if there are so many stars and planets out there, why haven't we found life on any of them and why haven't they come here?

"According to Greek legend, eighth century BC: Orion, the giant hunter, the celestial warrior. In Homer's Odyssey: supernaturally strong, the tallest and the most handsome of all... Carolyn paused. *"Earthborn men."*

The bejewelled stars of Orion twinkled innocuously at their stunned observers. Carolyn caught her breath as she read out Allison's digression into the Classics.

"Blinded by the King of Chios. Stung by a scorpion sent by the Earth goddess Gaia, when Orion boasted he would kill all the animals of the Earth. Shot dead by the arrow of Artemis. Placed by the gods in the sky forever, in retreat from Scorpio, chasing the Pleiades – the Seven Sisters – in perpetuity."

Blinded. Lethal scorpion in Iraq. "I'd like to kill every terrorist on this planet," he had said. *Seven Sisters? Road...*

Carolyn struggled to keep it together. If she had read something like this on any other occasion, she would be laughing herself shitless.

Not here; not now; not this.

"The Descendants.

"During this period – when we were beginning to interpret the signals – separate reports came into the Orion Programme, via our military and security services, of a certain few individuals manifesting highly unusual skills and abilities such as telekinetic, telepathic and extrasensory skills, the ability to see in the dark, hypersensitive hearing, and extraordinary powers of recovery from illness and injury.

"A separate, even more secret, investigation began, which concluded that these individuals were receiving further transmissions from Asteroid Station, aimed exclusively at them.

"Their physiognomy and anatomy is almost identical to those of humans. In some cases, they have one specific physical difference: their eyes, which can be covered by perma lenses."

Carolyn began to feel faint. Those beautiful, hard blue-grey eyes… ruthless, boring through anyone he spoke to, made love to... and hiding behind them…

She steadied herself on the podium. She wasn't trained for this.

"Most are normal at birth and later develop into an oval, cat-like pupil structure. They have phenomenal vision, although they may be photophobic. The telekinesis appears to emanate from the eyes.

"These unusual manifestations were kept secret. When noticed by family, doctors and others, they were thought to be a physical feature caused by a genetic mutation. It was assumed that they were high-achieving humans with extra-special qualities.

"We concluded from interpretation of further communications with Asteroid Station that they are the direct descendants of the original visitations and settlement by…"

Carolyn held on to the lectern to steady herself as she said the 'e' word.

"...extraterrestrials..."

She breathed in again.

"...from Planet HD8889 b. These visitations took place several times from the original landings in the eighth century BC up to as recently as the nineteenth century in an uninhabited part of southern England."

The location, on an old map of England, appeared on the screen. A 200-mile-radius red circle, its nucleus somewhere in the middle of Bedfordshire. The landing site was marked with a black blob, away from nearby towns, just before the southern counties started becoming built up.

"These descendants are very human-like; in fact, in several ways they are superhuman. But they are not human; they are of extraterrestrial origin.

"Transmissions received last year from Asteroid Station confirmed that the most recent..."

Carolyn suddenly stopped. The next word had been redacted. Catching her breath, she had to improvise in a split second.

"... descendant... from Planet HD8889 b is a British Army bomb disposal veteran from north London.

"His name is Major Adam Jerome Armstrong, GC."

Chapter 51

"…behold Orion rise
His arms extended measure half the skies
His stride no less. Onward with steady pace
He treads the boundless realms of starry space."

Marcus Manilius

The screen flashed up the wall-sized picture of Adam in fatigues, assault weapon in his strong, capable hands, standing on the red desert of Iraq. Next to him was an astronomical image of HD8889 b. An innocuous little planet with two moons.

Gasps resounded. Intakes of breath.

Carolyn felt like ducking to avoid the verbal rotten tomatoes. Grunting laughter was emitted at the most outrageous presentation anybody had ever delivered.

"Oh shit. Not him!"

"Oh my God." Times ten.

"What the fuck?"

"I don't fucking believe it."

"I do. I've met him. I'll believe anything."

'What did he land in, then? A C-5A Super Galaxy?'

"Is it April the First today?"

"Is this a charity stunt?"

"I think I've seen him on TV."

"Is he standing on the surface of Mars, then?"

Carolyn waited another moment for the comments to pass. Then she shouted, "No, he fucking well is not! Sorry, pardon the language. And it's Iraq, not soddin' Mars!" The murmuring persisted.

Carolyn yelled, "*Quiet!*" She wished she was back in her pre-MI5 life, pounding the beat on the streets of Newcastle.

"This is the... back story of Major Adam Armstrong, now VC!"

At the top of her voice, she cried out above the chatter and banged the table with her fist.

"VC. The Victoria Cross! For Gallantry in the Presence of the Enemy!"

That shut them up. Everyone in that room knew that Adam had prevented an improvised nuclear device from levelling London. North London, at least.

"My colleague, who wrote this report, was highly respected in our Service and in the science community. We shall all miss her greatly." Her voice cracked.

"And Major Armstrong may die in the service of his country, of... of... all of us! So, if I may continue.

"Subject of Special Interest.

"Planet Orion now holds clues not only to our past, but also the salvation of all our futures. As you will see below.

"Major Armstrong was first reported by members of his unit and his commanding officer to apply what appeared to be telekinetic energy during bomb disposal operations in Iraq and other theatres. He has also shown distinctive signs of ESP – extrasensory perception – which in extreme events has been predictive.

"Some are visual communications, manifesting themselves in dreams, visions and what we would call hallucinations. Some are actually transmitted messages from Planet HD8889 b, and have increased since 2012, when the signals were first identified.

"One would expect people receiving 'signals' to be suffering from some form of mania, schizophrenia or drug abuse. But

exhaustive work on the signals from Asteroid Station prove that they are genuine, and that this subject has received them.

"I and my colleagues observed this subject and found that he has also transmitted these visual communications to others, mostly randomly. I reported these observations, which were then taken on board by the Orion Programme.

"He has also shown unprecedented powers of physical recovery from gunshot wounds and lethal scorpion stings during service in Iraq."

Carolyn said, "I should add that Dr Hardy died before the counter-terrorist operation in north London in December, when Major Armstrong sustained multiple gunshot wounds to the chest and one to the head. He has survived several episodes of cardiac arrest and is fighting for his life.

"On admission to hospital, the paramedics discovered his eyes while they were treating him for his head wound. The senior surgeon reported this several levels up until the information reached the Orion Programme. It was confirmed that his eyes fit the description of an Orion… extraterrestrial."

There was silence at last. Medical verification. That nailed it. Deathly silence. Carolyn took another deep breath, then stopped. She noticed that a woman on the front row was staring, transfixed, at Adam's image on the screen. She recognised her as being from the Security Ministry. Her face was lined with tears.

The lady stood up and spoke, her voice shaking with emotion. The room stayed silent.

"Has he recovered? Is he going to be all right?" She cleared her throat, trying to correct the quiver in her voice. She cried out,

"If this… hero is from another world, he's bloody well gone and saved this one!"

Then it came.

Wave after wave. Applause. Deafening, resounding applause. Cheers from hearty military throats. Someone put their arm round the woman as she cried. Some stood, clapping, not cheering. Like people do when a coffin goes by.

Carolyn briskly brushed a tear away. *Another poor cow, mesmerised by this… bloody hero… from… And me an' all. I must be goin' soft.*

The applause died down. She continued.

"In 2018 Armstrong was brought into the defence project known as Double Felix, to create so-called 'supersoldiers' with extraordinary skills, strength and resilience. It was the tests he passed on the Double Felix project that spurred us to investigate him further. I was involved in this project, which is how I was able to further research my theories about this subject, based on our findings.

"We then carried out full sequencing of his DNA. We found the impossible: he possesses eight-base DNA. That is, eight protein bases rather than the normal four that all humans have. Something that has only been synthesised in a lab. His DNA structure was checked with every known genomic database. Full genomic profile details of this subject are in Appendix B."

A model of Armstrong's DNA helix flashed up on the screen, the impossible spiral rotating hypnotically.

"Eight-base DNA has unlimited possibilities in a living being: a vast capacity for information, exponentially higher levels of performance and resilience, and more will emerge as we study this subject further."

Carolyn looked back at his service photo on the screen. Such a normal British Army officer's face. A face so handsome. So *human.*

"Only now can we fully analyse the human genome. Sequenced DNA can carry information about ancestry, mutations and hereditary illnesses, and look back many centuries. We also enquired whether horizontal transfer of

genes had been carried out under the Double Felix project. This has been completely ruled out.

"We also ruled out or chromosomal disorders like Cat's Eye Syndrome, or genetic manipulation to change his eyes - as this is an ongoing experiment in the US and here on the UK project to enable soldiers to see in the dark. Neither applied to this subject."

Carolyn wanted the Earth, the galaxy and that little distant planet out there in the constellation Orion to open and swallow her up. She took a deep breath and read out Allison's words.

"My own initial analysis of this officer's DNA and special characteristics, however, brought me and other experts in the Orion Programme to the shocking conclusion that Armstrong is not human, but humanoid.

"Charts we received in the mass of data from Asteroid Station confirmed this. They included a detailed pictorial depiction of this officer and his eight-base DNA profile. These arrived in lines of code that took several days to decipher."

The wall-high dot-matrix composite of Adam's full form that had graced Orion Mission Control appeared, line by coded line, on the screen.

"In 2020 it was confirmed by the Orion Programme teams that Major Armstrong is a Subject of Special Interest."

Carolyn read on in a numbed, impassive tone, as though in a trance.

"This is because Transmission OR8089 and Major Armstrong's pure eight-base DNA confirm that he originates from a much more recent visitation.

"This is still under investigation."

Chapter 52

"Orion's beams, Orion's beams, his star-gemmed belt and shining blade
His isles of light, his silver streams
And glowing gulfs of mystic shade."

The Sphere of Marcus Manilius

"But wasn't he *born* here? Are you sure?"

Carolyn paused. Her stomach churned and her head was spinning.

Still under investigation.

"Of course, yes – North London," she said, with more hesitation than she would have preferred.

"The original ancient arrivals intermingled with humans."

Carolyn welcomed a moment of desperately needed light relief. *Intermingled. Our Adam's done plenty of that, by all accounts.*

"Their descendants all carry regenerated eight-base DNA. Details of this are in Appendix D. We do not know how the descendants of the original landings during the times of ancient Greece survived over generations. They also intermingled with humans.

"The biggest mystery emerging from our discoveries and still under investigation is how the subjects under our examination have DNA that has somehow been reactivated in this eight-base form in the current generation. The DNA of the original visitations had become hybridised with humans.

"Armstrong's DNA, however, is that of a pure Orion."

Carolyn gasped as she read this. *You kept all this dark, didn't you, Major? Every time you went out there in the desert,* dismantling devices. *Walking through minefields. Fighting for your country. Risking your life. Getting drunk. Rescuing your mates. Picking up bits of them. Knowing this crap. Maybe you got the message when you were out there. And what if you had PTSD as well?*

"*At first, we did not know if Orions were aware of their ancestral identity. It was then confirmed that they received a specific communication revealing their extraterrestrial provenance. This would have been shattering and deeply disturbing for them. They could not announce or reveal their extraordinary origins to a living soul. This would in any case have aroused ridicule and, in the UK, possibly got them sectioned under the Mental Health Act. They had to keep this secret at all costs.*

"*For Armstrong, as a serving and now veteran Army officer, this would have been a tremendous burden to carry.*

"*As for taking this subject and others through the trauma of this discovery, our Service's involvement in the Orion Programme does not include responsibility for counselling.*"

Suddenly, she realised the enormity of what he must have gone through – what he was still going through – battling critical injuries.

"*Other Subjects.*

"*We discovered that the Orion descendants are very rare. They are also not physically alike. Some are able to communicate telepathically, while others have fewer of the extra qualities, and some do not have the feline-type eyes.*

"*The signals have had other effects. Reported sightings of unexplained light phenomena have been seen over several countries, especially the Middle East, despite aerial bombardments and constant warfare obfuscating oddities in the skies above those countries.*

"*Sightings have also occurred over London, specifically north London. As far as we know, the sighting locations coincide with a high level of electromagnetic energy near to where subjects live or visit for long periods. They mirror in miniature the vast shock-waves spread throughout the Nebula, the magnetic fields of Orion."*

That was what Dan had seen. The lights. Over Highbury Fields. Where it all began, way back in July 2005. And where it could have all come to an end nearly sixteen years later.

"We also believe that some are senders and others are more likely to be receivers of telepathic communications from other Orions – or of the asteroid belt transmissions."

Carolyn interjected. "Dr Hardy died before such an example of an Orion receiver was later confirmed."

"Please don't say it's Vladimir Putin," quipped a wag in the audience.

Carolyn sucked in air, held onto the lectern and surprised herself by feeling some pride, along with total disbelief and some welcome amusement, in announcing the next revelation. At least she already knew about this bit, uncovered after Allison died.

"According to Transmission OR 8889, and subsequent DNA results, it has been confirmed that the prime Orion receiver discovered to date is the other operative we recruited and sent in to work for us as an undercover agent with the Adrestia terrorist group.

"He is the man who successfully sabotaged the dirty bomb for us in central London. He also somehow transmitted a warning signal to Major Armstrong as the police sniper on the roof was about to detonate the nuclear device at the back of Highbury station."

The room fell quiet.

"His name is... Daniel James Patrick Boland."

Chapter 53

"I wanted to be a secret agent and an astronaut, preferably at the same time."

David Byrne

Flashing up on the screen was a passport picture of a fair-haired, angular-featured Dan frowning at the camera, trying to look tough. Another showed him sharply lean in combat gear, firing a handgun in training. Another, taken covertly, was of him leading a counter-IED workshop in a hotel in central London, smartly suited. Adam was seated at the boardroom table, the MI5 officers opposite. The ones who didn't carry cards.

Next to these pictures was Dan's DNA profile alongside a prettily coloured dancing helix of eight-base DNA.

"That bloody idiot. The David Bowie fan? That's the only thing that's made sense so far."

"Hasn't he got previous with the IRA?"

"Five reduced to recruiting men from Mars, then?"

"And we thought the Russians were a problem."

"Are these two related? Cosmic twins?"

"No they are *not*! Come on, people, this is serious. Dan did a great job for us. He *is* an Orion, I mean a subject, but more distantly descended than Major Armstrong. Several generations back. His DNA reactivated in the last century when he was born. He's a different type. Just like *we* are all different types."

Like I'm a Geordie, but she left that out. The questions cascaded again.

From the back: "Not that I believe any of this rubbish, but if this Boland chap of yours is a receiver, how come he transmitted that message out of the ops room to his fellow Martian, the incident commander?"

"We don't know, sir. And Major Armstrong is *not* a Martian! He was born in north London!" Carolyn longed for the good old days of the Russians hacking and poisoning everyone.

"Boland was an easy target for an Orion sender. They were on the same circuit, if you'll excuse the pun. It would have been accidental contact at first. Then Boland gave evidence about premonitions, scenes, and other comms he received from Armstrong. Out of the blue – and, I can tell you, very disturbing for him. This is all under investigation. Just a coincidence that they're both based in north London. Chance in a gazillion. As likely as me and everyone in this room winnin' the bloody Lottery in the same draw.

"Listen, I know it's all pretty wild and shocking. But it isn't rubbish. I wish it was. And if you think all that was off the scale, I've saved the best til last. Five-minute break. Coffee's at the back. Sorry we've nothing stronger."

Carolyn drank down two of Dan's favourite triple espressos. She resumed.

"This is the final part of Dr Hardy's report, which describes the unparalleled importance of our imminent mission. The reason you have all been called in."

In an emotionless voice, she read on.

"As the translations proceeded, we learned about their senders, about the visitations here, and specifically about an impending catastrophe.

"The most recent are warnings about a vast object that has re-solidified below the site of its original landing. This occurred in the western Iraqi desert, then Mesopotamia in the eighth century BC, around the time of the ancient Greeks – so, over 2,800 years ago.

"The signals confirmed what has long been feared: that this initial landing left behind a huge disintegrated craft. In the

millennia that followed, it sank below the desert of what is now western Iraq.

"The underground legacy is of a material not seen before, and partly disintegrated one hundred yards or so below the desert surface. Over centuries, it has coalesced. The time for this underground legacy device to blow, like a huge volcanic eruption, is now.

"It began to solidify a year or so ago, and earth tremors are now a regular occurrence in western Iraq. Normally they occur on the Iraq-Iran border. Translation of the asteroid belt messages indicate that geological changes on our planet have enhanced the legacy craft's volatile nature.

"This underground device is set to explode not unlike the long-predicted eruption of the supervolcano located under Yellowstone Park in the US."

"This object covers five square miles. If it explodes, it will destroy much of Iraq and surrounding territories, with catastrophic implications both there and worldwide.

"The messages are warnings, to try to save us from a legacy craft that is about to become the ultimate weapon of mass destruction.

"It will explode at any time. It is like a vast underground mine on an extremely long-delay timer."

Somebody shouted out, "What about where Armstrong landed? In southern England? Is bloody Bedfordshire going to blow up as well?"

"That's under investigation." Carolyn felt a chill to the bone. *Parochial bastard.*

"And Major Armstrong did *not* land in southern England. Please!' She wished they'd landed down her road in Newcastle. They wouldn't have lasted five minutes. She struggled on.

"The main ancient visitation to the area that is now Iraq arrived in a massive spacecraft. Subsequent landings have carried far smaller numbers. The Orion Programme's geologists have conducted investigations in southern England.

So far, no unusual seismic activity has been detected at the southern England landing site. This is under investigation."

"The transmissions have told us that, due to their special skills, the Orion descendants on Earth are the only ones who hold the key to stopping the destruction of the Middle Eastern region.

"And this, ladies and gentlemen, is the big one. This is why you are hearing all of this about Adam Armstrong.

"Armstrong will be at the forefront as the most recently ...descended... Orion."

Recently descended.

Carolyn held onto the lectern and breathed in steadily.

"His extra skills will be invaluable, as they are less dilute than other subjects found so far. Transmissions have confirmed his special role. He has also received them.

"He will be leading the best bomb disposal units we can find.

"These transmissions must be viewed as an enormous breakthrough for humanity, for us to prevent the destruction of the Middle Eastern region."

Carolyn was beginning to realise, with a sinking heart, that Allison had not been killed by Adrestia. It was because of Orion. She had been sitting on the world's biggest ever discovery and its biggest secret, and its implications were beyond alarming.

"Orions of ancient and recent descent are all in high-risk, dangerous occupations. They have so far been in military service, and specifically in EOD. One is an Iraqi Army officer, also a bomb disposal expert, who has been active in operations against ISIS. Our US colleagues have notified us of two high-ranking female officers in the US Marines, one a decorated bomb technician. There may be more in other countries. It may take years to establish who and where all the Orions are."

Then came the crunch.

"Another suspected Orion is a former ISIS leader – believed to be a key operator in that terror group's second appalling incarnation. The Orion Programme received intel on this individual from testimonies of former ISIS operatives and Kurdish and Iraqi soldiers. Appendix C details these separate subject investigations."

Up flashed the photos of the Iraqi Army officer and the two US Marines. Like Adam, they all looked completely human. Next to them, the ISIS leader. The cries and yells of horror and disgust resounded, only much louder.

"As an apocalyptic mass-murdering cult, Daesh Mark 2 wants the underground device to blow. They lost, and they want to drag the region down with them. The deposition of hundreds of mines and IEDs by ISIS in this area and their destruction of archaeological sites was also to greatly hamper any operation to deal with the legacy device."

And it got worse.

"There is also evidence that the eco-terrorist organisation Adrestia, which I infiltrated on behalf of our security service, has a rogue spin-off group of scientists embedded in the Orion Programme and other space research centres. They have been attempting to intercept transmissions from Asteroid Station and we are concerned that they have sent messages back.

"Their mission: like ISIS, to stop all means we could use to disable the underground legacy object beneath the Iraq desert.

"I believe that the discoveries from the investigations outlined in this report should be made public. I also believe collaboration with the Russians and other countries conducting equivalent Orion Programmes is of utmost urgency.

"This is because, as the final part of this report explains, enemies have been identified who will sabotage this world-critical mission. These enemies will be pitted against the other Orion subjects, primarily Major Armstrong as the chief emissary.

"These discoveries have long been awaited. I believe that they are not the property of any one state government.

"Therefore, international collaboration must commence now.

"Dr Allison Hardy, June 2020"

Chapter 54

"The journey is the thing."

Homer, The Odyssey

Underground facility, West London: 8 January 2021

Dan sat at a small desk looking simultaneously at the TV and his laptop in the spacious utilitarian quarters assigned to him. He wore his shades and a black T-shirt, beige cargo pants and boots. Straight after seeing Adam in hospital, he had been brought into a separate area within the underground Orion Programme facility. Here he had spent a sparse, lonely Christmas and New Year.

There had been much prodding and poking. The eye scans turned up nothing unusual. Every bodily fluid and even ones he hadn't even heard of were taken and analysed. He was X-rayed and given a brain scan.

As well as more earth tremors in Iraq, he saw an item on TV about what would have been David Bowie's 74th birthday. This made him feel even more estranged from his past life. And strangely connected to this one.

They told him that, to everyone's amazement, Adam had recovered. He had been awarded the Victoria Cross. Dan was privately thanked for stopping the Adrestia-linked nurse from injecting him with a massive dose of fentanyl. For a few long moments Dan cried quietly, alone.

He got up from the desk and started pedalling furiously on an exercise bike they'd given him. He wasn't allowed out to the gym provided for the cooped-up staff. Carolyn came into his secluded quarters carrying a bunch of files and a tablet. Dan noticed that a nurse and an armed police officer were stationed outside his room.

"You settled in OK, then?"

"Why aye, bonny lass. I've got the place looking nice," said Dan, mimicking her Geordie accent. "I'll recommend this hotel on TripAdvisor. I go to all the secret underground government facilities at Christmas. They maul you about a bit too much in the spa, mind. Can I get a free massage?"

Carolyn's eyes went skyward. Then she remembered that he had endured a week of constant tests after they had left Adam fighting for his life in the Whitechapel. He had protested about each one, demanding that they explain. They had kept him waiting for the results – as much a test of his mettle as anything else.

Carolyn had dreaded this moment even more than delivering the world-shattering revelations at the turn of the new year to the top-level security gathering. It was time to come clean. First, about his DNA. He got off the exercise bike and stretched his arms out to her in a mock hug. She ignored it.

"You need to be sittin' down, pet."

"I'll stand up and take it like a man," said Dan.

"Well, you've got form with that, at least."

"No need to get personal," said Dan.

She took a deep breath and handed him the DNA file. She told him, very briskly, the result. And what it meant.

A long pause. Then he burst out laughing, very loudly, a hysterical guffaw for several long minutes. Just like on the day he had been recruited in that bright basement MI5 office, when they told him he'd been recommended by Adam. Only louder. Then he stopped abruptly.

"Is this a wind-up? I bet you say that to all the Bowie fans you recruit into MI5. It's his birthday today."

"It's true."

"Haven't you mixed my results up with…?"

Carolyn looked at him, very seriously. "No."

318

For once, Dan didn't speak for several minutes. He breathed very deeply. He looked at the file. The comments, some redacted, were instantly understood, if not the charts. The room spun. His face began to prickle. He began to see those little sparkly green dots which indicate a sudden drop in blood pressure.

"Is this why…?" He started hyperventilating. He looked up at her helplessly. "The scenes? The premonitions? Why I need to wear shades… Why I can hear a gnat fart…"

"Yes."

"And Adam? Is that what the scenes meant, and the one you sent me in to record? All those visions? Like when we shook hands? That flashing nightmare vision of an ancient battle, somewhere? Those beautiful desert scenes of a people… somewhere?"

Then she told him where that somewhere was.
And that Adam was from that somewhere.
And so are you.

"And… I recovered after being run over…. because I'm an…an…" He was gasping for air.

"Yes." And Carolyn quietly said the 'A' word again.

Dan passed out on the floor.

"Bloody drama queen," said Carolyn. "I told him to sit down." She called to the nurse outside. "Bring him a strong sweet coffee. Oh, and a brandy. And one for me, love. I'm going to need it when he comes round." She mumbled, "You wouldn't think he's just shot five blokes dead without batting an eyelid."

She yelled at him to wake him up. "Oh, and by the way, your great-grandad *was* Russian!"

Carolyn and the nurse helped him up and sat him down at the table. He swigged the brandy and started gabbling.

"Orion?"

"Yes. Orion. Planet HD8889 b, it's called."

"The text… that message from Adam… on Highbury Fields! He said, 'Thanks, mate. Orion'."

"That's what you called out to Adam from the ops room. Orion. When he was approaching the van. As that cop on the roof were about to set off the bomb."

He fought back the urge to be sick. Although he was seated, the room began to rotate like the brightly coloured, tangled arms of his – and Adam's – impossible DNA helix. Both profiles were displayed on Carolyn's tablet. He stared blankly at the coloured spirals, spinning round and round like his head.

"But… I don't have those eyes! I can't be…"

"Not all Orions have them. You don't. But your DNA is enough to have cats eating out of your hand, mind."

"So *that's* why cats love me. Especially Blo-job's cat," chattered Dan.

"Excuse me?" said Carolyn. "Oh aye, the white cat, clawing Carl Murrow's face off. In the nick of time. You got lucky there, pet." She went on.

"You're a receiver."

"That's what Adam said. What a cheek. I'm always active!"

"I'm not talking about your colourful sex life, ya daft pillock. I mean, you're a receiver of scenes, of signals. And you sent one too. When it most mattered."

"We're both from…?"

"He's the most recent example on Earth. Well, from a more recent visitation…"

"What are you telling me…" Dan held onto a nearby chair.

"Well, the most recent documented arrival was in the nineteenth century, Allison said in the report."

Carolyn skipped over the part where she had seen the redacted word. *The most recent…blank… from Planet HD8889 b…*

320

"That is, based on the transmissions and the Orion Programme investigations."

"Nineteenth century? Fucking hell, that's like yesterday!" *I must be dreaming. Wake up, wake up...* But it was real; it wasn't a vision. He burbled on. "No wonder he has such an... effect."

"Aye, he has an effect all right," Carolyn sighed.

"Where the hell did they land? Not Newcastle, I bet. They wouldn't last five minutes there."

"Middle of Bedfordshire. The original visitations were centuries ago, time of ancient Greece, in what is now modern Iraq."

"Iraq? Oh, yes, all that ancient astronaut stuff. So that's why I kept seeing deserts. So not... Highbury Fields?" said Dan.

"Right in the middle of a bloody great capital city? Be your age! Too built up."

"Ancient Greece. Eighth century BC. The time of Orion..." said Dan. He was hyperventilating again. Then he started pacing.

"I used to see that constellation. Up on the Fields." He rambled on, his thoughts all over the place.

"Fields of Orion. That planet, it's in the vast magnetic clouds, the fields of Orion."

He was swaying, gasping for air.

"The beautiful eight stars. Sometimes you can see nine. Orion, the mighty hunter... who got stung by the scorpion..."

"So did our Adam," said Carolyn, watching Dan stride up and down the room. "In the desert. Iraq. A lethal double sting – and he survived without antivenom, then got shot the next day. Recovered in two days. And you survived that car smash."

"And the red lights in the sky? Is that... why...?" His voice tailed off. He was desperate to stay conscious. "Adam said they were just energy. That you would tell me, all in good time."

"Electromagnetic energy, yes. Wherever you Orions happen to be. Two of you, for a start, within five miles of each other. It's a miracle the whole bloody park didn't blow up."

"Well, it nearly did. And London with it," said Dan. "If it hadn't been for Adam." Carolyn heard the catch in his voice.

"You did your bit as well, pet." Carolyn sighed.

She wished he'd sit down. She was afraid he would faint again, despite his training. This was beyond training. It was going to be a long evening.

He looked at her, wide-eyed.

"Where did my lot land? And when?"

"Your Orion forebears go much further back. Centuries. But you've got the same DNA. Eight bases instead of four. It has regenerated in the past century. They don't know why. He's much fresher than you."

"Fresher? I bet he is," said Dan, desperate to lighten the most shattering news any person – being – can get.

"He hasn't... you haven't... with him?"

"No, I flamin' well haven't!" she snapped back. "He's not my type. Mind you, he's had everyone else. And anyway, that's enough questions for now."

Then she stood up and blurted it out.

"But I've got one. How come you two blokes, him a decorated army bomb disposal veteran and you a very, very annoying maverick civilian... both of youse, originally from some other sodding planet out there in the bastard Universe...

"*...Both end up in my fucking unit!*

"And Dan, if you dare bloody repeat this, any of this, to any living soul, I'll bloody well kill you myself, with my bare hands!"

Dan passed out again, spilling the coffee all over the table and Carolyn's lap.

Underground facility, west of London: 10 January 2021

Dan was left more or less on his own to amuse himself. He sent pre-composed messages to friends and relatives. Carolyn's unit had written to them separately to explain that he was now in permanent government service on a major national security programme.

He got his mobile phone back at last, which was monitored 24/7. He savoured the 'stay safe' valedictory messages he got back, which he used to send to his army friends and colleagues going out on mission. He saw an item on TV about the fifth anniversary of Bowie's death and joined in with him singing 'Starman' – very loudly and very badly. He missed Jane more than ever.

Further Q and A sessions took place in a guarded room in the facility. Carolyn was accompanied by a young psychologist who had received no training in how to counsel agents who originate from another planet. Mesmerised, she stared across at Dan with big brown eyes. Noting her dark fluffy hair, full red lips and hourglass figure in an undone white blouse and a short skirt, Dan smiled at her and gazed back.

"I think I'll need a lot more counselling," he said afterwards, cheerfully. "She's gorgeous."

Carolyn sighed. "Allison missed out the bit about you lot being sex mad."

"Well, it's a great way to pull the ladies. You should have told me years ago that I came from Planet HD Whatsit."

"Oh behave yourself, man. You're as bad as the other one."

"Thanks for the compliment," said Dan.

She hadn't told him why there were earthquakes in western Iraq.

"Get your factor fifty packed, mate," barked the heavily armed officer who banged on the door and entered without being asked. "You're shippin' out. Briefing. Look lively. Chop chop." Dan wondered if he'd watched too many episodes of *Dad's Army*.

"Roger that." He responded briskly with the military phrase that always set Bea and Jane off. If only he could see them again. "Who do I report to?"

As if she had read his thoughts, Carolyn walked in.

"Get them shades on, pet."

"Ooh, great. Am I going back to Brighton?"

"You're deploying tomorrow. Iraq. Next big assignment. Away, man."

Dan blethered on. "I've never been to Iraq. I hear it's very nice this time of year."

"Well, it's got a lot more sand than Brighton."

Then it dawned on him.

"What the hell are you sending me there for?"

"Major Armstrong will brief you when you land," said Carolyn, smiling. "Stay safe, Dan."

Western Iraq: 15 January 2021

A tall, fair-haired, strikingly handsome British Army officer clambered out of a massive Chinook helicopter and strode out onto the vast desert of western Iraq. His mesmerising grey-blue eyes were screwed up behind military wraparound shades; his big, muscular form was fully kitted out in combat gear. A ballistic plate remnant sat, hardened, over his pounding heart. The rapidly solidifying metallic legacy of his forefathers shuddered beneath his desert-booted feet.

His team, all the prime EOD experts Britain could spare, and joined by many of their ilk from allied forces and specialist units from across the world, marched resolutely with him all the way to the military camp.

Waiting for Adam was his once-opposite number, now brothers in arms, the Iraqi Army officer and EOD veteran Major Muhammad al-Yad al-Jauzā – 'the hand of Orion'. They embraced briefly and exchanged greetings. They had already communicated, mind to mind across continents, after they had received the messages from over nineteen light-years across space. And since, from signals that pulsed into their inner souls from the belt of a billion broken rocks beyond Mars.

A fleet of helicopters ferried in consignments of equipment. The two commanders walked together to the base across endless rocky sand, beneath a deep blue sky populated by a bright yellow winter sun. They winced and squinted against the blazing light.

The ground shook from occasional tremors. At times it was like striding a cakewalk. A hundred yards beneath their pounding feet, below fields of landmines left by Daesh, a five-mile-long, 2,820-year-old underground mine waited to defy their special skills. Extraordinary skills and abilities passed down through thousands of years from a people light-years away, who had left a devastating legacy.

Those skills were nothing without their sheer, unsurpassable bravery, grit, intuition and determination, which was all naturally their own. They would need every ounce of it.

"This is the big one," said Muhammad.
"Copy that, mate," said Adam, flashing back his brilliant smile.
"I'm back again. No dramas."

North London: 15 January 2021

Carolyn sat in the back of a heavily protected private car. The car radio was on, playing 'Moonage Daydream'.

"Turn that up a bit, would you, love?" she asked the driver. She smiled as she hummed along dissolutely to Bowie.

They approached a quiet terraced street in north London. "I need to stop here for a bit." Mick Ronson's glorious guitar outro screamed to its zenith as she stepped out of the car. The January air was freezing, but being from Newcastle, she wore a light jacket and loosely wound thin scarf. A pair of binoculars hung round her neck and she carried a small bouquet of flowers.

"Let's see what all the fuss is about, shall we?" she said, looking out at the green space, quiet in darkness. The sky was clear. She walked steadily down the majestic avenue of trees lit by antique street lights. She looked up. There were no red shimmering lights. Just a little park in north London.

At the avenue's end, she put the binos to her eyes and gazed up at the beautiful constellation. She espied the three brilliant stars and the great Nebula just below them – the blur in Orion's sword. Where Planet HD8889 b had been found somewhere in the vast magnetic fields of Orion. She quoted Allison.

"Orion, the mighty hunter, the great celestial warrior. Supernaturally strong, the tallest and the most handsome of all men born on Earth."

She took the binos away and sighed.

"Or wherever you're from, bonny lad. You've got a job to do."

She walked across to the Tree of Hope, big, stark and leafless, at the far side of Highbury Fields. As she laid her floral tribute to Allison's memory at the foot of the tree, she said,

"We'll need a bit more than hope. But we've got the best there is."

Then she got back in the car.

"We need to go to Site 8."

The driver took her on the long ride that she was dreading since presenting the most Earth-shattering revelations in history.

A ride that would take her deep into the heart of the world's greatest secret.

Epilogue

"Orion: a hunter of shadows, himself a shade."

Homer, The Odyssey

Underground facility, undisclosed location: 16 January 2021
A short stocky woman accompanied by two heavily armed special protection officers walked down several flights of stairs into an empty, concrete-walled room. It was secured by three one-metre-thick bombproof steel doors. She wore a lightweight NBC suit and mask. Trying to steady herself, she walked slowly up to a car-sized glass case in the centre.

A laboratory operative unlocked several combinations, revealing the case's contents. A large grey metallic fragment, about ten metres long and five metres square, torn, partially crushed, jagged and burnt at the edges, lay under bulletproof glass and a lead radiation screen. Next to it was a torn piece of discoloured cloth, stained with streaks of blackened blood. Like an exhibit in the Science Museum, but never to be displayed there.

Carolyn stood still and, hearing her amplified, unsteady breathing inside the mask, turned to face the secret of Site 8. Through tear-filled eyes, she read the lines on the wall screen.

ABOVE TOP SECRET IN PERPETUITY
ORION PROGRAMME UK Site 8 (MOD)
RECOVERY ITEMS OR/808, OR/809

Confirmed By Transmissions OR8080-OR8102

Description of Recovery Items:
Fragment of Reentry Space Capsule
Fragment of Parachute (Bloodstained)

Age of Recovery Items:
Unknown, Under Investigation
Structural Composition:
Previously Unknown, Under Investigation
Date of Impact:
c. Mid-1990s, Under Investigation
Area of Capsule Fragmentation:
c. 700 sq miles (1,126 sq km), Greater London & Home
Counties, Southern England, under investigation
Status of Fragment Recovery:
Civilian, Local Authority, Municipal Park Routine Renovation
Location of Fragment Discovery:
Highbury Fields, London Borough of Islington
Place of Origin:
Planet HD8889 b, Star Ref. HD8889, (19.5 ly, Orion)

Reentry Capsule Occupant[s]:
One
Physical Description:
Live Adult Male
Caucasian Type, Hair: Fair, Eyes: Feline Type
Height: 6 ft 4 in (1.95 m), Weight 244 lb/17.4 st (111 kg)
Biological Status:
Extraterrestrial Humanoid (Orion Type)
Eight-Base Genomic Profile
Terrestrial Date of Birth/Age:
16 January 1975, Under Investigation
Terrestrial Name:
Armstrong, Adam Jerome
Terrestrial Status:
British Army Officer; Rank, Major
Prime Award, Victoria Cross 2021
Test Facilities:
Orion Programme Site 8, Genomic Laboratory Porton Down
Double Felix Project (MOD)
Place of Origin:
Planet HD8889 b, Star Ref. HD8889, 19.5 ly (Orion)

DEDICATED TO THE MEMORY OF
DAVID BOWIE
(1947-2016)
wherever he is

AND TO ALL BOMB DISPOSAL TECHNICIANS
wherever they're from

Glossary

Alpha radiation: a non-penetrating type of decay from a radioactive element that is harmful or lethal if inhaled or ingested

Ancient astronaut theory: the notion that extraterrestrials have landed on Earth in ancient times

ATO: ammunition technical officer – British Army bomb disposal operator

AWE: Atomic Research Establishment – organisation responsible for the design, manufacture and support of warheads for the UK's nuclear deterrent

Cat's Eye Syndrome: rare disorder characterised by an extra chromosome causing eye malformation, often sporadic with no family history

CBRN: chemical, biological, radiological and nuclear weapons, often called weapons of mass destruction, but can also be used in small-scale incidents

Det: detonator, the vital component of a bomb needed to trigger the explosion

DNA: Deoxyribonucleic acid – the molecule composed of two chains that coil around each other to form a double helix carrying genetic instructions for the development, functioning, growth and reproduction of all known organisms

Eight-base (Hachimoji) DNA: a synthetic DNA created in 2019 that adds four synthetic nucleotides in addition to the four present in DNA that codes for life on Earth

EFP: explosively formed penetrator/projectile – a type of mortar with a concave disk covering the explosive charge that solidifies into a kinetic slug to hit armour surface at 8,000m/sec

EMP: electromagnetic pulse – a short, intensely powerful burst of electromagnetic energy from a natural occurrence such as a solar storm or weapons, most notably nuclear explosions

EOD: explosives ordnance disposal – rendering safe, dismantlement and disposal of bombs and explosives in military and civilian arenas

ESP: extrasensory perception – the ability to perceive by means other than the known senses, for example by telepathy - 'reading thoughts'

Gamma radiation: a type of decay from a radioactive element that penetrates the body and is often lethal

Glock 26: compact firearm carrying as much ammunition as a full-sized 9-mm handgun

GM: genetic manipulation – the direct manipulation of an organism's genes using biotechnology

GRU: Main Intelligence Directorate – Russia's largest foreign intelligence agency

HD: the Henry Draper astronomical star catalogue; planets orbiting designated stars take the letter b after the star catalogue number

ICP: Incident Control Point – a designated point close to an incident, such as the emplacement of a bomb, where crisis management forces will conduct operations

ICU: intensive care unit – hospital department providing life-saving treatment

IED: improvised explosive device – usually a bomb constructed and deployed not to military or commercial specifications, in an infinite variety of designs, usually by terrorists, insurgents or criminals

IRA: Irish Republican Army – the world's oldest insurgency and terrorist group; the Provisional IRA is infamous for its construction and deployment of IEDs in Northern Ireland and mainland Britain over several decades

ISIS, Daesh: the Islamic State of Iraq and Syria – Salafi jihadist militant group and unrecognised proto-state that follows a fundamentalist, Salafi doctrine of Sunni Islam and is regarded as the most dangerous terrorist organisation of recent times

MI5: The Security Service – the UK's domestic counter-intelligence and security agency

MI6: The Secret Intelligence Service (SIS) – the UK's foreign intelligence service

NASA: US National Aeronautics and Space Administration

PIR: passive infrared sensor – a sensor that can detect motion then trigger an alarm. When used in a bomb or mortar, can trigger detonation

PETN: pentaerythritol tetranitrate – a very powerful, stable high explosive, major ingredient of Semtex; favoured by jihadist terrorists, hard to detect

Plutonium-239: radioactive element that can be used to make nuclear bombs

Polonium-210: rare radioisotope used in early nuclear weapons; hard to detect as it emits alpha radiation; used to kill Russian dissident Alexander Litvinenko in 2006

PTSD: post-traumatic stress disorder – a mental disorder suffered by many serving and veteran services personnel

RDD: radiological dispersal device – a bomb or dispersal system that spreads radioactivity either through explosion, aerosol, or other methods, often dubbed 'dirty bomb', usually a combination of an IED and a radioisotope

RLC: The British Army Royal Logistic Corps – Its 11 EOD Regiment is hailed as the world's premier bomb disposal squads

RPG: rocket-propelled grenade – a shoulder-fired weapon system that fires rockets equipped with an explosive warhead

RSPs: render-safe procedures - methods used by bomb squads to make a bomb ineffective

RTA: road traffic accident

SAS: Special Air Service – special forces unit of the British Army

Schrödinger's Cat: paradox expounded by Austrian physicist Erwin Schrödinger. If you place a cat and something that could kill it in a box and seal it, you would not know if the cat was dead or alive until you opened the box. So it could be both dead and alive at the same time. This theorem illustrated flaws in quantum theory (which describes nature at the smallest, atomic level) when applied to everyday objects and situations

Semtex: very powerful, stable, odourless high explosive favoured by terrorists, most notably the Provisional IRA

SETI: Search for Extraterrestrial Intelligence – successive scientific searches for intelligent life on other planets through monitoring electromagnetic radiation or transmissions

Sitrep: situations report

SOP: standard operating procedure

TNT: 2,4,6-trinitrotoluene high explosive

UGV: unmanned ground vehicle – a robot; advanced versions are used by bomb squads

UAP: unidentified aerial phenomena – umbrella term referring to UFOs (unidentified flying objects) and other unexplained things seen in the skies

Uranium: radioactive element; its highly enriched form U235 is used to make nuclear bombs

VBIED: vehicle-borne improvised explosive device – commonly called a car or truck bomb

VF: ventricular fibrillation – a critical situation when the heart beats with rapid, erratic electrical impulses, causing the pumping chambers - ventricles - to quiver uselessly instead of pumping blood

WMD: weapons of mass destruction – nuclear, biological and chemical weapons and any weapon causing mass casualties, widespread injuries and contamination

Acknowledgements

Long before I became an author and consultant specialising in counter-terrorism, I worked for a futuristic science magazine. I met science fiction writers and scientists and began following the music and imagery of David Bowie. In this century I embarked on a totally different career, and had the amazing privilege to meet and work alongside bomb disposal operators. They have inspired me beyond measure. These experiences, separated by several decades – with all their multifarious, totally disparate influences – have brought me to write my first science fiction novel. My first book published over ten years ago, on the Irish Republican Army, was fact. My second effort is fiction, but some of it is real – and much of it, undoubtedly, surreal. I do hope you enjoyed it.

I am deeply indebted to Michael Jenkins MBE, whose novels have been inspiring and whose advice, help and encouragement has been invaluable in getting me through the challenges of a totally different kind of writing. A big thank you to Catherine Dunn for superb, sympathetic editing, and to James Gardner and Mike Liardet for showing me the nuts and bolts of publishing. To Dai Williams for wonderful support and the book's first reading over a customary tasty curry and wine; to Kate Bloor for encouraging me to write a novel, and that, with my fevered imagination, it should be science fiction; to Anna and Pete, Pat, Wendy, and my beloved Jane and Celia, who have seen and heard it all before; and to Olga Merrick, whose novels inspired me to write my first, and who hopes there will be a sequel. There will be. And to everyone else who kept me on track on my own odyssey.

Printed in Great
Britain
by Amazon